EFFIGY

EFFIGY

ALISSA YORK

RANDOM HOUSE CANADA

COPYRIGHT © 2007 ALISSA YORK

All rights reserved under International and Pan-American Copyright
Conventions. No part of this book may be reproduced in any form or by
any electronic or mechanical means, including information storage and
retrieval systems, without permission in writing from the publisher,
except by a reviewer, who may quote brief passages in a review.
Published in 2007 by Random House Canada, a division of Random
House of Canada Limited. Distributed in Canada by Random House
of Canada Limited.

Random House Canada and colophon are trademarks.

www.randomhouse.ca

LIBRARY AND ARCHIVES CANADA CATALOGUING IN PUBLICATION

York, Alissa
Effigy / Alissa York.

ISBN 978-0-679-31472-1

I. Title.
PS8597.O46E34 2007   C813'.54   C2006-905696-X

Printed and bound in the United States of America

10 9 8 7 6 5 4 3 2 1

for my father, Allen,
and as always
for Clive

There are sins that can be atoned for by an offering
upon an altar, as in ancient days; and there are sins that
the blood of a lamb, of a calf, or of turtle doves, cannot
remit, but they must be atoned for by the blood of the
man.

—BRIGHAM YOUNG, *Journal of Discourses*, Vol. 4

How I would like to believe in tenderness—
The face of the effigy, gentled by candles,
Bending, on me in particular, its mild eyes.

—SYLVIA PLATH, "The Moon and the Yew Tree"

UTAH TERRITORY

1867

SHE'S BEEN LOOKING OUT for them since the sun still hung over the Stansbury Range. Now, as they finally shimmer into view, it is night.

Standing in the open barn door, Dorrie peers out across moon-lit pasture, marking their steady approach. There's no mistaking Hammer, squat as a chopping block astride his giant black mare, his boot heels bouncing even at a walk. Behind him, the Tracker glides. It's a trick of the dark—the Paiute guide puts one foot in front of the other like any man. Seven years on the ranch, and he has yet to take hold of a horse's reins. When distance demands, he mounts up behind Hammer. When given the choice, he walks or runs.

As they draw nearer, Dorrie can see there's no room for the Tracker on Hammer's saddle tonight. His place is occupied by a draped and gleaming form. A jolt of pleasure shoots down through the base of her spine and beyond—as though, like the milk-white body that commands her gaze, she too is possessed of a magnifi-cent tail.

Beside the Paiute the bay pack horse weaves, its burden a multi-toned mound. The black mare trots up a little, perhaps in response to a hay-laden waft from the stable, perhaps just a cluck of Hammer's tongue. The Tracker keeps pace, close enough now that Dorrie can make out the ordinary motion of his feet trading forward and back. She steps out a little, broadening her wedge of lamplight as they enter the yard.

"Sister Eudora," Hammer calls.

Her shoulders ratchet up at the sound of her name in his mouth. "You're back." She never knows what to call him. Mr. Hammer? Brother Hammer? This last seems plain wrong—he's old enough to call her daughter, even granddaughter. She could call him Erastus. He would allow such familiarity, might even welcome it, but the name repels her, so coarse it threatens to abrade the tongue. Which leaves one choice—the word she uses sparingly, when she can't help but address him. *Husband.*

"Eudora," he says again, "see what I've brought you this fine night."

He draws his horse up closer than he ought to, its breath steaming her crown. Ink stands higher than sixteen hands. Dorrie ducks beneath her massive black neck, passing Hammer's boot hooked in its iron to stand where the head of the white body hangs. Its face is long, pouring down into an abrupt darkness of nose. Blood behind the left ear and all down the neck, covering the withers like a shawl.

"It'll be a job to clean," she says.

Hammer twists in his saddle. "Where would you have me shoot it, the tip of the tail?"

She doesn't answer, instead reaching up to push her fingers deep into a clean patch of the animal's ruff. As a rule, fur provides a temporary refuge for her afflicted hands. Not tonight. The plush of the white wolf's coat awakens a crackling discomfort beyond the usual burn. She grabs her hand back, dropping her eyes.

"Stand back now," Hammer tells the top of her head, and she

does so numbly, thrusting both hands deep into the front pocket of her smock.

He dismounts, the mare's height causing him to land hard and sway on his heels. Reaching out to cup the she-wolf's chin, he thumbs her upper lip back to reveal a yellowed fang. "Pretty thing, ain't she?"

Dorrie nods.

The Tracker says nothing, busy at the bay's side, quietly loosing knots. His hands work fluidly in the corner of Dorrie's eye, and she turns in time to watch him slide a second, larger wolf from the pack horse's back. Drawing it by the forepaws over one shoulder, he twists, squatting slightly to assume its grey bulk. The bay stands unmoving, despite the stink of predator jangling ancient bells in its brain.

The Tracker sways a little on the first step, then finds his balance and proceeds, Dorrie taking sharp, skipping steps before him to open wide the high barn door. Once inside, he bows over her workbench, ducks his head and lets the animal roll from his shoulders. As he straightens and backs away, Dorrie moves in close.

Standing over the wolf, she feels an unfamiliar fluttering beneath her rib cage. She holds her breath a moment before reaching out to lift its tail. A male—no surprise there, given Hammer's preference for family sets.

As though privy to her thoughts, the Tracker returns with the second load clutched to his chest. Dorrie can make out multiple ears, paws, a couple of tails. This time he opens his arms as he bows over the bench, allowing the bundle to separate into three pups—two the size of well-fed cats, the third smaller, an iron-grey runt.

Hammer enters now, staggering under the mother's weight. He lurches toward them, barely in control of his load, but when the Tracker steps forward to help, he lets out a grunt, the meaning of which is clear. The Paiute nods, hands at his sides. A few steps more and Hammer crashes against the workbench, the white wolf slithering from his shoulders to fall across mate and young. For a moment no one speaks—Hammer breathless, leaning on his knuckles, Dorrie standing to one side of him and slightly behind, the Tracker retreating to his station by the door.

They are alone together, the three of them, and they are not.

Behind them the collection looms. Tiers of straw bales ascend the western wall, each of them crowded with Dorrie's creations. Hunter lies alongside hunted—fox and pocket mouse, lynx and grouse, mountain lion and deer. She can feel them there, every beast, every bird.

Hammer draws himself up, holding a fist to his running nose. The chemicals of Dorrie's trade have troubled him from the beginning. After three years of marriage and countless specimens preserved, the very air of her workshop is a poison to him. Already his eyes are glassy with tears. "Get on with it, will you."

She reaches past him to where her measuring cord hangs on its hook. Unwinding its coils, she can hear him begin to wheeze. She holds one end firmly over the dark sponge of the she-wolf's nose and lays the cord down over skull and withers, following the spine to its base. Her hands hum. Her stomach jumps. She takes the tail's length next, root to tip, pinching the cord to keep both measurements true, then laying it over the inch marks etched along the workbench. Stepping to the small table where her lamp sits flickering, she takes up a stubby pencil and sets the information down—first on a clean page of her notebook, then again on a scrap of paper Hammer can take with him back to the house.

Female, she writes in her tight, careful hand. *Head and body 51 inches together. Tail 15 ½.*

Wolves. Of all the cursed creatures to drag home.

Ursula Hammer shakes her head, her long white-blonde plait tugging where she's trapped it between pillow and spine. First among four wives, she sits up tall in her bed, dipping her needle through a circle of linen stretched taut. For every stitch the eye records there exists a shadow, the underwork that goes on where only the fingers can see. They may be large and blunt as any man's, but Ursula's hands are equal to the most delicate of work. She sinks her black thread quickly, giving each loop a little jerk as she brings the last leg of a *W* to a close.

Wolves. Isn't that just like the man. Four days gone and not even any meat to show for it. The pelts will be fine enough—even looking down from the nursery window, Ursula marked the white one's gleam—but what did that signify when Hammer will neither sell them nor allow any member of his family the benefit of their warmth. Every kill he makes goes straight to the fourth wife. He got the better of Ursula all right, the day he brought that one home.

Imagine sleeping all the daylight hours the Lord sends, then rising to rattle through night after night in that old mud-walled barn. There was a time when Ursula's cows kept the space sweet and warm, but Sister Eudora is alone out there summer and winter alike, save for a host of lifeless beasts. Ursula shudders. She might almost know a moment's pity for the wretched creature, if only Eudora didn't make more work for her. If only she ever did a stick of work around the place herself.

O, Ursula begins now, a slanted, ropy circle, two-thirds the *W*'s height. For a moment she imagines abandoning the text she's chosen, and stitching out *Wolves* instead. Then a sobering thought. Hadn't they called them wolf hunts? A Gentile term for a series of

Gentile crimes—burnings, lootings, killings, a year of them in the wake of Brother Joseph's death. His persecutors once again driving the Saints from their homes.

It's an old story, more than two decades now, but the rage remains vital, a systemic force. Ursula jabs herself with the needle, sucks the bright sprout of blood. It wasn't enough that they'd goaded us from Ohio to Missouri, from Missouri to Illinois. They had to murder our Prophet. They had to take Nauvoo, our beautiful city, too.

The night a trio of unbelievers came riding, Ursula did as her husband directed and ran for the woods. She took cover in a half-rotten log—a hidey-hole rife with the tickle of spiders, pungent with the threat of bear. When, after what felt like hours, Hammer finally came for her, she emerged to find her house burnt to the ground. At least he hadn't let them get away. He said nothing of it, but she wasn't such a fool as to overlook drag trails in the dust of the smoking yard, charred bones in the blackened wreckage she insisted on sifting through. Her husband was putting his gun to good use in those days.

Ursula draws another stitch, the thread pulling true, smoother and more lustrous than any she might hope to purchase in town. There's no denying the calibre of Sister Ruth's silk—a gift first given when the two women were good and used to one another, having shared house and husband for some half-dozen years.

She ties off the topknot of the *o*, lays down her needle and takes up the Book of Mormon from where it lies on the bedside table. Parting it at the purple ribbon's mark, she rereads the passage, making certain she has it right.

Wo unto those—"those," not "them." It's as well she checked. Her knowledge of Scripture is formidable—more than once she's mentally corrected the Bishop of the ward during Sunday

Meeting—yet it wouldn't do to let pride be her ruler and chance setting Holy Writ down wrong.

Ursula closes her eyes. For an instant she sees the words laid out as they shall be, three by three.

Wo unto those
that worship idols,
for the devil
of all devils
delighteth in them.

It's then that she hears him, cracking the kitchen door beneath her bed, pausing to remove his jacket and hat then wrestle free of his boots. Several minutes pass while she listens to him rooting around in her larder. She'll be cleaning up after him in the morning, wiping grease from the banister, sweeping crumbs from the stairs where, soon enough, he'll ascend.

Not yet, though. First, he'll pass through the front hall to the dining room. Ursula nods—a smug, chin-tucking bob—as the floorboards creak out this very pattern beneath her. As the dining room lies at the far end of the house, she has to strain to make out the following string of sounds—the chuck of the key in the sideboard's only locking door, the thwack of his book meeting table, the glassy grind of his ink jar coming to rest at its side.

Ursula opens her eyes. She'd make a fine hunter herself, her senses are so very keen. She has the steady hands of a hunter, too, the right one starting up again now, pushing down into the *u*. She must take care to keep its walls straight. Once, distracted by the unholy din Hammer and Sister Thankful were making two doors down, she worked an *n* off-kilter and had to prick it out.

Now comes the distant scuff and scrape of Hammer dragging a chair out to sit. And not just any chair. Ursula smiles to hear it—not with pleasure, but with a species of bleak satisfaction, a keeping of strict accounts.

❧

Opening to a fresh page in his kill book, Erastus Hammer writes, *13th of May 1867. Wolves. Full set taken on a stone apron outside the den. High ground. Stream running below. Took the mother first—all white—single ball to the skull behind the ear. Tolerably clean.*

He blinks, his eyes still watery.

Clubbed the pups—3—pelts perfect. Scarcely done when the father cast in his lot with the rest. Played upon me from the ridge at my back. Came flying from above and behind. Such a weight as would knock a man flat never to rise only a pebble's clatter gave him away. Swung up the barrel and spun to find him looking very sour at me mid air. Got a shot off on him. Used him up in one. Might still have taken me down with him only I stepped lively aside.

Erastus sits—as he always does when no eyes are upon him—not at the head of the table but at its tail. Ursula's chair. It's as close as he's come to touching her backside in years. Lord, the shock of it, bare against his palms that first time, hard as a man's thigh but infinitely smoother. Smooth and hard and cool.

His forearms lie on either side of the splayed kill book, dirty with curling black hairs, marked all over with the scars of a settler's life. His blue-eyed wife brings her elbows to rest here thrice daily, her pale arms knotted but somehow unmarred, longer than his own by half. How long now since he lined them up side by side in their bed, marvelling at her white and flawless size?

He screws his eyes shut a moment, then forces them to focus on the page. Reading over what he's written, he finds it wanting a line or two. He considers a moment, nods and wets his nib.

A fine weight of wolves. Not a dry hair on the horses by the time we made home.

Good enough. He fishes out the list of figures in Eudora's cramped, back-slanting hand. Hard to believe the tricks those scabby fingers know.

Was it providence, his overhearing the Burr woman's proud talk in Cedar City that day? He could scarcely help it, the way she was bleating on to the woman behind the counter. *She's so clever, my Dorrie. Just last week she made up a jaybird, dead one day, resurrected the next!* Erastus thought he'd travelled the more than two hundred miles south to Utah's Dixie to see about an exceptional mare, but in that moment the true purpose of his journey came clear. He lurked at the back of the store, fingering shirt cuffs and shoe leather, until she was gone. Then made his way to the counter, took out his purse and inquired as to where the good woman lived.

Driving out to the scrappy patch the Burrs called a farm, Erastus nurtured bright visions of every creature he'd ever killed. He pictured them arranged about his home—owls like vases, a grizzly like a gleaming desk—pretending for the moment that Ursula would stand for a wilderness dragged indoors. He imagined visitors stooping to examine teeth, or rising on tiptoe to marvel at claws, forgetting he was a man without the burden of friends.

Upon drawing into the dusty yard, he spotted the blur of a girl's figure through the open door of a shed. It was all he could do to keep his stride unhurried, matching it to that of her father, a man who ran like a slave to meet him then scuffed along babbling at his side.

At length Erastus drew near enough to get a look at her face. It gave him no pleasure—a shock of pleasure's opposite, in fact—but it wasn't her face he'd come to see. Her hands were a mess, nails chewed down, backs nicked, more than one narrow knuckle split. They were at work on a cottontail, divesting it of flesh and bone. The inner body was a headless, sinewy thing—plain meat. The pelt, on the other hand—face and feet and tail still attached—was all promise, a vessel to be filled. Those hands held secrets. He would have them, and the rest of her too.

Having copied the list of weights and measures, Erastus blots the page. A fragmentary inversion of his story appears on the blotting paper. He stares at it for a long moment before folding shut the book.

Not long now. She can hear him—no longer scribbling, sitting still a moment, directly below. Of course she can hear him. She's down on her knees, ear to water glass, glass to floor. A woman has a right to keep track of her man.

He stands, the chair scraping out behind him. Why does he sit in the first wife's chair rather than his own? Because he knows the witch wouldn't like it if she knew? Or because it's closer to the sideboard, the book he keeps locked away?

She hears the snick of the sideboard door. The chair shoved forward again. Any minute now.

She's been dressed for hours, face painted, ringlets set. Thankful Cobbs Hammer, third and favourite wife, standing at her window, staring into the night. Not that she expected him to approach from that direction, taking the track like a civilized man. Her husband is a hunter, a pioneer. More often than not he returns to her overland.

Soon she will hear his footsteps in the corridor. When they halt outside her door, there will come a slim silence before the handle turns in its works. It is this silence—this sound-not-sound of being chosen—that lends her every performance its edge.

Thankful rises, a curtsy undone. Returning the glass to its spot on the crowded vanity, she licks finger and thumb to pinch off her candle's flame, then sweeps herself to the darkest corner of the room.

Erastus slips the sideboard key into his waistcoat pocket. Instead of taking up the lamp, he lowers his mouth to its glass chimney and blows it out. He'll feel his way.

After the dining room's clutter, the front hall gapes. He built this house—eight bedchambers stacked atop kitchen, front hall, dining room and parlour. There's no angle of it he doesn't know. He's up the black stairs like a spider up its thread.

At the top he meets temptation in the shape of a door. His second wife, Ruth, lies behind it, probably sleeping on her back. She'd half waken if he went in. Let him push the silk shift up around her neck without protest, accept him with scarcely a sound. The nut-brown gloss of her hair, black in the blackness, the colour somehow still present in its slippery weight.

It wouldn't be worth it. The last time—the briefest of visits—earned him a month cut off from Thankful's favours. Quiet as he might be, he can be certain his third wife would lay her ear to the wall.

A left turn would lead him down the corridor to the large corner room, where his first wife lies alone in the tall brass bed. It's an idea he mustn't dwell on if he's to know any peace. Ursula's never actually barred him from their chamber, but years of trying have taught him there's no cold akin to that which her body gives off in their bed.

Erastus turns right. He runs the tips of his fingers silently along the wall, keeping low to avoid upsetting Ursula's framed mottoes, until he reaches the depression that signifies Thankful's door.

Maybe she'll have on that black feather ruff—the one that makes her look like a vulture would if it were a woman. Mouth red, eyes glistening. Erastus grins in the darkness. If he's lucky, he'll get the bounce on her, catch her off guard.

At the periphery of the Hammer ranch, the Tracker lies prone in his brush hut. His roof stands open above him, the night sky visible through a tangle of upthrust poles and, beyond them, the boughs of a scraggly oak.

The wolf den had not been new to him. He'd discovered the modest pack some five springs previous, the mother leading him there. He tracked her splayed toes back from a torn-open fawn, watched from a downwind distance as that year's brood spilled from the den to meet her. Ears flat, crouched and wagging, they chewed at her throat, licked and nuzzled about her lips. The Tracker watched her sides heave in response, saw her bring up a fair portion of kill. She sat back on her haunches as they fell upon the glistening pile.

He stayed on long after they'd finished every scrap, letting his belly join rock, his back lift off into sky. He witnessed the lolling aftermath of the feed and, some time later, the return of the silver-maned father. The white wolf roused herself to greet him, skipping forward with a pleasure so keen it cut the Tracker to his solitary heart. He took his leave of them then, but found himself passing that way every year at whelping time to see if they'd returned.

So it was that when Hammer spoke his latest wish aloud, the Tracker knew where to lead him. Not directly. He took a round-about route—roundabout by days—his misgivings bypassing heart and mind to settle in the soles of his feet.

The killing itself took little time. The mother he picked off with a lone shot through the skull. She made it easy for him, so bright in the gloaming, sitting guard over her babies, sitting still. The pups melted away when she dropped, vanishing into the den. He had foreseen such an eventuality, had brought with him the necessary tool.

He was down the slope in a heartbeat, Hammer hedging behind him, not trusting the grade. Leaving the white man to stand guard against any pack member drawn by the shot, the Tracker dropped to his knees and wriggled face-first into the wolf-scented dark.

When he was in up to his ankles, he felt the gape of a side tunnel at his cheek. From its mouth came a waft of collective, meaty breath. They were down there, keeping quiet, scenting him back. The willow stick with its square-nail tooth was designed for fishing out rabbits, but it sunk just as readily into the plush of a six-week-old wolf. A yelp, a twist to anchor the nail, and he dragged the first pup from the whelping chamber. Clamping a hand over the snoutful of needle-sharp teeth, he backed out into the falling night.

He thought Hammer might want to get in on the clubbing, but the white man held his nervous post, blinking and squinting into the brush. The stream sang quietly below as the Tracker killed the first of the three pups. It might as well have been Hammer doing it, for all the sensation it invoked.

He took care not to splinter the thin skull, unwound the rabbit hook without tearing the pelt. One, then another dreamlike repetition—crawl, jab, drag, club—and the job was done. Four bodies lay at their feet, three of which would have fit nicely inside the skin of the fourth. The Tracker took up his Henry repeater from the crag where he'd propped it. The rifle was a gift given in welcome not long after he and Hammer first met, the white man having traded horseflesh for two of the fine weapons with a Mericat soldier passing through.

Hammer spoke then. "Pity we didn't get the daddy."

As though summoned, the shape of a big male rose up from the outcropping behind the white man's head. The upswing of the Henry's muzzle nearly caught Hammer in the chin. There was just enough light to make plain the terror in his eyes. Seven years' service and still the white man imagined himself betrayed.

Leaping, the male was all chest, so that was where the ball caught him—the heart a hidden mouth, stopped and opened in one. He was already dying when he landed on Hammer, knocking him face-first to the ground. The Tracker took a step back and lowered his barrel, watching the white man wrestle madly with the shaggy corpse.

It took Hammer an age to catch on, roll out from beneath the lifeless animal and stand. He said nothing at first, marshalling his breath, avoiding the Tracker's eye. Then, after nudging the wolf's rump with his boot, he squatted down to feel beneath the long brush of tail. He showed a happy flash of teeth.

"Ask and ye shall receive."

He was wrong, of course. Even as it hurtled toward him through the gloom, the Tracker had recognized the yearling. He was the only pup kept on from last year's litter, the others turned loose in the world. A babysitter. Aid to his mother, companion on the hunt.

The yearling had reached full height and length, but Hammer had to be blind not to notice the young-dog stretch of his limbs, the lack of years about his throat and face. And the white man wasn't blind. Not entirely.

Hammer rose, staring at the dead male, dusting off his hands. Beside him, the Tracker held his tongue. It was a comfort to him, keeping something from the white man, holding a piece of the story for his own.

The kill was unlike any he had made before. His aim was as keen as ever—a hair keener, perhaps—yet he felt no pride. Nothing of pride's dark reflection either, much as he knew a wolf wasn't just any animal. Even seven years' fealty to a white man couldn't wipe that understanding from his mind.

The shame came later. After they'd led Hammer's black giant and her companion down from where they'd tethered them in the trees. After they'd piled the male and the three pups onto the pack horse and slung the white mother flush against Hammer's backside. One small blessing—with such a load, the white man couldn't insist the Tracker ride.

The feeling, when it came, registered not in the Tracker's guilty arm, not even in his chest, but in the string of bones at his back. A chilling presence pressed up against his spine. In his thoughts he welcomed his poor dead wife.

In the past, he might have snapped his head round to try to catch a glimpse of the slender whirlwind that was her spirit, but he'd learned such disrespect would only drive her away. So it was that he continued to trot along in the gap between horses, his gaze pinned to the white wolf's dangling paw.

Disgrace, the whirlwind wife breathed coldly down the back of his neck.

In defence he spoke sternly to her in his mind. *A skilful hunter is to be prized by the People. He is one whom the spirits have blessed.*

He received no reply, Hammer's voice cutting between them, sending her spinning away.

"Your people got any wolf stories, Tracker?"

The Tracker hung his head. He should have been used to Hammer's bald questions by now, the depth of the white man's unknowing. Imagine never having heard tell of the Father, Coyote's wise and provident elder brother. More than that, imagine thinking any man might recount those sacred tales, that they might be uttered, not by winter firelight, but out there in the open, on a warm spring night. Like as not a snake would hear, rear up and bite the teller.

"No stories." The simplest answer a lie.

On his back now, alone, the Tracker recalls the whirlwind wife's chill. He could light a fire to soothe himself, but that would require rising, separating the clay of his body from that of the hard-packed ground. Instead, he frees a hand from the knot of his arms and reaches down to unbuckle his belt.

His trousers aren't a bad fit—he's worn them and other hand-me-downs of Hammer's for as long as he's lived on the ranch. Before that, a series of anonymous castoffs. An Indian in white man's clothing is still an Indian, but the rags work like scraps of their unwieldy language, allowing him to move among them. There are times, though, when he can still feel the ghosts of his own bare legs in the air, the skin of the double apron flapping, the breechcloth snug and soft.

Inside the right trouser leg, the picture book lies curved against him, lashed to his thigh with a leather thong. Its cover has long since ceased to chafe, having formed itself to his contours like a familiar palm. He lays his own hand over it now, just resting, leaving the knot be. To untie it now would be senseless. He hasn't the strength to turn the whispering pages, let alone gather brush and summon up the light to see.

2

SOMEHOW IT'S DAWN, red light filtering through her cloudy windows by the time Dorrie lifts her thin knife and stands poised over the largest of the wolves. She'll have no choice now but to deny her nocturnal tendencies and work through the day.

The bodies are neatly arrayed—both adults on the long workbench, their pups nearby, lined up on a bale. Hammer and the Tracker laid them out according to her wishes before they left. She saw them to the door, where Hammer sucked deep, grateful breaths of open air. Partway to the ranch house, he pinched the bridge of his nose and shot a glimmering stream of mucus into the dust. The Tracker went the opposite way. By the time Dorrie turned her head after him, he was a smudge of deeper darkness against the field.

She lingered at the door long after both men had disappeared. When she finally returned to her workbench, she took her time over the finer measurements—those which Hammer had no use for, but which were essential to her. Girth front of hind legs, girth back of forelegs, girth at neck behind ears. The mother wolf was far thinner than her mate, all muzzle and legs. Older, too.

Once Dorrie had set down the numbers, she went on to make five detailed sketches, noting the placement of every ridge and hollow—anywhere the inner workings showed through. When she could fuss over the drawings no more, she busied herself with the arrangement of materials and tools. Her skinning knife and scissors, the razor-fine scalpel, the toothy saw. These she laid out within easy reach, along with a pot of arsenical soap, a stiff-bristled paintbrush and a tall, battered tin of finely ground salt.

As a rule she dispensed with these necessary preparations in a fevered rush, impatient with anything that stood between her and the primary cut. Tonight she moved as though ploughing through silt. Even when all lay in readiness, she stalled by taking down Major Greene's *Collection and Preservation: A Taxidermist's Guide*. Paging through the section on large mammals, she found nothing she didn't know by heart. After that she pored over the specimen itself, her eyes tracing the big male's particulars—the dark saddle mark over the haunches, the blunt, bluish snout.

By rights she should begin with the mother, get the blood out of that snowy ruff before she does anything else. She'll have to rub the stain with a wad of benzoline-soaked cotton, dust the damp shadow with plaster, beat out the chalk powder once it's dried. She knows this, just as she knows she'll skin the white wolf last.

She rolls the male onto his back. His legs are sufficiently pliable, hours having passed since the initial stiffening. She presses them apart. Using the blue muzzle as a lever, she turns his head to one side and parts the fur midway between the forelegs with her finger and thumb. The skin beneath it she parts with her blade.

One long, clean cut brings her to the anus. Next, a steady incision across the chest and up the inside of the right foreleg. Gaining speed, she skins all four limbs down to the last joint, dislocating and folding them free of their skin. The paws she leaves entire, suddenly huge on empty lengths of fur. Her fingers are in charge now, and she begins to feel something of the familiar delight in their skill.

Having peeled the tail and skinned out the back and neck, she slows a little around the ears. These turn inside out as though it's a trick the animal knows, skin giving up cartilage with so little fight she need use no tool beyond her own chipped and brittle nails. She burrows down to just above the left eye, stretching the brow taut until the eyelid reveals itself in a thin white line. Guiding her scalpel along this delicate limit, she leaves the lid intact. She does the same on the right side, then presses on to negotiate the whisker roots, the black fringes of lip and, finally, the dark apex of the nose.

A body oozes when it's flayed, a fact Dorrie has been unconsciously addressing from the first incision, scattering handfuls of sawdust on and around the pelt. Rolling the raw wolf onto its flank, she works the skin out from beneath it, bunching it up to one side. Forelegs come free with a cut at the shoulder joint, hind legs at the hip. She strips every scrap of muscle before setting the heavy bones aside.

She feels almost entirely herself now. Only a ghost of unease remains, and then only when her gaze slips sideways to touch on the female's creamy paw.

There remains but one task to be performed before she can roll the male's carcass to the edge of the workbench and let it fall. Closing her fingers around the handle of the saw, Dorrie drags it toward her over the bloodied bench. After a moment's pause, she draws it softly across the back of the wolf's skull, marking out the cut. A burst of effort and the brain will show. It never ceases to amaze her, the power of those fine metallic teeth when married to her own thin arm.

Standing alone in the little silkhouse, Ruth inhales deeply, closing her eyes. The place smells of forest. Resin seeps from the rough log walls, and from the planks beneath her feet. A green perfume lingers over the worm beds, mulberry leaves still verdant, still refreshing to the nose. The lavender she threw down yesterday heightens the atmosphere discreetly, like harebells at the foot of an oak. The silkworms themselves supply the odour of life—a gentle funk somehow evocative of insect, animal and bird.

In their feeding, the worms make a low music of water upon leaves. At two weeks old, they mimic a gentle rain. As they grow, so too will the force of their downpour.

Ruth opens her eyes. A shaft of daylight, thinned by the trees beyond the window, shows up a whirl of motes. She contemplates her own hand against a bed of juvenile worms. Fifteen days ago they emerged from vein-coloured eggs too tiny to handle; today they're half the length of her forefinger. A fortnight more and they'll be the finger's equal. It will be all she can do to keep them fed in those final days—she'll be run ragged. Such good little eaters. It's tempting to pick one up and raise it to her lips, bestow the reward of a kiss. Instead, she nestles a fingertip in among them. They accept its presence, continue feeding without cease.

Dorrie takes special care in sewing up the mother wolf's bullet hole. It's a tricky turn, just there, behind the ear. The male was no trouble—a clean shot through the chest where the fur stood thick and dark. The hole fit nicely into her ventral cut. The pups were even easier. Two of the skulls showed cracks, but none was dented, let alone crushed. The small pelts came away whole.

The salted skin eats at her finger pads, but fine work such as this doesn't allow for gloves. In any case she's accustomed to working through pain. Pushing her needle into the bullet hole's verge, she draws the silk thread taut, a lone stitch already minimizing the tear. Her sister-wife's product is both strong and fine.

You let me know if that's a good weight.

Ruth delivered the first of many spools to the old barn not long after Dorrie came to live at the ranch. It took months for the second wife to beg a favour in return. Or not beg. In fact, Dorrie's fairly certain the request was never spoken aloud. She can recall only Ruth's hand reaching into her apron pocket, producing a fat caterpillar gone still.

"He wouldn't like it," Dorrie said after a moment.

Ruth treated her to a soft smile. "I should think it would be a challenge, a pleasure to you."

Dorrie felt a jabbing sensation in her chest. The thrill of having one's nature even partly understood. *A challenge. A pleasure.* She held out an upturned hand.

Major Greene clearly held the preservation of insects to be a lesser art. He also held, however, that the true professional must be able to handle any specimen he is presented with, and so he had included a slim chapter on the subject toward the back pages of his invaluable treatise—between "Collection and Preparation of Eggs, Bird and Reptile" and "Essential Materials and Tools."

The bulk of the section dealt with mounting winged specimens, but at length Dorrie came upon a paragraph headed "Caterpillars and Worms." She was to squeeze the innards out through the tail end—an act requiring considerable delicacy and, more often than not, practice. But Dorrie's were not just any hands. Ruth had brought her one specimen only, and that was the specimen she would mount.

The silkworm was cool, smooth along its back, bumpy with leg-nubs below. It gave up its insides grudgingly, but Dorrie was patient, beginning again and again at the head, kneading gently, easing its substance along. In the end, skin and innards came apart, the one a flaccid slip, the other a slippery clot. Next, through the exit of the tail-end hole, she entered with a length of hollow straw. It was really that simple. Nothing to measure, nothing to construct. She would blow the shape into it, breathe back its living form.

As per the Major's instructions, she held the caterpillar over a lamp's soft heat while she did so, rotating the straw in her lips so the skin might harden on all sides. One could either remove the straw or cut it off short. Dorrie chose the former, judging it to be the more difficult, and therefore the more professional, choice. Caterpillars marked with vivid designs often required retouching with paint—not a consideration in this case, as her sister-wife's worm was grey.

Dorrie wasn't sure how fragile the finished specimen would prove to be over time, so she prepared a bed of tow for it in a squat and spotless jar. Ruth came for it before the breakfast bell. Her face took on a glow as she held the jar to the window's weak light. "Such a gift," she murmured, and Dorrie felt the jabbing again.

Never having made a friend in her life, Dorrie harbours no illusions about making one of Ruth. It's enough to know the other woman is there across the yard, working through the day just as Dorrie works through the night.

Drawing the last stitch through the white wolf's pliable skin, she ties the thread off in a tiny crystalline knot. Before snipping it, she turns the pelt over, laying it fur-side up across her knees. It's strangely light, insular yet cool, a blanket of fresh snow in her lap. No sign of the bullet's path. She runs a finger up the underside, feeling for the puckered scar.

🔥

What a crew, Lord. What a sorry crew. All the thousands of times Ursula imagined herself presiding over a supper table of her own, she never once pictured it looking like this.

As a girl and then a young woman, Ursula spent every meal-time ladling and fetching, in fealty to the bitter, exacting Harriet Pike and, later, the helpless Elsie Simms. Both of them slave-drivers in their own way. The moment Ursula took her seat, Mrs. Pike or one of her lumpen sons, or the original lump that was their father, would call for more pickles, more cornbread, more stew. The Simmses were no better—Saints or no, they never let her forget they'd taken her in after the Pikes had turned her out. The children were weaker-willed, and every order was preceded by, *Oh, Ursula, dear, would you mind?*, but little else had changed.

How could she have guessed then at the bloated shape her own household would assume? If it weren't for the children—her five industrious little angels flanking her left and right—Ursula doubts she would still walk the earth. Strong though she is in both body and mind, she would likely have dropped dead of work, like so many of the women who came westering.

The thought narrows her eyes, and she sweeps them past her daughters—little Josepha earnestly buttering her own bread, her elder sister, Josephine, taking small, neat bites of stew—to rest on the most recent, and perhaps least supportable, of her husband's wives. That filthy smock. And that hair, like a mule tail that's never been groomed. Sister Eudora is bleary-eyed. She's missed two meals already today, and Ursula was obliged to send Josephine to fetch her just now. *You knock until she comes. Don't you go in there, mind, don't even open the door.*

Truth be told, Ursula despaired of the fourth wife the moment she first clapped eyes on her. Doubtless thinner girls had managed to force babies out from between the pincers of their hips, but few of them would have lived to tell the tale. For more than a day she was at a loss as to the motive behind Hammer's choice. It couldn't have been carnal, as the last two had been. She wondered about a possible alliance with a family of note, but found upon questioning the girl that she came from nothing—a hardscrabble farm somewhere off the southern road, people by the name of Burr.

It was only after their sealing, when Hammer took his child bride shopping for needles and knives, that Ursula understood. It was no longer enough to keep a record of every animal he shot—now he wanted to stockpile the creatures themselves. To think a man could be so ruled by vanity.

A hank of Sister Eudora's hair slithers loose to dangle in her stew. She takes no notice, lifting another in a series of indelicate mouthfuls to her lips. Ursula can stand to watch her no longer. She shifts her gaze to Sister Ruth and feels her eyelids relax.

It's hard to credit now, but Hammer's second wife was also thin as kindling when he brought her home. Even harder to imagine is the flush of bad feeling Ursula experienced when he first led Ruth into her house—not jealousy, exactly, but something very like. Ruth was warmly, quietly beautiful, a fact Ursula found she could not entirely take in stride.

Five children and a decade later, she's come to regard her sister-wife as, if not an ally, then at least no threat. Ruth helps around the house throughout the winter months, but come spring she spends every waking moment with her worms. She's happy enough to produce bobbins and hanks of thread, but despite years of weaving in the land of her birth, she refuses to make cloth. Ursula learned long ago that any talk of procuring a loom will meet with silence and a lowered head. A stubbornness as soft as it is enduring. Never mind how it galls Ursula to peddle the surplus unfinished product in town, then turn around and pay premium for a bolt of inferior twill.

Still, she wouldn't trade the second wife. She knows full well not one in a hundred would have borne five strong, squalling babies and turned them over without a fight. Five and counting. Ursula can't help but smile at the idea—a sixth little lamb to be welcomed before Christmas of this year. And more after that, even if she has to peel Hammer away from his worthless third wife every time.

Ursula turns her attention to Sister Thankful now, making her eyes like open winter windows, letting them linger on the round of a fat ringlet until the other woman feels them there. Not a finger lifted in the six long years she's lain about this house. What's worse, despite endless nights abed with the husband they share, not a single new soul to show.

Ursula doesn't bother to meet the third wife's kohl-rimmed eyes. She looks instead to the table's head, and for an instant considers calling Hammer to account for his wives. But to what end? This is old territory—she's trodden it until every inch of her is sore.

What can you mean, Mother? I never see Sister Ruth or Sister Eudora but they're about their work.

Work? Ruth is never to be found when I want her. And when did Eudora ever churn the butter or knead the bread? I doubt she even knows how. As for the other one—you're not going to tell me she's anything but bone idle!

Here he might smooth his moustaches, tilt his head as though mystified by what she's said. How she hated it when he kept his temper while hers began to fray.

Charity, my good wife. He could smile so unkindly when he wished to. *You know Sister Thankful is a martyr to the megrims.*

Ursula closes her eyes rather than continue to regard him or, worse, look one seat further to Lal, her poor excuse of an eldest son. None of it—not one of her husband's choices—would be so galling if she hadn't instructed him to the contrary in nearly every respect.

After a dozen years of managing a household alone, Ursula was ready for help. Hammer was taken up with breeding and trading horses, and Lal was as useless at eight years of age as at any other. Housemaids were few and far between on the frontier, and those who were about commanded too great a price. Wives were cheaper and easier to control—or so Ursula imagined at the time. Besides, was it not a man's sacred duty to people Zion with his seed? Hammer must take another wife, at least one. Ursula made it clear to him—sat beside him on the parlour settee and spelled it out.

"She must be in excellent health—look for a good complexion and carriage, colour in the cheeks, a sturdy spine. Young but not a child. Cheerful but no idiot—I can do without prattling in my ear. She should be orderly, industrious, clean. And mark this, husband: she must be easily governed."

Hammer stared at the floor while she talked. "Anything else?" he muttered when she'd had her say. As though she'd been browbeating him rather than urging him to marry again.

Ursula knows she must open her eyes soon. The children will begin to worry, one of them—Joseph, most likely, bless him— asking, *Are you all right, Mother? Are you well?*

❧

Chancing Thankful's wrath, Erastus slides his eyes past her to rest for a moment on Ruth. Even as she lifts her fork, his second wife radiates stillness. She could be a glossy parlour plant, the kind a man can't help but finger when he's left alone with it in a room.

More than a decade has passed since the first time he held Ruth in his arms. Her English skin was chapped and sullied then, her brown eyes those of a heifer much abused. She was one of many he lifted into waiting wagons that day—women and children, even several men too weak to rise, lying dusted with snow on the iron ground. They were converts on the trail to Zion, victims of a poorly planned, ill-fated migration scheme. The handcarts they'd been dragging for months stood over them where they lay.

It was no great feat to lift her. He felt little evidence of the soft creature she would become, the hips and breasts she would redevelop in his care. Then her bonnet fell away, and her hair tumbled free to clothe his shoulder, his cold, bare hand. Such a slithering. How could it shine so, when the wick of her life's force was clearly guttering? How could it give off such a scent— flowers grown in the bed of a woman's hidden parts—when the rest of her already smelled of death? Mysteries then and now. He knew only that he would have her. It would be necessary to pay out her bond, but he would have her. And Ursula would have her wish.

"What's your name?" he asked, after laying her down alongside another near cadaver in the wagon's box.

"Graves." Her voice was reedy, threaded through with air. After a slow, skipping breath, she added, "Ruth."

"Ruth Graves."

She did her best to nod.

"My name is Brother Hammer. Erastus." He paused. "I have one wife, but she'd welcome another. There's a good-sized house and plenty of land. You'd want for nothing."

She watched him from inside all that hair, a bleak portrait in a polished frame. "Trees," she wheezed finally.

"Cottonwoods, scrub oak, pine up in the hills. There's a peach orchard out front of the house."

She fumbled beneath her blanket, withdrawing a hand wrapped around a stubby length of stick. "Mulberries." Quiet but crystal clear.

He straightened his spine, as much as any man might when he's bent double in a squat. "I'll plant some first thing."

She nodded again, her eyes falling shut.

Coming back to himself, Erastus retracts his gaze to find Thankful staring straight ahead, unaware of his wandering. Out of habit, his eyes flick to her bosom, shoved up high for his pleasure, bare almost to the nipples' rosy rings. Necklines unknown anywhere else in the Territory, a scandal in Ursula's eyes. He rests there a moment more. The pale flesh sighing, beating with her cinched-in breath. Always a suggestion of panting about his third wife. She catches him looking and makes slits of her little grey eyes.

The air is stagnant in Dorrie's barn, daylight gone now, trailing its warmth. The skulls have taken hours. She's proceeded in order of descending size—adult male down through female runt—

scooping out brains, severing optic nerves, prying eyeballs out whole. Careful work, but nothing compared to removing all traces of facial flesh. When bone was all that remained, she applied a thorough coating of the creamy arsenical soap, making certain to force the bristles deep into every dimpled fissure, every hinge.

As always, the Tracker sounds a single knock. Dorrie learned long ago not to waste her breath calling out for him to come in. He'll wait there until she comes, stepping back when she pushes open the door. She takes up the lamp. On her way she passes the five new skins drying fur-side down over bales, salt drawing out the moisture so they seem to sweat.

As she returns to her workbench, the Tracker follows close. His nearness no longer troubles her. It may be that the sight of a strange Indian would cause her pulse to lurch and patter, but he's the only one she's set eyes on since coming to the Hammer ranch.

He drops into a squat before the pile of skinned wolves, fingering a pink off-cut from a pup's tender thigh.

She watches him. "Would you eat that?"

He turns up his eyes.

"I never thought. I would've used cornmeal. Instead of sawdust, I mean." She forces a thin smile. He makes no pretence of offering one in return.

"Eat." The Tracker drops his gaze, then shakes his head slowly, imparting something weightier than a simple no.

"All right." She moves to a set of standing shelves, where five bundles of leg bones lie interspersed between five open-backed skulls. Picking up a small paper tag, she feeds its knotted string through the bone circle that lately housed the runt's eye.

The Tracker rises. He should be preparing to spirit away her leavings. Instead, he stretches out his hand, a single finger pointing to what he desires. Second largest, second from the left. The

Tracker turns up his palm. Dorrie draws on her heavy gloves, reaching for the female's skull.

"It's poison now. You can't touch."

Still his open hand.

"Poison." She moves past him to the workbench, setting the skull down and taking up her pot and brush. These she uses to mime painting the skull. When he still doesn't move, she acts out painting her own hand, then holds the pot up near her face, letting her tongue spill out of the corner of her mouth as she rolls her eyes back in her head. A moment is all he requires. Upon letting her vision settle, she finds he's plucked up the skull. He holds it to his chest in a doubled grasp.

"No, Tracker."

He meets her gaze, his eyelids contracting to form the chilling squint she's chanced to see him turn Hammer's way. The skull faces her too—open sockets, teeth. The tip of the Tracker's thumb dips down into an ear niche and flinches back. Dorrie takes a few quick steps to the nearest specimen—a blacktail buck—and knocks three times on a spot between its antlers.

"See," she says, "I need it."

His eyes leave hers to play over the form in his hands. Freed from his narrow stare, she approaches, reaching out her hand. He nods, but instead of handing over the skull, he returns it to its place on the shelf.

"Eyes," he says softly.

It's beginning to dawn on her that the Paiute has in mind some greater purpose than the decoration of his hut. "All right. You have to wash your hands first, though." He turns to her, his face blank. She can never be sure how much he understands. Again she mimes, falling water, scrubbing hands. To her relief, he follows her to the wooden crate she uses for a washstand. She empties the tin jug into the basin and hands him a yellow lump of soap. "Wash." She points to a shallow cut in the heel of his hand. "Wash hard."

He accepts the soap, bends and sets to work. Once it becomes clear that he means to be thorough, she leaves him to it, returning to her workbench. On the floor down the far end, abutting the pile of carcasses, three gallon pails brim with brains, clots of fat and other scraps. She knows without thinking which one she must delve into—it sits a little apart from the others, giving off a soundless hum.

Discarding her gloves, she kneels down beside it, pushes up the sleeve of her smock and reaches in past her elbow. There's a good deal of waste to feel through, but the shapes she's after seem to co-operate, one and then the other brushing her fingertips like fat little fish. She palms them carefully, drawing her fist out of the pail with a sucking plop. When she glances up, the Tracker stands over her, hands dripping at his sides.

"Here." She holds up her hand, suddenly too tired to rise. Two dark eyeballs glisten on her palm. "These are hers."

Still hungry, Lal Hammer hunkers in his mother's larder, cutting himself a wedge of her bread, loading it with the tallow she collects in a jar. He saws roughly, gouges deep. She'll spy out what's missing and finger him either way, so why not leave his mark? Nineteen is too old for a beating—she hasn't taken her spoon to him in earnest in over two years—and what kind of a fool fears a mother's unloving gaze?

The bread goes down slippery, the fat edging on rank. He hacks and slathers a second helping. Certain to be noticed now.

The last time his mother took him on, she did real damage, cracking the little finger on his left hand so he had to bind it to its neighbour, nurse it close to his chest for weeks. If only that had been the worst of it.

The second slice down his gullet, Lal stands contemplating a third. The loaf looks like a bear's been at it. One by one, he sucks his fingers clean.

It wasn't as though he'd done anything so terrible. Wasn't it the eldest's duty to share with his younger brother, to teach him the ways of the world? He'd wondered if Joseph would follow him at all—the poor kid strangling in her apron strings—but the boy came readily enough. A quick look round to be sure she wasn't watching and they were away.

Joseph was seven then, plenty old enough to learn. He worked like a grown man, worried like one too. Wasn't it only fair he should come to know some method of blowing off steam?

Lal had the tobacco rolled and ready—no sense wasting time while the pair of them might be missed. Or one of them, anyway. Lal could wander as far as he liked without Mother Hammer troubling herself on his account.

The smoke rose thick and fragrant, climbing the afternoon light, clinging to the stable's back wall. Joseph hacked like a consumptive but kept at it, taking goodly pulls and forcing them down. For the first time ever, Lal entertained the notion of warming to his suck-up of a little brother. Despite the decade between them, he might make a pal of the kid after all.

She made no sound coming down the long side wall. Not a whisper. Burst on them like an Indian—a pale, blue-eyed savage in a speckled dress. Joseph dropped his soggy butt. Didn't run, though, knew better than to add cowardice to his crime. But it wasn't Joseph she was after. The kid pelted off the moment she released him—like a witch freeing an enchanted man, she did it with a wave of her wand. Or rather, her long-handled wooden spoon. She'd brought it with her, knowing that if Lal was leading his little brother anywhere he was likely to be leading him astray.

Unlike Joseph, Lal kept hold of his smouldering butt. He took a pull on it in the full of her gaze, clenching his teeth about its papery tail to keep them from rattling in his head.

"Is that tobacco?" The spoon at her side now.

He couldn't stop himself. He sucked another lungful, let it colour what he said next. "What do you think?"

He'd known all his life she was strong, but never to what terrifying degree. She thrashed his smoking hand until it was a curled cupful of pain. He was big for seventeen. She was his mother. Struggle though he might, he could not break her hold on his arm.

That evening he came to the table and found his place unset. She pointed behind her to the kitchen without a word. Confused, he left the dining room, found his portion sitting on the kitchen table in a battered tin bowl. He ate quickly, set the bowl beside the basin and carried the pail of kitchen waste out to the mound. After that, he hauled the next day's water—slowed but undaunted by his useless hand. Wounded or no, he busied himself with a dozen other chores he hadn't seen to in years.

That night Lal worked long after his brothers and sisters were tucked up in bed. When he dragged himself to the kitchen door, she was waiting. To forgive me, he thought, his heart leaping. Then he saw the grey mass draped over her arm. It must've been the roughest blanket in the house, a relic from their first years in the Territory, when they were still just making do. She pointed the way to the horse barn. She wasn't speaking to him. No one was.

The next morning the tin bowl held porridge—no molasses, no cream. He spent a fortnight eating alone in the kitchen, sleeping in the stable loft. It wouldn't have been nearly so bad if he'd known it would come to an end—if he hadn't been convinced this proximate banishment described the new limit of his life.

When, after those two long weeks, he came to the kitchen and found no bowl awaiting him, he felt his heart sink further. Now she wouldn't even feed him. How long before she flushed him from his sorry bunk with a hay fork and sent him packing?

When she called him, her voice distorting as it filled the front hall—*Come to table, Lal*—he had trouble making sense of the words. Luckily, he'd made a friend by then, somebody who could set him straight. He brought his left hand to his mouth. Not the pinky side—the bent little finger was weak. The strong one, the one he could count on, was the thumb.

"Huh?" he asked it.

You're in, the thumb cried, *you're back in!*

"Lalovee Hammer!" his mother yelled.

Hurry up, clot, the thumb hissed, *you'll miss your chance.*

And Lal felt the legs beneath him move.

He gives a jerk, remembering. Finds himself still in the larder, his pinky finger—the right one, not its crooked partner—still plugging his mouth. He pulls it free. A soft, wet pop and, with it, the surfacing of a green idea.

Ruth will be in the silkhouse. Aunt Ruth, he should say properly, but as there's no one to hear him, he whispers only, *"Ruth."*

He could use a smoke about now, to singe the taint of stale fat from his tongue. Where safer than among Ruth's mulberry trees, where his mother has yet to set foot. Anything not purely practical is a waste in her eyes. Never mind that Ruth gleans silk from her labours.

Lal had his initial feel of the stuff when he was fourteen. It was the first year Ruth wasn't heavy with his father's latest brat, and it coincided with her first decent crop of mulberry leaves. She ran a length of newly spun thread across his palm, proud of what she'd made, unaware that she was altering the lined inside of his hand with a new, invisible groove.

Now that she's with child again, Lal watches Ruth whenever he can. There's a lovely new shape under her apron. Her profile is softening, causing him to lie awake nights, sweating. To take himself roughly in hand.

It's a sin to touch himself so, but with a religion that forbids so many comforts—liquor, hot coffee, even tobacco—how can a young man help but put a foot wrong? Yes, he could definitely use a smoke. And if he should happen to pass close by the silkhouse in his travels, well, he could use a little of that, too.

A stone's throw from his empty hut, the Tracker crouches in the brush. In his right hand, a digging stick—a tool so versatile, so scorned by white men looking down from their mounts. *Digger.* A single word to cover Paiute, Western Ute, Shoshone and more. Untold camps, untold peoples lumped into one.

He jabs and gouges, pausing to scoop the loosened earth away with his cupped hands. When the hole is elbow deep, he sits back on his heels. Closing his eyes, he feels tempted to call up a prayer. Instead, he reaches into the pocket of his waistcoat—sweat-stained, hanging open about his chest—and retrieves the she-wolf's eyes.

He sets them, one after the other, into the hole. Pupils down. This is part kindness, to keep from dropping grit into their unprotected gaze, and part cowardice, to avoid meeting that gaze with his own. He covers the eyes gradually, gently, but it is still dirt, still a burial. Patting the infill flat, he finds himself reluctant to apply much pressure, picturing the balls bursting, leaking away.

He stands and goes looking for stones. A pile, even a small one, will remind him. Besides, if the ground is left bare, anything could scrabble down through the loose pack and spirit the eyes away.

After an absence of an hour or more, the Tracker returns to load Dorrie's waste into the barrow. She doesn't know whether he will burn or bury it, or simply lay out a scavengers' feast. She's never asked.

He bloodies his front with the flayed, headless wolves, saves the brimming pails for last. Then, finally, she is alone.

Standing at the foot of the straw tiers, a pair of ground owls in stasis by her knee, Dorrie becomes suddenly, crushingly aware of her fatigue. Her arms dangle at her sides, hands stinging. It makes no difference how long she soaks them, how many coats of tallow she applies before sleep—they remain a torment to her, a pair of bony crosses to bear.

In her stillness, she becomes aware of the gentle nausea brought on by the scent of her arsenical soap. The stuff only makes her truly ill when she has to cook up a new batch. It's a simple recipe. Slice clean cakes of white soap into boiling water and watch them melt to slime. Add pounds of powdered arsenic, ounces of camphor, stirring to make sure the mixture doesn't scald. There are fumes and, no matter how gingerly a body pours the powder, fine particles that hover in a noxious cloud. Like any living creature, Dorrie can only hold her breath for so long.

She glances out the window, gauging the silky dark. Perhaps an hour or two until the first lightening, then another until Mother Hammer raises the alarm on her hollering bell. She should snatch a little sleep before breakfast, she knows, but the shelves stand between her and the cot, and she finds herself reaching for her gloves so that she might handle the mother wolf's skull again.

It's the teeth she can't seem to get past. The canines bristle when she hinges open the jaws, interlock like yellowed fingers when she eases them shut. Built to clamp and hold fast to thrashing prey, they can puncture even the toughest of hides, crack through to marrow, sever spines. The flesh teeth come together further back—paired sets of scissors for shearing off chunks. Behind them lie molars designed to crush pelvises, femurs, the densest of ungulate bones.

Dorrie turns the skull face-on and brings it closer—crossing her eyes slightly to maintain focus on the weave of teeth. Again she works the formidable jaws. Open. Shut. Open. It's all right. The only way she could get bitten now would be if she willed it. Snapped the mother wolf's mouth shut on herself.

She's not thinking right. She sets the skull back where it belongs and drags herself to the far corner of the barn, wheezing audibly as she hits the cot.

3

DORRIE DREAMS:

Wingbeats, deep and slow. The sun flares off my back feathers, firing my blood as I row through the grass-sweet current forced up by the escarpment below. The story stretches out beneath me, plain. Crow's-eye view.

To the east, the nesting humans lie low—the females huddled with their wounded and their young, the able males on guard. Circled wagons or no, it's a foolish place for a nest, the heart of a long meadow, open to predators on all sides.

They must be parched. The same sun that plays over my dark gloss will have shrunk their pink tongues to stubs. It's been three or four days since their wide-open camp curled in on itself like a grub—and all the while the nearby spring calling to them, saying *wet, clear, life*.

Several gaunt, red-eyed males have tried their luck, bursting from the circle into the waist-high grass, buckets held high, striking their ribs as they ran. Time and again they drew fire, black smoke tracery from the hills. Time and again they lost heart, abandoning their buckets, hurling themselves back into the nest, panting and dry.

The breeze, shifting now, bears up a carrion perfume. Around the circled camp, the grass shelters countless dead. Horses and cattle by the score, humans by the handful lie unmoving in its sway. Drawing near, I breathe deeply, but do not dive.

Today the human nest shows white, something hoisted, flapping high. Birdlike, but a sorry excuse—all glaring light, in service to the wind. I could show it a thing or two, bend the air to my will and not the other way round. Curious, I tilt a wing tip to carve a rent in the space beneath me, contract and slip along its spiralling length.

Swooping close, I learn the white is no bird, but a thing human-made, a rag on a pole—like one of those set out to flash among corn forests, unnerving my kind. No living thing at all, no threat. Still, the bird-heart in me cries out for safe vantage. I flap, climb to comfort and veer.

On the turn, a stirring. A figure emerges from the scrub to the north, advancing with the stiff-legged stalk of a male. He bears a second not-bird, this one a shade whiter, held aloft. I pump his way. The white flutters, but I am high enough now not to answer its rapid pulse with a quickening of my own. Instead I turn again, lay a bead on its quavering and hold it in the crook of my eye.

Now the curled camp spills a rag-bearer of its own, my vision split until the pair of them come face to face in the waving grass. Talk now, as always with the humans, talk. In the lull I become sensible of my wings, growing heavy now, each pinfeather crying at its root. The high current calls. Better yet, a juniper's jagged shade.

But wait. From the mouth of the same northern draw, a second figure appears. For a moment the distance plays tricks, showing a hound on its long hind legs. On the next wingbeat I see true—human, also male. This one comes empty-handed, arms swinging to feed his rigid stride. His aspect in slanted shadow as he passes below. The scent he gives up is close to canine—ravenous as crow, but nowhere near as clean.

The camp accepts both strangers, opening just enough to take them in. I dip and drift, settle on the taut, ribbed skin of a wagon's back. It stinks of humans, dead trees, broken-minded mules.

Ill omen. Normally, one of the females would catch sight of me and hiss—*sssssssttt* or *shoo*. Her brood would scoop stones and hurl, forcing me to lift and land, perhaps even shingle away. Not this day. This day they lie weakened, turning up their faces like a clutch of newborns, looking to the two outside males, especially the upright cur.

Only one of those nestled in the centre returns my gaze—a female with a fine fall of darkness down her back. Not feathers, but as close as any human might hope to come. Beside her, slumped in fitful rest, her young. Female, if I'm any judge—more of the same dark hair. Its over-skin is paler than the mother's, perhaps once as white as the call-and-answer rags.

The dark mother watches me for several breaths, then drops her eyes to the outsiders, disregarding the rag-holder, focusing on the dog man, the one with all the words. One after the other, the females around her rise and go to him. Weep and smile at their seeming-saviour, reach out to him with their filthy hands. Not the dark mother. Like me, she has eyes, a nose. She keeps to the depression, drawing from beneath the folds of her draping skins a dark brown block. Under her prying fingers it opens out doubled and blank.

Her eyes fixed on the dog man, she touches the tip of a thin tool to the blankness, drawing out black as a claw draws red. Unable to resist, I open my wings and drop, land soundlessly atop the barrel that supports her back. Risky, yes, but the vantage is clear.

The bird brain reels to witness it. First the sloping shadow of his gaze, and now, in a single cutting line, the terrible set of his jaw. She does him justice, recording not only the bowed lips, but also the teeth they hide. In time he stares up at me from her lap.

I hunch forward over her shoulder, my claw-hold precarious on the barrel's head. No one takes any notice of a lone black bird. All eyes on the dog man. He's silent now, cocking an ear to one of the nesting males. When quiet comes, he bobs his head, his hand snaking out to meet the other's in a clasp.

When I next look down, the line-and-shade face is gone. Doubtless she's tucked it away beneath her sagging skins. Do these humans never preen? Many of them are smeared red-brown as though they've recently danced through an abandoned kill. Their smell, too, speaks of old blood, fresh fear, the tangy promise of rot.

At a word from the dog man, his partner squeezes out through the same chink that allowed him in. I lift and follow, touch down on the same wagon's back, this time above the tail. Below, the rag-bearer raises his white signal and brings it tearing down. In answer, the northern draw disgorges two wagons, each bound to a pair of straining mules. What ails these creatures, that they allow humans to use them so?

Beneath my claws, a shifting—not of the wagon alone, but of the whole nest writhing, coming to life. I'm torn, tail to the chaos, beak and beady gaze to the slow advance. The wagons grow larger with every rolling step, cutting a wake down the wide river of grass. The bird eye describes two more human males, each seated astride a wagon's protruding tongue.

The dog man moves into the open as they draw near, the females following him with their broods in tow. Mules and wagons halt. I watch along my beak's black slope as, one after another, the mothers let go of the smallest among their young, allowing them to be hoisted into the shadow of the first wagon's mouth. The nesting males follow with their own offerings, feeding the wagon their long, glinting guns. Better to store these with the little ones than to trust them to the second wagon's load of injured adults.

The dark mother comes last, her single offspring stumbling at her side. The child gives out a wail that lifts my softest inner down. More mountain lion than human. Her hold is a cat's too. They have a time of it prying her free.

4

MOTHER HAMMER'S BELL.

Dorrie wakes to a simple vision, the sole remnant of what feels to have been a lengthy dream. The image is harmless enough—a white flag in a stiffening breeze—so why does her flesh crawl so on her bones?

She'll be late to the breakfast table if she doesn't rise soon, a further transgression she really shouldn't chance. Still, the white flutter lingers. Without planning to, she rolls onto her side and reaches beneath the cot. Feeling over the plump rise of a pillow, she closes her fingers around the feathered body resting there. Here is yet another sin against Mother Hammer's divine order—a good feather pillow wasted, stuffed away underneath a bed.

The first wife kicked up a fuss when Hammer dragged the cot out to the old barn after Dorrie had spent a week sleeping on straw. Scarcely wide enough for one, it was a husband's unspoken promise—she'd be left alone so long as she kept up the good work. Two wool blankets, a lone pillow and a worn set of sheets followed, sent on Hammer's orders, but borne in Sister Ruth's arms.

When requesting a second pillow didn't work, Dorrie lied, complaining of congestion, a need to prop herself up in bed.

"Is it any wonder?" Mother Hammer directed her reply to the far end of the table, as though she and her husband were dining alone. "Sleeping out there like a barn cat. She belongs indoors."

Hammer looked up from his plate, folding a strip of roast into his mouth. His silence was impossible to gauge. While Dorrie had yet to see him openly take Mother Hammer's side, he was not above deserting the poor soul who'd angered her.

He laid down his knife and fork. "Give her the pillow."

"I have enough to manage without babying the likes of her." Mother Hammer set her mouth, only to gasp when Hammer brought his fist down hard on the table. Dishes jumped. The first wife let the quiet billow and swell. Then punctured it. "As you wish."

It was childish, Dorrie knew, all this fuss so she could provide a stuffed crow with a comfortable bed. It wouldn't have been necessary if he could have perched on the crate beside her cot, standing guard the way he had on her bedside table back home. But Hammer had been perfectly clear on that point: every specimen on his ranch would be one that met its end by his hand. The collection they would build together would stand as a testament to his skill.

She hadn't minded leaving behind the weasel, the yellow cat, the mice. Not even the bright jay, so difficult to skin over the head, or the sharp-shinned hawk she'd mounted on the wing. Cruikshank Crow, however, she couldn't bear to part with. He was the first specimen she'd mounted, the only one she'd blessed with a name. She smuggled him along, swaddled in a petticoat at the bottom of her trunk.

Drawing the old crow out from beneath her bed, Dorrie lies back and stands him up on her chest. Black claws at her breastbone. His head sits slightly askew—an error she'd never make

today, but as luck would have it the effect is fitting. Cruikshank
Crow is curious.

If anything about the black bird seems unnatural, it's his gaze.
It wasn't Dorrie's fault—Mr. Cruikshank had a great many sup-
plies in his bulging leather case, but he'd run clean out of bird
eyes. He fingered through those he did have—fish, dog and deer,
all wrong in colour and nowhere near the right size—then sent
Dorrie on a hunt, showing her how to measure likely prospects
against her baby fingernail. A pair of pebbles were the best
replacements she could find. Both were black with a slaty sheen,
one round save for a tiny nick, the other slightly oblong, making
Cruikshank Crow a bird forever on the verge of winking.

Dorrie could replace the pebbles—pry them loose from their
sockets, chip out the hard putty and push in fresh, set in a shiny
pair of number nine browns—but it's an idea she's never seriously
considered. It would render the old bird more lifelike, more like
all the rest. Something he is not.

Mr. Cruikshank came out of nowhere that day—or rather
everywhere, the wide world beyond the farmyard she'd called
home since she was seven years old. His long legs carried him
down the Burrs' dirt track, a fat carrying case hampering his
stride. Mama took off her apron, told Dorrie to go into the
kitchen and walked down to meet him at the gate.

Dorrie slid down in her chair when her mother led the stranger
in through the kitchen door.

"Dorrie, this is Mr. Cruikshank. He's come to speak to your
father about some work. Sit down, Mr. Cruikshank." Mama
crossed to the cupboard and took down a glass.

"A pleasure to meet you, Miss Burr."

Dorrie said nothing. She was thirteen years old but built like a
riding quirt. His tone showed he'd taken her to be the age she looked.

The three of them sat in silence for a time, the visitor sipping the plum juice he'd been given, Mama seating herself before a pail of potatoes, turning one after another against her knife. The spotty ones she passed to Dorrie, who dug in her knifepoint to twist out bruises and sprouting eyes.

Mr. Cruikshank held his tongue until they'd peeled close to half the pail, then reached down to the case at his feet. "Do you mind, Mrs. Burr?"

Mama glanced up. "Go right ahead."

A leather tongue held the two halves closed. When he thumbed its brassy hasp, the case sprang wide, a hairless creature that had been holding its breath. Reaching into the nearest half, he withdrew a glossy wooden box. Its dimensions were those of a modest jewellery case. Its contents proved infinitely more precious than any locket or brooch.

The bird would have fit snugly in the cup of her hand. It was neat-headed, chubby, perfectly preserved. Heavenly blue marked with a cirrus waft of white. Mama smiled. Dorrie felt herself stand and draw close to the stranger and his prize.

"Budgerigar," he said softly.

"Budge-eri—"

"Or just plain budgie."

"Budgie." Her mind was racing. "How—"

He grinned, patting the open case at his feet. Dorrie knelt for a better look. Glint of bottles, gleam of blades. Mama set her potato aside and peered over the table's edge. "Why, Mr. Cruik-shank, what on earth?"

It turned out that what appeared to be magic was in fact the result of a series of physical acts. Once Dorrie had secured Mama's permission, she led Mr. Cruikshank around back of the barn, finding to her delight that the crow Papa had stoned that morning had yet to be carried off in the mouth of a fox. She stooped for it, and Mr. Cruikshank, comprehending, laughed.

"Very well. Have you a table where we can work?"

The butcher block in the shed would do nicely. He was a generous teacher, talking her through the process step by step, letting her learn with her hands. They began by loosening the wings.

"Bend them back until you feel the shoulders touch. Gently now, you don't want to break any bones."

She obeyed, easing the feathered limbs together across the crow's back.

"You can mount a bird with broken wing bones, but it's sloppy work. A professional takes every precaution to avoid mutilating his specimen. Remember that."

The initial cut taught her much—how to slide the knife like a finger's feeling tip, deep enough to sunder skin while leaving the flesh beneath it intact. Mr. Cruikshank kept up a steady stream of instructions, sprinkling handfuls of cornmeal over the crow's body from time to time. "You can always clean the feathers later if you must, but it's better not to spoil them in the first place."

She smiled at the ease with which the skinny legs pushed up out of their skin. Mr. Cruikshank handed her the heavy scissors, and she snapped through each of them at the knee. After stripping the toothpick bones clean, she thrust them back inside their leathery socks.

Next he talked her thumb and forefinger down either side of the ribs until they met at the small of the back. "Sever the tail at its root. Use the scissors. Careful you don't cut into the quills—your tail feathers will drop out if you do."

The skin could be peeled back now. The crow became a raw hand emerging from a glossy glove, its skull the final joint of the middle finger. Dorrie cut through both shoulders cleanly, releasing the black fans of the wings. Which left the delicate work of the head.

"Never pull," her teacher said quietly. "Use your thumbnail. Push the skin gently from the bone."

Dorrie felt her way. The folds that were tucked into the ear holes came out with a combination of prod and pluck. Mr. Cruikshank took over to work around the eyelids but allowed her the satisfaction of skinning down to the crow's black bill. Stooping to his case, he retrieved a heavier knife, with which he sliced deftly through the back of the bared skull, separating it from neck and tongue. The body adhered nowhere now. The skull, like the wings and leg bones, would remain with the hollow skin. Mr. Cruikshank laid the stumpy torso aside.

Dorrie was surprised when he told her to guide the tip of the fine knife around the socket of an eye. Her hand shook a little, and she was grateful when, for the first time, he reached in over her shoulder to steady it with his own. Together they loosened the dark brown balls, scooping one, then the other, out whole.

"Never, ever burst an orb, Miss Burr. Treat your specimen with respect."

After the eyes, there remained the small matter of the brain. Three secret, judicious cuts and out it came.

He taught her a great deal in those few short hours—how to poison skin and bones with a coat of creamy soap, rendering them resistant to both insects and rot. "Take extra care about the wing bones, Miss Burr."

She learned how to ease the skull back inside the skin, to tease the face and head feathers flat with the tip of a pin. Mounting the black bird then became an exercise in restoration—all they had removed, they now constructed anew. A brain of wadded cotton, a trunk of tow wound firmly with thread. Wires anchored in the new body gave shape to the neck, wings and legs. A fourth curved out beneath the tail, this last to be snipped off at its base in a week or so, once the skin had dried, allowing the tail feathers to set.

Threading a needle's narrow eye, Mr. Cruikshank showed her where to sink the four small stitches that would hold the crow's breast closed. When the last of these was tied, she bent its neck and limbs into a modest roosting pose.

"Be sure the flight feathers overlap one another cleanly." He folded the wings, pinning each to the body at the wrist joint, then shoving a further two pins in either flank for support. Withdrawing a pair of pointed tweezers from his breast pocket, he handed them to her. "Neaten him up. Whatever state he dries in, that's how he'll remain." She nodded and began picking over the crow, teasing every stray quill into place. Together they wound thread in complicated patterns about the pins that held the wings closed, further assurance against any hint of disarray.

It was then that he sent her to look for the eyes. She was only gone for a few minutes, but by the time she returned, both sockets were lined with moist putty, and Papa had come in from the fields. His moustaches were wet with labour, lank. He sucked at them, his eyes blazing. Mr. Cruikshank stepped away from her side to meet him.

Her memory of what followed is incomplete—she was so intent upon the crow, the final, unsupervised step of setting its ersatz gaze. Fragments of heated discussion filtered through.

"I don't understand you, sir."

"Don't come the innocent with me. You Gentiles are forever sniffing around our women—"

The crow was black, yes, but not only. A shimmer of green about its shoulders, blue along its cawing throat.

"You think—my God, man, she's a child!"

What more there was to it, Dorrie never knew. In truth, after doing the decent thing and naming the crow after him, she seldom spared her teacher a thought. His departure signified little, as he'd already set her on the path. Her mind was alight. So many creatures in the world, and all of them going to die.

Saddling Ink for the thirty-odd-mile ride to Salt Lake City, Erastus keeps his back to his first-born son. Can't help hearing, though, the overeager rattle of him rigging up that blasted horse. Erastus bought the pretty, difficult gelding in a moment's softheadedness, made a first anniversary gift of it to Thankful. She kept the red sash he'd tied around its neck—turned it into a surprising set of drawers, in fact—but refused to go near the horse.

He never actually gave the palomino to Lal. Just left it festering in its stall, let it grow desperate for the field while the boy got up the guts to ask.

"Can I ride him?" Voice cracking over a few short words.

"Suit yourself."

"Can I name him? I picked out a name."

Erastus left this last unanswered. Days later, he heard the boy whispering his choice in the gelding's ear. *Bull*. Not many could've gotten it that far wrong.

Erastus feels his upper lip contract. He plays with the notion of changing his mind. *I believe I'll go on my own*, is all he'd offer, let Lal's face fall as it may. And wouldn't it be fine, riding out for the city alone. Fine, yes. If only he could make out the terrain that lay more than a few yards beyond Ink's nose.

He tried spectacles, some four or five years ago now. It was a bit of a trick getting his hands on a pair. The nearby town of Tooele was out of the question—a crack hunter could scarcely wander through the front door at Brother Rowberry's and declare to all and sundry gathered there that he was getting on for blind. He knew of an apothecary's in the city, though, tucked away down a side street, quiet in the late stretch of day. There were no other customers in the place, but he locked the door behind him all the same, dragging down the blind. The man behind the counter stood steady. There were reasons besides robbery why a man might visit an apothecary on the sly.

Erastus tried on pair after pair, drawing them from the straw nest of their crate, settling them straight-armed and precarious across the bridge of his nose. He couldn't see far enough within the shop's walls for a proper test, so he opened a gap at the blind and peered down the dusty lane.

One pair did it, a bit slithery around the edges but the centre crystal clear. He could think of nothing but dropping his first quarry—something tricky, an antelope maybe, or a bighorn. That and the look on the Tracker's face when Erastus told him to hold his fire.

The thrill lasted until the city fell away behind him—houses thinning out, yards expanding to become farms. At the first unpopulated stretch, he tried the spectacles on. They stayed put while he kept Ink to a careful walk, but threatened to fly off at any kind of speed. Closer to home, he cut across country, dismounting when he was well into his own land but still a good distance from the house.

The damn things made a fool of him then and there. Without

them he couldn't discern the target. With them he couldn't line up his sights. He hurled them down as a child might and crushed them beneath his heel. Once mounted, he grinned bitterly to hear Ink follow in his footsteps, grinding the lenses beneath her hoof.

His vision is much deteriorated since that day—back then he could still trust himself to make a journey alone. He might take the Tracker with him to auction, if only the mulish devil would ride. There's no way in hell he's drawing up to that crowd with an Indian sharing his saddle, hugging his back. Besides, being Paiute, the Tracker doesn't know the first thing about handling horses. Lal tends to come down on the nasty side of things, but at least he can keep a string of colts and fillies under control.

On the up side, the pair of them will turn heads together. Erastus is a man of reputation, mounted on the finest-looking horse in any crowd. Bull makes a good contrast to Ink, an eyeful in his own right, so long as he chooses to behave. And there's no denying Lal's the sort both women and men watch. His mother's son. It's as close as Erastus will come to parading Ursula around Temple Square—the city no lure to her, even if it is the City of the Saints.

Truth be told, Erastus would just as soon not go himself. It'll be a day spent feigning interest in gaits and bloodlines, followed by a short night in a shared hotel room and the chore of the return ride. Hard to believe he used to have trouble sleeping the night before an auction. He can recall lying awake in a kind of fever, wondering how much his best colt would fetch, or whether a promising mare or even a stallion would catch his eye. It's been five years since he felt moved to buy a new horse. Last night he slept like a stone.

Ink stands waiting, kitted out. Mounting up, Erastus feels a familiar rush at assuming her height, a pride that encompasses both the horse and the springing strength extant in his fifty-two-year-old thighs. Once seated, he nudges out a stately, long-legged walk with his knees.

At his back, Lal opens the corral gate, cursing as he organizes the young horses in their string. When he finally takes his seat, grunting, the palomino paws and blows. Erastus gnaws at his lip, keeping himself in check. Ink trots up at his signal, the track disappearing before him as they leave the waking ranch behind. They'll do fine today, just fine. Lal manages well enough in town—it's in the wild that he's no earthly use.

Erastus used to let him tag along on hunts or roundups from time to time, telling himself the boy would harden into something worthwhile. It must be three years now since he last spun himself that particular line—yes, three, because Eudora had lately come to stay. In that case Lal would've been sixteen, old enough that Erastus should've been able to count on him. He shakes his head, recalling how his eldest son blanched at the sight of blood on that stark morning.

Erastus had heard talk of horse thieves at work in the region. Twin brothers, once good Saints, now apostates, were headed out the back door of the Territory, grabbing what horseflesh they could on the way. It was the Tracker who brought word that they were cutting favourites from the herd on the far pasture.

Erastus rode out at a gallop with the Indian clinging to his waist, while the boy floundered along behind them, kicking the palomino's ribs in to keep up. He drove Ink hard, but running was a joy to her, and before long the herd hove into view. Or what he understood to be the herd. What he saw was a particoloured, shifting copse. As they drew closer, he could make out a pair of forms that jutted above the canopy, wheeling to and fro.

The brothers fancied their odds. They held their ground and started shooting. Erastus turned loose on their wavering forms, his revolver bucking in his hand. The brown arm that swung up from behind him worked its weapon like an extra digit. Gesturing with muscular precision, it picked one twin, then the other, out of the panicking herd.

If the boy got off a single shot, Erastus didn't hear it. Chances are he had both hands around the saddle horn, hanging on like a slip of a girl.

The twins' own two horses were full-blood trotters, a chestnut gelding and an iron-grey mare, both welcome additions to the herd. The brother who fell first had a set of saddlebags tooled all over with a western vista—jagged peaks, trees clustered along a riverbank—the neatest bit of leatherwork Erastus had ever seen. The bags were wet with blood, enough so it ran in the many licks and hollows that made up the scene. To let the colour sink and stain would've been a shameful waste. Having quieted the spooked horse, Erastus worked the buckle loose and hailed his son.

There were dirtier jobs going than rinsing a pair of saddlebags in the nearby creek. Dragging a pair of matching bodies to a single grave, for instance—the Tracker didn't need telling, he was already breaking ground with his pick. You wouldn't know it, though, to see the look in Lal's eyes. It wasn't like Erastus to justify his actions—especially not to one of his own issue—and yet he found himself muttering something about sins beyond saving, apostasy being at the top of the list. Had the boy never heard of blood atonement? Didn't he know there was only one substance that could wash those brothers' souls clean? Brother Brigham himself had asked the question—*Will you love that man or woman well enough to shed their blood?*

In the end the boy did as he was told, but he handled the bags as though they were a pair of lungs still breathing. After that he helped the Tracker cover the twins with dirt and gathered brush to build a fire on the spot—thereby throwing animals off the scent and hiding any change in the earth. The whole time dropping things, stumbling over his own two feet.

Since then any outing that included Lal commenced and ended with the wheel-cut trail they follow now, known hereabouts as the Hammer Track. Ink knows the road and wants to run it. After a mile or so Erastus lets her.

"Hold up," Lal cries, already falling behind.

Dorrie's rhythm is all off. It's mid-afternoon and she ought to be sleeping—or if not sleeping, then working on the wolves. Instead, she paces from the small window at the back of her barn to the smaller one beside the door. The back view sprawls southwest down the greening valley. The front looks northeast into the circle of yard. On perhaps the twentieth pass, she halts to watch Sister Ruth exit the main house and cross to her stunted trees.

The swelling under Ruth's apron troubles Dorrie. How will the second wife carry on with her work next year? Can she possibly pick leaves and bear them to her worms with a baby dragging at her breast? True, she can look forward to Mother Hammer taking over once the thing is weaned, but by then she will have lost an entire season.

Babies are a deal of trouble, but at least they can be laid down and left to cry. Ruth's older children are dutiful—Mother Hammer has made them so—but they still require tending. Someone must feed and wash them, teach them to be virtuous, to warble out songs, to read. Endless trouble. Endless need.

Once, in the dead of Dorrie's first winter on the ranch, the eldest daughter made the mistake of bringing that need to her.

Hammer had dropped off a frost-stiffened snowshoe hare only an hour before. Dorrie was just getting to work on the thing when she felt a sudden blast of cold and looked up to find Josephine standing mutely in the crack of the door. The stove threw its heat her way. Stupid child, holding a door ajar in January. Telling her to close it would be risky, though. She might take it as an invitation to step inside.

Dorrie crossed her arms. "Mother Hammer doesn't like you being here."

The girl didn't budge.

"It's dangerous."

Still nothing. Josephine stood shivering, snow sifting in around her, dusting the raw wood floor. Her eyes wide and wary, she took in the hare, the knives in their neat array. What harm if she did come in and warm her small hands by the stove? None, except that Dorrie had come over all gooseflesh. From the wind, yes, but only in part.

It was something about the girl's size—perfectly normal for the six- or seven-year-old she was then. Dorrie had worked on smaller specimens, creatures whose translucent ribs would seem mere filaments alongside the finger bones Josephine harboured in her mittened fist. Still, the child's body seemed insufficient, vulnerable in the extreme.

A nauseous ache took hold of Dorrie by the shoulders. She reached for the hare and held it out at arm's length.

"Run away, little girl," she squeaked, bobbing the rigid ears. But her stepdaughter was already long gone.

There's a dream Ruth has—not often, perhaps once a month. Save the past four. Save any she's passed while in the family way.

It will return, she tells herself. Once I am delivered of my burden, it will return.

Lying atop the covers, she cups a hand to the rise of her condition. Still months to go and already the thing is stoking her blood to blazing, weighting her steps, making a dull sponge of her brain. She shifts onto her side, her temple seeking a fresh spot on the pillow. How is she meant to rest? More to the point, how is she meant to work?

She's seen through five whole seasons, egg to moth, but never while carrying a child. Sister Thankful gave her those good years, arriving when Ruth was fit to burst with Baby Joe and thereafter keeping their husband to herself. It was all but painless, being cast aside. Five babies in as many years had gone a long way to dulling what little wifely feeling Ruth had known. By the time Hammer took his third wife, his second was dwelling more and more frequently on the life she'd led before meeting him. Or, more precisely, on the sense of future she was then possessed of, the promise she had yet to fulfill.

Of her actual life, she missed nothing. Not London—though in truth she knew little of the great city beyond her home district of Spitalfields. Certainly not the close quarters she'd shared with her mother until her sixteenth year, when the older woman died gasping in her sleep.

Every day but Sunday, Ruth navigated the pinch and racket of Brick Lane. Weavers' cottages stood chockablock, their high banks of windows fitted not for anyone's pleasure, but to keep the workers within from going blind. Mr. Humphrey ran as good an operation as any. Ruth knew a decade's employ there, from the time she was nine years old. Her mother had started six years before that. The pair of them would sit back to back in their corner of the attic loomshop, each tying on a warp. Until Ruth sat alone. Fifteen thousand threads give or take. A donkey's workday. A pauper's wage.

As she turns to cool the other temple, the face of her employer rises unbidden, long and wavering as a wraith's.

Miss Graves, you strike me as an intelligent young woman. Tell me, are you interested in silk?

I am, sir.

She answered without pause, without gauging the layers of his intent. He was old enough to have fathered her—to have fathered her poor dead mother, come to that. And he was married, even if Mrs. Humphrey, martyr to a trick heart, rarely left her bed. Ruth sees now how it ought to have been clear to her. It was fitting that an employer should stoop close to inspect his worker's technique, but no man's eyesight is that near.

"In that case I shall instruct you in the subject. It is, as you can well imagine, a particular passion of mine." He smiled thinly. "Come down to my office when you finish here."

So began an education. Weeks passed without so much as a hint of suspicion to cloud her mind. This was in part because Mr. Humphrey advanced upon her at a glacial pace—knuckles brushing her elbow, then nothing for days—but in the main because the matter of his talk so stirred her imagination that she grew dull to her actual surrounds.

One lesson in particular impressed itself upon her mind.

"You will recall, Miss Graves, the topic of our last discussion, the domestication of *Bombyx mori*."

"I do indeed, sir."

"Excellent. Now, common as this little fellow is, you mustn't imagine his to be the only species responsible for producing the world's silk."

Mr. Humphrey had in his possession a selection of books, the pages of one of which he now laid open. Coming to stand alongside Ruth in her chair, he lowered the exposed folio into her line of view. The engraving thereon was so delicate, so compelling, she couldn't help but trace it with her finger's tip.

"Life-size, if you please," he murmured.

Here were no pale, captive insects. The Tusseh silk moth of India spanned an entire page, fully six inches from wing tip to wing tip. The caterpillar was an arching monster, strung together out of sacs rather than segments, bristling with starry tufts of hair. What was more, the species was untamed, untameable. Those who would harvest its fine produce were obliged to watch over the great worms wherever they chose to spin.

In the dream it is Ruth who stands shepherd to the pendent cocoons. The jungle is hot and dark. For a time all is quiet.

The bats come first, chittering patches of night. Then their opposites, the white and whistling birds. Snakes brighten the leaf litter. Cats—several times tabby-weight—balance in the overhead boughs. *Mangrove, crepe myrtle*—marvellous names for mysterious trees. There are even dogs, thick-shouldered, bristling with copper fur. To reach the cocoons they must leap to heights quadruple their own. And they will, if no one stops them.

But this is no nightmare. The dream-Ruth is fearless. She plucks leathery wings from the vine-draped vault, crushes hissing tongues beneath her heel. She is equal to the leaping red dogs, equal to everything that comes on.

Close to sleep now, Ruth shifts her loosely shut eyes, bringing the ghost of that engraved page clear. Such moths. Bodies like furred, truncated thumbs. Wings made lovely by brave design— primitive figures of stark, unblinking eyes.

Thankful wakes with a start, her neck awry. She's alone in the parlour. Night has fallen and no one has bothered to wake her— they haven't even left her a candle. The half-worked bodice lies across her lap. She can't fathom its colours in the gloom—black appliqué on velvet of a midnight blue. A garment her mother's milk-and-coal colouring would have rendered lethal. One she would have judged sinful to wear.

Thankful may not have the complexion, but there are other ways to make a dress work. She has a character firmly in mind: a French noblewoman driven by circumstance to depend upon the charity of strange men.

In the dark, Thankful locates her last stitch, knots the thread and bites it through. The pincushion is a cool and spiny thing. She sticks the needle in deep and sets her work aside, making sure to arrange it bosom-up on the side table, where it will rankle in Mother Hammer's eye. Rising, she finds her neck is well and truly cricked. She must carry herself with care or risk a headache. Foolish to have dropped off like that, upright in the midst of them all.

She navigates across the parlour, arms waving like the fronds of some underwater weed. Once through to the dining room, she feels her way from chair back to chair back, pausing to turn and peer at the hunched shadow of the clock. Its face is silvery, the placement of its hands unclear. She suffers a wash of imbalance, clutches the chair at hand—the youngest boy's place—and clings there a moment.

Overhead, a floorboard sounds its weakness. The room directly above Thankful ought to be empty, it being the bedchamber she calls her own. It can't be Hammer—he's away in the city overnight. Letting go of the chair, she moves blindly into the front hall. Before her the kitchen stands in darkness. Mother Hammer abed then. *Or not.* A quarter turn, half a dozen sliding steps and the toe of Thankful's slipper touches stair. She gropes for the banister and ascends.

Light-footed or no, she's not fool enough to imagine sneaking up on the first wife—there may as well be bat's ears under that whitening hair. Still, she proceeds softly. At the round of the landing, the wall before her bristles with framed mottoes. She sets three of them askew before continuing on.

Ruth's door stands at the head of the stairs, then more of the first wife's embroidered words. Thankful takes a breath and steps into the wash of weak light escaping her chamber's open door. Backlit by a lamp, Mother Hammer rises up on her knees before the gleaming dresser. Every drawer gapes, several spilling their bright insides. Thankful pictures the front-heavy dresser toppling, crushing the first wife where she kneels.

It's not the first time Mother Hammer has run her big hands over Thankful's things. God knows what she thinks she's looking for—a length of rubber piping, perhaps. A bottle of vinegar or soapy spirits. Some pronged, indelicate device. *What does she take me for?* Thankful leans against the jamb. Let the witch snoop, watch her slink away.

Mother Hammer keeps on about her business as though unobserved, rifling through the bottom drawer, shaking out item after item as though searching for insects in their folds. She stands with the last of these still in hand, assuming her full height fluidly, like a lamp wick turned up high. The garment is a precious one, a bed jacket of buff and grey feathers worked in a cunning design. Thankful fashioned it four years ago—she remembers, it was more than a month's work. Its front panels mimic the face of an owl. Two well-placed holes allow her nipples to stand in for the glowing eyes.

"Careful with that." She smiles. "It's one of his favourites." Then she sees that the other hand too holds something in its grasp. A shape like an unnamed organ, pale pink and shimmering. Thankful feels her smile stiffen. Mother Hammer lets the owl jacket fall and, in a counter motion, brings the small, scented pillow hard against her nose. Thankful's breath deserts her. She's grateful for the support of the jamb.

"You think this will hide it?" The first wife gives the sachet a violent squeeze before casting it to the floor. "You think a few petals can cover the stink of your sin?"

Silence swings like a footbridge between them, and then Thankful giggles, a sound that surprises them both. It shakes the older woman. She snatches up her lamp, says nothing as she pushes past.

Thankful watches her shunt away down the hall. "Sleep well, Mother Hammer," she calls softly. She can't help herself. The first wife hasn't a clue.

The Tracker sits cross-legged before his fire, loosing the leather-bound book from his thigh. It's been in his possession for a decade, and though he has paged through the journey it depicts a thousand times, he has yet to do so by the light of day. Tonight he confines himself to those drawings that move him distantly, taking care not to smudge the dark lines of which they're made.

One, about a third of the way in, shows a wide plain peopled with giants. It is the only buffalo herd the Tracker has known, his own land closed in by mountains, the great beasts present there in legend alone. So much meat, so many heavy hides. Little wonder the people of the plains are mighty.

Turning several pages in one, he lands on a drawing that never ceases to make him frown. A stone-faced Mormonee stands with his arms knotted across his chest. Behind him countless sacks spill corn. His stance is familiar to the Tracker, a certain stiffness that comes of refusing a hungry stranger food.

Closer to the end of the book, the Tracker finds a picture he cannot help but like. A white man, young and keen, drives a path through waist-high grass. The Tracker is neither white nor nearly so young, but he has lived this drawing untold times. His earliest memories are set in such meadows, deep sinks of grass girded by slopes of juniper, piñon, sage.

The first time he was allowed along on a rabbit drive, he plunged into the high growth to one side of the path and found himself in over his head. A panicked spinning on the spot wound the four directions into one. He came close to yelling, reducing himself to a nuisance—or worse, a funny story to tell the women and elders—but managed to bite back the cry.

Only then, heart in his mouth, hammering at the backs of his teeth, did he remember the fifth direction—sky. Suddenly all was open. The sun hung where he'd left it, climbing up from the land beyond the camp. Turning the back of his head to its glow, the Tracker brought his palms together and parted the way, keeping on until his own thin path met the beaten-down track of the men. Rabbits are not buffalo, but still he gloried in the hunt that day. Still the People were fed.

— 5 —

May 15th, 1867

Dear Daughter

Forgive my wretched lettering. My every finger has puffed up fat
as a field mouse. Do you recall the set you left behind Dorrie?
The papa mouse sitting up on his heels begging. The mama
with her cheeks full of seeds. Such fine work. Such a clever girl.
But I lose my thread. The way my thoughts wander these days
your poor mother cannot help but fear this cursed swelling has
found its way to her brain.

Why on earth should they call it dropsy? A word better suited
to a skinny creature with hair falling out in clumps than to this
bed-load of lard I have become. If only it were true fat and not
fluid. Do you know I pressed the pen to my forearm before I
began writing and the pit is still there. If I could reach my sewing
basket and pluck out a needle I should be sorely tempted to auger
holes in this flesh of mine. In any case it would do no good. The
fluid does not run like the water in a creek but settles like that in
the creek bed. I am drowning yes but not in water. In mud.

Dorrie there are times when I can scarce pry up an eyelid
and why should I wish to when all about me I see nothing but

disorder and dirt. The girl has made her mark on the place all
right. You would not recognize the kitchen. The last time I
managed to drag myself out there the sight gave me such a pain
up under my ribs I was certain I should faint dead away. Do not
think me ungrateful. I know it is she who turns me in the bed
and lifts me onto the pot and washes my most secret parts
without a single unkind word. But must the cloth she washes
me with always be left to moulder in the basin when it ought to
be rinsed and wrung out to dry? Must the sheets when she
finally comes round to changing them always be stiff and
scratchy straight off the line? Must they be grey?

Do you remember how white you and I brought the linens
out my girl? Mother's little laundry maid. The first time you
helped me pin pillow slips and tea towels to the drooping line
I so looked forward to fixing the pole and hoisting the laundry
high. I was certain the sudden fluttering would delight you.
Forgive me Dorrie I should have thought. I never would have
dreamt a child of seven years could cover such ground. It took
all the breath I had in me to catch you and gather you up
wailing in my arms.

You were always such a help to me. Even after you started
work on your animals you never once troubled me with your
mess. I don't believe I picked up so much as a curl of down or a
tuft of fur. The girl could take a page from your book. I can see
her out the window now standing on a potato plant watering in
the full sun. But why concern myself when I feel certain I will
no longer tread the earth by the time she's grubbing up her
stunted crop.

Dorrie can I hope to set eyes on you before I die? I do so
hate to harp but you are three years married now my girl and
you have never once come home. Will Mr. Hammer not allow

it? You never say if he is a good husband to you. You write so
seldom and when you do your letters are so very thin. Always
you mention your latest specimen. I believe a badger was your
last. The rest I am left to guess at.

Daughter are you well? Have you one friend among Mr.
Hammer's other wives or perhaps among their children? You
were a child yourself when you married him after all no matter
what your father claims. Dorrie I cannot bear to think of you
living as your mother does in the midst of others and yet alone.

Is Mr. Hammer kind to you? Does he treat you with any sort
of care? He did not impress me overly with his character. You
will know this Dorrie. You will have heard me argue the point
with your father. That was before he gave up all right to the title
by bartering you away.

My girl I should not write this but I do. On my wedding night
I bled so I believed I was dying. ~~Your father~~ No I shall call him
Mr. Burr from here on. To think I ever called him by his
Christian name. Lyman. I have not spoken it aloud in three
years. I shall never do so again.

On the night of the day that saw me sealed to him Mr. Burr
rose from the bed and left me to my bleeding saying it was not
for a man to have knowledge of such things. The flow stanched
in the end but not before I had watched myself turn pale as a
lily in the mirror that stood across from our bed. The same bed I
lie in now. So many years I shared this rickety iron boat with
that man. So many nights I woke to his howling and lulled him
back down only to lie staring myself.

But Dorrie your mother was a woman when she married.
Nineteen or twenty I can't think which. You were fourteen years
of age. I pleaded with him. I told him time and again how it would
break my heart and when that didn't work I tried to frighten him

by saying you were too frail for the marriage bed. I insisted you could not possibly weather the trials of confinement let alone the tortures childbed can bring. I should have known by his answer. And what would you know of it woman? Confinement? Childbed? What would you know?

I should have seen then that he had but little feeling left for his family. That he had already plucked out his heart to bestow it elsewhere.

Dorrie these pages are all I can manage for now. I will not send them yet. You have only ever written one letter to my dozen so I might just as well save up a bundle before I send them and hope for one in return. Do not think I mean to blame you Dorrie. If ever a blameless soul walked the earth it is you.

> All a mother's love
> Helen Burr

— 6 —

HAVING SLEPT through the breakfast bell, Dorrie has taken the unusual step of joining the family for the midday meal. A mess of cornbread, greens and gravy eaten in haste. She's shuffling back to her barn when the sound of hoofbeats spins her on the spot. Along the track three riders bob into view. She moves into the privy's slim shadow and looks out.

As always, Hammer rides in the lead. Behind him, Lal pinches the toffee-smooth gelding between his overgrown thighs. And behind Lal, a stranger.

Loose-waisted in the saddle, the new man sways. His horse looks to be a mare, heavily muscled about the haunches, built to go hard and far. Hip bones set too high make for a fair jolt in her gait—she'd be a bone-rattler to most, but the new man rides her mildly, a thin bird trusting its tree.

The mare is a chestnut, unusually dark. Dorrie knew another like it once.

Since forever—or at least since she emerged from the fevered landscape of her childhood illness and began the life she can recall—Mama had taken her to visit the horses in their stalls. In the beginning she went wrapped in the yellow blanket, carried through blinding brightness to gentle gloom. As her strength returned, she began to cross the yard at Mama's side. Once there, she would stand before one of the stalls and hold up a trembling hand, half a red apple wobbling on her palm—fingers flat, or the teeth might mistake one of them for an additional gift. "They're like chisels," Mama reminded her. "Not all the grass in this world is tender."

The red-brown mare Papa called Shade was the tallest on the farm, long in the leg, almost spindly. Dorrie portioned out her favours to all—the muscle-bound paint she would later learn to ride, Pepper, the salt-coloured gelding that was Mama's favoured mount—but in her heart of hearts she loved the gangly Shade best.

She remembers the dark eye descending, lips muscling over her apple-scented palm. She was thrilled almost to the point of terror the first time she stepped onto an upturned bucket to stroke Shade's long face. She took great pains to avoid the vulnerable blind spot between the mare's eyes, the white snip there Mama had warned her not to touch.

Heaven only knew where Shade came from, or even how long she'd been on the farm. Mama couldn't seem to recall, and the first time Dorrie asked Papa turned out to be the last. He too had no answer for her, just a sudden stillness, a stiffening along his spine. He was balanced in a squat over the washing-up pail on the porch. When he finally did twist her way, he said only, "Fetch me a cloth."

The next morning he saddled up Shade and led her prancing from the barn. Dorrie couldn't help but feel pleased with herself—clearly her questions had reminded him it was high time he let the thin mare stretch her legs.

They heard the shot, she and Mama both. They were bent over a lesson in pie crust, the two of them white up to their elbows with flour. They thought nothing of it, or if not nothing then *a rab-*

bit, maybe, and Mama might have said something about setting aside a chunk of pastry in case they'd be making cottontail pie.

Papa broke the news as though it was nothing. Not when he first arrived, his dirty boots echoing over the porch, not even during the meal, but afterwards, when all three of them were full. He told it from behind his napkin, wiping his mouth as he rose.

"Shade bust a cannon bone." He laid the soiled napkin over the plate he'd rubbed clean with a wedge of bread. "I had to put her down."

For an instant Dorrie could read her own horror writ large on Mama's face. But only an instant, for then Mama too was standing, reaching for the empty stew dish and clutching it to her chest. "What a shame." She said it almost brightly, addressing a spot on the wall behind her husband's back. Neither of them looked in Dorrie's direction. Papa ducked away to the parlour. She could picture him in there, assuming the fat armchair, reaching for the month-old *Deseret News.*

"On your feet, miss." Mama's skirts brushed up against Dorrie's dangling leg. "Help Mama clear away this mess."

Dorrie did as she was told. Stacked up the greasy dishes, cutlery in a tangle on top. Dipped the rag and wrung it out and scrubbed the kitchen table's planks. Not right away, though. Mama had stoked up the coals and set the washing-up water on to boil before Dorrie felt able to slide down from her chair and stand. It wasn't her legs—thin though they were, they felt sturdy enough. It was her throat. There was something inside there, forcing its way up from below. Like a hand, but blunter. Furrier.

She swallowed it. Just as she swallows the ghost of it now. Just as Hammer's stable swallows the rump of the new man's mare.

Hammer's horse barn is vast and dim. Riding in on the heels of
the eldest son's horse, Bendy Drown smells the way of things—
piss-soaked straw, droppings left to grow mushrooms, here and
there a furtive whiff of mouse. Sure enough, in the shadows of
the second stall, a rodent-toned flash atop a sizable mound of
manure. Feeding there. Plucking out seeds.

Hammer dismounts in the midst of things, seemingly unaware
of the scuttlings now audible in the cessation of clattering hooves.
Strange that a man who rides such a magnificent horse—a man
known for having supplied mounts to those in the highest
positions—should allow his animals to suffer such neglect.
Hammer's reputation had preceded him to the auction; Bendy
caught wind of it before he ever set eyes on the black mare and its
rider. At the time it seemed enough to single his new employer
out from the press of ranchers offering him work.

He'd done little enough to warrant the attention of so many
men. When a twitchy three-year-old had dumped its fourth rider
in a howling heap, he'd jumped the gate, if only to save the colt
from the other young men rising up at the fence rails. Approaching
the colt at an even pace, he kept his eyes to the ground and mum-
bled a low refrain. He introduced himself before reaching for the
reins, making sure to breathe a good part of his name into the animal's flaring nostrils. *Here I am. Bendy. It's only me.*

In the end the colt was willing enough—Bendy felt the fine back
accept him the moment he took his seat. It was the crowd he didn't
like, the bellowed bids and queries, and in particular the auction-
eer's rapid-fire drone. Bendy compensated with a close-hugging ride,
drawing the animal's attention back to the red comfort of its own
heart. He built up the steady counter-thrum of a trot, filling the
spaces between hoofbeats with a guttural hum. Two turns of the
corral and the colt was a champion. The bids flew thick and fast.

And now he's here. Miles from where he woke this morning, stable hand on the Hammer ranch. The man who hired him lingers at the off side of the great black mare. The top of his hat scarcely crests her withers. It's a wonder he can ride her at all.

The son and his horse make a better match. Dismounting with a sodden gracelessness unexpected in one so good-looking, Lal Hammer straightens to stand shoulder to shoulder with his flashy ride. The palomino sidesteps to put distance between them and commences sucking wind. Lal's fist whips out to jab him in the barrel. The horse ceases gulping, but Bendy marks the glint of his rolling eye.

Swinging down from Stride's back, he feels his every joint protest the hard fact of the floor. Now is not the time for the freakish, hyperextended stretches that will bring him relief. He contents himself with a discreet backbend of the knees, invisible within the denim bulk of his britches.

Nor, it seems, is it the time for questions. Hammer's already on his way toward the gaping door. "Lal'll show you the ropes. Come for supper at the bell." Passing by closer than necessary—closer than is customary among men in the wide-open West—he cocks a black eyebrow. "Got a wife needs seeing to."

For a short man he covers a good deal of ground in a few strides. The moment he veers left, disappearing from the door's wide frame, the son clears his throat and spits. "You'll bunk up top in the loft."

"Right. Do the others sleep up there too?"

"Others?" Lal's smile is slow, unfriendly. "His Indian'll duck in of a winter night, but only when it's really cold. He's horse-shy."

It takes a moment to sink in. All these stalls. Bendy reaches absently for the buckle of Stride's girth.

"Uh-uh." Lal crosses his arms. "You see to his horse first." He's younger than Bendy by perhaps three or four years. His eyes are impressive—huge in his well-shaped skull, cornflower bright. Only they can't quite hold their ground.

"Okay." Bendy lays a reassuring hand on Stride's rump, then steps past Lal and the palomino to where Ink stands motionless. "Which stall is hers?" He takes a light, respectful hold on the big mare's reins.

"Take a guess."

Looking round, Bendy spies a double-sized enclosure down the far end. "You want me to do Bull next?"

"When I want something doing, I'll tell you. I'll be back directly." Lal swivels and makes for the open door, leaving the palomino unsure, shifting on his overgrown hooves. Horse breath and echo. Then the sound of Hammer's son pissing hard against the outside wall.

Bendy leaves the big mare, crossing quickly and quietly to Bull. The gelding is wary at first—neck levering up in answer to his firm hand taking hold of the reins—but the moment Bendy reaches down to loosen the over-cinched girth, the horse inside it seems to slacken and give.

"All right, boy. All right now." A muttered accompaniment to the swift work of his hands. Reaching up under the saddle, he feels over the blanket, smoothing the thick crease that will have been a torture to Bull's back. Next he shifts the whole rig forward up onto the withers, then eases it back, redirecting hairs that have lain the wrong way since early morning. Stride stands where he left her, looking on with what he can't help but feel is an approving eye. He fixes the buckle of Bull's girth two holes looser, his reward a double lungful of grassy breath that bottoms into a sigh.

He's leading Ink back to her station when Hammer's son calls to him from the door. "Do Bull next. Then you can get started shovelling stalls."

Feeling his heart begin to sink, Bendy fixes his attention on the animal in his care. Ink is oddly placid for such an enormous horse. She flows easily into her stall, headed for the few stray wands of hay still clinging to the rack.

Seated at her vanity, Thankful pinches blood into her cheeks. She has several pots of colour but none that achieves quite such a becoming hue. Of course it fades. And there's the threat of bruising—she's done it twenty times already today, imagining she's heard hoofbeats in the distance.

This time he's really home. She watched him ride up the track minutes ago with Lal and a new man following hard. A young, gangly man, undeserving of a second look.

As soon as Hammer can get past the first wife and her accounts book, he'll be up to see her. She inspects her face in the mirror. How is it she inherited not one of her mother's features? For such a bleeding-heart ninny, Eliza Cobbs was terribly selfish, hoarding those good looks to herself. *"Ninny."* It helps a little to utter it aloud. A beauty like that. Her mother could have had any man in Chicago, but fell instead for a nobody who bred her the second he got her home from the church. Surprise, surprise— the landlord came calling and Daddy was never seen again.

Thankful pulls a grimace, lets it go slack. Nose too sharp, lips too thin, eyes too small, a nasty pebble-grey. All gifts from her long-gone father, polluter of his wife's perfection. Eamon Cobbs. *Cobbs*—even the name he saddled them with is ugly. Her mother wept buckets for him over the years, long, wet lashes framing her clear green eyes. She might have called herself a widow and married again, or at least taken a wealthy lover. Instead she took in laundry. Let her legs grow slack standing over a washboard, turned her hands into a pair of boiled puddings, built her right arm to bulging with the weight of the iron.

Thankful was seventeen the day she decided they could no longer get by on the pittance her mother earned. She'd passed the Limelight often enough; to effect the change she had only to turn and walk in. The theatre adored a beauty, but it required ordinary women too. The clever sisters, the maids-in-waiting, the nuns. All the better if those lesser players could fill a costume well.

Thankful takes solace in her figure, which is better than the ninny's ever was—better than most. High, full breasts, a girl's hard waist and a nicely bustling behind. Dancer's legs. Her mother suffered wormy, painful veins, but Thankful knows better than to let her blood sink and pool. She puts her feet up whenever she can, sleeps with her heels on a pillow plumped up fatter than the one beneath her head.

She had her admirers, men in ill-fitting coats who sat partway to the back. They were generally good for six months to a year before they tired of her or ran low on funds. One, an overseer at an ironworks, was missing five teeth—three top and two bottom—where a grapple hook had caught him in the cheek. The flesh there sunken as though sucked from the inside. He begged Thankful to push her tongue through the gap, moaning when she worked it slowly over the bumpy gum. She did what she had to. The better men, the ones who brought roses backstage, never brought them for her.

When Hammer approached her in the theatre's back lane, he bore a clump of ox-eyed daisies in his fist. Thankful had been at the Limelight for half a dozen years by then, and if anything, her parts were getting smaller. Of late a girl with a heart-shaped face, formerly assistant to the wardrobe mistress, had been cast as Audrey, a Country Wench—a role that had been Thankful's on the last run.

She knew the sound of a door opening when she heard it, and in this case it sounded like a terse proposal offered by a short, uncultured man. He was father-aged, no drawback to a girl who'd made do without one. He let her know right off he was a man of property. The best grazing land in the valley. The finest horses. A beautiful eight—*eight!*—bedroom house. The fact that two of them already held wives came as a surprise, no denying, but she'd never let wives stand in her way before.

Backstage the following night, she couldn't help but crow.

The heart-faced girl piped up. "Utah? He's never one of them Mormons?"

"Saints," Thankful corrected her icily. "And yes, he is. He's in Chicago on a mission."

"A *Mormon?*" This from Charlotte de Courcey, perpetual lead. She was Cleopatra that night, haughty in headdress and bird's-wing eyes. "Thankful, you silly slut, how do you know he hasn't got himself a wife already?"

Shrieks of laughter.

"He does, Charlotte." That shut them up. And then the line she'd been practising all day: "Just like your Mr. Webb."

If Thankful had any doubts, they died during that night's show. A house half empty, a few hoots for Charlotte, smatterings of shabby applause. And her rancher. Front row centre, leaning forward in his seat whenever she set foot on the stage.

Following Lal into the dining room, Bendy finds himself herded to a seat on the table's left flank. He's surrounded by sons—the sullen eldest on his right, the younger boys to his left. Three sets of eyes, three heads oiled and combed, a single equine shade. Beyond them, at the table's tail end, sits the woman who can only be first and foremost among Hammer's wives. Her gaze is unnerving. Even seated, she's clearly inches taller than any woman he's known.

Bendy pays little attention to Hammer's muttered grace. He knows he should keep his eyes closed, even as he cracks them to take in the facing female side. On the first wife's left, the youngest girl wears her hair in stubby plaits. Beside her, an older sister has hers dragged back into the severest of knots, though she can't be more than ten. They match their three young brothers in colouring. A third, the eldest girl, has inherited Hammer's jet-black hair.

Letting his eyes linger a moment, he finds she resembles her five look-alike siblings in no way. Where they're sturdy and well groomed, she's sinewy, unkempt. Her loosely clasped hands are raw, afflicted with angry scales. Her age is difficult to judge—her build adolescent, her bone structure adult. Between her and the eldest son there exists no point of comparison. Lal is a masculine recasting of the first wife—the same cornsilk hair and startling eyes. As she is handsome, so he is beautiful.

To the left of the black-haired girl, the source of the chestnut-haired children becomes plain. The woman seated directly across from Bendy is quietly lovely. The second wife, he guesses. It's not such a difficult idea to get used to. Women were a rare commodity in San Francisco, where he grew up—it only made sense to share. Here they do things differently again.

Beside the second woman sits a third and possibly favourite wife, given her position at Hammer's right hand. She's dressed entirely out of keeping with her surroundings, her dress fly's-wing green, the bodice cinched tight, spilling a powdered helping of breasts. Painted lips between hollow cheeks between two great clutches of dirty-blonde curls. A complexion along the same yellow tones, though here too she's been generous with the powder. She's no beauty, but holds herself as though she were. On the word *Amen*, her eyes snap open, fixing not on Bendy but on the young man beside him. On Lal.

The first wife lifts her head and orients it his way. "Brother Drown, you know my husband and our eldest son." She gestures to the boys on Bendy's left. "This is Joseph, Joe and Baby Joe."

Bendy nods, keeping his face a blank. With such a woman, there's little chance she's pulling his leg.

Two fingers touch down briefly on her bosom. "You will address me as Mother Hammer." The hand sweeps on. "This is Josepha, and my eldest girl, Josephine." She leaves him hanging for a moment, confused. Then, "My husband's fourth wife, Sister Eudora."

Wife? She watches him through a slide of black hair. For an instant he feels his face betray him—the very instant confusion gives way to alarm. She looks away before he can wipe his expression clean.

"Sister Ruth is Brother Hammer's second wife." Mother Hammer concludes the round of introductions with a flick of her long fingers. "Sister Thankful is number three." The third wife cracks her mouth as though to speak, but Mother Hammer holds the floor. "Tell me, Brother Drown, how do you come to live among God's people in Zion?"

Her gaze is blade-like. He fights an idiotic urge to lift a hand to his face and feel for the warm, wet evidence of its touch.

"Well, ma'am—"

"Mother Hammer."

"Mother Hammer. I lived in Utah once before."

"Deseret. It is the Congress of the United States that refers to this Territory as Utah, men who have never set foot on its blessed soil. They named it after the Indians who were content to leave it a barren wilderness. The Kingdom of Deseret, that is the rightful name."

"Brother Brigham's name." Hammer sits back, smug-faced in his chair.

"Taken," Mother Hammer adds, "from the Book of Mormon, which, as you know, was translated from the ancient tongue by Brother Joseph, the *original* Prophet and President of the Church. You know the meaning of the word, Brother Drown?"

Bendy does. Or did. Knows he's been told. "I—"

"Honeybee." She looks hard at her husband, directing her voice to Bendy out of the side of her mouth. "A creature that knows the sweet reward of industry, that works not merely for its own selfish gain but for the benefit of the whole." She smiles, her lips drawn out long. "In any case, you were saying, Brother Drown? Some years ago . . . ?"

Hammer answers for him. "Brother Drown rode for the Pony Express."

A change comes over the children, sudden, palpable. On the far side of the table both girls look up at Bendy with widening eyes. To his left, the boys turn their heads as one.

"I see." Mother Hammer nods. "I believe the ponies stopped running in '61."

"Yes, ma'am."

"Six years ago, then, you lived in Deseret."

"Just about."

"Yet you've only just been baptized."

"That's right. About a month back." Seeing she's less than satisfied, he adds, "In Iowa."

"Iowa."

"Mother," Hammer says darkly.

She meets his stare. "I'm only inquiring, husband. If Brother Drown is to live among us, I believe I have the right to inquire."

"It's all right." Bendy looks from wife to husband and back. "I don't mind."

Mother Hammer is the first to break deadlock, her eyes shifting to pin Bendy anew. "And during those six years?"

"I carried the mail."

She raises her pale eyebrows. "You drove a stage?"

"No, ma'am, I—"

Hammer's fork rings out against his plate rim. "For pity's sake, woman, not every one-horse shithole's on a stage line."

The children lower their eyes.

"Language, Mr. Hammer." His wife lays down her longest silence yet. When she speaks again, her voice is several notes closer to a man's. "I imagine you volunteered for the Union." She pauses. "Or perhaps you waited for the draft."

Bendy feels himself colour.

"My wife the patriot," Hammer sneers. "Abe Lincoln's girl."

She doesn't spare him a glance. "Well?"

"No, ma'a—Mother Hammer."

"Don't tell me you had the means to buy yourself a replacement."

"No, we were exempt."

"We?"

Bendy swallows. "A war can't run without the mail."

"Hah." Hammer grins. "What do you say to that, Mother?"

Her gaze buckles, and Bendy takes the opportunity to look down at his plate. She's put her finger on a sore spot. He did hide behind the job, holding on to the numbingly dull route from Ottumwa to outlying settlements far longer than he would have if the South had never attempted to secede. The war terrified him, the official news paling in comparison with the flesh-and-blood horrors that travelled by word of mouth.

"The war's been over two years," Mother Hammer says, breaking in on the thoughts she's woken. "Did you carry the mail all that time too?"

He nods. It's a small enough lie, born of a vague sense of shame. It's not as though he's done anything wrong over the past couple of years, committed any crimes. Like so many cut free after the war, he drifted, first on foot, then on horseback—Stride the second mare he'd owned, solid dark where the first had been patchy, pale. Together they crossed streams and rivers, unseen county lines. Bendy hired on driving cattle, breaking colts, riding flank on a wagon train that dissolved when it was only a fortnight under way.

He could list these and half a dozen other jobs if he had to. Instead, he focuses on the space between salt cellar and gravy jug, and tells a portion of the truth.

"This one Sunday I came upon a man preaching by the river. I'd heard the story before, back when I lived here—it was all about Brother Joseph and the Angel Moroni, how Brother Joseph went and dug up the sacred plates. I don't know, somehow hearing it called out in a clearing like that, the sense of it finally sank in." He pauses. "After he was done talking, he started leading folks into the water. Before I knew it, I was in up to my waist."

The first wife makes a close-lipped sound of comprehension. He hazards a glance her way, meets a look that couldn't hurt a fly.

❦

Ursula empties the hissing kettle into the dishpan and plunges her hands in past their wrists. No pain, thanks to the slow numbing of years. She grabs a glass by its bottom, her mind returning to the story of the hired man's conversion. From there it's but an easy sidestep to the memory of her own.

Mrs. Pike liked her to be quick about the morning errands, and so it happened that Ursula was walking at a fair clip when she first heard the Prophet speak. Preachers were common as pigeons in the town square of Independence, Missouri, and Ursula knew Mormons to be the worst snake oil merchants of the lot, but Joseph Smith had a voice that would not be denied. It stopped her with a jerk—like a pair of hands gripping her suddenly, almost brutally, about the waist.

Realizing she's still washing the same glass, Ursula dips and passes it to Josephine, who dries it carefully, setting it mouth down on the tray.

The Mormon Prophet had no real need of the stump he stood on. He was tall—her own six feet of corporeal height plus another of pure presence. The voice that had so firmly halted her progress now turned and drew her close. She made her way forward through the schooling faithful, growing sensible of the body inside her dress—feeling it turn slippery, sleek as a trout's.

She got close enough to learn that his eyes, like her own, were blue. Darker, though. Water to her air. He kept them shaded under lashes as long as a calf's. How Ursula ached to stand directly beneath that fringed gaze. She strove against the throng, but the Prophet's people were gathered tight about him, and in the end she had to content herself—if such a state of rapt agitation could be called content—with a distance between them of some half a dozen feet.

He didn't colour up as lesser men did when speaking before a crowd. Instead, the blood seemed to leave his face entirely, allowing the vessels therein to fill with a serum of liquid light. His topic was the persecution of his people—and rightly so, for the Saints were driven from Missouri less than a year later—but it wasn't the theme of Joseph Smith's oration that held Ursula fast; it was the man himself. Every part of him was perfect, save perhaps the nose-heavy profile he revealed when blessing the crowd's flanks with his gaze. Even this she loved instantly, taking a flawed feature to mean he was not a god come to ground, but a creature she might one day speak to, even touch.

She feels the weight of another clean, wet glass against her fingers and hands it off absently, letting go before Josephine quite has it in her grasp. The girl reacts with an all-over spasm, snatching and clutching it to her chest. Ursula says nothing, fishing in the basin again.

Until that day—that voice, that man—Ursula's life had been mouse-coloured. The spongy bread dough and dingy quilts, the endless soiled diapers of the Pike babies, the shuddery, ill-constructed barn, even the nubbled udder she yanked daily. The time before she turned eleven and entered servitude had been little different. She had toiled for her aged parents in a state called Pennsylvania. Coming west to Missouri with the Pikes, she had simply traded one unkind family, one rodent-grey farm, for another.

So it was that when the gift of conversion came, she experienced it in biblical terms, as the falling of scales from her eyes. And when, as leaders will, Joseph Smith concluded his fine speech and rode off in the company of his lieutenants, she knew with a bright certainty that she would look upon his radiance again.

It took little effort to cut free from her life—apprising her employers of her new-found faith was all that was required.

Harriet Pike did her best to berate the religion out of her house-maid, and when that didn't work, Walter Pike drew his belt from its loops and did his worst. Ursula limped from their house purple from her buttocks to the backs of her knees. She asked the way to the Mormon Meeting House in the street, eliciting half a dozen sneers from unbelievers before she happened upon a Saint. The plain little woman did more than direct her. She looked into Ursula's burning eyes, caught hold of her hand and led her the whole way there.

Crouched hard against the silkhouse wall, Lal breathes slowly through his mouth in a bid to quiet his blood. At length its foamy rush subsides, withdrawing from his ears to pool thickly in his heart. He listens. A low hissing—the feeding worms still too small to produce a hard-raining racket. Ruth is close by, her weight playing over the floorboards not far from the log at his ear. Sooner or later she'll cross to the stacks that line the far wall, and he'll rise to the window and watch.

For now he lays a hand to the wall. Logs he helped haul and fit. Not cut, though. Hammer chose to share the crosscut saw with the Indian—who'd clearly never laid hands on one—rather than trust his own son with anything sharp. Lal was fourteen when they built the little house, still uncertain of the strength in his burgeoning limbs, the dimensions of his own two feet. Hammer barked at him every step they took together on opposite ends of a log. He was on edge, in a hurry to finish this favour for his second wife and get back to his third.

Lal fits his grip to the humped round of a log, finger pads nosing for the strip of adobe chinking, silty and cool. His father left him to it when it came time for the sloppy, skin-peeling work of mudding up the gaps. It was early spring. At times the mud formed a glassy skin he had to break through. His fingers cracked and bled, and still Hammer said nothing but, *Get on with it*, the few times he strode over to check on the progress being made.

Ruth worked alongside him. She needed everything ready before the mulberry trees came into leaf, and there were still the shelves to be constructed, and four small corner hearths to be bricked in, in case of unseasonable cold. It was to be her first year keeping silkworms—that much Lal understood, though he had no clear notion of what such an endeavour might entail. Left to his own devices, he imagined a mass of spidery creatures with slimy pink legs.

What mulberries had to do with it he couldn't guess, and he wasn't about to give himself away by asking. It turned out there was no need. Ruth, who seldom uttered more than three words together, told him everything—not in one go, but portioned out through the days' toil.

When the trees were ten days or so from turning green—look for leaf buds three-quarters of an inch long—it would be time to set the eggs to hatching.

Eggs? There would be chickens involved as well?

Ruth would fetch them up from the cellar, and wear them here—she touched her bosom, giving Lal a brief, confusing jolt in his britches—keeping them warm against her heart.

How many eggs could she mean? Surely even one would crack.

A week and a half later, the eggs would hatch, giving rise to tiny silkworms.

Not chickens, then. Worms, too, could be born in this way.

These hatchlings would feed on the first, tenderest leaves, chopped fine for their baby mouths. As the leaves swelled and strengthened, so too would the caterpillars. *Caterpillars.* Finally something Lal could make sense of. The grappling creatures of his fancy fell away, replaced by an image nearer the truth.

The month of May would be devoted to the gathering and laying down of leaves—it was shocking how much the little fellows could put away. Then, after four weeks or so of gorging, the worms would climb up into twigs stooked for the purpose and begin to spin. For two or three days straight they would draw silk from their mouths, until they closed themselves off entirely from the world.

Once ensconced, the worms would become chrysalides. Lal heard *crystal-ids* and pictured the glasses his mother kept in the sideboard—one let fall from the fingers, reduced to wriggling shards—but Ruth described hard little cases full of a sort of living soup. This would be the end for most. When the time was right, she would pluck the cocoons from their branches and boil them alive. Why? So they wouldn't spoil their silk in the process of being reborn.

Only the lucky few would be suffered to emerge. The look on Ruth's face when she spoke of this final phase—as though she were stroking the unfolding wings, when in truth her fingers wedged red muck into the rift between two logs. The jolt returned to crackle through him, searing a blackened path. And then she scolded him—*No, Lal, not like that*—and he was himself again, put-upon, enraged.

He returned to the mulberry copse often that May. The first time he carried a sack of new leaves inside and saw the stacks of writhing beds, he felt a boy's disgusted delight. He stood and watched Ruth mince leaves, then distribute the green hash over several trays. She'd warned him to be quiet, but his voice came out chalky and loud. "Don't you need a lid on them or something?"

"They won't wander," she whispered. Then held a finger to her lips, a gesture that somehow made it harder for him to keep still.

He left soon thereafter, closing the door carefully behind him before walking, then running, through her trees. Reaching open pasture, he hammered on until his heart gave him pain. He couldn't understand what was wrong with him. He wouldn't until some three months had passed and those same low trees cast a mottled August shade.

There was a good crop of mulberries, ripening to black. Lal came with a pail in each hand to help his aunt. He found her lying propped against the thickest trunk. She was marked, splattered all over with what he could only conceive of as blood. Red at her throat, her pale dress filthy with splashes. Ruth was hurt, possibly even dead, and the shock of it taught him he loved her.

Then a dark berry came loose, falling to explode brightly across the back of her hand. She stirred, and Lal clenched his teeth hard to keep from howling his relief. The stains were sweet now. What he wanted more than anything, what he kept himself from doing next, taught him the nature of his love.

When Ruth moved in her sleep again, he set his pails down softly and fled. He didn't kneel down by her side and clean her like a mother cat would, one lick at a time. Or not like a mother cat. Not like a mother at all.

Tonight the Tracker opens to what may be the finest drawing in the book. As always, he is torn. Part of him wishes desperately to turn the page. Another, slightly stronger part insists he fill his eyes.

The child wears little—a stringy vest, a pair of the swollen pants they call drawers. Her face, neck and forearms are painted with streaks of dust. She is young, perhaps six or seven years on the earth. Innocent of all that is to come, she crouches in the shallows of a stream. Her shins angle off beneath the surface— water's trick of bending whatever it holds. Her gaze is open, direct. She looks out at the Tracker from the moment between dipping her tin cup and raising it chill and dripping to her mouth.

It's a mouth, a gaze, a head of dark, unruly hair the Tracker would know anywhere.

He knew them instantly three years back—even though the girl's age had doubled, even though her grimy, eager expression had narrowed and soured. Knew without a doubt the day Hammer brought his fourth wife home.

— 7 —

WHEN DOES A LIFE BEGIN, if not with its first memory?

Bendy would've been four years old. He remembers his mother kneeling on the floor beside him, her broad palms cupping his heels, pushing his feet back over his head the way he liked. Not three feet distant, his father perched on the lip of the sunken couch. Beside him sat a man twice his girth. Something lay open on the steamer trunk before them. A book? A newspaper? *A map.*

Such a crowded scene wouldn't have been unusual. Two ground-floor rooms were all the Drown family had claim to in that converted New Orleans mansion—one a glorified closet that housed the parental bed and wardrobe, the other a kitchen, parlour and nursery in one. The washstand hulked in the corner nearest the door. The privy lay down a dim hallway. Three heavy doors and there was still the yard to cross before you got there, the only path a spider-slung gully hacked through yellow, sweating leaves.

The air in that old house clung wetly to the lungs. It made no difference if his mother hoisted the window; when there was any breeze to speak of, it only delivered the delta's ooze, the human fetor of the port. Close quarters. On his father's shipping-clerk wages they could afford nothing else.

The steamer trunk served as a table, a desk and, before he grew too long for it, Bendy's bed. He'd resisted moving to the couch—drawing his shins up alongside his thighs, forming a tight W with his lower half—but his mother wouldn't hear of it. Bend all you like, John James, but you need to sleep straight. Nighttime's when little bodies grow. *John James.* The first half all his own, the second the name his mother gave up when she married a man called Drown.

While she folded him in half, easing his aching joints, his father talked business with his thick-bellied friend. "Three hundred!" Bill Drown thrust an ink-bruised finger into the air. "Three hundred dollars a day, just waiting to get spooned up out of the ground!"

It was the first time John James saw gold in his father's gaze. The man beside him showed it too, albeit a milder case. That was when his mother let go his heels and sat back against her own. "Thirty," she said, her own eyes grey and clear. John James held the shape she'd made of him, sensing it was no time to move.

"What did you say?" His father's voice was quiet.

His mother rocked a little on her knees. "Thirty dollars a day. That's what you said this morning. That's what you told me you heard."

The look Bill Drown gave his wife remains hard and true in Bendy's mind, the shaft around which the memory spins. Still the golden gleam, but beneath it a fathomless, fish-eyed stare. Chances are his mother realized then and there what she'd married. She may even have seen the future open out before them like a roiling sea, herself and her precious boy bobbing, hitched by their necks to a rowboat with broken oars.

In truth they bid farewell to New Orleans from the hold of a cotton boat, Bill Drown having filched a mound of coin from the warehouse's inner office and dispensed the first part of it crossing palms—beginning with a longshoreman's, rope-burnt to a glassy pink, and ending with the cotton boat's second-in-command. The boatswain's palm bore a scar in the shape of a crucifix, the ruched inversion of a deliberate gouge. Whether he'd done it for simple adornment or as a kind of devil's bane, it was clear the fool had gone too far. He'd cut clean through the tendon near the crux. His middle finger curled useless and grey.

These and countless other images the boy inherited from his father. Always the darkest of details, related most often in the dark—John James under a scrap of sacking on a rooming-house floor, or rolled up against the damp inner slant of a tent when they hadn't the price of a bunk. *Night stories.* At times they were part of a call-and-answer ritual involving the disembodied voices of other prone men. Mouth after mouth opening to gild the grim present—stories of strikes up this river or that stream, so-and-so sinking every last penny into pick and shaft, going down broke but coming up glittery with the real stuff, not a word of a lie, covered head to toe with the dust.

Now and then Bill Drown uttered one of the tales John James stayed awake for, a snatch of what lay behind them, the life that came before. In this way he learned the rough plot of his past, a short, jagged line along which he arranged the few scenes he could recall.

The three of them had ridden high on the cotton bales, the dark of the hold alive with fibres, ghostly wisps that clogged his nose and caused it to leak blood. They put in on the eastern flank of Panama's narrow waist. Chagres, a port hotter and more sulphurous than New Orleans, or, as John James was still foolish enough then to think of it as, *home.* They journeyed by canoe as far as the Chagres River would take them, then onward by mule. The isthmus, a thin, serpentine twist on the map, became five days' journey through a stinging, biting fog. His mother began to lag.

She batted John James away from her while she still could, but on the night before they were to reach the Pacific coast she no longer possessed the strength. He clung to her despite her whispered, delirious warnings, felt her twist and sizzle, then slide away into a calm blue cold. Meanwhile, Bill Drown cultivated a western campfire squat with several other San Francisco hopefuls, not one of them fool enough to bring a woman and child in tow. He kept his distance until the first disturbing cries of a tropical dawn, then kicked a sullen path across the camp to find his wife dead and staring, wrapped in her wide-eyed son.

Bill Drown said nothing at the graveside, leaving the stunted prayer to one of two young brothers with whom he'd shared the previous night's fire. They'd refused to move on with the rest, staying to help dig a hasty grave. *Lord bless this woman and keep her always for one of your own. Ashes to ashes. Amen.* The three men shovelled hard and fast, wedge after wedge of pungent, sticky earth.

"Make haste, boys," Bill Drown wheezed, "the *California*'s on her way. Keep back, John. You'll take a shovel to the face." Just like that, he cut his son's rightful name in half.

John James sat pressed up against his mother's straw suitcase in the heaving cart the last leg of the way. They heard the mayhem first. Then, from half a mile distant, they caught sight of the roaring throng. *Forty-niners.* There were hundreds of them, a vast herd bristling with gun barrels and blades. Steaming towards them, the high black hull of the *California*. Virgin vessel on a historic trip, she was the Pacific Mail Steamship Company's shining pride, bound to commence service between the Isthmus and Oregon, with a stop at San Francisco along the way. Having set off from New York harbour in early October, she'd successfully navigated the clawed toe of Cape Horn and come steadily up the Pacific side of things—only to put in at Panama and be mobbed.

Bill Drown tore their luggage from the cart and broke into a run. John James struggled after him, the straw suitcase snagging in the mud. He began to cry, eyes only—he needed all his breath to try to keep up. At the verge of the crowd his father whirled, pounded back and snatched the soiled case. As John James stared, he popped the hasp, dumping its contents on the trampled ground.

Her good black silk. The grey-blue gingham, plain but not when she wore it, not with those eyes. It was the sister to the dress she'd died in, cut from the same thin cloth. Her under-things, yellowed despite effort. Her shoes gone lumpy with wear.

"Get in," said his father.

The suitcase gaped. It was perhaps two-thirds as long as the steamer trunk and not nearly so deep, but John James could feel where he would fold, see precisely the angles it would take. Just as he could see his father would wait only a few seconds more.

His fingers were the last part of him in, withdrawn moments before the lid came slicing down. On their way, they raked the loose mound of his mother's things, the index hooking a handker-chief by its lacework corner and dragging it along.

Perhaps half the crowd managed to crush aboard, a human storm more forceful than any gale. John James witnessed the boarding through the suitcase's weave—men's trouser legs a fran-tic darkness, here and there an impression of coloured light. In the thundering rush up the gangplank, he felt certain his father would have second thoughts. A suitcase was an easy thing to discard. Let it drop over the guard rope, sink and settle to the ocean's floor.

John James kept mum for an age in the woven case, Bill Drown finally remembering to free him hours after they were under way. The *California*, California bound—a voyage pared down to departure and arrival by his childhood mind. They slipped through the Golden Gate on a radiant day in February '49. Arriving as they did in the company of the mail, they were heralded like a cargo of kings. Ships at anchor showed bunting. The bay was an oscillating table, festive with floating cakes.

A thunderous volley of welcome caused John James to cower at his father's knee, convinced the ship was being fired on. The guns raised a shout from the men at work on the yards, a rolling cheer that spread ear to mouth through those gathered along the surrounding hills.

On board the dark steamship, John James felt the press of bodies tense and sway, and heard the mass of mouths—his father's among them—belt out a cheer of their own. He was attempting to worm a pathway up along his father's hard, sour-smelling thigh when Bill Drown reached down and grabbed him beneath the arms. Dragged up painfully through the crush, he screwed his eyes shut, felt himself hoisted aloft and swung. Then felt the shaft of his father's neck between his legs. Instinctively, he looped his bare feet back under Bill Drown's armpits, twisting and locking them in place.

It was the right idea. They were only one row of bodies back from the rail, and Bill Drown needed both hands free to wave like mad. John James opened his eyes on a forest of thrashing arms. Many flew standards—undershirts, rags, whatever came to hand. His father's whipped by brighter than most. John James had rolled his mother's handkerchief up tight in his trouser pocket, but Bill Drown must have plucked it out while he slept. To look at or to hold. More likely to swaddle a finger with and clean out his nose.

Now he was ripping it back and forth through the air. John James made a grab for it too late. His father relaxed his long fingers, let it catch on a gust and fly.

— 8 —

DORRIE DREAMS:

The human nest is emptying. From my post atop the wagon's back I watch the adult females and their walking young advance in loose formation, following the wagons that carried their injured and their little ones away. The dog man's pack has grown, forty or so males having trotted from the northern draw. Like a stand of sucker saplings, they form a line across the land. Each holds a long gun across his chest. Each lowers his eyes as the females and their charges pass.

The dark mother moves at the flock's leading edge, eyes fixed on the wagon that swallowed her child. For all their wide-ribbed sway, the mule-drawn loads are gaining ground. There is little the dark mother can do. Even if she were capable of breaking into a run, she would butt up against the pack member that leads their group.

Below, the last of the nesting males leave the circled wagons behind. They snake through the grass in a column, following their females at a distance, moving north. At the tail end, a male on horseback herds them on. Flanking them on the east, the line of pack members falls in step. I drop from my station, climb twenty, forty wingfuls, let go in a jagged glide.

I sweep along the doubled line, winging on to where the females and young advance in a shifting pool. The wagons follow their mules over a rise. They're still visible to me, but lost to those below. I hear their disappearance in the dark mother's inhalation, sharp with fear. Tied to the undulating earth, there is much she cannot see.

Such as this.

The hollow I fly over is choked with scrub, bristling with hidden life—human males, both Originals and Pales dressed to resemble them, smelling of horsetails and grease. The true Originals hold still, making their brown bodies so many slender, harmless trees.

Sensing an end, I'm tempted to set down on one of the scrappy oaks and count the ragged females as they pass, beak nodding over every bare or bonneted head. But the bird brain jumps to the dark mother's young, so I tilt and pump hard to where the shambling wagons roll on.

Having overshot the lead wagon's mules, I bank to meet a wave of change. Back along the trail where the males walk two by two, the mounted pack member has broken ranks. His horse skittish beneath him, he lets a shot ring out, followed by four human barks.

The far meadow explodes in rolls of thunder, the doubled male column sliced down its length, the western half falling before the glinting guns of those who met and matched them on the field. In the same instant the Originals, true and false, burst from the scrub. They too show metal, some lifting guns, others unsheathing knives like long, single claws. They fall upon the females and their young, meeting the shrieks of their prey with blood-thinning cries of their own. I climb and witness all.

At the head of things, the dog man and the two wagon riders buzz around the second wagon's tongue. With a heave and a squeal, they lead it off to one side of the track. I can hear its cargo—an infirm adult female and three bloodied males—calling out from inside. Then more flash and thunder and they are quiet, their bodies dragged from the wagon and dumped.

From the lead wagon no such silence. The sky shudders with sound—the frightened wails of the young left unattended inside rising to meet the howls of those being cut down back along the trail. Curiosity should send me wheeling that way, not to mention the scent of fresh blood, so thick it can almost be seen. Instead, I pace the air, awaiting I know not what.

Until it comes. Just as the second wagon gave up its dead, the first gives up one of its living. A small body, blurring white and black. Compact, quivering, it slips over the wagon's tongue, dropping to land in a crouch. It scuttles hard, turns serpent when it makes the grass. At the scrub line it disappears, but not before I've gotten a good look. There's no mistaking it. She was the last one in. The only one to make it out.

9

DORRIE WAS EIGHT YEARS OLD the first time the Burrs took her to town. Cedar City. She knew she was meant to be delighted, and so she made sure to keep her trembling hands hidden, twisting them beneath her shawl. She rode sandwiched between them on the front seat—Papa's jouncing hip bone, Mama's giving haunch. When the track hit a flat stretch, Papa let her take the reins. Or not let, exactly. She had no real interest in assuming control.

He'd shown a fine mood all morning, harnessing the horse early, then coming to stand at the bedchamber door and watch Mama brush and brush Dorrie's black tumble of curls. "Leave it loose," he said when Mama began dividing the dark mass into braidable hanks.

Mama turned on her chair. "She'll get terribly tangled."

At that he delved into his trouser pocket, withdrawing a length of silk ribbon, the purest white. He tossed it onto the bed.

"Oh, Lyman." Mama reached for it, smiling. "Look, Dorrie, see what Papa's bought you."

Dorrie stepped out from beneath the shadow of the stilled brush and stroked a finger down the ribbon's length.

The ride made Mama happier still. She crowed to see healthy

colour in her daughter's cheeks, and indeed Dorrie could feel it there, soft and spreading, nothing like a fever's immovable daubs. Papa turned his head their way. He looked Dorrie up and down, his moustaches dragging up at their ends. How could she tell them the idea of a street bustling with strangers horrified her? Or that sitting up high on the buckboard—even in the midst of an unpeopled meadow bisected by a narrow track—made her feel like a lump of living bait?

As they neared the ragged Indian village at the edge of town, Papa drew up to let a wagonload of young Saints pass them going the other way. He lifted his hat with one hand, the other flat and insistent at Dorrie's spine. "Sit up straight, girl. Who's gonna see you slumped down there like a sack of corn?"

After he'd helped his wife and daughter down in front of the dry goods store, Papa slapped the reins along the paint's sway-back and drove on. Inside, Dorrie clung to Mama's skirts like a much younger child, dropping shallow curtsies whenever someone stared long enough to elicit an introduction. "My late sister's child, Eudora." Then, "Eudora, this is Brother Oates." Or, "Dorrie, meet Sister Creel."

More than one of them couldn't wait until she and Mama had left the shop before they began whispering. *Orphan.* A sinister word, hissed across flour barrels or between bolts of webby muslin down the back.

The woman behind the counter pinned Dorrie with a look and said brightly, "Well now, Eudora Burr, what would you say to a peppermint stick?"

Nothing if she had her way, but the spasm in Mama's hand told her different.

"Yes please, ma'am." A small enough response, but it pained Dorrie to give it. Pained her and delighted everyone else—the woman grinning like an idiot as she plucked the long candy from its jar, Mama squeezing her hand again, but softly this time.

On the boardwalk outside, the two of them sat surrounded by parcels on a hard-backed bench, awaiting Papa's return. Mama insisted upon exchanging words with every passerby. Dorrie's guts swam with sugar and nerves each time a skirt or a pair of trousers halted before them.

Then came a collection of bare, brown feet—not on the boardwalk, but beyond, on the dusty street. A flick of the eyes set Dorrie's heart skittering. Indians. Two men, a woman and a boy. The grown-ups were dressed in charity, one man's trousers cinched with rope, the other's with a red necktie. The woman's hem dragged in the dust. Only the boy was dressed in the old way, which was to say, scarcely at all.

All four kept their eyes lowered, a kinship Dorrie might have picked up on if she hadn't been at the mercy of her thundering pulse. There was nothing to fear, she knew, especially here, in the centre of town. Like any good Saint, she understood that Indians were in fact descendants of the original Twelve Tribes— descendants gone astray, mind, but not without hope. Those who'd been saved come Judgment Day stood to be reclaimed by God. Dorrie knew this. And still she shrank inwardly at the sight of those brown feet shifting past.

She said a quick prayer for Papa's return. Peering down the dusty street, she imagined every set of brown moustaches and faded grey hat was him, never mind if the cart was drawn by a mule or a black draft horse, or even if the man came on foot.

When Papa finally did arrive, pulling up in front of the rail, she chanced to be looking the other way. The man who'd caused her head to turn was clean-shaven, hatless. A hardened aspect, a crop of greasy, dust-coloured hair. Amid this river of strangers, here,

Dorrie felt, was someone she knew. She knew his mouth, full of bright teeth when he opened it to greet a man who crossed his path. Knew his blunt, extended hand. Knew especially the teary gleam, the doggy slant of his smiling eyes.

Perhaps he had visited the farm while she was ill—she might have glimpsed him then, mightn't she, through the slit of a blood-shot eye? It scarcely mattered. She recognized him, and felt certain he would recognize her, too. Forgetting her manners, forgetting even that she could speak, Dorrie stood and pointed, singling him out.

Papa engulfed her. He bent her arm down harshly at the shoulder, as though it were a branch he would separate from its tree. "Get in the cart." His voice hot in Dorrie's ear, turning icy when he repeated the order to his wife. "Get in the cart, Mother."

Mama obeyed, her movements jerky. No sooner were they settled on the bench seat than she was tucking Dorrie's head beneath the brown wing of her shawl. The day was warm, but Dorrie didn't struggle. Instinct told her to go limp, to breathe shallowly in the musky damp beneath Mama's arm. She heard Papa load the parcels hastily behind their backs, felt him jam in beside her and bring the reins down hard.

The mulberry copse is private, enveloped in shade. It's just the two of them, Ruth one tree over, two rungs up the ladder, reaching into green. Lal tears loose a fluttering handful, suddenly recalling what she's told him a dozen times—a gentle twist to spare the twig. These trees must do for many years. He proceeds with greater care, switching to a different branch so he can watch her over the tops of his hands.

When his sack is full, he drops to the ground and crosses to stand close by her skirts. Her hand hangs at eye level, graceful and stained. Reaching up again, she causes her hem to rise, revealing her bloated feet. They're bare, dark pink and satiny, slung like steaks over the rung. She catches him looking.

"Do they pain you?" he blurts.

She sighs. "They do."

He drags his eyes downward, fixing them on a clot of bunch-grass.

"Lal?"

Ordinarily he would thrill to the sound of his name in her mouth. Just now, though, he's distracted by an even sweeter voice. *Sssss. Rrrrrr.* The sly, secret rubbing of her underthings, cotton on silk on skin.

"Lal?"

She twists to look down on him. *Sssrrrrr.* He'll touch her. No one will see. He'll close his arms about her legs, press his face into her apron's dirty lap.

"Lal."

He looks up, startled.

"You'd not say a word to your mother. About my—my not wearing shoes."

"Oh, no. Never."

"Good lad."

It hurts him to meet her gaze. He lowers his eyes again. "My bag's full."

"Well, lean it up by the cottage—the shady side, mind."

He nods. "Will I do another?"

"If you like." She turns back to the mulberry—*rrrrr*—moving one big foot—*rssss*—then the other—*ssrrrrr*—up a rung.

Mounted on Stride, Bendy takes the near pasture at a walk. He begins by hugging the margins, making mental note of every rotting post, every dangling rail. From there he works a narrowing spiral, looking down Stride's neck—near side, off side—now and then slipping down to investigate a suspicious plant or kick dirt into a potential trip hole and tamp it down. Spying a frayed lick of twine, he reels up a tangle capable of jerking the most sure-footed of animals off its hooves.

At the verge of a shallow sink, he comes upon a thriving clump of hemlock. Unlashing his spade, he digs it up, hooking it by the roots through the buckle on his saddlebag. Several smaller clots come up easy, giving way with a good yank. He weaves them into the mother bush, to be burned later in the day. All this and he's still nowhere near the pasture's heart. He shakes his head. It's a wonder Hammer's got any horses left for him to tend.

Mr. Humphrey clearly held his subject dear. His lessons followed no set plan, at least none Ruth could discern. He might just as soon dwell upon the Catholic persecution that drove Huguenot weavers to British shores as on the manner in which the *Bombyx* silk moth spends its brief and flightless life.

The female's perfume is irresistible to the male. He is equipped with a pair of feathery antennae, which sweep the air in search of her scent. Her abdomen swells to the point of rendering her immobile. Up to five hundred eggs, can you imagine, Miss Graves?

Often he focused on the wondrous fibre itself.

"Certainly one might tear a thin scarf along warp or weft, but

catch hold of two corners on the bias and you test the true met-
tle of the thread." Mr. Humphrey rose from his armchair and
drew just such a scarf—flesh toned, translucent—from his jacket
pocket. Bending awkwardly from the waist, he laid it across her
hand. "Pull. Go on, Miss Graves, exert yourself."

She obliged him, eliciting a smile that seemed oddly pained.

"You'll never tear it, will you? And see what it weighs? Nothing.
Scarcely more than a handful of air."

She pinched the scarf between finger and thumb, gauging its
negligible weight.

"Ball it up. Go on, ball it up in your fist. Stuff it away." His
eyes were bright. "Feel it give?"

She nodded.

"Feel it—" He groped for the word. "—resist?"

Her answer was a smile.

"Good. Quickly now, one motion, open your hand."

She gave a little cry as the scarf sprang from her grip. Splayed
and fluttering, it shrouded her upturned palm.

"Such delicacy of draping. Unmatched, unmatched!" He
snatched up the scarf, a clawing motion that made her jump.
Beads of sweat stood out on his cheekbones, his bone-white
brow. He blotted them, the scarf darkening with every dab. It
was plain something ailed him, but she never dreamt what it
was. He shuffled back and, in a slow collapse, resumed his
chair.

"Silk will absorb up to a third of its own weight in moisture."
He spoke softly now, directing his voice to the crumpled dampness in his hands. "It is warm when warmth is required and yet it
breathes."

He looked up at her then, his eyes brimming. And still she
didn't see.

Ursula begins counting at her own end of the upstairs corridor. If asked, she would deny any reckoning. Would say instead *looking in on*, or *checking*.

The first door along the western wall represents zero, the nursery empty for another five months yet. The second opens in on her slumbering girls. A stooped, cover-smoothing inspection of each—*one, two*—and then she's on her way past the head of the wide staircase to the chamber that holds her boys. Their cots form a triangle for her to walk. She hunches briefly at each of its points—*three, four, five*. It's rare to find one of her lambs wakeful.

The last door on the children's side Ursula leaves alone. Lal is far too old for a mother to check on. The Lord only knows what she might find.

Opposite Lal's room lies the door to Sister Eudora's empty chamber. Unaired space, a reminder of every wifely duty the girl leaves unfulfilled. Ursula lays an ear to Sister Thankful's door. Too late to catch them in the act, she hears nothing but the rumble of Hammer's snores. She straightens, her next embroidered motto springing fully formed to mind.

> *Whosoever bringeth forth*
> *not good fruit,*
> *or whosoever doeth not*
> *the works of righteousness,*
> *the same have cause*
> *to wail and mourn.*

At Ruth's door she thinks fleetingly of looking in—not so much on the woman as on the promise of the child to come—but decides it wouldn't do to risk disturbing her sister-wife's sleep. Not when the idiot woman spent all day picking and hauling leaves, and will be up at least once in the night to lay down more. Ursula turns and descends the stairs.

At the back kitchen door she trades her slippers for boots and steps outside to find the moon lofty and full. Its distant light renders the yard in extremes, yet she feels no quickening in her chest, no urge to lengthen her stride.

Inside the cow barn she turns a slow revolution, holding her lamp high. Four, five, six good milkers, safe in their clean, dry stalls. She turns a similar circle in the cramped chicken house, adding only a nodding of the head to take in all three levels of roosts. Satisfied, she lowers her lamp. From here she'll proceed to the larder, to tally her stores.

At the low sill of the kitchen door, something silver flashes in the corner of her eye. She turns her head to find stillness. Hers is not a mind to cling to glimpses. Stepping inside, she dismisses all conjecture as firmly as she closes the door.

She crosses to the larder, fits her body like a key into its narrows. Sacks and bushel baskets crowd her skirts. The honey cask nudges her knee. Down the far end the cured side of pork dangles. Ursula turns to face the left-hand bank of shelves. Bundles of candles, crocks and cakes of soap—all put up by her, stirring the stinking kettle while Joseph fed the fire and Josephine set wicks or added lye. Above these, neat lines of bottles and jars. A comfortable sufficiency, even surplus, though such words hold little meaning for one who's known brutal seasons. Besides, she can't afford to grow complacent with Hammer selling fewer horses every year.

At eye level, halved yellow fruits press against glass. One, two, three jars of peaches, Ursula tells herself, but her heart's not in it.

In truth, she can scarcely focus on the jars before her, let alone count them, for the idea of what they hide.

She's four jars deep before her middle finger makes contact with the tin. She brings the little box to her nose, flipping open its hinged lid. Inhaling deeply, she gives a small shudder. She closes the lid to avoid sacrificing so much as a morsel, nearly tripping on the hem of her dress in her haste to reach the stove. The coals still have life in them. Ursula prods and jabs them, centres the kettle and turns. She owns no teapot. She'll steep it loose in a cup as always, add the cream and sugar direct, strain through her teeth as she sips.

Her parents would have cringed at the very idea. Like many an English commoner come to the New World, they'd made a religion of tea, warming the pot like their betters, setting out saucers and wedges of buttered bread. Ridiculous to be sensible of their disapproval even now. Ursula was Josephine's age the last time either one of them drew breath, let alone brewed up a pot of best black Ceylon.

The stuff is hard to come by in the Valley of the Saints. She's chanced ordering it in to the post office in Tooele, even stooped to trading with Gentile emigrants seeking butter and cheese. More than once she's gone months at a time without. She digs out a heaping teaspoon. It's greedy, right enough, but there's no sense bowing to temptation if she doesn't go all the way. The kick of it will tingle. Its heat will connect throat to heart, heart to vitals. She sets spoon, sugar tin and cream jug at the ready, listens hard for the water's happy roll.

It is wrong to partake of stimulants. Sinful. It weakens the soul.

Surely, given all her labours, the Lord will see fit to overlook this pettiest of trespasses. Brother Joseph would—Ursula's certain of it. She gives a sharp smile at the idea of him. The Prophet was a man of flesh. Were he present, he might even join her in a cup.

Wary of horse thieves and other predators, Hammer insists the entire herd be stabled at night. Eighteen head. It's less work than it would've been the week before—Bendy's boss having pried half a dozen colts and fillies from their dams and taken them to the city for sale. Still, Bendy ought to be tired by the time he's seen the last mare to her stall. His body knows it, every stretch of over-giving gristle burning as he mounts to the loft. It's his brain that refuses him rest. What he wouldn't give for some of his fatigue to settle in the grey weight behind his eyes. Wakefulness is a curse he's known since boyhood.

Two days on the job, and any notion that this place might be different is already beginning to fade. What's worse, he suspects the same might be said for this entire leg of his life. He's taken oaths, learned secret signs, pledged himself a believer for life—and still he finds he is possessed of an isolated soul.

He might as well face it. Hammer shows only a surface inter-est in the horses, and Lal is lazier than an overfed dog. It's not the idea of working on his own that troubles Bendy—he was never happier than when he rode the ponies—but he had hoped to become part of something larger than himself again, a brother-hood of shared purpose, if nothing else.

As for that other something larger, the elusive family life, it's here, all right. He's sat at many tables, but never one that boasted so many women and kids. The battles are quieter than most he's witnessed, but they're clearly raging all the same.

Sister Thankful, you'll help clear away.

I would, Mother Hammer, only I believe I can feel one of my megrims coming on.

Oh you can.

I believe I can.

Pause. *I see it hasn't affected your appetite.*

No. Grey eyes cutting to the husband they share. *No, I appear to have appetite enough.*

Lying atop the blanket—a saddle blanket by the smell of it—Bendy drags down his eyelids and longs for sleep. Mere seconds pass before his eyes snap open, plumbing the blackness that is the barn's ribbed vault. His joints howl. With a frame so loosely hinged, the muscles have little choice but to take up the slack, clutching and clinging about the bones. He sits up, folds himself lengthwise like a doubled slip of rope. Taking a boot sole in each hand, he bends his elbows out wide and draws his face down between his calves. Holding, breathing the blanket's funk until his hip sockets begin to ease.

Rocking up on his buttock bones, he rolls through onto his back, hauling both legs with him. Shins alongside his ears, he grabs hold of his elbows behind his thighs. A further degree of easing, the burning almost benign. Hooking his fingers to his boot heels, he opens himself butterfly-wide. Lies there as though pinned, listening as a bad case of stable cough starts up below.

Hinging his body closed, he rises and steps to the opening in the loft's floor. A lightless, tactile descent and he's back on horse level. He lands with care, quiet on his leather soles. He considers lighting a lamp, but the gloom is thinner down here, leavened by moonlight falling through the windows he's left unshuttered to clear the air.

Bendy follows the cough six stalls along to where a plain brown nag stands wheezing. Her every exhalation comes in halves, the suffering too great to find release in a single stream. He rubs her damp brow for a time before unlatching the stall door.

"Here's your neck," he says softly, laying an open hand there. Then, with the other palm, "And here's your back." A course of skating strokes along her shuddering spine and he slides his fingers down her barrel. "There's your ribs, girl." He feels further, discerning the irregular ridge of a heaving line in the muscles of her gut. "Chronic, huh? Don't worry, I'll get it cleaned up in here for you. Get you some better air."

He straightens and draws his outspread hand once again along the nag's back, letting it rest on the high point of her hip. He might be fooling himself, but he could swear her breath is clearer, the cough shallower when it comes. He lays an ear to her sloping side. Finds himself thinking there might be something to this job after all.

Four pages before the picture book's end, the Tracker comes upon a dark inversion of the portrait he lingered over last night. It shows the same small girl, half hidden under a bonnet's drooping rim. She sits in the dirt, dustier by far than she was pages before. In this drawing there exists nothing so hopeful as a crystalline stream.

The child's eyes are obscured, so the Tracker looks to the true focus of the work—her hands. As in the earlier, happier scene, the right one grips a tin cup. The left lies on its back in the lap of her filthy skirts. The cup holds nothing. The artist, possessed of no water with which to fill it, has instead darkened its mouth with a shadow of lack.

Beyond the thirsting child, three slumped figures and the back of a man on his knees. There is no horizon. The kneeling man fills

the gap between two wagons, his arms hoisted, neck compact—
the pose a man assumes when sighting down a rifle's length.

No matter how many times the Tracker turns to this page, it
unbalances him to assume this point of view. Ten years have
passed since that bright autumn day, and still he can close his
eyes and look down on the circled wagons from above.

The People had come together in the hills, men from his own
camp and countless others answering the call. The Tracker had
taken part in large gatherings before, but never like this—so many
assembled at a white man's behest, and not a single woman
among them. Their purpose was different too. Not a grass-seed
gathering or an antelope drive or a piñon harvest, the dance and
all its couplings to follow. Not a harvest at all.

Yet another Mericat wagon train was moving southwest across
the People's land, its stock eating a broad swath of what little good
grassland remained. Yauguts and the other Mormonee captains
had schooled the braves along the road, and again in buzzing hud-
dles once a goodly number had arrived. More than ever, they
claimed, the Mericats were the enemy of the Mormonee and the
People both. Mericat armies from the East were massing in the
mountains, preparing to make war on all those in the Territory.
Red and white must band together against the common foe.

For hours the Mormonee captains stirred the People's blood
with their tales. One told of how this particular wagon train had
poisoned the Pahvants at Corn Creek with the gift of a contami-
nated ox. No, said another, not an ox—these Mericats had sunk
so low as to poison a spring. In any case, Kanosh's people, who
had done no worse than to come begging for bread, had doubled
down over their cramps, turned circles in the dirt and died.

By the time all stood ready for the initial raid, the Tracker,
Younger Brother and a hundred other braves were fairly dancing

to descend. It was the last and deepest dark, known to the People as second night. Filtering down from the sage-fragrant hills, they followed the ravine's cut out into the black sea of grass.

In the way of whites, the camp had loosed its greedy herd. The meadow groaned with tearing teeth—horses, mules and oxen, thick-witted cattle by the score—beasts that were no match for men who had hunted pronghorn, mountain sheep and deer. They ran off hundreds. The Tracker followed the dark, boxy behinds of a dozen cows back down the draw. Watching them scramble and totter as the terrain grew rough, he felt a contempt colder than any he had ever known.

Yauguts and the other Mormonee, painted in crude imitation of the People, held the braves back until the pre-dawn gloaming. The long wait in that high-country cold only served to quicken their desire. Smoke rich with the fat of rabbit and quail drifted up from the Mericat camp. At long last, with the sky like deep water stirring, they returned to the valley bottom, again following the gully of the creek bed to within range of the sprawling camp. This time they made their presence known with a trilling howl, a great volley of singing arrows and leaden balls.

They killed a handful, a child among them, and wounded a handful more. Stray stock added to the numbers, animals shrieking and lowing as they fell. The surprise came when the sleepy sprawl of the encampment answered the attack. After a brief skirmish the People swallowed their battle cries and ran.

While the Tracker and his number were dragging their wounded back to the rocky cover of the western hills, the wagon train turned in on itself and sealed up tight. The Mericats worked on, throwing up breastworks, digging holes into which they would lower their wagons' wheels.

All this the Tracker would comprehend hours later, looking

down on the closed camp in the dying light of that first long day. While the retreat was actually happening, he had no awareness of anything beyond the gunfire behind him, and the body of Younger Brother, by turns rigid and writhing in his arms.

Death by shattered knee is cruel. The pain is blinding—the Tracker witnessed this, watched Younger Brother's eyes veil over and cease to see. The blood persisted against all pressure. The sun tracked steadily overhead. Death came on the heels of darkness, the chill of mountain nightfall stopping Younger Brother's heart.

As dawn broke over the second day, his body lay covered in rocks not far from where the Tracker crouched. Near enough for his spirit to whisper and be heard.

My wife, Brother. My wife.

The shame the Tracker knew then surpassed all vengeful blood lust, all grief. He knows it now, remembering—a keen, sick-making pressure at the backs of his lowered eyes.

Younger Brother was barely cold under his weight of stone and already the Tracker was warming himself with the idea of her. Younger Brother's woman. Younger Brother's widow now.

There would be no driving that warmth away. The best he could do was to feed it, stoke it to roaring, turn it loose on the valley below. Over the next three days many would leave with their dead and their wounded, but the Tracker would stay on till the bitter end. Somewhere inside the Mericat camp lay the hand that had shot Younger Brother's leg out from under him. The eye that had guided the ball.

The Tracker touches a hand to the page before him, willing himself into the present day. There is no gazing upon the picture without being there. Not where he was—crouched among boulders, nursing his rage—but *there*, inside those circled wagons. Inside the thirsting girl.

He closes the book. Feeds another black, twisted stick to the fire. The flames rise up in thanks, dulling for the moment the sense of his own dimming. His is no ordinary sickness. He has appetite enough. His limbs serve their purpose. His heart thuds on. Still, whenever he turns his gaze inward, he meets this gradual darkening down.

The fire spits, sending up a cinder that lifts the Tracker's eyes. They meet their match in the firelight cooled and returned, the steady yellow-green of a lupine gaze. The rush in the Tracker's rib cage is not fear. Nothing like. The wolf is well known to him— thick silver mane, black markings about the eyes. Once a pack leader, half of a breeding pair, he is now a solitary beast. The Tracker reaches out without thinking, turning the Father in his tracks. Night swallows his tail tip. The Tracker's hand gropes and falls.

10

EIGHT MONTHS after Bill Drown and his trembling boy passed through the fabled Golden Gate, San Francisco had mushroomed to the point where it could no longer be called a town. Fall rains had melted the streets. Crouched toadlike in the dark, John James closed his hands around two cold fistfuls of mud. He was five years old, wedged beneath the solid fact of a boardwalk, out front of the third gambling house Bill Drown had graced with his presence that night. Through the boom and press of boots, the flexion of planks, he kept alert for his father's stride—at once hastier and more burdened than that of other men.

Not three days after they'd traded the shifting deck of the *California* for dry land, Bill Drown had lit out for the goldfields. John James had stayed behind in the rooming house they now called home, left to the dubious care of its owner, a one-time mountain man who saw only the ghosts of things through the pearly skins of his eyes.

Bunks were at a premium, so John James bedded down in the potato cupboard, his nights passed among sacks that breathed a dirt sweetness even as they threatened to rub him raw. Those same potatoes kept him barely fed, served floating in broth that stunk of fish or mutton or both. The mountain man doled out supper at sundown, cornmeal porridge at dawn. Shallow wooden bowls, slick with grease. No seconds—he stood guard over the stove with his starch-stained knife.

Milk-eyes or no, he could make out movement well enough. John James learned the hard way when, after a week of near starvation, he scuttled close and swiped his bowl into the bubbling kettle. The mountain man's blade came down flat and nasty across his knuckles. He let out a yelp that met with laughter all down the table's length.

Only the mountain man kept a straight face. "Next time you'll catch 'er edge on."

John James nodded, coddling his fist.

On the odd night when there was a bed going spare, John James still chose to climb into his cupboard and draw shut the door.

"Men'll do things to a boy when he's sleeping," Bill Drown had warned him the morning he left. He spoke it darkly, bent over his packing while John James hopped and fretted behind. "Be sure and bed down with your back to the wall."

John James could summon only the vaguest of pictures—a bearded, eyeless creature sneaking up on him from behind. He could cry out, but the most that would do would be to turn the miners in their bunks, so many grey-blanketed waves. The mountain man wouldn't come—the mountain man might well be the transgressor. Whoever he was, his arms would be too thick to reach way back into the cupboard. Back to where, pale fleshed and dirty as a potato himself, John James curled.

In the weeks that followed, he learned to look further afield. Hunger transformed him, twisting a tentative child into a skittering, thieving thing. It turned out a boom town had its blessings:

those who struck it rich quick could be relied on to be foolish with their goods. More than once he came upon a provision-stocked mule tethered out front of a saloon, its owner drinking hard inside in an effort to dull his delight.

Bill Drown's first strike was minor, but it was enough to bring him in from the fields. He staggered into the rooming house long after the lamps had been snuffed. After convincing the mountain man to lay down his gun, he dug his drowsy son out of the cupboard and carried him to a corner bunk. Keeping his back to the rows of snoring miners, he lit his camp lantern, nudging the wick down low. He draped his arm over John James's shoulder and drew the boy close. "See here now." He reached inside his stained waistcoat and produced a balled-up rag, tied so it wore floppy grey ears. Undone, it fell open to show a palmful of starry sand.

John James had been ill for some time, the potato cupboard racked nightly with what sounded like a dowager's deadly cough. Sensing it would please his father, he hunched forward for a closer look. Gold dust entered him on a breath. He sneezed hard, scattering the top two-thirds.

The marks he earned that night put the welt left by the mountain man's knife to shame. Bone bruises to a one, his back and legs turned to fruit flesh—hard and green, then yellow, stretched shiny with juice. Of the men who raised their heads to his howling, not one lifted a finger in his defence. When the mountain man yelled down from his high bunk, it was for quiet, dammit, and nothing more. Bill Drown got in a last wallop before he drew back from the whimpering bundle and spun away. He left the door gaping behind him. Only then did one of the miners shift himself, dragging his dark blanket around him as he rose to kick it shut.

John James didn't lay eyes on his father again until long after the bruises had healed. When Bill Drown finally did blow into town, he headed straight for one of a hundred card tables to burn up whatever wealth he'd managed to unearth. It might've been that night—or one of several others like it—when he carried John James to the same corner bunk and presented him with a knife of his own. It was stubby, stuffed in a dark leather sheath that had been tooled with the crude face of a dog.

"A man is called upon to protect himself in this world." Bill Drown turned his face to the fissured wall, thrusting his sharp behind out to take up the lion's share of the bed. Balanced at the bunk's edge, John James shoved the gift down his bootleg, sheath and all.

He'd worn it against his calf ever since. It was there now, worrying his ankle as he crouched beneath the boardwalk, awaiting the footfall he knew.

John James looked out on a world made of boots. Knee-high and filthy, they drove pathways through the ooze, this pair reeling, that pair careful, the owner sober or, more likely, drunk to a blank-faced stun. A blunt brown toe caught momentarily on a swag of brush, hacked from the surrounding hills and dragged down by the cartload to quell the rising muck. Thick heels thundered over a stretch of unopened tobacco crates. Rendered worthless in a moment of oversupply, they'd been thrown down to plug a sink-hole. In the dark, racing heart of the gold rush, value was a quick-silver thing.

Dead ahead, a slender pair flashed buttons below a sullied froth of hoisted lace. John James felt his heart skip. Women were few and far between in the city, dearest of luxuries to be had. Such a sight could set even a boy's pulse racing—a motherless boy's more than most. A glint of street lamp showed the overskirt to be a feverish shade of pink. A working woman, then, one of the dark beauties shipped up from beneath the world's wide belt. Not one of the rarest, the kind that came wrapped in grey or sparrow brown.

John James blinked, his eyelids hot, the balls beneath them cold. His limbs might pain him, his position trouble him, more if he allowed himself to think ahead a day or two, perhaps even so long as a fortnight, to the morning when Bill Drown would once again take to the yellow-veined hills. Not thinking ahead was the trick. There was this body—the body of John James Drown—at play or at peril or at rest. Beyond that, there was the next best chance at a meal. Crouching, waiting, he had eaten his fill within the past eight hours, and so was less than desperate for food. The cold wouldn't kill him and nobody knew he was there. Comfortable or not, this was rest.

Sooner or later his father would come. John James would know him first by ear, then, as Bill Drown forsook boardwalk for boggy street, by eye. His state of mind would be easy enough to gauge: high plunging steps told of a manic mood upheld, whereas a dragging gait warned of its aftermath, the rampant, unknowable slope. If it were the former, John James would show himself, caper a little, openly tag along. Otherwise he'd keep a safe distance. When Bill Drown had lost a pile, and sometimes even when he'd won, he'd been known to strip out his belt and chase his son through the streets, forcing John James to take refuge in one of a hundred slits and crannies—the whole dank district a honeycomb he'd made his own.

So why hunker beneath the boardwalk at all? Why not slip off, find a way to fill his belly, return alone to the mountain man's and bury himself deep among the clustering spuds? He knew only that he ached. From the pressure of the boards above him, from the chill of the mud below. From hoping for a glimpse of his father, even if it was just the back of him, winding away.

—

Bill Drown shoved open the mountain man's door two days shy of Christmas—their first in the slanting city on the bay. John James and a dozen flea-sore men looked up from their breakfast bowls. The man in the door frame was soaked. Behind him, a slate scree of rain. His eyes skipped the length of the crowded table, alighting briefly on the son he hadn't seen in a month much as they did on everyone else—mostly new blood, one or two still having troubled themselves with a morning shave. Bill Drown let a rift open in his own dark beard.

"Gripp," he said, stepping inside and clapping a palm on the mountain man's shoulder, "my arrears." A clerk's term, plainly out of place. It fluttered in John James's ears, an echo of that other life, his father's blue-black fingers at the close of every day.

Gripp may not have been familiar with the word, but he knew well enough the meaning of the small buckskin pouch Drown let drop on the table before him. A suspension of spoons at the thud of what could only be the real stuff hitting plank. The mountain man nodded, beard to breastbone, his whiskers and wool shirt two grades of bled-out grey.

Bill Drown widened his wet smile. The sight of his teeth hurt John James. He lowered his eyes, focusing on the last yellow lump in his bowl. His father loomed, his fingers a sudden, blunt rake through John James's hair, water streaming from his coat cuff to shock the boy's scalp and waken its host of nits.

"Will I serve myself, innkeeper?" The voice cheerful, the combing fingers hard. In the corner of John James's vision, the colourless bulk of the mountain man rose.

After eating his fill, Bill Drown ploughed into his bunk and slept for twenty-two straight hours. John James came and went, never straying far. By the time his father woke, dawn was near and the rain had let up for what felt like the first time in memory. The two of them walked out together in their customary way—Drown neither inviting John James nor objecting when he tagged along.

It was a short stroll to the docks, where they stood staring out over the darkened bay. Abandoned vessels bobbed, their crews having legged it for the hills.

"Fools," Bill Drown murmured. "Madmen."

John James held his tongue, knowing to let the explanation, if there was to be any, come on its own.

"That's what easterners call those of us who leave the daily grind for the goldfields." His father spat, foamy by his boot tip. "Grunts and bosses, not a freethinking man among them. And the South is no better. Maybe if your daddy sets you up on the family plantation, but even then, what kind of sorry bastard wants to be tied to a plot of land?" He dropped into a squat, taking hold of John James by the wrist. "I dug one hell of a hole this time."

John James nodded, shoved his tongue up into the tickle behind his front teeth.

Bill Drown grasped and twisted, exposing his son's louse-pale inner arm—the skin there like a skimming of cooled lard over dark prongs of vein. "There was this crevice laying longways down the rock, packed with clay, some gravel in there too." His breath was coming fast. "She was a bitch to open up, but the thing is—" His face broke wide open. "—I knew. I just *knew!*"

John James fought the urge to wrest himself loose. Much as he hated the sight of it, he stared hard at his forearm, preferring it to his father's molten gaze.

Moments later both arms hung free, Drown having released him to reach deep into his coat. It was a gesture John James had come to know. He used to think it signified, that his father's small strikes would result in a home, or at least a room in one. Bill Drown behind the counter in a shop of his own. The goods for sale scarcely mattered—John James generally envisioned an array of clean white lumps. The counter, and his father's hands on it— strong and solid, fingers spread wide—that had been the thing. He was wiser now. He was six.

Glancing about, Bill Drown hauled out a pouch several times larger than the one he'd given Gripp. He jigged it on its draw-string, weighed it in his palm. John James held his breath when his father flashed him the gold. Fat grains of it, a miniature sack of wheat. He willed himself to smile.

Behind him, too young as yet to breach the skyline, flames. Soon those who owned buildings would run mad with buckets, while Bill Drown and a thousand others stood idle, watching the business district burn.

May 17th, 1867

Dear Daughter

The girl has just fetched me in a bowl of her soup the steam off it so foul I have directed her to bear it away again. Have you any bread I asked her. Yes Mother Burr. She will insist upon addressing me so. And cheese? Yes. Then bring me a little of each and no mould on either. Dorrie you will judge me peevish to have added this last but you cannot conceive of the specimens she has delivered to this bed. You may imagine her spiteful as I once did. I will confess I took a kind of bitter pleasure in the idea. But my girl you would be wrong.

She is a slattern no denying but the home she was raised up in schooled her so. The mother you might recall is famous for riding to Cedar on mule back with her house apron flapping and flour in her hair. Her dozen or so children could grow a fair crop of cabbages on the muck in their ears. The girl was the same when she came to us. I doubt she had ever washed there and many another part besides. I know because it was I who bathed her on the day of their sealing.

Can you credit it Dorrie? We were in rooms at the Salt Lake House Mr. Burr having determined to strain our finances sorely and do the thing up in style. Yet he would not brook our stopping to visit you on the way home. He was so good as to inform me that we had taken holiday enough and there was work to be done back on the farm.

The girl had passed the previous night in her own room while I bunked in with Mr. Burr. That night after the ceremony we would switch places myself returning alone to the smaller room. But before that she had to be made ready. I stood her unclothed in the washtub and scrubbed her head to toe. I suppose I could have left this work to the women at the Endowment House but I chose not to. In this matter I cannot seem to explain myself except to say that I wanted to get a good look at her. Or more truthfully that I didn't want him seeing any part of her I had not.

To this end I found myself faced with a particular challenge. While she didn't pretend to any modesty when removing her dress and everything under it she clung stubbornly to her right stocking going so far as to step into the tub with it bunched about her ankle like a man's sock.

I wonder Dorrie if you ever had occasion at Sunday Meeting to take notice of the girl's limp. Perhaps not given the way you kept your eyes to yourself when in company. Suffice it to say she favours the left foot as the right is not entirely formed. This was no secret of course. Mr. Burr would never have rated such yellow locks if they hadn't come part and parcel with a consider-able flaw. The girl would have been snapped up by at least a Ward Bishop long since.

I was impatient with her perhaps even a little harsh. You

must remember I was on my knees before the glory of her eighteen years. I will admit to yanking at the stocking even to the point of threatening her balance but that was before I looked up and saw her face twisted and streaming with tears. Now child. The words were out before I thought them. Your mother is a tenderheart by nature Dorrie as I believe you know. I shan't hurt you I said. Then I saw it was not pain she feared and I told her she must not be ashamed.

Plain enough sentiment but the look of wonder on her face told me she had never heard the like before. She bit her lip and shifted her weight to her good foot without a word. I peeled the stocking down to find a curled and filthy thing. Its smell was that of some poor creature crawled off to die. My girl you will judge me a liar when I tell you I felt nothing akin to disgust. When I tell you my throat was so swollen with pity I feared for a moment I would choke.

I would know that sensation again. Months perhaps even a year on when I was already beginning to suffer from a pooling in my feet and legs. The hour was late. I had been abed and sleepless in my discomfort for some time when I decided a poultice might afford me some relief. I was creeping to the kitchen each step a punishment when I spied them through the crack of the parlour door. This time it was ~~Lyn~~ Mr. Burr who was on his knees. The girl was in my armchair a fact that would have irked me had it not been for the way she was holding her face in her hands. He had the stocking off. He was lifting the fist of her bad foot and touching it to his mouth. Dorrie you will pardon my plain talk. You are a married woman now and so I believe you will understand. A man's feelings do not always spring from his heart. Do you take my meaning? Mr. Burr's interest in that foot was unhealthy. The girl knew it. She kept her face hidden the entire time I stood watching. She held herself rigid as a corpse.

Dorrie I know well how such a scene will trouble you now you have witnessed it through my eyes. I know you must cry inwardly that a mother ought not to burden her child with such a story most especially with regard to the man she has called Papa. Do you think me cruel my daughter? This is nothing to what I must tell you before I am through.

Doubtless you imagine your mother to be a virtuous woman unshakable in her faith. You will recall how I polished the table upon which the Book of Mormon and the Bible and the Doctrine and Covenants lay. This last my favourite and yours too I believe for its recounting of the many revelations that came to Brother Joseph direct from God. How many lines of Scripture have passed from my lips into your ears? As many and more into the ears of Mr. Burr. At times I confess I have fancied myself a kind of bottomless pitcher pouring out the word of the Prophet and with it the word of the Lord. But there is a bottom. I can see it now.

It turns upon this point. I am Mr. Burr's wife in this world. It cannot be helped. But to be sealed to him for all eternity is a fate I cannot brook. The idea sticks in my throat. I cannot swallow it and so my girl I spit it out.

Some three decades have passed since Mr. Burr and myself were baptized by Brother Joseph himself at the temple in Kirtland. Decades during which my faith has been tested and tempered more times than I care to think on. And yet I can still recall a time before I made bold to call myself a Saint. At that time I was acquainted with a vision of the hereafter that was a good deal vaguer and in my dark hours I find it is this Heaven and not the Prophet's upon which I dwell. I tell myself I will be admitted entry. Mr. Burr may or may not but I believe I shall be rid of him in either case. God willing I shall tread upon the clouds alone.

Dorrie yesterday morning Brother Creel came to say a blessing over me and to heal me with a laying on of hands. It was all I could manage to lie quiet while he jabbered on. Words even holy ones can lose their worth if you hold them cheap. Just as if one were entrusted with an innocent body and allowed strangers to make free with it until the flesh ceased to feel. Am I frightening you? Forgive me. It is my own fear that leads me to so dance about the matter.

Let me begin with a small truth and see if it won't loosen my pen. The girl as I have always named her to you is called Katherine. Her family called her Kitty and Mr. Burr has followed suit. A sly ridiculous name he utters at every chance. I have refused to do so just as I have refused to call her Sister which as you know an obedient wife is called upon to do. Katherine is the best I can manage. I would call her Miss Ells but she no longer is. She is like myself Mrs. Burr.

But I promised you a truth and here it is. Kitty suits her. Not because she is sly or ridiculous but because she is warm and demands little more than her keep. Because she belongs and she doesn't. Because she turned up one day and never left. Nor would I have her do so. I would not be without her. There now. All this fuss over a name. But a name holds meaning my girl. Shall I keep on while my ink still flows?

Eudora I told you time and again you were named after your real mother my poor sister who perished on the road to Zion. That was a lie. I had a sister called Eudora yes but she died before her seventh birthday of poison blood from a blister overlooked. Poor child she was always a secretive thing. She said nothing until a vein the full length of her leg had turned black. She was like you in that way but she was not of course your mother. I don't know who your mother was. And yet I still presume to write these words. Not because I claim the right but because I cannot bear to give them up.

All a mother's love
Helen Burr

12

THERE HAD BEEN NO COURTSHIP as such. Hammer came to the Burr farm on a Thursday. Dorrie looked up to find him staring— not at her face but at the work in her hands. She was turning a rabbit's hind leg out of its fur.

The eyes that watched her were small and dark, set in a weathered face. His hair was black like her own, his moustaches greying. He shifted his gaze to the butcher block before her, taking inventory of her rudimentary tools. He was short, so much so that Papa's entire face showed above and behind him. Dorrie expected to find irritation written there, or the prickling shame he often betrayed where she was concerned—but found instead a beaming smile. The stranger took a step toward her.

"Tricky work." The first words she heard her future husband speak.

"Yes, sir."

"Brother Hammer," Papa said, thrusting his face forward over the man's shoulder, "this is my daughter, Eudora."

Hammer nodded. "Done many others?"

"She has indeed." Papa's voice came out squeaky. "Eudora, come inside and show Brother Hammer your animals."

She hesitated. Did he mean for her to take the stranger into her bedchamber, the only place Papa allowed her to display her work? He said it gave him the shivers to have them hanging around. No fit way for a girl to amuse herself. *She's artistic, Lyman,* Mama would remind him. And if he grumbled further, *It gives her joy.*

Dorrie set the rabbit down, wiped her hands on her apron and followed the two men across the yard to the house. To her relief she saw Papa was showing Brother Hammer into the parlour. It would seem he wished her to present her collection to them where they sat.

Mama had done more than stand up for Dorrie's chosen pastime—it was she who had made it possible in the first place by sending away for the best Christmas present any daughter had ever known. Never mind that it hadn't arrived until March. *Collection and Preservation: A Taxidermist's Guide* came bound in thick red leather, still smelling faintly of the beast on the hoof. Opening it, Dorrie came close to wailing, so keen was her joy.

She'd been in possession of the book for some months when Hammer came calling, and had been making do with limited materials and blunt, unwieldy knives. Still, she felt a silent thrill of pride as she carried in her work. First the mice, then the weasel, then the birds. Cruikshank Crow, convincing though he was, she left on the bedside table. She saved the yellow barn cat for last, setting it down in the midst of the others, turning it by its arched back so the men could make out the teeth she had so skilfully bared.

Brother Hammer sat with his boots planted wide, right hand raking his moustaches. "Well, now," he began, just as Mama appeared at the parlour door.

"Oh." She was fresh from the garden, dirt to her elbows, her apron a sight. She took in the stranger, the menagerie laid out before him. "I didn't realize we had company, Mr. Burr."

"This is Brother Hammer." Papa left off the second half of the introduction, the part that included his wife. "You won't have had your dinner, Brother Hammer," he added. "Eudora, help your mother in the kitchen. Leave the menfolk alone to talk."

The following day, when Hammer returned to the Burr farm, it was he and Dorrie who were left alone. Sitting opposite her suitor, she could hear Mama's protests vibrating in the walls. Papa's voice came only once, loud enough to bring about the quiet that ensued.

Hammer wasted no time in wooing. "Eudora, your father has given his say-so for you to become my wife."

Dorrie nodded dumbly. Her head felt curiously off-kilter.

"You won't be the first."

She nodded again. A sensation of slippage, as though her skull were somehow improperly anchored to her spine. She stared at a dark flower on the rug.

"There's an old adobe barn," he went on. "I'm something of a hunter, see." Then the words that lifted her eyes. "It'd be yours. Your workshop."

"Workshop?"

He grinned. "Thought you might like that."

She twisted her hands. He held his peace while she thought. Her answer, when it came, was firm. "I'll need materials. Proper tools."

It was Hammer's turn to nod. "Anything you want."

It wasn't until perhaps an hour after they pulled away from the gate that it dawned on Dorrie—she was now entirely dependent upon the near stranger at her side.

Hammer drove the buggy long and hard, his black mare scarcely blowing. Squinting down the long track before them, he talked of life on the Hammer ranch—the best grass, best horse-flesh for miles around, the three wives who got there before her, the small herd of children who all appeared to be saddled with the same name. Dorrie said little, but pricked up her ears when he spoke of the game he'd bagged in recent years.

She'd travelled the same road only a year before, Papa driving her all the way to Salt Lake City, seat of the Lion of the Lord. They'd rolled right past the impressive edifice of the Beehive House, home of President Young and his host of busy wives. The Endowment House was a plainer affair, two storeys of adobe with a four-windowed front—three staring, one blinkered, obtuse. She entered alone, Papa pulling away smartly, off about his errands without a backward glance. In one hand she bore the ceremonial robes Mama had sewn for her, parcelled in brown paper and tied with curling twine. In the other, a bottle of oil.

Once inside, she removed her shoes, then whispered her name, date of birth and several other particulars the clerk desired to know. Before long, a white-haired woman with the split lip of a hare came to escort her within. Together they entered a vast, steamy room cut down the centre by a curtain hanging limp on its rod. Like all young Saints, she was to be cleansed of the blood of this generation.

The surface aroma of the place was fresh, strong soap and a bundle of herbs. Beneath it, like a layer of good air in a room full of smoke, ran a current of more personal smells, the boldest of which—a metallic tang reminiscent of the barn at calving—set Dorrie's skin crawling.

In moments she found herself surrounded by female elders, women Mama's age and older, whose practised hands made short work of removing her clothes and half carrying her to the waiting tub. They left no part of her untouched, scrubbing as vigorously between her legs as they did between her toes. She was a raw thing by the time they towelled her down.

Next came the heavy yellow oil. Crown of the head, eyes and ears, mouth and feet made unctuous. Her breasts and loins greased so that she might bring forth a numerous race. Her arm anointed so that it might be strong in the defence of Zion and in avenging the Prophet's blood.

By the time they began to dress her, Dorrie had gone numb. The muslin shift fell about her like an exhalation, warm and stale. Then the undergarment every Saint wears as a guard against disease and violent death. A long skirt over that, and finally Mama's linen robe. On her head a square of muslin, pinched at one corner to form a veiled cap.

She can never quite recall the sacred name bestowed on her that day—familiar Old Testament syllables that ran through her like a tablespoon of fat. Other details elude her as well. She knows she sat witness to a play, a stilted enactment of Creation, the Fall, the final restorative Glory of Man. For this portion of the proceedings there were other initiates present, young men and women in similar garb to her own. Also present—can this be true?—was President Young himself, goat-eyed, bearded, built like the carpenter he used to be. Can she be remembering things correctly? Is it possible Brother Brigham himself acted the lead, pacing and thundering before her, clumsy in his depiction of God?

After the play came signs and passwords, arcane grips. In the end she knelt exhausted with the others in a ring. Right hand raised, she moved her lips in a series of oaths. She would avenge the death of the Prophet upon the Gentiles who murdered him and would teach the children of the Church in this wise. She would obey without question any command of the priesthood.

She would consider all that transpired within those walls to be a secret inviolable unto the grave.

And now she was to enter the Endowment House again, this time as a bride. First, though, there remained a distance of some two hundred and fifty miles to be travelled, including a detour to the ranch, to collect Hammer's first wife. Mama had told her what to expect during the ceremony—the first wife positioning herself between Dorrie and Hammer, taking hold of Dorrie's hand and placing it in the hand of the husband they would share.

The miles rinsed through her. They reached the town of Beaver that first evening and stayed with a family Hammer knew, Dorrie bunking in with a pair of plump daughters while her husband-to-be stayed up talking with the man of the house. They would make stopovers at the towns of Fillmore, Nephi and Lehi before they reached the ranch, and each night Hammer would see to it that she slept with other women or alone. He had yet to trouble Dorrie with so much as a brush of his lips against her cheek. She began to imagine herself becoming a daughter of sorts to him, a wife in name alone.

They drew up to the Hammer ranch in the waning of a warm, dry day. A pair of orchards flanked the track. To the left, strict aisles of peaches fanned like an apron from the hips of the main house. To the right, lines of unfamiliar black trunks ran at doglegs. Barely visible in their midst stood a log house large enough for one.

The yard opened out before them, Hammer reining in the black mare before a scene of some industry. A boy of perhaps six years of age sat in the crook of a limb, handing peaches to a smaller brother and sister below. Such care, such competence for children so young. In a nearby swath of sun, a girl who looked to be the eldest stood partway up a ladder, laying halved fruits on a scaffold to dry.

Only the youngest in evidence—a moon-faced little boy—sat idle in the grass. Every one of the children had skin the colour of butter and hair that looked polished, like expensive wood.

In the shade of the long verandah two women sat on rail-backed chairs, bowls in their laps and bushel baskets at their feet. Both were running knives down leaky fruits, separating flesh from stone. The younger of the two—butter-skinned, wooden-haired—worked slowly, taking pains. Her companion's blade darted and flashed. She sat erect under a mound of white-blonde hair.

The woman Dorrie took to be the first wife waited until the buggy had come to a full stop before she looked up from the work in her lap. Even at a distance, Dorrie felt the measuring instrument of her gaze.

Hammer swung down from the buggy, sniffing the air. "Peach-cutting," he said, presumably addressing Dorrie, though he didn't look her way. Then, in a sudden bellow, "Lal!"

Down the far end of an orchard corridor, a young man dropped from a tree. Here too the bloodlines lay plain. Advancing with a jerk, he stumbled against a near-full basket, causing several tender fruits to leap its woven lip and roll. He froze for a long moment, then came at the buggy in a dead run.

"Haul that trunk in when you're done," Hammer shot back over his shoulder, already striding toward the pair of women—the younger rising now, smoothing her skirts.

It was then that Dorrie realized no one meant to hand her down. The son, having snatched up the reins, stood watching her, saying nothing. Mama's training told her to ignore his rudeness and extend her hand, but she couldn't help feeling it might come back damaged, like a finger pushed through the wire of a cage.

She chose to back down on her own, the buggy jolting into motion before she could get both feet beneath her. Righting her-

self, she stared after Lal. Even his back was sullen. She had a
nasty thought: come tomorrow, she would be his stepmother.
Notwithstanding the fact that he was clearly her elder by at least
two years, if all the other wives somehow dissolved, she would
have to learn to call him son.

Still the first wife had not risen. Taking small steps toward the
foot of the verandah stairs, Dorrie lowered her head. The air was
honeyed, pitted with small cyclones of flies. She didn't look up
until she had to.

The younger wife, still standing, offered an unfocused smile.
Hammer had taken her chair and was sliding a peach-half into his
mouth, the flesh red and riven where it had clung to the pit. Dorrie
dropped a shallow curtsy. The first wife looked her up and down.
She laid her paring knife across her apron, entwined her sticky,
discoloured fingers and made a steeple of her sizable thumbs.

Stew. It's all the woman ever makes. You'd think there was never
a decent cut of meat on hand the way she boils every chunk to
mush and strings. A man likes to sit down to a recognizable portion of flank or loin at his own table from time to time. Something
he can get his knife into.

Erastus looks down the long table, this small distance enough
now to make him unsure whether his first wife's eyes are meeting
his. He glares dully in the event that they are.

"Pardon me, Brother Hammer."

Erastus shifts his gaze to the hired man. A face long and wanting, too knowing for its twenty-odd years. Bendy. Fairly named
from what Erastus has seen, his frame more rope than bone.

"Brother Drown?"

"Well, sir, I was just wondering, that picture, there."

Erastus draws his lips back in a smile. Knowing he won't see true—a furry frame around grey-green darkness, moth-white daubs of collar and cuffs, yellow smudges of face—he does what's expected and angles his gaze alongside Drown's. "A pretty piece of work, wouldn't you say?"

"Yes, sir. Those people, are they your kin?"

Erastus clenches the smile in place. He hasn't long to wait. The sound his first wife lets out is somewhere between a cough and a goose's honk.

"You'd need a sight coarser paint to do justice to his people."

"And you'd know, would you?" Erastus hears the strangled tone and smoothes it out. "You who never laid eyes on a single one."

"I know the country, all right," Ursula spits. "I know the stock."

The old weapons are the keenest. He's a Missourian born and bred, the cruellest persecutors of God's people thus far. Never mind how he hated that river-soaked swatch of land. Not the river itself, though, the silty Grand muscling its way through his childhood, calling out to him from its catfishy snags. He only rarely penetrated its depths. He was too busy coughing up yellow batter in the Hammer Gristmill, or getting bitten raw by mosquitoes when he was lucky enough to work outside. Even his father's bloodhounds had time to nose through the grass or lie panting in the shade. When Erastus wasn't hard at it, he was crumpled in bottomless sleep.

Salvation came in the guise of a straggling crowd. He stood at his father's side that bitter morning. Lalovee Hammer and a handful of others gripped their guns for the look of it, but knew better than to fire on such a numerous host. They kept their violence verbal, punctuated by the occasional high-lobbed stone. Erastus had heard plenty of talk about Mormons—a plague of souls more trouble than Indians and slaves combined—but the day they came filing down the track that bordered his father's land, their heads bowed against a hail of insults, he felt his heart twitch with pity. It was January, a cutting wind off the river, squalls of snow. Some dragged alongside wagons or stock, but many came with nothing but a blanket over their shoulders, a bundle in their arms. More than one came on feet that were bare and blue.

The moment he spotted her, his heart left off twitching and began to burn. His vision was still perfect then—he took in every inch of Ursula Wright as she passed. Beneath her bonnet's rim, hair like a cloud bank, eyes like two glimpses of sky.

Lalovee Hammer saw her too. Unlike his son, he didn't stare in mute astonishment. He stooped for the sharpest, unloveliest stone at his feet. It was a boy's reaction—spy out beauty and mar it, quick as you can. Erastus had his father by the wrist before he knew what he was doing. It was only then, as a young man of twenty-three, that he became sensible of his own strength. He squeezed long enough to render Lalovee's grip useless, then a moment more to bring a glimmer of pain to the old man's eye. He brought his lips within an inch of his father's bristling cheek.

Did you never think I might want something of my own?

Erastus left home without a penny to his name to join that river of bodies, walking among their number clear to Illinois. The largest stone flew straight from the hand of his own father to catch him square in the back of the neck—a spot that pains him to this day when it rains. Still, in Ursula's books he remains a Missourian. The lowest of the low.

Erastus ratchets his smile a finger wider. "My good wife speaks the truth, Brother Drown. That fine couple are no kin of mine."

"I see, sir."

It's clear Drown is wishing he hadn't spoken, hoping the talk will take another turn. Erastus hunches forward.

"You old enough to recall the forty-niners?"

Drown's face darkens. He nods. "Yes, sir."

"Most of them had never crossed a county, let alone a continent. No idea what they were signing on for. They come hauling dresser drawers, grandfather clocks—" He pauses for effect. "—paintings. The minute they hit hard country, they start shedding their goods. Myself and a few companions, we worked a stretch of the trail east of the Sweetwater. You wouldn't credit it. Wash basins, harnesses, gunpowder. Like an auction house blown sky high."

Again the hasty nod, a movement Erastus scarcely registers. He's talking for his own ears now. "Not that everything they dropped was treasure. They'd come through some bad water a ways back. Dead cattle every other step, blown up so you could pop them with a pin. Graves, too. Shallow as cat scratchings."

Eudora drops her fork. It glances off the verge of her plate, eliciting a hard click from Ursula's tongue. The girl neither excuses herself nor looks up, only reaches out with that strawberry claw of hers, clutches the fork and resumes eating in her joyless way.

"It took a strong stomach, that work," Erastus goes on. "Strong constitution, too. Those that could still walk had every plague and ague going. We lost more than one good man ourselves." He shakes his head. "Their surviving stock looked like washboards on legs. We'd buy them at a low figure, keep the cream for breeding, fatten the rest and sell them on to the next sorry pack. That's how I got started trading horseflesh. Folks want oxen and mules when they're westering. A man settles, the first thing he buys is a good horse."

"Scavenging."

Ursula's voice startles Erastus. He's come close to forgetting table and family, seeing instead the long track of riches for the taking, the haggard ranks of gold-hungry fools. He blinks, her features refusing to come clear.

"That's the word for it," she adds.

Half a dozen retorts spring to mind, but not one of them does justice to the internal yowling her words have evoked. This woman he's scratched and scrambled for, her best milch cow descended from an emaciated black-and-white he led back to her from the littered trail.

The wife at his left hand speaks up. "I call it commerce. What do you think built this place?"

"Commerce." Ursula turns the word over like a lozenge. "There's a topic you'd know something about, Sister."

Thankful sucks air. It's Erastus's turn to take her part.

"Sister Thankful knows a great deal about many topics, Mother." He wipes the back of his hand over his moustaches, a habit he knows she abhors. "Topics a simple country woman might not understand."

Thankful knows better than to laugh out loud, but her bright lips widen in the corner of his eye. Ursula sits erect, her indistinct face the colour of something boiled. It seems he can still call her blood up, after all. He clears his throat.

"The fact is, Brother Drown, my own mother, may she rest, was a good deal plainer than the lady you see pictured there." The hired man has lowered his head as though praying. Erastus waits until he raises it before adding, "My daddy was uglier still."

Tonight Ursula needn't lay her ear to Thankful's bedchamber door to witness the noisy goings-on within. All the same, she does.

It's a variation on the usual theme—a good deal of tousling, then a sharp avian *screeee*, followed by a thud that becomes thudding, rhythmic and obscene. Hammer wheezing on the offbeat, "I've—huh—got—you—huh—huh—now." Thankful replying with stuttered whistles, another long, strangled squawk.

Ursula's heard enough. She doesn't wait for Hammer to finish the job, knowing full well the string of curses he'll emit, the last and foulest dwindling to a groan. She glides past Ruth's door and carries on to her own.

Once inside, she crosses to her dressing table and sits, regarding herself in the mirror's swimming dark. Hammer lets himself go shamefully with his third wife, though, to be fair, she's the sort of woman to invite profanity. It was a different story the first and only time he lay with Sister Eudora in her bedchamber. Hammer was so quiet about his business that night, Ursula caught nothing but the final disembodied grunt. The girl's silence lay thick, muffling the proceedings like a blanket of snow.

With Ruth, he whimpers and moans. The second wife answers as though she were a bolster repeatedly compressed, releasing a chain of soft, exhausted sighs.

In his first marriage bed, Hammer neither whimpered, nor grunted, nor swore. He whispered endearments. What was worse, upon reaching his end, he wept. Doubtless he told himself Ursula didn't notice—it was never more than a tear or two—but she wasn't the kind to let weakness go unremarked.

Her face in the looking glass is without feature. She doesn't bother lighting a candle to let down her hair, instead plucking out pins and dragging her brushstrokes by feel. Next she must undress, another chore she'll manage, perversely, in the dark. She won't sleep, she knows it. Still, she'd be a fool not to lie down and try.

The Father has kept mainly to hard ground. He's left a trail so staggered that the Tracker, tracing it about the darkened ranch yard, gets muddled time and again. Often he has only scent to go by, one promising waft among a thousand airy ribbons of not-wolf—hardly more telling than a single shapeless scuff. Still, he tracks. Catches a whiff and follows it to a well-formed print, the Father's broad forepaw preserved in a patch of damp out back of the privy. After reading its direction, he grinds the print away with his boot heel.

Setting off in a line defined by the two middle claw marks, the Tracker moves into scrubby grass recently disturbed. The Father's scent condenses into a discernible stream, flowing on to a spot beneath the back window of the child wife's barn. There, in the spill of her night-burning lamp, faint but undeniable, a pair of more compact tracks mark the place where the Father rose up on his hind legs like a man. The Tracker fits his own two soles over the prints, obliterating them. Standing where the wolf lately stood, he peers through the warped and cloudy glass.

The child wife sits on her stool, hands still on the workbench before her, face hidden behind a fall of hair. When she fails to move for minutes on end, the Tracker shifts his gaze to the crowded western wall. The gleam of a black horn beckons. Viewed through the wavy pane by the lamp's low flicker, the stuffed antelope behaves as stones do in the bed of a creek. It moves. The Tracker drops, twisting to flatten his back against the old barn's wall.

There can be no forgetting the day he brought the pronghorn down. It was around this time last year. Hammer didn't accompany him so much as dog his steps, and then only until the grade steepened and he began to fall behind. After that it was just the two of them—the animal wounded in its haunch from the initial long shot, the only way the Tracker stood a chance of keeping up.

It felt all wrong. Though it wasn't unheard of among the People for a lone hunter to stalk a single antelope, the Tracker had never done so, and neither had any of the men in his camp. As a rule, the spring-footed beasts were taken communally, with several years passing between culls. A pronghorn hunt required one who was gifted to call the animals down, keeping hold of them by their spirits until they could be killed. His father's elder brother was such a man. He would haunt the verges of a herd for days on end, singing to the beasts by daylight, sleeping among them by dark. When the time was right, he would lead them to a brush corral. Once encircled, the pronghorns would run themselves ragged, then cede without struggle to a rain of clubs.

Despite its bleeding haunch, the antelope maintained a good lead. It gained an open cliff and, judging itself to be safe for the moment, paused to crane back and nuzzle its wound. So doing, it cut a sharp profile against the sky. The Tracker had a clear shot, but somehow failed to centre the heart. Knocked to the ground by the force of the ball, the pronghorn lay stunned a moment before rolling back up onto its hooves.

Again the Tracker gave chase. Following the weaving, blood-spattered trail, he jogged a memory loose. His father's face, lost to him for years, hung before him, underlit by fire. The known mouth moving. One of the old, old tales.

A hunter, tracking his wounded quarry, entered the mouth of a cave. Soon enough, he found himself in the world below. Like the finest of underground streams, this world ran sweet and pure—a meadow green and waving, veined with water, rich with game.

While the story-hunter descended into that good valley, the Tracker climbed. Hammer must have been a good mile behind him by the time he ran the antelope to ground. When he stooped over the animal—collapsed and quivering on its side—he did so alone. Bright red bubbles whistled from the hole in its heaving chest. The sun was hot, the scene barren. He watched the antelope's keen eye turn skyward, then turn to stone.

It's not the first time a wolf has howled within earshot of the house. A body grows accustomed to such sounds, comes to appreciate them even, living on the frontier. It is, however, the first time a howl has yanked Erastus bolt upright out of a black ditch of sleep, palms wet, pulse thundering.

The wail is dying now, his waking mind gripping fast to its quavering tail. No braiding, declarative harmonies here. This wolf is alone—perhaps somewhere on the far pasture, paws planted in his best grazing grass.

In the silence that is the howl's wide wake, Erastus wipes his palms on the quilt and wills his heart to slow. Each moonlit hand rests on a silky diamond. Finding his backbone too rigid to let him lie, he turns his pillow on end against the headboard and shuffles back on his buttocks to meet it. A burning under his ribs alerts him to the last breath he swallowed gone stale. Let it out. Drag in another. He looks for comfort to the face on the pillow beside him. Thankful is not a pretty sleeper. Her long nose whistles, the mouth beneath it a toothy gap. Erastus looks away.

Every inch of him is listening—the horned heel callus, the hairy belly, the clammy hands. Good sense to the contrary, he feels the whorled cups of his ears yearn forward, drawing taut the thin skin at their backs. This despite knowing the wolf will leave the sky quiet for a time, open for reply.

A lone animal poses the greatest threat to a ranch. Bereft of a pack to hunt with, a rogue wolf will turn his bright eye to a man's livestock. Being neither a sheep nor a cattle man, Erastus has less to fear than some. It takes a gang of them to bring down a healthy horse, especially one rich with mustang blood. Still, there are the milch cows and the chickens to be considered. There are the foals.

The cry will come again. Unless the creature has moved on— and he finds himself hoping fervently that it has—it will sound its existence, unreel its ringing question again. No sooner than a quarter of an hour. Perhaps as long as three-quarters. Erastus listens. Outside, the wolf listens back.

Standing with her arms folded across her chest, Dorrie moves her gaze over the dimly lit collection. Three tiers up, the lantern-eyed lynx sits tonguing its paw—a pose that came to her the moment the Tracker rolled its snow-caked form onto her workbench. And there, the blacktails stand precisely as she imagined them upon her first glimpse of antlers protruding from a distant flank—buck and doe like a pair of hands sheltering their dappled fawns. Even the flying squirrels suggested their own scene as Hammer drew them from his bag. The female landing, clinging to her branch, her mate behind her, open wide in flight. It was the same with the birds. The turkey vulture insisted on being strung from the rafters in a tilting, soaring V. The mergansers chose to demonstrate phases of takeoff, the lead duck climbing, two followers still skating, flapping hard. It was simple—Dorrie saw the scene and made it. Until now.

Turning on her heel, she crosses to the door and pushes it open into flooding moonlight. The yard is large, but hemmed in by human structures and therefore safe. She sets off counter-clockwise along its margin, making her best attempt at a shuffling stroll.

The ranch—at least all she knows of it—rotates past. The privy, then the slat block of the washhouse, wafting lye. The vegetable plot. The house's silent sprawl.

She skirts the redolent dark of the peach orchard to where the track bleeds off into blackness. Taking a breath, she crosses its double cut and veers to hug the mulberry copse's verge. In its shadows the silkhouse sits quiet, the worms about their business in the dark. Ruth will have checked on them recently, or will be rising to do so soon.

As the last of the broad-leaved trees falls away, outbuildings stand in order of increasing size. First, the chicken house with its warning fox nailed flat. A waste of a good pelt, but Mother Hammer had insisted. Never mind the effect of that star-shaped skin on the already nervous birds. Their every day flavoured with its constant tang, the promise of a squawking, mangled death.

The cow barn seems peaceful by comparison, its inhabitants dark-eyed and dull. Dorrie continues on to the stable's massive facade and lingers there a moment, steeling herself before rushing the last, curving leg of the way—the corral a tame gateway to a terrible expanse.

Which brings her back to the old adobe barn. Its high grey door is so worn as to seem furry. She lays her palm to it, lets it slide in a single downward stroke. Nothing awaits her inside. Only the same set of questions she's been struggling with since the wolves arrived, the same maddeningly blank internal slate.

Behind her, a sound. She's heard it a thousand times, but tonight every sense is tempered by the spectral light. The moan of the stable's great door is the utterance of something alive.

She turns in time to see the new man lead Lal's palomino out into the corral. There's no mistaking the horse. It's the only one of its colour on the ranch, coat caramel-brown, mane and tail pure cream—ashen now in the lunar wash, but the eye, adjusting, translates. *Bull*. An unkindness of a name. The rider's is scarcely better—Brother Drown. Or, as he informed the family at table that first evening, Bendy. Whatever his name, he's got his work cut out for him. Bull tends to bear a man's weight like a grudge.

As though in defiance of her thoughts, Bendy Drown hooks his boot in the iron and mounts in a baffling, elastic surge. Dorrie blinks. Limbs like so many whip lengths, and then he's settled between cantle and horn. He lets Bull stand for a moment before nudging him into a walk, nice and easy, clockwise around the corral.

Dorrie hasn't been on a horse in years. Doubtless Hammer would have allowed her if she'd asked, but the truth is she dislikes riding. Taking to horseback means taking to the open. A body has to be content to progress across a valley bottom like a stitch across a massive quilt, having no fear—no notion, even—that at any moment the quilt might buckle into smothering folds.

Dorrie knows full well a field can't swallow her. Knows it and doesn't, all at once.

Chances are she never would have climbed onto the paint's back if Papa hadn't insisted she do something to put a little colour in her cheeks. *Little wonder she looks like the dead up and walking. Does she ever even set foot outside?*

Mama took the time to join her long after Dorrie was proficient enough to ride out on her own. Notwithstanding a dearth of sidesaddles on the property, Lyman Burr expected a lady to ride like one. Dorrie's unease doubled when her seat was off-kilter. Sensing this, Mama held a trot until they were out of Papa's sight, then slowed to a stop so the pair of them could rearrange themselves astride. *Better, my girl? Now you can get a proper grip.*

Mama knew to avoid the open without ever being told, keeping to the maze of cottonwoods or making brief, speedy bursts between clots of scrub. Dorrie followed close, tucked deep in her drooping bonnet. Whenever she felt a wash of panic, she stared hard at a spot midway down Mama's back. More often than not, Mama would turn in her saddle and smile.

Coming back to herself, Dorrie finds she's flattened her back to the workshop door. Her eyes refocus on horse and rider just as Drown presses Bull into a trot. It's something to see. Normally an eye-rolling, lip-flaring mess, the palomino obliges him with a steady three-beat stride, ears forward, head high. For a good half-circuit. And then he shies.

Drown holds to the animal like a second tail, rippling along its length but firm at the bony root. He clings fast while Bull skips and reels, eventually quieting him to a shuffle. Sliding down from the saddle, the new man resembles nothing so much as a bucket of some dark liquid upturned. He takes a few steps and crouches, his hand disappearing in the grass. Behind him, Bull holds rigid, wheezing his fear.

When Drown rises, he does so slowly, in his hand a long black stick. He lays it flat across both palms, taking a narrow step then another toward the horse. He says nothing—at least nothing loud enough to reach Dorrie's ears—yet his meaning is crystal clear. *A stick, see? Only a stick. No snake here.* Bull understands him, too. Relief passes over his handsome bulk, redrawing him in kinder lines.

Drown hurls the stick hard and far, his arm flailing. End over end, it cuts a fluid arc, disappearing as it crests the fence. He remounts with a spring, Bull catching him in the grasp of his back and breaking into a joyful run. Dorrie stares after them. There's no denying the evidence of her own two eyes. Under a new man, the palomino is a whole new beast.

13

IN THE HEYDAY of the gold rush, San Francisco drew hard men from the far corners of the globe. Australia, land of red earth and venom, gave up some of its worst—abused, brutal men known about town as Sydney Ducks. Others came steaming from the green wedge of continent to the south, still others from the eastern states, a land cankered with civility, rotten with farms. In a few short years the golden city had nursed up an underworld to be reckoned with. Eight-year-old John James walked softly, grew eyes in the back of his head.

Neither strong nor particularly fleet of foot, he learned to adopt the ways of the crabs he looked down on for hours from the wharves. Snatch what you need. Scuttle short distances. Hide. It became a kind of genius—the spring and give of his limbs extending clear up to his brain, his kelp-green eyes. He was forever scanning, picking out shadows that told of unoccupied space. They were everywhere once a body started looking—here between piles of siding, there among coils of jute. The shape of each potential refuge registered internally, dimensions translating into terms of his own design. Elbows hooked around ankles, knees tucked behind ears.

Hiding was what he should have done—would have done if he'd had his wits about him—the day he came face to face with the stray. But his wits were on holiday, taken up with a good half panful of pork and beans, slung out in a clot on a refuse pile, out back of one of the better rooming houses in the district. Rich with a bubbly sheen, the beans had clearly turned. Not so far gone they wouldn't stay down, though. The mountain man had served up worse.

They called to John James, a slow-slipping, come-hither ooze. He felt his saliva run and pool, and, in the keen pleasure of anticipation, let a trickle escape his thin smile.

Looking up, he found his expression mirrored by a dripping grey muzzle, a pair of narrowed eyes. The dog stood equidistant to the beans, assuming the third point in the ancient triangle of human, beast and food. It bared a pink reef of gum, eased out a snarl. John James glanced about for a hidey-hole, but aside from the muck of the refuse pile, the lane stood solid, flooded with light. Garbage could cut you, seep poison into the wound—he'd nearly lost a foot that way only a month before. Besides, his guts were twisting with hunger. And he'd gotten there first.

He saw now the stray was a bitch, bald black nipples dragging low. He met her gaze. She bristled, took a stiff-legged step his way. He allowed rather than willed what happened next—his malnourished corpus pitching forward, assuming another's form. Arching his spine, he felt the transformation take. As near as any human being could, John James turned himself into a dog. He knew it. The bitch knew it. She winded him, turned tail and ran.

John James woofed. He was weighing his next move—whether to rise up and stride manfully to the prize, or keep low, gobble and growl—when he heard an unfamiliar sound. It was a pair of hands meeting, a hard, happy racket that echoed the bright length of the lane. The doorway to the rooming-house kitchen stood wide. A woman in a fat-soaked apron came close to filling its frame.

"Clever, clever." She left off clapping. "Never seen the like."

John James stood warily, wiped his paws—his palms—on his britches. When the woman shifted out onto the stoop, he took a matching step back.

"Don't run, child."

The word arrested him. *Child*. Of course. Not a dog. Nowhere near a man.

"You live round here?" she said.

He stood quivering.

"Hungry?"

He bit back a grin. Talent could do more than save your skin. It could fill your belly, too.

He was drawn to the company of women long before he ever dreamt of holding one in his arms. Kate Blakey, the rooming-house mistress who'd applauded his first-ever trick, had rewarded him with enough bread and bacon to choke a pig that day and several since. On fine mornings, he'd sit on the stoop by the trash pile. When it was raining, she'd let him inside to eat by the stove. He knew better than to wear out his welcome—once a fortnight or so kept her glad to see him.

Other times he would wander to the foot of Telegraph Hill, skirting the violence of Sydneytown to wind his way through the tents of Little Chile. The women there hadn't much to give, but buckling himself down into a roosterly strut and scattering their chickens generally earned him a bowl of spicy soup. That and an hour or two in the light of their keen laughter, the sound, rather than the sense, of their talk.

He'd been alive for a full decade when he came within spitting distance of Red Meg, a rare beauty whose company commanded a staggering sum. John James was on his back on the boardwalk, ankles knotted behind his head. He'd drawn a small crowd that afternoon—seven miners, a merchant and a man in black who was likely a preacher of some kind. Meg came up catlike, the only sound the sudden rush of nine men sucking air. They opened a chink in the circle for her skirts to fill. Eyes the colour of whisky, comfort and havoc in one. A weight of copper curls. John James caught his breath along with the rest of them. He craned his neck upward, gaping at her over the twin points of his behind.

"Bendy." She spoke softly, thoughtfully, as though the two of them were alone. "Bendy boy."

"You know that one, Meg?" one of the miners said into his beard, breaking the spell. The rest of them laughing their relief.

Meg's yellow eyes turned to glass. She let the howls die down as she smoothed the green silk about her ribs. "Open your purse and find out."

To a man, even the one she'd bested, they roared. Red Meg drew back with a kind of curtsy, swivelled and sailed away. John James let go the pose, rolled up and hugged his knees. Around him the men howled on.

"Bendy," he whispered to his kneecaps, and smiled.

— 14 —

DORRIE DREAMS:

Clearly the child is strong. Witness how she clung to the dark mother, her bold, slithering escape. Then there's the force with which she holds me to this stunted oak, making my feathered body a black mark above her huddled form. True, I've flown a few slow loops over the greater scene, but each time she drew me back to her, her pull like the call of a mate, or larger—the call of the roosting place, the flock.

Being crow, I should make my way back to the killing field. I might have to haunt the margins for a time if the humans are still at work. On my last circuit I winged all the way back to the circled wagons. Between here and there, the dog man's pack hunkered over the dead. They were stripping the bodies, revealing even the blue-white underskins of their feet. One yanked a glitter-string from a female's wrist. One plucked shimmer-discs from an overskin he'd peeled away. The crow eye sparked and buzzed.

A third sank to his knees as I flapped over his head. He regurgitated heavily into the grass, though there was no sign of him having partaken of the kill. They tend not to feed on their own kind, or on other predators, come to that. Someone should tell them the flesh of a meat-eater is more storied—veins of every creature it's run to ground still marbled throughout.

Some Originals stooped alongside the pack members, others gone to gather up the cattle and horses they ran off into the hills some nights since. How is it the freed beasts don't know to keep running? They wait only for their hearts to slow, then forget their captors, drop their noses into the green and feed. Herbivores. So often at a loss in the face of the true nature of things.

Such waste, such feast the humans leave behind. Those inner skins exposed to the sun, great softener, great opener of the dead. It remains to be seen how long they will protect their kill, standing over it jealously like wolves. At least the silver ones desire the flesh for their own consumption and, once sated, will often share. When humans kill humans, they cache every scrap, cry bloody murder if any creature dares dig it up.

Were I to alight on one of those bodies, they'd welcome me like a plague. I might manage to hop to its chin, slip the fine tip of my beak beneath an eyelid. I might even pierce the rich salt jelly, but before long one of them would cast the first of many stones. So unjust. They'll never unearth the cache themselves, so why not let the other blood-lovers feed? Still, eventually night will fall. The humans will build a fire and cower round, or, better yet, beat a hasty retreat back to their lairs.

The pattern of bodies shows the killing was swift. Here and there lie signs of a few short chases, bursts of panicked speed, but most fell not far from where they were surprised. The females and their walking young form a loose flower head, fully blown. Some distance away, the line of fallen men marks the poor bloom's severed stem. It's a picture rendered all the more striking by sprays and welters of blood. To pick a path between the corpses would be to wet my claws, to paint a tail-feather trail.

The air is heady—wafting from the field to where I bob and wonder on this scrubby branch. The light is long. Time to follow the thread of a flight line to the gathering tree, to hail the others, the mate among them, build numbers before carrying on to the roost. For days now I have resisted evening's draw. I tell myself nothing could be more crow than to be trapped between carrion and curiosity. I lie. The child's gravity is great. She controls me as my own deepest nature cannot.

My perch affords perspective. A string of humans, Originals and pack members, moves through the scrub close by—near enough that an open-winged glide would bring my claws in contact with scalp. The child's eyes, if she dared open them, would make out human hooves and legskins flashing between trees. Perhaps even the swing of a bloodied hand.

I drop my beak, staring down through the leaves of the sad oak, already burnt with the gold of their own dying. She curls white and black about the base of the trunk. Mammal surely, but human? I watch until her dark eye opens and meets my own. Then tuck my beak deep into my wing and select a secondary flight feather, one I can make do without. I tug it from its bony mooring and let it fall. Its path describes the mystery that has grown up between us, this undeniable, spiralling thread. Despite the black point of its quill, she watches it through her open eye.

MOTHER HAMMER has a mania for sage. She adds it by the fistful to her every soup and stew, so that, more often than not, a perfumed cloud hangs over the table during the supper hour. Dorrie has learned to take small sips of air between her lips, holding her breath while she chews. She's had little choice. The first wife put her foot down early on when it came to the subject of Dorrie eating with the family.

"Bread broken together is a covenant." She addressed their husband as though the crowded table were a tunnel, the two of them crouched at either end.

Hammer smiled. "Judas broke bread, Mother."

Her gaze took on a gilding of frost. "She'll come for breakfast and she'll come for supper, or she won't eat a blessed thing."

So Dorrie came. Took her place between eldest daughter and second wife, and endured Mother Hammer's glare.

For three years now the first wife has been obliged to set aside a portion for Dorrie before seasoning the rest. Dorrie has no wish to vex her; she simply can't stomach the dusty herb. Not that stomaching was ever an option—she's never once managed to force down so much as a mouthful of anything that bears its taint.

She was fourteen years old, a bride-to-be come morning, when she encountered her first taste of Mother Hammer's stew. She spit it out. Brown and slippery, it landed with a plop in her bowl. Mother Hammer was on her feet in an instant.

"I'm sorry—" Dorrie began, but her explanation met the first wife's leathery palm. A person might be expected to tremble, even colour up, after delivering such a blow, but Mother Hammer stood steady, her creamy complexion unperturbed. No one—not Hammer, not his wives or his children—made a sound. After a long moment, the first wife folded her height gracefully, resuming her seat.

Dorrie raised a hand to her cheek, felt blood, or possibly a hot stream of drool, escape the corner of her mouth. She wasn't crying. She very rarely cried. Her eyes had remained perfectly dry some five days previous while Mama sat weeping, watching her pack her trunk.

Mama hadn't minded Dorrie's aversion to sage. There was never even a question of setting portions aside—once she discovered the reason behind the frequent upsets at the supper table, she dumped a full jar of the vile stuff down the privy, never had it in her kitchen again.

It was clear Dorrie could expect no such kindness in her new home. Mother Hammer was watching her. Eyes lowered, she loaded her fork carefully—a glistening disc of carrot, a stringy clot of beef. Raising them to her lips, she felt her gullet constrict. It was no use. She laid down her fork.

"Mother Hammer," she said quietly, "I mean no disrespect—"

"Don't you dare." The first wife's tone was confusing, more suited to a request for the salt cellar than a threat.

Dorrie took a deep breath and held it, snapped the stinking forkful back up to her mouth. Shoving it between her lips, she bit down hard, striking a sharp note across the tines. Her throat wasn't fooled—it flinched shut, the sheer force of rejection propelling meat and vegetable in an exceptional arc. Both morsels hit the floor somewhere behind Joseph's chair.

Who knows what Mother Hammer would have been capable of, had she not been suspended in disbelieving shock. This time it was Hammer's turn to rise, and once he had, even the first wife had to keep her seat.

"Are you ill, Sister Eudora?"

"No," Dorrie choked.

"Something amiss with your supper?"

The first wife gave a noise as though she too were in danger of gagging.

Dorrie rubbed her throat. "It's the seasoning, the—" She hesitated, even the word nauseating now. "—the sage."

Hammer nodded, working his gaze down the table in a slow stitching motion. "Mother," he said, locking eyes with his oldest wife, "you know the Church counsels all good women to welcome their husbands' wives."

Mother Hammer's eyes grew wide in what seemed a supernatural gesture, a calling down of the sky.

"From now on you will cook something simple for Sister Eudora. Something plain." Hammer resumed his seat, grabbed his roll and tore it in two. "You must be tired, my girl." It took Dorrie a moment to realize he was addressing her. He pushed the smaller of the two halves into his mouth and talked around it. "Sister Ruth, be so good as to fetch Sister Eudora some bread and milk, and show her to her room."

The first wife has been holding forth on the life of the Prophet, letting her supper grow cold.

"That's enough of that, Mother," Hammer says abruptly. He shoots Bendy a look. "My wife holds but one subject dear to her heart."

"You know of one more deserving, do you, husband? Hunting, perhaps? Or horses? Or—hunting?"

Hammer breaks the following silence by working his knife across the china with a squeal. "I suppose you've got a tale or two from your days on the ponies, Brother Drown."

"Not many, sir. I had a pretty smooth time of it."

"You in on any of those mustang roundups Brother Egan ran?"

"Once or twice."

Hammer nods.

Seeing more is expected of him, Bendy chews and swallows. "Well, there was this one time just after I signed on, we took a dozen or so down around Topaz Mountain."

"Uh-huh." Hammer pulls a stretchy, close-mouthed smile.

"They were watering at creek there. We let them drink their fill."

"Slow them down a piece."

"That's right." Bendy feels himself warm to the memory of that late spring day. The herd was still winter-scrawny, patchy with moult, but they were a sight to behold all the same. The saddle horses knew they were there long before any of their riders got wise. Bendy felt his mount quicken beneath him, wondered at first if they might be in the vicinity of a snake.

"We were lucky," he tells Hammer. "We came up on them downwind, got a good look from a ridge maybe half a mile off. It was a pretty steep cut. We split up and got the jump on them from both ends."

Hammer nods his approval. "You listening to this?" He knuckles his son's well-developed shoulder, three sharp backhanded raps.

Lal bristles. "More than enough mustang blood on this ranch already."

"This again." Hammer wipes the gravy from his moustaches. "My boy here thinks I ought to donate my hard-earned dollars to a pack of Gentile swindlers out east. Used to be quarter horses were the be-all and end-all, but what is it now—Kentucky Saddlers? Blooded Morgans? Or should I get a pair of thoroughbreds shipped direct from the Queen's stables?"

"What do you ride?" Lal mutters.

Hammer's expression cools. "What's that?"

"Stride's three parts mustang." Bendy surprises himself by wading in. "She's not the prettiest horse, but she's pretty near perfect."

Lal gives a snort.

"Not some notion of perfect," Bendy says. "Really perfect. For their world."

Hammer's son swivels to face him. "She's weedy, hammer-headed, tied in at the knee. They all are." He grins at the good sense he's making. "Never mind that they're devils to break."

"Depends who's breaking them," Hammer puts in.

Lal ignores his father, bringing his nose an inch closer to Bendy's. "I've seen them so stubborn they won't even feed. Starve themselves rather than get broke."

Bendy nods. "I've seen them like that too. You have to coax them."

Lal flexes his upper lip. "More trouble than they're worth."

Bendy holds his tongue for a long moment. Then speaks, his voice firm in the service of something finer than himself. "They might look cow-hocked, but their legs are sound. They're more likely to drop from a burst heart than a broken bone. The same goes for their feet, and they know how to use them, too. Walk a mustang into muck and he knows to stop, back out slow. A blooded horse'll panic, kick in deeper, get mired." He shakes his head. "No, for my money you can't beat a touch of the wild. There's not a dog living with one-tenth the grace or cunning of a wolf."

Hammer's youngest wife flinches, the movement large enough to draw Bendy's gaze her way. She meets it with her own—steady, deep-socketed, black. For a second he can't be certain where he is.

"Well spoken, Brother Drown." Hammer brings an open palm down hard on the table. "We'll go out later in the season and see if we can't haul in a few. Just the two of us, mind. Lal's not much use in a roundup, are you, son? Gets confused."

In the plate-scraping quiet that follows, it's as though Lal—still now, deathly still—is nonetheless emitting a sound. Imperceptible to the ear, Bendy hears it through the skin of his right cheek, right forearm, right hand. Like fat hissing in a fry pan, popping and threatening to catch.

The silkhouse is light within, dark without. So long as Lal resists moving, there's no reason he should attract Ruth's eye.

Her dress is a discomfort to her—he can see that much through the window, her hands crabbing along its seams, moving now to her belly, now to the small of her back. It's gift enough to watch her fret and fidget in this way. He doesn't dream his luck will ripen to the point it does now.

The first button—the one at her throat—gives way easily. There are many others, though, a trail of tiny stepping stones leading down. His patience is beginning to fray by the time she slips the last of them—the one that hints at the navel beneath it—free of its hole. A double shrug out of the sleeves and the dress drops in a dark ring to the flower-strewn floor.

Faced with the pale bonework of Ruth's stays, Lal finds it difficult to breathe. The ties oblige her fingers. Lace by lace, her beautiful body grows. The corset falls, a mess of angles atop the gentle dress.

Her shift is simpler than any woman's garment he's seen—not a gather, not a detail from neck to hem. Its colour is close to none at all, the yellow of fresh cream, but thin as the wateriest whey. When she moves to step out of her fallen clothing, he knows a sudden clutching in his chest, as though some creature has made a mouthful of his heart. The shift floats, then lies flat against her. He can see everything—the ghost of her drawers, the swell of life expected, the dual, moving beauty of her breasts.

It's too much. Lal feels his knees turn to water. His head hitting ground rouses him. Minutes pass before he trusts himself to rise.

Crossing to her little window, Ruth fingers the silk shift where it drapes against her thigh. She's conscious of a deeper discomfort now, her flesh troubled not by the strictures of fabric but by her own impropriety, the sense of vulnerability that comes of acting outside a lifetime's bounds. Soon she'll stuff herself back into her clothing and return to the house. In the morning she'll dig out one of several roomy dresses she hasn't needed for years.

She transfers her weight from sole to sole, the shift whispering. It's the last of a trio Hammer gave her on their first night together as man and wife. The other two—one shell-pink, the other icy green—have long since worn to webbing. He opened the gift for her, shoving aside the white bulk of lace Mother Hammer had draped across her pillow before liberating the flimsy articles from their box. Their simplicity pleased Ruth, as did the quality of the weave.

It's not superstition that forbids washing the shift—or the body beneath it, for that matter—until the last cocoon hangs entire. Ruth's reasoning is simple, based on lessons learned during her first spring season on the ranch. At the time, she was big with the girl Mother Hammer would name Josephine. Hammer was busy breaking colts for auction, and Ruth would lean at the gate to watch him, fitting the bulge of her middle between the rails. He liked an audience, though in truth she paid little attention to his antics, letting her gaze turn unreceptive whenever the process grew overly cruel. The gate accepted her bulk, and so long as she leant there her mind remained quiet, soothed not by the scene immediately before her but by the greening country beyond.

Mother Hammer had made it clear that no Saint should seek to lie with his wife when she is with child, but there were times when the day's result—good or bad—produced in Hammer a state of agitation that knew only one cure. He took Ruth quickly on those occasions, leading her by the hand to an empty stall, propping her against a stack of bales before lifting her skirts and working her drawers down from behind. It wasn't the horizon that claimed her attention then but a chaos of compacted straw. He was kind enough to hand her up when he was done.

"Not too ripe for you, am I?" he asked her the third or fourth time.

She busied herself straightening her skirts.

"Can't wash, can't change my clothes." His eyes glittered in the stable's brown light. "Not even my smalls." He gestured in the direction of the corral. "Wash your smell off just when they're getting used to you, you might as well start all over." He stepped in close. "You're about used to me now, aren't you, my girl. Getting to like it a little, hmm?" For an answer she held her breath and smiled.

She'll be pretty whiffy herself come the end of four weeks' time. By then the shift will have come to feel like part of her, blood or some clear equivalent coursing through its fibres, warming its folds. It's not that she need tame the worms—they've been bending to the human will for thousands of years. All the same, she desires very much that they should recognize and trust her scent.

There's no doubt the shift is thinning. She'll need to break in another. Is it possible Hammer still harbours sufficient tenderness toward her to make her a gift? He'd never think to offer of his own accord, but perhaps if she were to ask . . . ? No, it would be as good as asking for his attentions, and, more than like, bearing the nine-month consequence thereof.

She could fashion her own. Finally agree to a loom, spend her every evening rounded over its workings until, like her own mother, she knotted her shoulder blades and spine into a painful, permanent bow.

Weaving is hard work, but it's not idleness, as Mother Hammer is wont to claim, that keeps Ruth from employing her skill. The truth is, the further those initial threads travel from the worms that spin them, the less vital, less meaningful they become. The great bobbins of madder red and alder bark gold she handled daily in Mr. Humphrey's bright attic seem poor relations compared with her plump cocoons. Once thread meets loom and lies flat or figured, it's but a cousin several times removed.

Ruth turns from the window and surveys her diminutive house, picturing herself a dozen days hence. She'll coax the worms up into their branches with a pan of spitting onions, a cloud of eye-watering smoke. Over a period of a few days, the dead brush will seem to come alive, producing a bumper crop of custard-coloured berries. Ruth will wash the pale shift and fold it away. It will last her through next year's worms if she's careful. Beyond that, she doesn't care to think.

The night is warm, yet Thankful descends, as is her habit, to fill the earthenware bottle for her bed. Not because she needs it, but because she would have her actions go unnoticed on those occasions when she does.

Her dress ripples wetly down the stairs behind her, seen in her mind's eye from above. The candle in her left hand is appropriate—it bathes her bare forearms, her throat. The bottle balanced on her right, however, is a dull, brown prop. She imagines it to be anything else—a cat on a crimson pillow, a man's head on a silver plate.

It wouldn't kill Mother Hammer to leave the kettle simmering for her, but as usual Thankful finds it shoved to the cool back corner of the stove. She struggles with the stove door, stirs the coals and draws up a chair to wait.

On the table at her elbow, a plate of Mother Hammer's biscuits lies covered with a checkered cloth. The bumps are unmistakable. Thankful didn't touch hers at supper. Well, touch, yes, but not to her lips. She weighed it in her palm, making sure to catch the first wife's eye before returning the leaden thing to the plate.

She's been waiting several minutes, her mind gone slack, when her husband's eldest son comes in out of the night. He opens the door by heaving against it. Seeing her, he makes a void of his expression, then lets it sour about the mouth. She says nothing, only stares back at him, letting her gaze soften when he bends to work out of his boots. His hair gleams in the candle's guttering. She could rise. Two, perhaps three strides and she could stroke it, grab hold of a hank and pull. Instead, she needles him.

"Where have you been, Lal Hammer?" An idle question, until he straightens to show a face gone rigid with guilt. "Oh-ho." She licks her lips. "What have you been up to?"

He takes a jerking step toward her. Her pulse doubles. Another step, and she can see up his nostrils. She fights the urge to lower her eyes. He reaches for her. No, not her. His hand snaking beneath the cloth for a biscuit. Without planning to, she smacks him, hard, just where the cords of his forearm narrow to bone. He turns on her, his face a battle scene now—shock and rage and, yes, there in the back quarter of those big eyes, something new. He's seeing her. Taking her in.

He grabs hold of her by the wrist, his grip nothing like a boy's. A fluttering thought—he'll break something—but he's already let her go. He flicks the cloth aside, helping himself to the biscuits, clutching four of them to his chest. "You're not my mother." His voice is raw.

"No." She holds his eyes with her own. "I'm not."

He wheels and stalks away, swallowed by the dark front hall.

Bendy can't help but admire Hammer's mount. Even setting aside beauty and size, Ink is a fine saddle horse—resolute, sure-footed, strong. At a walk her gait is flawless. At a canter she's a devil to keep up with, never mind at a run. The day Bendy followed his new boss home from the city, he could feel Stride churning beneath him with the strain.

All this plus an even temper, despite the fact that she's survived the worst terror known to her kind. The evidence mars her back. As regular as war paint, four scored lines cut on the oblique down each shoulder, each haunch. They caught Bendy's eye at the auction, long before the man on her back offered him a job. Unsaddling her that first time, he took the greatest of pains not to cross those lines, circling around them as he rubbed her down. Even so, he couldn't believe she didn't flinch. It was rare for a horse to live through a cat landing on its back. He's heard of only one other, and it never brooked a rider again.

Gazing on the stripes that mark her near-side shoulder, Bendy feels his hand slide toward them without the say-so of his brain. Beginning at their highest points, he fits his fingers to the leathery grooves. Ink tenses, seems almost to swell. Doesn't kick, though, doesn't even turn and bare her teeth.

Bendy musters all the gentleness his body knows. Slowly, ever so slowly, he draws his fingers down the tracks of the four long scars. He lingers a moment at their tails—her terror will be keenest here, where the claws punctured hide. Ink begins to tremble, a vibration so subtle that, for a moment, Bendy questions its existence. A moment more and he lifts his hand, initiating the second of many strokes.

The second wife spoke sparingly as she led Dorrie up to her bedchamber that first night, saying nothing until they stood together at the top of the stairs.

"Mother Hammer." Ruth gestured to her left where a single door divided a long stretch of the eastern corridor wall. "Myself." She laid a hand to the door before them. Turning to her right, she waved vaguely along the entire western wall and murmured, "The children." They carried on to the third door on the adult side. "Sister Thankful." Finally, at the far, dark end, "This is yours."

Ruth turned the brass handle and pushed, the plane of the door giving way to a well-furnished room. At the window, a shaft of waning light. The rug had a freshly beaten look. The bedposts gleamed. The quilt was turned down on the near side, revealing something left folded on the pillow—a garment of purest white.

Ruth followed her gaze. "Mother Hammer made it." She set the bread and milk down on the dresser. "Save it for when you return from the city—when you're married."

"Married," Dorrie repeated.

Only then did Ruth look her in the eye. A long look. "You must take everything off. Every stitch. Then put on the nightdress, get under the covers and wait."

Dorrie nodded, her tongue suddenly thick, a dirt-caked potato in her mouth.

"It will pain you." Ruth shifted her glance so it hovered above Dorrie's shoulder, as though there was someone standing quietly behind her back. "There may be blood, but there will be no injury." She paused. "You understand?"

Dorrie nodded again, the tuberous tongue swelling, pressing against the ribbed ceiling of her mouth.

"Good night, then." Ruth withdrew, her departure made final by the mechanical chuck of the door.

Dorrie stood still in the middle of the room. After a time—she couldn't be certain how long—she took a trio of steps to the dresser, pressed up against it and plucked up the bread. A drawer handle tormented her hip bone. She ate quickly, forcing small bites, taking mouthfuls of milk to help things along.

The following day proved long and trying, yet it was lost to her in the blink of an eye. They returned from the city by moonlight. Again she stood alone in her room, staring at the nightdress. There was no denying what was required of her. She would manage it step by step, like any other task.

She drew the heavy curtains closed and set about undressing in the gloom. Her boots she kicked under a chair. Dress. Petticoats. Stockings. She piled them on the dresser and shuffled to the foot of the bed.

Every stitch.

Step by step. Dorrie climbed out of her drawers. Unbuttoned her vest. After a moment's dull panic, she wadded her underthings into a bundle and shoved them beneath the bed. Straightening, she lifted the nightdress by its shoulders and let it fall open before her. Lace at the neck and wrists, fine as the foam on a dipper of new cream. Hard to believe the first wife's hands were capable of such delicate work.

The nightdress might have been fetching if it hadn't been several sizes too big. It dropped like a pale tent down the pole of Dorrie's shivering form, inches of excess length puddling about her feet. Her arms, prickly with gooseflesh, disappeared inside the bulbous sleeves. Between them lay an absence—the space where a bosom should have been. The neckline sagged, revealing to anyone who might care to look down it a drop that was unnervingly sheer. Dorrie hugged herself. Clearly, Mother Hammer had expected her husband to bring home a woman. Not a flat-chested, terrified girl.

There was nothing to do but do as she'd been told. She climbed into bed, thrusting her legs deep between the sheets. She'd never

listened so hard in her life. An agony of waiting bled into fitful
sleep, cracked open wide by the hallway light, the slow inward
swing of the door. She let out a cry.

"Hush, girl, it's your husband."

She bit her lip and sucked it. Hammer set a candle down close
by. Slipping out of his braces, he let them hang in two black U's at
his thighs. He took his time unbuttoning—his manner casual, as
though he'd forgotten she was there—then shucked out of shirt
and trousers, letting both lie where they fell. Reaching for the lip
of the bedspread, he tugged it out from under Dorrie's chin. She
couldn't have cried out then if she'd tried. And what use? Her
protector in this world was no longer mother or father, but the
very man who loomed over her in his smalls.

"What have you got on under there?" Hammer plucked at a
protruding tuft of sleeve.

Dorrie misunderstood him. "Nothing." She formed the word
with some difficulty.

He twisted the pinch of sleeve, gave it a yank. "What's this,
then?" His knuckles came to rest on the pillow, inches from her
eye. "Take it off, there's a good girl."

It was the next step. Dorrie wriggled beneath the covers,
gathering endless folds, catching her thumbs in the lace. Finally,
after a moment of near suffocation, she worked the nightdress
free over her head. Rather than let him see it, she shoved the
frothy thing aside, forming a legless lump on the far half of the
bed. She needn't have bothered. Hammer got a good look at
everything when, with a snaking flourish, he hauled the covers
down. It both helped and hurt that he appeared not to like what
he saw.

Only Mama had ever seen her like that, and only on bath day.
How Dorrie had dreaded that weekly stripping down. It was near

torture to stand trembling in a foot and a half of hot water, lathered from head to knee.

Or no, not only Mama. There were the others, the women who took charge of her that endless day in the Endowment House—countless pairs of hands, or so it seemed, scrubbing every living inch of her, only to undo the clean with palmfuls of stinking oil. Dorrie knew now what harm such rituals could do. She had entered that ugly building a girl, but had walked out a woman. A woman could become a wife. Could find herself lying on her back before a man of parent age—a man she hadn't so much as laid eyes on a fortnight before.

Pinned beneath her husband's gaze, Dorrie knew a nakedness too vast to be housed in a single form. A host of thought-bodies radiated out from her own, each of them stripped painfully bare. Some, like Dorrie, lay on their backs. Others lay face down or curled pitiably on their sides.

Climbing onto the bed, Hammer forced her to scoot sideways and butt up against the nightdress. On his knees now, he fumbled with the front flap of his smalls. Dorrie shut her eyes a second too late, a moment after he'd drawn the thing out in full. She lay dead still. The pain was such that she could think only of cutting—and therein lay the idea she would cling to until he was done.

What if, by some miracle of doubling, she were able to stuff and mount herself? The notion was calming, almost soporific. She felt her limbs give up all resistance, felt her heart check itself and begin to slow.

What a thing to peel back her own thin skin, rid her body of its messy insides. To scoop the grey-blue matter from her own domed skull, peer into that pure space through sockets that once cupped her own eyes. What size eyeballs would she need? She could paint a pair for accuracy, human blackish brown, or she could do something daring—select a pair of deer eyes, perhaps. Such a gentle, forgiving gaze.

Other changes would be possible. She could bring the eyes—deer or otherwise—forward in their sockets, pad out the cheeks and nose. It wouldn't be lying, only setting her specimen to best advantage. Hadn't she mended the crook in the barn cat's tail, set the bone in the hawk's bent wing?

Another question. Her legs—held apart now by Hammer's blunt knees—what size rods would they require? She searched her mind. Quarter-inch would do for a good-sized dog, but a deer took half-inch or better. Half-inch, then, especially if she was to be mounted upright. Not that she need be. She could mount herself crouching. Even flying, if she so desired.

If asked, the Tracker would be hard pressed to explain his nocturnal visits to Hammer's yard. Last night he destroyed all traces of wolf sign he came across, even going so far as to grind a handful of sage into every discernible scent mark. Trees and fence posts, certain corners on certain barns. Tonight he finds the same spots redolent with urine, claimed afresh.

The Father is tempting fate. He's dropped a goodly pile of scat by the corral gate—a pungent, moonlit message even the blue-eyed son couldn't fail to remark. Like everything about him, the Father's leavings are oversized. The Tracker squats and breaks one open between thumb and fingers. Downy fur, gentle bones. A cottontail. No serious hunting, then, just enough to keep his four legs beneath him. Even here, on white man's land—the neighbouring property rich with helpless lambs.

Scooping up the pile in both hands, the Tracker carries it to a nearby mound of horse droppings and inters it within. Then stoops again, reaching through the corral rails to plunge his hands into the still water of the trough. Thinking of the horse that will first lower its head to drink there in the morning—nostrils wide, eyes rolling—he feels the tug of a smile.

He wipes his palms on his trousers, the right discerning the rise of the picture book. The Father's freshest trail leads away from the yard—long back and tail hairs furring the underside of the corral's bottom rail, a discreet belly-drag in the dirt. The Tracker takes a different path, following the fence's arc around back of the child wife's barn.

Her window spills gold through the mudded wall. Beneath it, a new set of prints overlay the ones he scuffed away. The Tracker crouches, erasing the telltale configuration of pad and claw. Then rises to fill his eyes. Again the child wife sits unmoving. Before her on the workbench lie scraps of wood, a block of paper, a single pelt. She is the very picture of isolation. Watching her, he feels memory overwhelm him, dragging him backwards into the life he left behind.

As had always been the custom among the People, the first-blood hut was built by the girl's relatives, situated at a little distance from the main camp. She was to live alone there for four long days, after which she would emerge a changed being, no longer a child.

Even then he wanted her. Even then it was too late.

He didn't know it yet, but she was Younger Brother's from the beginning, the skein that bound them having formed when they were small, sending its first fibres out as they passed a clay deer between them, hand to hand. The Tracker was too busy hunting to take notice of her then, dreaming of the day when he'd claim a man's privilege and lay his kill at the feet of his parents—or perhaps even those of a girl. When he would no longer be restricted to feeding the old ones, who took food because it was due them, never remarking on a young hunter's skill.

He'd achieved manhood some years previous by the time the girl began to bleed, and had already established himself as one of the finest hunters in the camp—fleet of foot, steady of hand, clear of mind. The day her mother and the other women led the girl away, he happened to glance up from the rabbit net he was mending as they passed. Until that moment, he had sometimes wondered why no woman had ever caught hold of him in his dreams. Now all was clear. He'd been biding his time.

He could scarcely contain himself until dark. When the night finally came down, he crept from the camp to lie in wait among the sagebrush, not far from her lonely hut. One vigil became four. Each morning was the same. Just before dawn, she burst from the low dwelling like a cottontail flushed, her dark shape growing deer-like as she ran.

The Tracker came during daylight, too, whenever he could risk it. He watched the hut when she was inside it, imagining her confined within, going without meat, without salt, without cool water, even, to quench her thirst. Forbidden to touch her own scalp, her face. Lying stretched and sweating on the hotbed her relatives had built for her, live coals smouldering beneath a blanket of earth.

From time to time she would emerge from the mouth of the hut, all limbs and belly and breasts. Her face when it flashed his way showed ghostly streaks of clay, as did the dark cap of her hair. It only added to her allure. As though her head were even more naked than the rest of her, baring that which lay beneath her skin, her bright and lovely skull.

He wasn't fool enough to approach her. To do so would've meant risking everything he had to offer—his strength, his vigour, his ability in the hunt. What kind of a husband would he have made for her then?

The question is painful to him, dangerous. He runs from it, returning to the scene before his eyes. Inside the old barn the child wife takes up her block of paper, stares at it for a long moment, lays it back down. The Tracker drops in the breath before action, before she swivels her head his way.

— 16 —

JOHN JAMES WAS TOO THIN by half to act the part of a harbour seal, but he had the flippers down pat, and his flop-bellied shuffle made the show. Falling coins provided a low music. Those that landed on the frayed lining of his upturned cap sent a clothy *thp* resounding through the planking of the wharf. Those that struck other coins shivered and rang. One missed the mark, hit the wharf edge-on, leapt and wheeled. He could have snatched it back before it plummeted beyond reach, but to do so would have meant betraying his role. In the eyes of those watching, he was a creature of the sea. No need, no notion even, of money— a silky, brown-eyed baby for whom the glint of silver spoke only of a jawful of fish.

Instead he barked, a hard, carrying yelp that covered the coin's small splash. The crowd let fall a brief metallic shower—a sweet sound trampled by a sudden din. John James felt the noise in his chest, a thunderous, building swell. In seconds his audience was gone. He flopped a tight semicircle, peering after them down the wharf. A shipment of mules was unloading—far greater spectacle than any produced by an eleven-year-old boy, even one with rubber for bones. He rolled onto his side and pushed up through a crouch to his feet. Scooping up his take, he hopped back onto the covered walk of a floating warehouse, leant on its railing and waited for the long herd to pass.

At its head a towering man stood in for a stallion, whip curled at the ready in his hand. To mules, men were the understood leaders, but the snorting train also showed an occasional flash of horse—black then red then grey. John James found himself tallying up their number. Seven. Nostrils stretched wide, ears swivelling, they called to one another across the thick brown backs of the mules. When the last of the animals was by, he found himself following in their cacophonous wake.

He kept pace with the herders, hanging back out of range of their whips. Coatless men in untucked, wringing shirts, they pumped their hard right arms, drawing leather S's in the air. The herd made an open plain of the dockyard, forcing carts and their drivers aside.

John James had passed Wicklow Stables a hundred times, but never when the great front doors stood wide. The space breathed a deep welcome as it swallowed the snaking parade. Standing to one side atop a hay bale, a man with a gleaming pate and a thick blond beard oversaw the proceedings. Apart from the odd bellowed order, he stood silent, eyes roving, hands clasped at the small of his back. Drawing closer, John James saw he was bald in the purest sense, his scalp slick as a pickled egg.

"Am I blinding you?"

"No, sir." John James darted a glance along the stable wall. A warren of feed bags and grey-green bales, countless avenues of escape. He let his eyes slip back to take in the last of the high, shining rumps and shivering tails. A pair of stable hands followed, each heaving shut an enormous door.

The bald man was Bill Drown's age or older—a father's age—

but he hopped down from his platform with the keen-bodied spring of a boy. It made an impression, that youthful leap. John James found he was neither sidling toward the feed bags nor whirling and pelting away.

"Fond of horses, are you?"

"Fond?" John James echoed.

The man lifted two fingers, signalling to one of the stable hands to hold his side ajar. "Best come inside and find out."

It was the beginning of a softer time. Robert Wicklow kept John James clothed and fed, and allowed him to bed down in one of the narrow back stalls. Clean straw, three walls, a door with an audible latch. John James wriggled himself a nest and slept more soundly than he had in memory. In exchange, he cleaned and cared for the stalls, then the equipment, and finally the animals themselves. It turned out he was indeed fond of horses, profoundly so. Mules too, though the feeling was blunter—strength and iron will paling in comparison with grace.

Wicklow worked him hard, but also took care to teach him a thing or two. Pressed side-on to the gunmetal flank of a mare, the stable owner ran both hands down her shank, several loving passes before he stooped to lift her foot. "Give her leg a little rub, get her used to the idea." He began carefully to pick out the hoof. "They fear terribly for their feet."

John James learned horses the same way he learned their tack—piece by piece. He'd been at the stables for nearly four months before the boss allowed him to saddle up and mount. Even then he scarcely got hold of the reins before Wicklow barked at him to get down.

"Clean your tack."

John James opened his mouth to protest—what was there to

clean? he hadn't even made it to the stable door—but clamped it shut when he saw the look on Wicklow's face.

Wicklow stood over him while he shined the bit. The moment he set it aside, the bald head tipped into his line of vision and a hand came forward to pluck it up.

"Open your mouth."

John James felt the knot of his innards drop. He'd come to expect kindness from this man—the terse, distant variety, but kindness all the same. Sucker, he thought dully. Then closed his eyes and parted his lips.

Wicklow didn't bother to fit him with the crownpiece. He let the bridle dangle loose, easing the bit between John James's teeth, holding it in place with a light, even pressure on the reins. It was a jointed snaffle, designed to subdue a rising tongue while dragging icily at the corners of the lips. Wicklow held steady a moment, then gave the right rein the mildest of tugs. John James felt the bit's message all down his right side. He braced himself for what was undoubtedly to come; Bill Drown tended to start off with an open hand, building his way up to boots.

Wicklow let go the reins. John James felt the weight of them, slack against his jaw. He stood perfectly still until Wicklow took him by the shoulder and turned him round, holding his hand up like a dish beneath the boy's chin. John James tilted his head downward, let the bit roll. His boss caught and held it in his open palm.

"It's for talking. For telling them what you want them to do."

John James nodded.

"And you were yelling at that old boy, weren't you. Fair screaming in his ear."

To his shame, John James felt his eyes—dry in the face of hunger, of beatings, of impenetrable dark—fill instantly with tears.

A drop escaped the left one's duct before he could blink it back. Wicklow had the decency to let go of his shoulder and look away.

Even after he'd proven himself competent in the saddle, John James rarely got the chance to break a trot—never mind feel the creature beneath him run. Once when he delivered a draft horse to one of the milk ranches beyond Leavenworth Street, once when he walked the toll road out past the Mission to the Pioneer Racetrack and rode back on a pregnant mare. These were exceptions. He counted himself lucky if an errand gave him cause to breach the business district, let alone the city's ragged verge.

Wicklow took a similarly careful approach to acquainting him with the written word, beginning with A and inching forward from there. "Maybe one day you can help me in the office," he murmured through his beard when, after several botched attempts, his pupil spelled Wicklow across a clean white page. John James felt a sudden internal swelling. For a moment he didn't dare breathe, in case whatever it was might burst.

He felt it again the day Wicklow took it upon himself to keep Bill Drown at bay. The one and only time John James's father set foot in the stables, he was fresh from the Monte table, where he'd heard over a particularly sour hand that his son had taken a job and, with it, a home. He'd been gone six months, breaking his back at a hydraulic operation in the foothills of the Sierras for precious little payout, only to return and find himself forsaken. When he shoved his way in past one of the other stable hands, John James was five stalls back along the western wall, saddling a placid mare. At the first familiar bellow, he dropped into a squat.

"John!" Bill Drown shouted, the truncated name more chilling than any threat. John James's train of thought gave way to the dull surge of his pulse. He scuttled, reached for the stirrups and swung, clinging to the underbelly of the mare.

"JOHN DROWN!"

The horse held steady. He pressed his cheek flat to her chest, listening to her heart thud while Bill Drown howled for him, lurching from stall to stall. More than one animal reared, a colt of no mean value bruising a foreleg, coming close to splintering bone. Wicklow led the pack that came hammering—men and boys armed with rifles, shovels, whips. John James let go and fell into the straw. Rolling up onto all fours, he pressed his eye to a knothole and watched his father run.

From then on, Bill Drown sent word for his son to meet him at his latest hotel or rooming house, or at the foot of Long Wharf, or at the barber's, where John James would like as not find his father lolling in a big brass tub. If Bill Drown's luck was running clean, they might meet up at Noble's Coffee Saloon, where he'd stand his son a boiled egg or a hot roll, maybe even a black chaser of tea—paid for with a pinch of yellow grit.

John James didn't always answer his father's call. Early on, the pull was still strong in him, but by the time he'd been at the stables for a year, it had died down to a tug he could choose to ignore. He had responsibilities. He couldn't go running off just because some bastard he used to know was tearing another strip through town.

John James was a young man of thirteen years when, once again, the docks of Yerba Buena Cove boiled with fevered men. Some were green, but most came bowed under the miner's packs they'd been shouldering for years. Picks and shovels, dented pans. A scant decade and California was played out. British Columbia beckoned. Ho for the Fraser River, the promise of virgin streams.

Already five foot eight, John James was growing so the pains in his legs woke him nightly. He stood like a beacon atop a creosote barrel at the crowd's edge, looking down over the swell of hats. One caught his eye, familiar in its battered slant.

"Father!" he heard himself shout.

Dropping down from the barrel, he slid backwards through the story of his life. By the time his boots met plank, he was a little boy, blind with panic and tears, stumbling after one among hundreds, only to be folded into a mother-scented suitcase and swung violently aboard.

"Father!" It came out in a wail this time, and a host of hairy faces turned his way. All but one. Bill Drown kept his eyes forward, trained on the gangplank, a bottleneck clogged with men.

Father. John James almost bellowed it a third time, but as he drew the necessary breath, he drew with it a gutful of truth. It was the wrong word. Bill Drown would never turn at the sound of it. He hadn't answered to it for years.

Weeks later, John James was leading a pack mule loaded with farrier's nails back to the stables when a display in a shopfront window brought him up short. He'd seen human bones before—a fingertip, even a skull—but never the whole story at once. The skeleton stood with arms akimbo, legs ever so slightly bowed. A hand-lettered sign leant against its bony toes: *A Returned Frazer River Miner.* John James felt the mule's hot breath on his neck. He knew then and there.

A year would pass before he heard anything definite. When word did come, it spilled from the lips of a green-eyed miner old before his years. John James braced himself the moment he saw the stranger come limping. Laid down the harness he was mending and turned to take the brunt of it face on.

"You Bill Drown's boy?"

He nodded dumbly.

"Your father's dead." Then, in the worn-away lilt of his mother country, "I'm sorry for your troubles."

He was halfway to the door, rendered buglike by the stable's cavernous insides, before John James managed a word. "How?"

The miner spun slowly, a move oddly graceful in the midst of his halting gait. "Shovel to the back of the head. Undermined his neighbour's claim."

Again the waltzing turn, the hobbled stride. John James closed his eyes. When he looked out again from the dark of his own making, the miner had gone. He let out his breath. All of it. Even the bit he normally kept by.

17

May 19th, 1867

Dear Daughter

How to begin a letter when the last one ended upon such a
note. At the beginning surely but which one? My own was unremarkable. I was one of eight children born to the good soil of
an Ohio farm. Mr. Burr's was much the same only the soil and
everything else was several grades poorer. What did I see in
him? Everything he no longer is. Also I was the plainest of five
sisters including poor dead Eudora. Chances were good I would
be the one left to tend my parents in their dotage and though I
served them to the best of my ability the truth is I bore my father
little love. My mother for all she tried might as well have been
his dog. You know the rest. Marriage followed by conversion
followed by more persecution and toil and abandoned crops
and forsaken homes than any life ought to hold.

And all of it nothing to the fact that I had no child.

Dorrie from the time I could walk I was stealing kittens from
their mothers and feeding them with a finger dipped in milk.

All those years I imagined myself to be the barren one but look at him now. Nearly three years with his sturdy young thing and not so much as a false start to show. I tell myself I might not have minded if our marriage had been the sort to fill a woman up. It was not Dorrie. Not by half.

The beginning that matters came when you did my girl. Ten years ago now. I was forty years of age. I had given up hope.

You were sick when you arrived. You know this well enough. You have been told a hundred times but I wonder do you remember how you pitched like a mad thing in the bed? For more than a fortnight I dribbled water and weak broth between your lips. Anything more than a few spoonfuls and you would bring it back up. You went from ice to coals soaking the sheets and soiling them. I never slept so little in all my days. I was never more awake.

It was during those weeks that I began to tell you stories and one in particular. After many letters of entreaty from myself my sister had finally seen fit to join God's people in the valley of the Great Salt Lake. Widowed young she brought with her her only child a girl seven years of age. This same child was delivered unto Mr. Burr and myself by the captain of the handcart train my sister had joined. It was he who told us she had given up her spirit unto God. A sad tale. I told it every time I washed you or fed you or freshened the cloth on your brow. More than once I came within a hair's breadth of believing it myself. Fatigue I suppose. That and the wish that this and not the other might be true.

You came out of it in the end. Shaky and pale but you came. Is it any wonder you were a quiet child? There is silence my girl and there is silence. Yours was visible. You will think me fanciful but I swear at times the air about you took on a bluish cast. How it wrung my heart. How I worked to draw forth if not joy then at

least a hint of interest in the world around you. Help Mama make
a pie Dorrie. Here you pop the pits from the cherries. Why don't
we go for a ride my girl just you and Mama. You obeyed but you
never really took part. Not until he came. Dorrie you will know of
whom I speak. Surely you must have felt the change his presence
worked on you.

Coming from England Mr. Cruikshank might have been hoping for a cup of tea or perhaps even a glass of beer. Or he might
have been in the Territory long enough to know he would receive
no such refreshment in a Saint's home. In either case he
accepted the glass of plum juice I offered him with thanks. He
was looking for work though what labour those stems of arms
were suited to I could scarce imagine. So soft spoken for a young
man. Well born I thought from his way of talking but down at the
heel. I knew Mr. Burr would have no work for a Gentile but
decided to let him rest a little and wait. A decision lightly taken
and largely felt.

Dorrie you came to life the moment you laid eyes upon that
sky blue bird. It was clear to Mr. Cruikshank and even to my
own unschooled eye that you possessed a gift. He took me aside
when I carried a plate of corn bread out to where you were
working in the shed. Mrs. Burr he said to me you must
encourage her. She must have instruction. The look on my face
brought him down a notch. At the very least she must have tools
and a book or two. At that he drew pencil and paper from his
waistcoat pocket and wrote in the neatest man's hand I had
ever seen *Collection and Preservation a Taxidermist's Guide* by
Major Thomas Greene.

I wonder Dorrie did you even notice how I ran after Mr.
Cruikshank when your Mr. Burr so unkindly sent him away?
This was not as I later told my husband to apologize for his

rudeness but instead to beg a favour. I pressed the scrap of
paper back into that young man's hand and with it all the money
I had put by in the kitchen crock. I wouldn't have the first idea I
told him. Won't you help me? No letter. Just have it sent to the
post office in Cedar City. He said nothing only nodded. How he
pitied us. I could see it in his eyes.

Mr. Burr was to know the depth of my feeling. Can you really
think he wished her harm? I cried. He was teaching her Lyman.
She's thirteen years of age.

Marrying age. He wouldn't look at me when he said it but he
said it all the same. And worse. Brother Sykes has a wife of fourteen. Brother Turner took his youngest when she was twelve.

It shocked me Dorrie. It stunned me dumb but it should
not have. I see now how he always had one eye on the day
when he would marry you off to advantage. How he crowed
over your milky skin and so-black hair when you were small.
How he complained as you grew out of your childish good
looks. I hope the truth of this does not pain you my girl. I have
never known a woman who benefitted of thinking herself a
beauty when she was not.

As you know the book arrived the following spring. It came
direct from Greengage and Smythe Book Merchants of San
Francisco along with a note from Mr. Greengage himself
beginning Dear Mrs. Burr as per your inquiry. Mr. Burr handed the
parcel to me already opened though the direction bore my name
alone. I knew only joy that he would allow you to keep it at all.

The way you looked at me when I gave you that book. The
way you pored over its pages your fingers trembling. I had not
known a body's love could double in an instant. Would I have
taken my gift back if I knew then how the secrets between its
covers would draw Mr. Hammer's eye?

Dorrie why did you offer no protest? I know you are a dutiful girl but not one word? You left me to fight for you alone. I could hardly argue forever when you yourself had already agreed.

But I torture myself. I torture us both. As fate would have it a man of wealth and influence set his sights on you. A man who could see to it that despite Mr. Burr's low standing he should receive permission to take a second wife. But the truth is Mr. Burr would have seen you off sooner or later. He had another reason to wish himself rid of you. And of me. I will explain myself Dorrie I swear it. But for now I must rest.

All a mother's love
Helen Burr

18

THE COW BARN is Mother Hammer's territory, and it is for this reason alone that Bendy has been on the ranch some four days before he darkens its door. He's only here now because there's something he needs, and chances are this is where it'll be.

Joseph and Joe are hard at it on their little stools, milk ringing in their pails. The air is body-warm. Sweet, too, not a hint of the sourness Bendy's come to associate with milking. If these boys spill a drop, they know damn well to wipe it up.

"Morning, Joseph," he says, "Joe."

Both neat, gleaming heads draw back from their cow flanks and rotate his way.

"You boys know if your mother keeps a cat about the place?"

It's an odd question, he knows—where there's one barn cat there are twenty—but if he's taken the first wife's measure correctly, she's the sort to tolerate only one or two. He's just as sure she won't be entirely without. It's a fair bet a woman like her would regard a scattering of mouse turds not with apathy or even disgust, but rage.

"Tom," the older boy says. "Up in the loft."

"And Kitty," Joe adds.

"No." Joseph returns his brow to the cow's side, resuming the task at hand. "Kitty went in the flour sack with the last litter."

"Oh." Joe nods, following through until his forehead too meets flank. "I forgot."

Bendy feels this in his gut, as though for several seconds the writhing sack is located there. Foolish. It's the way of things. Perhaps if the boys—the younger one at least—seemed to feel something about it, he wouldn't have to. He shifts his weight to his toes and back. "You don't mind if I borrow him for the morning, do you?" He forces a smile even though neither of the boys is looking his way.

"Go ahead."

He can't be certain which one of them has spoken. It scarcely matters. He proceeds to the ladder and climbs.

Tom is massive, thickly muscled, white. Bendy pokes his head up through the loft floor and meets him eye to opening eye. A trout-green gaze. Ears intact, tail supple and full, lifting now, drawing the hindquarters after it in a rising stretch. Without a doubt the handsomest cat Bendy has laid eyes on—no kin to the toothy, wire-legged wraiths he avoided as a child.

With a hand the cat can't see, Bendy reaches into his trouser pocket for the chicken leg he kept aside the night before. Tom has a good nose on him. He's easing forward, responding to the offering before it appears. Bendy peels off a swatch of nubbled skin as a teaser. Spreading it on the hayloft floor, he backs away down the rungs. Tom stands chewing, impatient above him. Once the way is clear, he springs down the ladder as though it's the gentlest of slopes, landing in a dearth of sound.

Bendy holds the chicken leg at hip level, waving it like a stubby tail, leading the snowy brute past the wordless boys. Striding to the horse barn, he imagines the picture the pair of them make.

Once inside, he leads the cat directly to the largest of several mouse nests he's found.

"Not yet, boy." He pockets the leg. "Don't want you too full to do your job."

But Tom is already wreaking havoc, tossing a blind baby into the air.

❧

The Tracker wakes suddenly, awash in early light. He crawls from his hut, rises and sets off eastward. In the early days, Hammer would fetch him when his presence was required, but seven years at the white man's side have made a limb of the Tracker—he flexes when the impulse comes. The first few times he showed up on his own, Hammer betrayed surprise. *How in the hell?* In reply, the Tracker employed a white gesture, turning his empty hands up to the sky.

This morning the wide pasture glows. The Tracker moves through its shifting brilliance into a time long gone.

Small Sister was newly a woman, proud to wade with the others deep into the grass, lifting her seed beater high. It happened that the Tracker was within shouting distance that day, he and Younger Brother setting snares. He felt the hoofbeats through the bark soles of his sandals, looked up to see the Ute braves high atop their mounts—ten, maybe twelve of them thundering from the northeast draw.

The Tracker might have been a horse himself, so fleet were the legs upon which he ran. Not thinking to shed her burden basket, Small Sister pelted toward him with it bouncing on her back, spraying a trail of seed. Her new breasts leapt and jangled. At the extremity of her arm the seed beater flailed, a wide and woven hand. He reached her—almost reached her—as the Ute slaver leant wide and low. A knotted arm encircled Small Sister's waist, and the Tracker's goal was gone.

He drove his heels deep into the ground to keep from throwing himself under the churning hooves. It was a dark horse that flowed past him, the deepest, richest brown, glowing with the lather of many miles. Its mane was true black, a windswept, rippling wash—not unlike the Ute's tresses, falling over Small Sister's face.

Black nostrils too. This the Tracker would remember later, the horse's nostril flaring above him. He would remember the Ute's nose, too. The flash of eyes above it, the broad, strong bridge, even the tiny white protrusion—the nostril cartilage home to a shard of polished bone. From a deer? A bird? And there were fish bones in the Ute's necklace. And bear claws. The swinging scoop of it rattled and shone.

It is this more than anything that pains him. If he was close enough to take note of the Ute's nose pin, close enough even to hear that fine rattling above the drumming of hooves, how is it he couldn't catch and keep hold of her, his own dear flesh?

Seven women taken that fine summer's day. Try as he might, the Tracker can only picture one.

As always, the Tracker finds whatever summoned him to the white man's side wasn't wrong. Trading the morning light for the ribbed insides of the horse barn, he finds Hammer oiling his gun. Nearby, the new man eases a bit into the black giant's mouth. Their gazes cross, the new man offering a nod over the horse's lowered nose. The Tracker keeps all expression to himself.

Between them, Hammer's mount is somehow changed. The Tracker can't help but remark the difference—nowhere more evident than in the cant of her massive head. It's as though she desires nothing more than to surrender its great weight, skull and senses, to the new man's hands. The Tracker focuses on the horse's right ear, cocked his way now, measuring him despite her bliss. He follows the black column of neck to her shoulder, the barred marks there a memory they share.

He and Hammer had followed the fat tracks for miles, the Tracker losing the trail repeatedly. The pale cat was playing with him, padding through water, taking to trees. At last it split off from the river and led them in a steep ascent.

The air, close and curdled in the bottomlands, began to move. The Tracker scented then caught sight of the cat's leavings, a partially covered pile. Dense with hair and bone, the stools spoke of hunger, a goodly stretch since the last fresh feed. Reaching country too broken for horse hooves, he waited while Hammer tied the animals in the shade of an outcropping before carrying on.

He should have known better. The mountain lion doubled back, the promise of tethered horseflesh too sweet to resist. The pack horse would have been the safer bet, but the cat knew good meat from tough.

A horse under attack makes a sound impossible to forget. They hadn't made it far—Hammer holding him back, cautious among the rocks—when the scream spun the pair of them where they stood. The Tracker ran on goat legs, leaving the white man behind. Rounding the last dogleg of a narrow cut, he brought the Henry's sights up in line with his eye.

The scene beneath the outcropping entered him with the slow-flowing force of a dream. The pack horse hauling back into its haunches, the black giant thrashing, all hooves and whipping spine. For now, the fight was enough to keep the cat from biting, working its long teeth between bones to snap the hidden cord. It was holding on tight, though, a fat, cream-coloured saddle with a glaring face. Spotting the Tracker, it added its own voice to the squealing song of its prey. The black horse rocked forward, baring the cat's white chest. On the back-surge the mare's head and breast obscured the shot. The trick was in the timing. Crooking his finger, loosing the ball a hair's breadth before the next plunge.

It was a kill for the telling, the first shot rendering a second one unnecessary. Claws let go, retreating into their sheaths the moment the Tracker's ball met heart. The lion was airborne on the following buck. It landed in a crease of the outcropping, both horses dancing in the wake of its death. Hammer broke upon the aftermath through the thin smoke drifting from the Henry's muzzle.

The Tracker felt something akin to respect for the black mare that day. Once she'd quieted enough to see the predator was well and truly dead—Hammer showing her, kicking it in the belly where it lay—she stood rock-steady, seemingly oblivious to the blood escaping the four corners of her back.

On the white man's command, the two of them heaved the mountain lion up onto the skipping pack horse. While the Tracker lashed it down, Hammer shucked out of his coat and laid it across the mare's shoulders to blot the worst of the wounds. It was a long ride back, the first third of it a straining downward grade, but the big horse never flagged. The pack horse eventually took his cue from her lead and settled into the rhythm of burden and track.

It was the finest kill they'd delivered to the child wife so far. Her eyes caught fire when she opened the door to them. When they laid the body out on her workbench, she bobbed over it like a crow.

"Meat," the Tracker said over his shoulder, following Hammer to the door.

The white man turned. "You'd eat that? Marmot I can see, even beaver. But cat?" He shook his head. "You hearing this, Eudora?"

She didn't look round, saying only, "Come back in the morning. Before the bell."

"Tracker. Hey, Tracker." Hammer's voice now, jabbing down from the great horse's height. "What're you waiting for?"

As always, the Tracker takes a moment to harden himself before assuming his place at Hammer's back. His people never took to riding—a body's own two legs made more sense in a country of river, sagebrush and rock. They paid for it when the Utes came thundering, scooping up slaves.

The Tracker accepts a hand up. He knows a familiar wash of panic as he leaves the ground, feels it ebb as he settles in. It's an uneasy intimacy, this riding groin to buttock, belly to back. Often a good grip on the cantle behind him is all the Tracker requires, but there are times when Hammer can't resist urging his horse on. At a full gallop the Tracker has no choice but to wrap both arms around the white man, squeeze his eyes shut and hold on.

The new man draws wide the stable door. As the black horse gains the yard, the Tracker stares over Hammer's shoulder straight into the lifting sun. He blinks, the skeletal scene imprinted on the backs of his eyelids. Drawing them open again, he spies the first wife framed in the kitchen door. In the People's camp, the *Niav* stood just so each morning, poised at the threshold of his hut. The Tracker blinks again, harder. The old life is stretching itself inside him today, breaking through.

Meanwhile the scene before him evolves. The smallest boy bursts from the chicken house, gripping a shallow basket to his chest.

"Walk, Baby Joe," the first wife calls out sharply. "They're no good to me smashed."

The child halts abruptly, nearly upsetting his load. Then proceeds on tentative feet.

"Joseph!" she yells over the boy's head. "Joe!"

From the depths of the cow barn, a united, unintelligible reply.

"What's keeping you?"

A second muted answer brings her broad hands to her hips. She is nothing like the *Niav.* He was the People's voice, yes, but never their ruler. Such gentle, sensible exhortations. *Today we hunt rabbit. Hunt well or the People will go without.*

The first wife has ignored her husband until now, but as Hammer turns his mount's head westward, she raises her voice his way. "Husband!"

The Tracker feels the word kick and ripple through the white man's back. Hammer goes so far as to halt the horse, but draws the line at turning back her way. Behind them, she hollers again. "See if you can't bring back some meat this time."

Hammer answers with a nudge of his heels. The black horse tenses and flies.

For nearly two months Ruth descended to her employer's cramped office at the close of every workday. It wasn't until his lesson on mulberry trees that she awakened to his true design.

Morus nigra, the black mulberry, was preferred in England. *Morus alba,* its pale-berried cousin, was the Continental choice. It was here that Mr. Humphrey touched her. On the leg, just where the knee's hard cap subsides into thigh. He hadn't the nerve to use his hand. Instead, he drew a hard little stick from his trouser pocket and nudged her with its point, talking all the while.

"Mulberry truncheon, my dear. Cut this very winter." His voice had a rattle in it. "Strike it in the ground and *Morus nigra* before you know what you're about." He looked her full in the face, and she saw that his eyes were leaking. "It's yours."

"Mine, sir?" In her confusion she said just the wrong thing. "But where would I plant it?"

Mr. Humphrey caught his breath. "Oh, my darling girl!"

Ruth leapt to her feet as the old man dropped to his knees before her. She ran from his office as though it were on fire, knocking a bolt of mourning crepe to the floor on her way through the shop. Fumbling at the lock, she found the truncheon still clutched in her hand. The impulse to fling it away was powerful, the urge to shove it down her dress front stronger still.

It had to have been fate. Ruth ran the cobbled half mile home through a filthy spring rain to find every woman and girl in Mrs. Stopes's house crowded into the parlour. A stranger sat among them, his chair drawn up to the hearth. He was not a young man, nor was he so old as Ruth's ardent employer—the reddish hair at his chin and temples only salted with grey. While he wasn't ugly in the full sense of the word, no one—not even a mother—would call him handsome. A man, in short, unremarkable in every way. Or so Ruth thought.

He glanced up when she paused in the doorway, but only for an instant, as though the sight of a wet and breathless female signified little when compared with the elemental vision of the fire. It was odd that he should sit like one who belonged so entirely, addressing himself to the blaze. Odder still was the form of his address. He would speak to them by and by— spinning tales of a New World Zion, a beloved prophet struck down—but as Ruth stood dripping on the hall carpet, he chose instead to sing.

Ruth attended church like anyone. She'd witnessed men in the act of raising up their voices to God every week of her life. As a rule, the male parishioners who filled the pews of a Sunday sang as though they were barking orders to the Lord. Chests came forward, moustaches buckled and flexed. By contrast, the man by the hearth scarcely moved. A parting of the lips was sufficient. The melody was martial, uninspired. The lyrics, too, made little impression. *Come, come, ye Saints, no toil nor labour fear; but with joy wend your way.* It was the man's faith that moved her, the simple purity of his tone.

The Widow Stopes loved nothing more than to carry tea and cake to a weary man, and so it was that the missionary sat talking past the stroke of ten. There were girls who took to their rooms in a show of Anglican or Methodist fealty, as well as those who retired in the knowledge of shuttles to be taken up come dawn. Ruth was among the core that stayed. She listened carefully to every promise the young religion held—from adventure to renewal to belonging. When the missionary spoke of the packet ship *Thornton,* due to depart Liverpool for New York in a matter of days, she made a mental note of the name. In the end she harboured only a single question, kept to herself until the moment he rose to go.

"Sir, do they manufacture silk in Deseret?"

"Not yet." He regarded her closely. "But it is a keen desire of President Young's that his people should."

Mrs. Stopes kept him talking by the front door, but Ruth heard nothing of their conversation over the groaning of the stairs. Her room was cold, dark as a coal chute and nearly as narrow. To think she'd halved it with her mother for so many years. She closed the thin door behind her and knelt beside the bed. Reaching beneath its iron frame, she wakened spiders, felt one scramble across the back of her hand. The carpet bag was where her mother had shoved it after unpacking their things. *I know it's a squeeze, love. We won't be staying long.*

Ruth beat the dust out of the bag's drooping flanks. Then stood and began slowly to pack.

Four walls. One with a window, a nothing view. One with a door leading nowhere. The third crowded with wardrobe, dresser and vanity, the fourth blocked by a bed. And what a bed—canopied and grand, twice the width of any Thankful had lain in before she consented to hide herself away from the world. Hammer had it built to her specifications, which were based, for lack of any other example, on the stage bed at the Limelight. The bed Desdemona breathed her last on night after night. Pillars and tassels and satin. Ugly as sin.

Thankful can't stand her bedchamber. All day long she's trodden its garish carpet, descending only to take her place at the table beside her husband's empty chair. She might walk out, at least as far as the privy, but why bother, when Mother Hammer will send the eldest girl up for the pot before long. Thankful bested the first wife in that particular arena early on, letting the horrid thing fill to capacity and beyond. She didn't marry a wealthy man only to straddle the same hole as a dozen others, breathing the swampy rot of their leavings while wood bugs took refuge in her skirts. Never mind the walk there and back, the yard—mud or dust, depending—doing its level best to destroy her shoes.

All true, yet none of it the reason she rarely leaves the house.

She made an effort in the beginning, badgering Hammer to take her into the city, or what passed for one, sometimes settling for a ride into Tooele, turning her nose up at every button Brother Rowberry stocked. Sundays offered another chance to show herself. She'd spend hours fussing before the mirror, only to be shunned by every gingham-swaddled female she passed.

At first she no longer asked to come along. Then, after a period of some months, she began to refuse when Hammer offered of his own accord. She was taken up with her lacework. The track made her teeth clatter. She could feel a megrim coming on. How else to explain it? She knew only that thresholds—those marking the passage between indoors and out—had somehow become threatening. The ranch and everything beyond it no longer welcomed her. In fact, it wished her harm.

As do these four walls. She has to get out. A last searching evaluation in the looking glass. Her dress is the fourth she's tried on since supper, purplish and vaguely regal. Her curls are holding up well. She glazes over the disappointment of her face.

On the stairs she imagines music swelling from the pit. *Lord of lords! O infinite virtue, com'st thou smiling from the world's great snare uncaught?* Not Thankful's line. She had played Charmian, attendant to the Egyptian queen, and had been lucky to get the part.

She hesitates at the bottom step. Should she go left, to the deserted kitchen, or right, through the dining room to the parlour, where Mother Hammer will be holding court? It's a terrible weakness, this longing for company, even that of those you despise. All right. She'll sit in her corner. Take up her sewing and pay them no mind.

Ursula works the pulse of the high-backed rocker, unconsciously drawing it in line with her own. The children flock and settle about her skirts. She ignores Sister Thankful in the nearby arm-chair, letting her gaze soften in the glow of their burnished heads. Her angels have heard tonight's story before—countless utterings, to say truth—but she can be sure they will strain forward as though it's the first.

In the midst of the preparatory quiet, the third wife stirs, shifting the dark garment in her lap. Ursula drops her eyelids against the distraction, maintaining silence as she wades into the legend's wash.

The twenty-seventh of June, 1844. A humid day, a spacious second-storey cell. Brother Joseph and his own flesh-and-blood brother, Hyrum, unjustly imprisoned therein. Treason? What means country to a man who is the darling of the Lord?

The mob came with the lengthening of day—faces blacked, the cowards—waving gun barrels, bayonets, knives. They stormed the gate, the faint-hearted guards firing high over their heads. Flooding the stairwell, they rose like bile in the prison's throat. Brothers Taylor and Richards were present too, visiting the blessed prisoners, bringing hope in the form of smuggled guns. And now the four of them were trapped.

The mob forced open the door. Brother Hyrum, possessed of a single-barrel pistol, took three balls—head, chest and leg—and promptly gave up his ether unto the Lord. Brother Taylor took four— one that would have stopped his heart if it hadn't stopped his pocket watch instead—bled terribly and somehow, along with Brother Richards, lived to tell the tale. But enough of the minor players. Brother Joseph, bright star of the world, threw down his spent pistol amid the mayhem and leapt to the window's ledge. Frame him there. A tall, beautiful man in his shirtsleeves. In his glory.

Those behind him shot him in the back. Those gathered below fired skyward, as though they would murder the sun. The Prophet pitched forward, falling twenty feet to land curled like a babe on his side. His last words the only words they could be—"Oh Lord, my God!"

He died among villains, men who, unsatisfied with the end they had dealt him, propped his broken body against the well in the courtyard and fired into it, execution style. Some say even this was insufficient for one among them—a brute who approached with his bowie knife unsheathed and a jagged beheading in mind. They tell, too, of how he scuttled back like the insect he was when a shaft of the Lord's sorrow illumined that drooping head.

It is this—the picture of that sudden light rinsing over those boyish, bloodied curls—that calls Ursula back to herself. Or, more precisely, the moan that picture evokes, uttered softly but nonetheless aloud. Her eyes flicker open, glazed with tears. The children sit patiently at her feet. She has only the vaguest notion of how long she has obliged them to wait.

Such obedience. She will reward them, surprising them now with the privilege she normally keeps by until after the story's end. She hunches forward, the chair's motion arrested beneath her, and extends her left hand into their midst. The third finger bears the bulk of an unwieldy ring, a great oval of some dull grey stone set in silver. It is so plain as to belie the term jewellery, calling to mind instead skillets and stoneware, hinges on cupboard doors.

Comprehension remakes the children's faces. One after another they extend their own hands, each folded into a delicate fist from which only the smallest finger protrudes. Ursula fixes each of them with a brief but solemn stare, then fits her fingernail under the lip of the stone and folds open the ring. Inside lies a lock of the Prophet's hair. She pinches it where it's bound with a length of black thread, plucks it up from the silver bed. Always the minute spring as it clears the walls of its setting, then still-ness, a lone curl sprouting from between finger and thumb.

The children know to take a single stroke, and do so in order of ascending age, silently waiting their turns. Baby Joe is yearning forward, his pinky a stubby, searching thing, when the third wife clucks her tongue.

"What next."

Stung, Ursula holds out her hand to halt her youngest, thereby breaking the ritual in two. "Sister?" She strains the word, chill and livid, through her teeth.

"Got any redskin scalps you want to show them?" Thankful gives her brassy curls a shake. "You'll give them night terrors with that thing."

Ursula stands in a rush, the chair bucking behind her. She tucks the lock away and takes a step, planting her boot between her two daughters. Another step, and she smiles inwardly to see Thankful's hands seek cover beneath the work in her lap.

"'The Lord saith,'" Ursula begins, her pitch low and clear, "'because the daughters of Zion are haughty and walk with stretched-forth necks and wanton eyes, walking and mincing as they go, and making a tinkling with their feet, therefore the Lord will smite with a scab the crown of the head of the daughters of Zion—'"

She comes to the border of Thankful's skirts and looks down on the crown she's just named, for the third wife hasn't the forti-tude to lift her eyes. The most she can manage is to force a small, disdainful sound out through her nose. Ursula unhooks her gaze from the complex dressing of Thankful's hair and drops it to her lap, watching her needle hand work free from its hiding place and attempt to execute a stitch. Again, the Scripture fits.

"'—and the Lord will discover their secret parts.'"

Thankful freezes.

Ursula draws breath and hisses, "'In that day the Lord will take away the bravery of their tinkling ornaments—'"

"I don't have to listen to this." Thankful stabs the needle into her pincushion and shoves her sewing aside.

"'—and cauls, and round tires like the moon—'" Ursula doesn't entirely understand this line, so she ups her volume to deliver it. "'—The chains and the bracelets and the mufflers—'"

The third wife cannot rise—she hasn't room. Neither can she sit and take it. Like a dog, she ducks and scuttles. Ursula quells the urge to bring her knee up hard under that sharp little chin.

"'—The bonnets, and the ornaments of the legs—'" She's shouting now, in pursuit of her enemy—not running, though, the mistress of a house never runs. Thankful's dress shows to advantage in the dining room's low light, her hind end flickering from barn-swallow blue to plum. Shot silk, the best money can buy. Dearer by far than the whore deserves.

"'—and the headbands,'" Ursula bellows, "'and the tablets, and the ear-rings—'"

The list goes on and on, tumbling entire from Ursula's lips so that even she is surprised by her own capacity to recall. The children have stayed put in the parlour, and for once she finds herself wishing they weren't quite so well behaved. Thankful stumbles twice on the stairs. *Rings, nose jewels, mantles, hoods*—item after item becomes insult, becomes threat.

"'—veils!'" Ursula shouts the last of them to Thankful's bedchamber door, moments after it slams shut in her face. The sliding of the bolt signals defeat, but never let it be said that Ursula Wright Hammer is one to leave the work of the Lord unfinished. She delivers the last verse in dulcet tones.

"'And it shall come to pass,'" she informs the ignorant, wilful creature listening on the other side, "'instead of sweet smell there shall be stink; and instead of a girdle, a rent; and instead of well set hair, baldness; and instead of a stomacher, a girding of sackcloth—'" She pauses, long and pregnant, before uttering the final phrase. "'—burning—' Do you hear, Sister? '—*burning* instead of beauty'!"

❦

Thankful would pace, but the run upstairs in her stays has winded her. She considers flinging herself across the bed, but such a flopping impact would be dangerous. She can feel the megrim now, frothing behind her eyes, threatening to congeal. They're coming more often of late, staying longer when they do.

Burning instead of beauty.

The witch's words have found purchase, not because Thankful believes them—it's her nature to believe in little—but because she's heard the like a thousand times before, from the time she was captive in her cradle to the day she announced her coming union with a heathen polygamist from the West. She smiles to recall how her mother gaped like a fish at market upon hearing the news. For once, for a good five minutes at least, Eliza Cobbs held her tongue.

Not that she was ever one to harangue as Mother Hammer does. Hers was a soft-spoken crusade, Methodist murmurings without cease.

"It's no place for one of the Lord's faithful, Thankful."

"Mother, the Limelight is a *theatre*." Thankful sighed it, shrilled it so many times. "We do Shakespeare!" It was true, to a point. They played the Bard, among others, but only the most popular plays—and those were pared down to scenes of swordplay and poisonings, cross-dressing and lovemaking and war.

"But I've work enough for two, dear. You could help your mother right here at home."

Countless such entreaties filled the cracks between readings from the Good Book—when all Thankful wanted was to soak her feet, or to rinse the week's sweat and powder from her one good set of drawers.

Wealth gotten by vanity shall be diminished . . .

Who can find a virtuous woman? for her price is far above rubies . . .

And the woman was arrayed in purple and scarlet colour, and decked with gold and precious stones and pearls, having a golden cup in her hand full of abominations and filthiness of her fornication . . .

Only words. But her mother made a pattern of them, as delicate and deliberate as any spider's. Its lines—plucked and jangled by Mother Hammer just now—describe the fretwork of Thankful's nerves.

Ursula returns to the parlour with blood in her cheeks. Resuming her chair, she goes on to recount the story of the Prophet's martyrdom—the children wide-eyed with horror to the last. They file off to their beds quietly, planting dry little kisses on her lips as they go.

Alone now, Ursula fingers the cold hump of the ring's stone. Her chin drops. She exhales his holy name along her breastbone. "Joseph."

Jailed for such a trifle. Doubtless he had indeed ordered the destruction of the *Nauvoo Expositor*'s offices—the type hurled like so many pebbles into the street—but it signified little. Those who lived by rights in the blessed city knew the rogue newspaper to be nothing but a tool of vengeance for the Church enemy, William Law. Still, the first and only edition had brought a secret gladness to Ursula's heart.

Like anyone possessed of a pair of ears, she'd heard the rumours concerning the Prophet's many wives. Law's editorial—reviled though it was among loyal Saints—gave credence to that which she had long hoped to be true. If, like ordinary men, the Prophet had only one wife, then Ursula's sole chance at happiness was dependent upon that woman's death—and the thin-lipped Emma Hale Smith seemed the kind to live on and on. If, on the other hand, Brother Joseph was indeed married to many, who was to say his eye might not one day alight upon her?

She cracks the ring, the stone tilting to rest its round back against her middle finger. His hair is so very soft. Trailing the lock like a paintbrush across her cheek, Ursula closes her eyes.

Eighteen forty-four. She was twenty-two years old. She could have married a dozen times over by then—there had been Hammer's many proposals and others besides—but she was determined to wait for her heart's desire. Only now that desire was locked away in the Carthage jail.

She was fretting over her beloved's safety, hurrying to market with a basket of the Simmses' eggs, when Porter Rockwell thundered past at a gallop, howling the awful news. The Prophet's strongman resembled nothing so much as a madwoman that day—grey locks streaming, pale eyes bloody with tears.

Joseph is killed—they have killed him! Goddamn them! They have killed him!

Ursula felt her legs turn to serpents beneath her. They slithered in opposite directions, dropping her in a dead faint, a mess of eggs and straw.

—

It was a mournful contingent that carried the martyr's body back to the city he had dreamt into being—back through the wailing thousands to the mansion that had been his blessed home. *Martyrs'* bodies, to say truth, for Brother Hyrum came too, though his coffin might have held a hog for all Ursula paid it any mind. She had her strength back by then. Had her wits about her, too. She would need both to force her way to the front of the crowd and make use of the small scissors in her hand.

Bendy does his best to be a good Saint. He's started the Book of Mormon a dozen times, but never makes it past the Lord's commandment to Lehi that he *take his family and depart into the wilderness* before dropping off or recalling some task left undone and rising from his bunk. At such a rate it's plain he'll never make it through the book's catalogue of journeys and wars, so he takes to reading the way he was taught to—a page here, a passage there. This night, the book falls open at Alma, the final verse of chapter two.

And it came to pass that many died in the wilderness of their wounds, and were devoured by those beasts and also the vultures of the air; and their bones have been found, and have been heaped up on the earth.

A small enough morsel, but it's all he can manage. He allows his eyes to close.

The dream is brief, a hushed and vivid tableau. There is high ground, a hill independent of valley or cliff. He both stands and watches himself stand, barefoot on its grassy back. Before long a secret worms up through his naked soles. The hill is no work of the earth's. Were he to break through the turf beneath him, he would turn up a spadeful of bones.

〰

No cause to unlock the sideboard and fish out the kill book tonight. The entry would be a short one: *20th of May 1867. No luck.*

Instead, Erastus opens the door to his third wife's bedchamber. He has to squint in the half-light, but as always when Thankful treats him to his favourite of all her creations, there is the smell. A fox is a plush and pungent creature. He begins to make out the line of her, drawn back between wardrobe and dresser. She greets him with a high, inviting bark.

Before Eudora came to live among them, Erastus took his pelts to be tanned in Tooele. The finest of these he presented to Thankful. His third wife accepted the fox with ardour, closing her eyes to run a hand down its red length. Then met his gaze and demanded half a dozen more. His curiosity fired, Erastus set out directly, covering endless ground, spurring horse and Indian on.

Thankful took her time with the pelts, but waiting only honed Erastus's desire. When the unveiling finally came, it exceeded his every imagining.

That night, as tonight, his actress wife met him clothed in an unmistakable musk. Her limbs were bare, save for the burnished cuffs that clattered with claws when she moved. Her hair was bound up in a tawny headdress. In place of a blouse, she wore a bib of bushy tails, the slightest shimmy allowing glimpses of human flesh. A short cape covered her back, falling to the three-quarter mark of her bare behind—this he would discover when she turned to lead him in a frantic, restricted chase.

But the true revelation lay beneath the tips of those dangling tails. Erastus gasped like a child when he found it—he couldn't help himself. She had the narrowest of the pelts tucked up snugly between her thighs. Its eyeless face nosed her navel. He was loath to remove it. Driving once, twice into the pelt for pleasure, he found Thankful had thought of everything. The fur parted for him where she'd razored a tidy little slit.

Again the sharp, impatient bark. Erastus approaches his third wife with caution. She'll scratch him given half a chance. She's broken skin before.

19

JOHN JAMES MIGHT WELL have gone on to work in the office of Wicklow Stables, might even have followed in his father's long-ago footsteps and become a clerk, if only that father had remained among the living. As it was, ever since he'd received word of Bill Drown's comeuppance, he could feel himself coming loose from the moorings of his new life. Could a boy—a man, really, he was closing in on fifteen—could a man one day up and begin to float? A fool's notion. But in the war between sense and sensation, the latter inevitably holds sway.

He took to keeping his hands full at all times. Feed sack, water pails, saddle—in a pinch a pair of horseshoes would do. Anything to keep his boot soles in contact with the stable floor. At night he draped himself with heavy saddle blankets, woke sweating, certain he'd dropped into consciousness from a position several inches above the straw.

For months the feeling dogged him. Then, just when he was beginning to resign himself to a private, circumscribed lunacy, it left him in the midst of a bright day. He was propped up against a hitching post on Montgomery Street, both hands keeping a firm grip behind him. The stable owner had sent him out with a list the length of his forearm. *And mind you don't take all day.* It was a warning Wicklow wouldn't have issued before the change, one John James wouldn't have needed to hear.

Two blocks down, a disturbance erupted into the street. Intially John James thought *fight,* at least one man bellowing in the eye of the throng. Then he caught sight of something brilliant—wheeling through the air, a succession of bright red balls. Wagons swung out next, their fringed tops visible above the advancing crowd.

The bellowing came clear in scraps. "Beasts the likes of which you've never seen!" And then, "Equestrian feats—that's horse tricks, folks—to halt the beating heart!" Soon the seams met to form an endless ribbon of words, half shouted, half sung.

John James let go his post. He had to if he was going to press in with the rest of them for a better look. The ballyhoo issued from a tall, thin source—a reed of a man in a dark yellow top hat, his velvet tailcoat and trousers the same unpleasant shade. He led a well-muscled grey—a real beauty, dappled and heavy-lashed. From a distance the pair seemed otherworldly. As they drew closer, the horse remained lovely while the man betrayed a moth-eaten fatigue. John James watched him pass, heard his monologue dissolve into the general din.

In the wake of the grey mare came a white-faced, juggling clown, his suit of loose ruffles soiled, his boots bulbous and worn. The nose of one caught on a warped plank in the road, jerking him in a four-step stumble. Twisting through an off-kilter whirl, he recovered, keeping all five balls aloft. He cracked a painted grin, the crowd rewarding him with a roar.

The first cage was horse-drawn—a dark brown gelding alongside a bluish nag that could've been its grandam, one part horseflesh, three parts glue. John James let his gaze slide over their sweat-dark backs to where a smallish black bear rocked on its haunches in the shifting space between bars. Its plaque read *Rocky Mountain Bear*—golden letters on a background of hunter green. A creature common as played-out claims in the surrounding hills.

A pair of mules hauled the lion. Neither golden nor maned, it was one of the biscuit-coloured giants from the mountains not far to the east. A *California Lioness*. Deaf to a chorus of miners' jeers, it lay motionless in a doughy heap, chin flat between its massive paws.

Two more mules dragged a cage full of cages. Suspended, swaying, they contained perhaps a score of exotic birds, lush and varicoloured as the New Orleans fruit stands John James had known as a boy. Banana yellow, banana black. For a moment he felt his mother's fingers gripping his, market-tense.

Next, hitched to a near-lame mule and its compensating partner, came a barred cargo of scampering forms. Seven silver-ruffed monkeys, three in grubby white dresses, four in miniature sombreros and little black britches. A man clung to the far side of the cage; John James saw only his arm, thrashing and grabbing at the monkeys, keeping them wild. Their screeches mingled with the shrieks of the birds, lifting the finest of John James's hairs. He'd endured a similar chorus one morning as a child. The morning he woke clinging to a mother gone cold.

He resisted clapping his hands to his ears, instead giving his head a prolonged and violent shake. When he finally left off, the last of the cages was before him. Behind its bars sat a beast whose fur was long and gleaming, coffee-dark. A hyena? A baboon? John James had heard tell of such creatures but had never laid eyes on so much as an engraving. He raised them now to the nameplate, shocked to find it bore an actual name: *Mena the Amazing Dog Girl*.

He gasped, and as though drawn by the minute vacuum his mouth created, the dog girl turned her face, and then the rest of her, his way. As near as John James could tell, she was unclothed. The hair on her head met and melded with the hair that adorned her body. A shorter, finer version sprouted from her chin and cheeks. Bare flesh peeked through in two creamy rings around wet black eyes. She met his look. Looked him straight in his dazzled eyes.

It had been four years since John James last tied himself up in knots. The performances had grown up out of instinct, a creaturely call to survive, and since Robert Wicklow had taken him in, he'd no longer seen the need.

That night, in the grip of a new instinct, he lay on his back in his hollow of straw and caught hold of the sole of one foot. In three tries he had the heel tucked behind his skull. It was a start. He reached for the other foot. Pictured himself shaking the ringmaster's bony hand.

20

DORRIE DREAMS:

Night, and the scuttle of a pocket mouse wakes me. I am ravenous, stiff, still rooted to this scrappy oak. Beneath me, the child stirs, the noise that spoke to me of potential prey speaking to her of threat. How can they be so at ease among their own killing kind yet so jittery in the wild, when even wolves turn tail at the sight of them? A grizzly could be trouble, true, or a mountain lion, but neither makes a mouse-sized scuttle in the scrub. Bears come crashing, the sound of wild abandon, an absolute dearth of fear. Cats are all silence until it's too late. A blessing both are too weighty to waste their time on birds.

The child sits up. Half a moon is more than enough to pick out her grubby, hanging skin. If she understood the dark language, I would tell her of my last flapping survey of the field. The ragged bloom of females and young lying separated from its stem of males. Bodies gleaming blue, dark patches where blood rose up gurgling like the water in the spring they never reached. Here a split skull, brain showing dove-grey through a starburst of bone, there an arrow still bristling. Such a temptation. To take wing and land at one of those gracious holes, dip the beak, grasp hold of something tender and tear.

It would be taking a chance. The dog man's pack are clinging to the field. They've bedded down, but their fire still burns high. And there is the child. She wouldn't like it, though she must be hungry too.

She stands now, trying out her legs. Knowing it's futile, I let out a rasping, tight-throated caw. *Not safe yet. Stay.* She looks up at me, hollow eyed, and I hear myself, *uh-uah, uh-uah,* the gentlest of begging calls. Still she turns, orienting toward the meadow, moving back the way she came.

Keeping her always in my eye, I hop along branches, glide from crown to crown. True flight takes energy, something I feel the lack of all through me, having gone a full day's distance with no food. The underbrush thrills with promise, but I haven't time. The child steps out onto the path, walking narrowly, fitting her feet to the track of a single wheel. She crests the slight rise. Brush crowds the trail as we approach the spot where the Originals lay in wait.

Poor earthbound thing. She'll never know the fine shape her flock has drawn upon the ground. On her level there exists only a mess of bodies, and one in particular—the female who held fast to the lead, staring after the wagons even as they disappeared.

The child halts. Makes no sound save a prolonged absence of breath, followed by several shallow gulps. I feel an urge to give up my vantage, glide and settle on her shoulder. It would terrify her, I know. She would scream and give herself away.

She takes a step forward, a step closer to the black fan of human hair. In the dark it blends with the stain around it, the life that drained out the deep slash in her gullet. Give humans their due— the bright blades they draw from nowhere make a clean, deep cut.

For a long moment the child stands staring, taking in the dark mother's stripped and moonlit form. Then she whirls, forsaking the wagons' rut and plunging into the brush. She beats a noisy, scrambling retreat, thrashing so I can't help but call out another alarm. I cannot say if she hears me. Only that she keeps on.

Low hills rise up beneath her, oak giving way to juniper and sage. When the grade grows steep, she makes feet of her hands, turning animal beneath the partial moon. I follow her up into the sharper air, longer glides between trees now, stretches of open ground. When the climb becomes too much, she veers south and follows the sloping range.

She overlooks it now. If she were to direct her gaze downhill, she would see the long meadow rich with dead. From this angle some are hidden, others plain, depending on how they fell, which way their bodies flattened the grass. She would see the smoking fire of the dog man's pack. Beyond all this, she would see what remains of her flock's camp, the circled wagons bereft of their white covers now, all shadow and rib.

But she keeps her eyes forward, stumbling on, and I begin to believe she will follow these hills to the desert lands, running until she drops and dies. What difference in the end? To the west, the smouldering camp. To the east, more unknown humans, Originals and Pales. To the north, the dog man and his wagons. She might as well cut a path over the punishing sands. I will stay with her if she does, at least to the line where the warm-blooded must turn back or burn.

It won't come to that, at least not tonight. A wrinkle in the hill's face sprouts a clump of sagebrush, grown fat in its protective fold. As though returning to the burrow she's always known, the child drops to all fours and forces her way in headfirst, finally hiding her white overskin away. She bruises leaves, bursting countless veins of scent. Suddenly I can no longer see, smell or hear her. My senses tell me the child is gone, but in my mind's eye she curls beneath the stinking bush just as she curled at the foot of the oak.

Nearby, a twisted juniper stands. I alight on its thickest limb.

21

TONIGHT THE BROWN BULK of a roast graces the table. The first wife is an expert carver. Everyone gets their due.

"Brother Drown."

Bendy jumps a little. "Yes, Mother Hammer?"

"I imagine your knowledge of Church history leaves something to be desired."

Hammer forces a loud exhalation out the side of his mouth. Says nothing, though. No longer a novelty, Bendy is on his own.

"Well, I—"

"It is my custom to instruct the children in that very subject of an evening. Perhaps you'd care to join us in the parlour."

He knows an order when he hears one. "I will, Mother Hammer. Thank you, I will."

Bendy's heard tell of Haun's Mill before, but never the damning details. Hearing them now, he finds himself sitting forward on the hard settee.

"Two dozen families and your poor mother among them. Not a mother then, though, children. Not even a daughter. A servant." Mother Hammer pauses, looking down at the children gathered about her feet. "Two dozen families working the fields, the sun low and red in the sky." Her rocking ceases. "What day was it, my lambs?"

"October thirtieth," they reply in concert.

"What year?"

"Eighteen thirty-eight."

"Eighteen thirty-eight." She nods. "Can you imagine, children, I was but sixteen years of age the day they came squeezing out of the woods all around us, raising up their guns. Missouri militia. Two hundred and forty troops, they say, though I can tell you, we none of us stopped to count. We cried surrender, but they fired on us all the same. I ran for the thickets after my mistress, the pair of us dragging her children by their wrists. They nicked the youngest across his calf."

Baby Joe gives a gasp, Bendy noting its effect in the muscles of the first wife's face—the briefest of contractions, a smile she doesn't allow.

"I had to tear strips off my petticoat to bind him up." She draws a breath to capacity, as though preparing to submerge. "But we were the lucky ones, those of us nearest the brush. Others sought refuge in the smithy's. How many, Joe?"

The middle boy sits up tall. "Eighteen in all, Mother. Three boys, fifteen men."

"That's right, my angel. Eighteen in all, shot through the chinks between the logs. One boy hid beneath the bellows and lived to watch the militiamen break down the door. His name, Josephine?"

"Sardius Smith, Mother."

"And what did he do? Joseph, now."

"Mother, he begged for his life."

"Begged for it. And the man who held a gun to poor Sardius's head, what was his reply?"

Again the full chorus, a shrilling Bendy endures in his bones. "'Nits will make lice!'"

"Good." Mother Hammer plunges back in the chair, three violent rocks before she brakes with her heel. "Think, children, on what kind of man—what kind of *men*—would be capable of committing such an atrocity. Close your eyes. Be quiet some minutes and think."

Bendy shuts his eyes along with the rest of them. He thinks hard—not along the lines Mother Hammer has dictated, but around and around a single word. *Atrocity.* He's come upon it only once before—in print, and so he sees it now. Eight black shapes to build a troubling idea, one Robert Wicklow had to explain to him once he'd sounded it out.

It must be a decade ago now. He was reading aloud from the *Daily Evening Bulletin,* the story one of those that made his boss's head shake slowly in time to the low tsking of his tongue. He can recall only fragments of it now—the parts Wicklow had him stumble over until he got them right.

. . . *the vile brood of incestuous miscreants who have perpetrated this atrocity shall be broken up and dispersed.*

. . . *a crusade will start against Utah which will crush out this beast of heresy forever.*

Here the image of newsprint folds away to reveal Wicklow's face, his expression one of saddened disgust. *Mormons.*

"Well?"

Mother Hammer's voice is jarring. Bendy feels himself colour, as though she's caught him in the midst of some disgraceful act.

"Baby Joe?"

"Bad men," the youngest blurts.

"Good boy. Josephine?"

The older girl bows her head. "Heartless men."

"Good. Brother Drown?"

The children twist to peer at him, bracing their hands on the braided rug. His mind is a pale blue blank, the same shade as the first wife's exacting eyes. Then suddenly, without a doubt, he knows exactly what she wishes, but does not expect, to hear. "Godless, Mother Hammer. Godless men."

This time she cannot contain her pleasure. She shows it in a flash of teeth, a taut and spasming smile.

The Tracker's nineteenth year promised to be a bright one. The boughs of the piñon trees dragged to the ground with the first bumper crop in seven years. Many camps came together to reap the reward—more young women than the Tracker had ever seen, and still he had eyes for only one.

What was stopping him? She had been a woman for two moons now. She wasn't his blood—her people having joined the camp only one generation before—so there would be no objection to the match. He had only to declare himself and, if accepted, lead her by the hand to his hut. *If accepted.* And if not? He had never known such doubt. Perhaps this was what came of spying on a girl during her lonely time, the price of breaking taboo.

The piñon harvest had come none too soon. After all that work there would be dancing, young couples sparking and pairing off. The air would be ringing with cries of courtship. To approach her with longing in his eyes would come as naturally as drawing breath.

He watched her at every opportunity during the long days' toil. Her right breast lifting as she reached for a cluster of cones with her long hooked pole. Pleasure crimping the corners of her mouth as she knelt with the others over the roasting pit, watching the hard green cones spring open, inhaling the nutty smoke. Her hands were strong and small, especially skilful in their manipulation of *mano* against *metate* when reducing the shelled, parched seeds to meal. The action causing the muscles of her back to dance.

Later, during the dance itself, she evinced an all-over sinuous grace. She moved directly opposite him across the wide circle, her beauty made luminous by a fine, continuous sweat. Looking her full in the face, he found it difficult to maintain rhythm. Her midriff was worse, so he stared at her feet, sweet and brown in their sandals, and he danced.

> *Lovely one, the piñon tree.*
> *Lovely one, the piñon tree.*
> *Dark of needle, hung with seed.*
> *Dark of needle, hung with seed.*

He lost sight of her when the circle broke and pooled. By the time he located her face again, he found it changed. She shimmered as though viewed through a bright curtain of rain. Her arm too was different. It still flowed down to her pretty fingers, but those fingers now lay hidden, tucked in Younger Brother's hand.

Life aboard the *Thornton* was an orderly round. The converted went about their business in orchestrated shifts—cooking, cleaning, praying to the rhythm of the ship's bell. Time between tasks took the shape of instruction from one of the returning missionaries in their midst. Quarters were cramped—nearly eight hundred aboard—but were divided into well-run wards, each with a bishop at its head. It took some effort for Ruth to apply this title to such ordinary men, a bishop being a creature of lacy hem and vaulted headdress in her former life. It was the least of many changes she would come to accept.

The days were made of ritual, so much so that actual rites such as baptisms—her own among them—took on a commonplace air. Not so funerals. There was no mistaking the gravity of a sheet-swaddled body slipping overboard. Some loss of life was to be expected during those long weeks at sea. The converted were poor. Many infants, many old. Schedules and scourings do not a magic vessel make.

It was after one such interment—a boy of twelve whose whip-thin corpse strove like an arrow for its watery mark—that Ruth found herself lingering empty-headed at the starboard rail. The sun had gone down, but the ocean still showed a residue of blood-red light. Her gaze glanced off the reflective swell, then pene-trated to where a shadow swam close against the hull. It was huge, the length of two lifeboats laid bow to stern.

In the pocket of Ruth's dress, a rind of bacon curled. She'd learned to save herself a morsel or two to sweeten the long hours between meals. Doubtless she would have been rebuked if any-one had seen—dropping good food overboard in the middle of an ocean, where every direction offered nothing but water meeting sky. What could she be thinking of? Only that the shadow required something of her, and that a curl of bacon was little enough to spare.

She did a wicked thing. Elbows on the rail, she clasped her hands before her, closed her eyes and began to murmur, as though she was addressing the Lord. The bacon slipped away as she loosened her fingers' clasp. Just then the ship's bell rang the gathering to prayer. When she looked down again, the water's dark was entire. She told herself the thing was sated. It had dropped to the bottom, or turned to follow its great mouth away.

Ruth was below decks when she first heard whispers of something called celestial marriage—a doctrine by which a Saint might take himself more than one living wife. Among the women of her ward, there were those who refused to believe and those who, horrified at the prospect, swore they would be on the next packet home. An empty threat. Most had paid only a small portion of the nine-pound passage, and had signed a bond promising to repay the Church's Perpetual Emigration Fund once they were earning in the New World.

Ruth neither denied the rumour nor cried foul. The notion of more than one woman in a household seemed natural. The only man she'd ever lived with was her father, and memory had reduced those early years to variations on a single scene. It centred on a bedridden body shrunk to nothing, wet and endless coughing, gobbets of coal-black phlegm loosed into a rag. *He hadn't the constitution for it*—the doctor's sighed assertion when the patient finally passed.

Her husband dead and gone, the Widow Graves did the sensible thing and moved herself and her small daughter south to where there were jobs for women and girls. Mrs. Stopes ran a safe, clean house. Many came and went—some marrying, some lighting out for greener pastures, some giving up the ghost—but Ruth and her mother stayed. A dozen years together, then another three with Ruth left to warm the bed alone.

In all that time, she'd given the idea of marriage little thought. She wasn't fool enough to imagine it would save her from hard work, and Mr. Humphrey's attentions had taught her a husband's loyalties might stray. As for children, another topic favoured by the girls who gathered around Mrs. Stopes's table, one glance about the below-decks village gave the lie to their tender imaginings. All around her lay mothers driven to near madness, women who hadn't slept a wink since dry land.

Of course, Ruth had known, however vaguely, that her life in Zion would include a husband. All the same, she'd never actually seen a couple—let alone a family—in her mind's eye. The forms she encountered there were a good deal simpler. The lobed, serrated figure of a mulberry leaf. The perfect oval of a cocoon.

Eighteen horses are too much work for one man. Since it appears Bendy will be left to his own devices more often than not, he's made of himself two stable hands—one working by day, the other by night. When the diurnal man isn't tending to fences and troughs, he's shovelling shit and spreading fresh straw while the stalls stand empty. The nocturnal version works by lamplight, cleaning and mending tools, washing sweat-stiff blankets, resurrecting long-neglected tack. Sleep finds the gaps and fills them, an hour or two at a time.

What little veterinary know-how Bendy possesses, he's already putting to use. Aside from the asthmatic nag, a round of cursory examinations revealed thrush in nearly half the herd. Turned-up hooves showed black, putrid sponges, the frogs gone yeasty from standing in piss and filth. As for Bull, in addition to his vice of windsucking, it turns out the troubled gelding is prone to bouts of spasming colic. There's little Bendy can do during these episodes. He stands close by while the palomino sweats and paws the stable floor, talking softly until the pain dies away.

After less than a week on the job he can see some improve-
ment in the old mare's cough, now there's some decent air for her
to breathe. Daily hoof scrubbings with dilute iodine, plus fresh
straw and clean, dry floors, are beginning to make a dent in the
epidemic of thrush. In the meantime, however, a two-year-old
paint has come lame—a case of pus in the foot as bad as he's
seen, swollen clean up the fetlock, the heel hot to the touch, alive
with a jumping pulse. Having brought the matter up twice with
Lal and once with his father, Bendy harbours no illusions about a
horse doctor riding up any time soon.

It's the dead of night when he decides to take matters into his
own hands. The paint puts her faith in him. She allows him to
bend and lift her bad leg, even tolerates his probing fingers,
flinching only when he hits the sweet spot and the pain is too
pointed to bear. It hurts him to betray her, to produce the freshly
whetted hoof knife from where he's kept it hidden in his belt and
make the scraping, plunging cut. He feels her cry all through him,
but takes comfort in the yellow spurt, the gust of septic air.

Straightening, he tells himself she understands—the release
of pressure a lesson in itself, a wordless treatise on the necessity
of purging poisons, airing wounds. And indeed, she does seem to
forgive him, holding fairly still while he pares away enough of a
hole to be certain the abscess can drain. His hands careful, he
ties on a poultice to encourage the ooze.

Stepping outside to clear his sinuses of the lingering stench, he
spots the square of yellow light in the wall that faces him across
the wide yard. He's noticed it burning before. It would seem the
youngest wife secretes herself in the old adobe barn at night, as
well as during the day.

What she does with her time, he's hard put to imagine. From
what he can see, Mother Hammer and her appropriated flock do

the lion's share of the work in both house and yard. The third wife keeps herself to herself—he has yet to catch sight of her out of doors. He's seen the second wife pitch in when pressed, but more often than not she spends her days in and around the little log house that seems to be all her own.

For the most part, Bendy finds he's already accepted these and other small mysteries about the place—what does Lal do with himself all day? where does Hammer go?—but there's something about this particular discovery that awakens his curiosity. It would be simple enough to see for himself what the fourth wife's up to. He could skirt the yard, sidle up to the bleary window and sneak a look.

The moment he thinks it, he puts the thought from his mind. If he goes over there—and he will, he realizes, soon—he'll go directly. Walk up plain as anything and knock on her weathered door.

In the clearing outside his hut, the Tracker stands naked before a smouldering fire. Some time ago—one hour, perhaps two—he awoke to find his waistcoat and trousers binding him close. He tore free of them in a dreamy panic, crawled gasping into the night.

The fire is low. He feeds it—a tangle of scrub that flares quickly—and, in the uprush of light, frees the picture book from his leg. Crouching, he flattens it on the ground before him, open to the second-to-last page.

Yauguts stares up at him. The Crying Man. His Mormonee name was John D. Lee, his title, Indian Farmer—as though the People were a crop to be tended and eventually cut down. In the portrait he is smiling, or near enough. Pinching his thin lips into a bow, softening those pale, pale eyes. No tears there—not now—but the corners slant down as though fashioned for the purpose, the blinding water to be whisked from his vision quickly, leaving it cold and clear. Not a cruel face exactly. Some might even find it fatherly—and hadn't the People turned to children in his shadow? Coming to him with their palms outstretched in hunger. Doing his bidding. Trusting his word.

Yauguts gathered a great many to the long valley that day, summoning them with promises of cattle and clothing, pots and guns. Cedar City men under Big Bill and Moquetas. Chief Ammon's Piedes from the country around Beaver. A goodly number from as far off as the Muddy and Virgin rivers. The Tracker, Younger Brother and many more from camps along the Santa Clara's banks.

They came expecting a raid, the killing swift and simple, the bounty great. They found instead a siege. It was clear from that first dawn attack gone wrong. As they retreated, some fell softly, swallowed by the grass, while others hit hard, bucked and wheeled in the spill of their own blood. Younger Brother one of these.

The Tracker felt his brother's absence growing keener as he ran, each threshing stride the tautening of a lifelong cord. He had yet to reach cover when it snapped him round.

He found Younger Brother without looking. Those long brown legs. As far back as the Tracker's memory stretched, he had envied those two fine limbs. The gift of grace they bestowed upon their owner, the way they lifted Younger Brother's head above a crowd. And now the right one was a ruin. The Tracker shouldered him and pounded for the hills.

The pair of them lay low behind a boulder, Younger Brother clawing at him, whimpering. A better man would have finished him off. Knelt to cut the straining neck, or at least stood back and fired. A better man would have had the clear conscience, the clean intent to help his brother die.

The Tracker should close the book. Instead, he turns the page.

One grief supplants another, the second finer, both delicate and deep. The final portrait, while impressive, was clearly drawn in haste. To achieve a likeness so true, the maker must have needed help, one of those fragile plates the whites call a looking glass—good for looking one way only, back at oneself. The Tracker imagines it tilted just so, held up by a pair of small, dusty hands.

It's a striking face. Thinner than that of the daughter laid down some pages before, it shows the same pinched evidence of thirst. The eyes betray suffering and more—the adult curse of foreknowledge. The hand that captured these features had done justice to the Crying Man's too.

The Tracker is suddenly cold, the whirlwind wife touching down for the briefest of instants, looking over his shoulder into the dead woman's eyes.

He cannot know for certain if the knife was his. He did slit throats—they all did, true Indians and painted Mormonee alike. Leapt from the thin cover and cut the women and walking children down, just as Yauguts and the other captains had planned. He recalls only skirts against his bare ankles, hair in his fist—one head dark like hers, another dead-grass pale, yet another red and glaring in his eyes.

Blood ran hot in those abandoned moments, washing over his hands, surging through him in hateful, joyful waves. The veins danced in his skin, full to bursting with his own red share and that of Younger Brother too—Small Sister a third pulsing presence, wherever her body might be.

It was only afterwards, when all but the very young of the Mericat camp lay quiet, that the Tracker felt his blood begin to cool. He moved among the bodies in the company of both Indian and Mormonee. Stripping the dead made sense—their belongings were nothing to them now.

White women's clothing was a puzzle to the fingers, so many layers in that heat. It took him an age to work the dark-haired woman free of her blood-wet dress. Further fumbling loosed her undergarments, revealing pasty, smeared breasts, nipples that had known a child. The patch of hair, so black against the fish-belly sheen of her thighs, seemed an opening, a triangular gateway to the night. Another darkness lay a hand's breadth further down— a book like a brown fungus, fixed to the top of her leg.

Yauguts had driven out of sight with the children, but the other white captains had been perfectly clear—any writing, any book or paper, was to be delivered up to one of them the moment it was found. The Tracker glanced about him. More than one Mormonee crouched close at hand, but each was blind to him, engrossed in his grisly work.

The thrice-looped knot held tight. He worried at it for several breaths, then slipped his knife from its sheath and made short work of the job. He held the book close, opening it in the shadow of his own chest. To his surprise—his delight, sharp and strange though it seemed in that desolate scene—he found not the baffling insect tracks of the white man's words, but a horizon of woolly humps and gleaming horns.

A second sweep about him revealed not a single gaze trained his way. Sucking in his belly, he opened a gap down the front of his trousers and slipped his find away.

Returning home from the blood-soaked valley that day, the Tracker knew Younger Brother's woman would take him in. It was possible she would have accepted him while her husband still lived. Younger Brother would have agreed—it was in his nature to share—but a portion of her would have been worse than no part at all.

Now it was the Tracker's duty to become her husband. His duty, his guilty reward. His heart leapt when she looked up at him from the weaving in her lap. He took a step closer, the picture book pinching where he'd tied it. Still she didn't rise. And when she lowered her head again, he saw there would be no need to speak the news aloud.

His eyes, greedy even in that moment, sought her lovely hands, motionless now, fingers frozen against the warp. Only then did he take in the shape of her design. *Cradle.* His joy was so terrible it threatened to separate his soles from the earth. The child would be Younger Brother's issue, but it would be down to her new husband to stoke the coals of her hotbed as she lay recovering from her labours. It would be the Tracker who would watch over her—not from afar this time, but lying beside her, joining her in the forsaking of salt, cold water, meat.

Looking through her fingers to the cross-hatching of willow below, the Tracker flashed on a story of himself. He saw a proud father walking with the stump of the baby's cord curled in his hand, carrying it high into the hills. Stooping down, he placed the precious object not on the track of a mountain sheep but in the hole of a pocket gopher. Despite himself, despite the heavy news he had come bearing, the Tracker smiled. The child would be a girl. Not a return of Younger Brother to haunt him, but an echo of the woman they loved.

22

GILLESPIE'S WASN'T the sort of hotel to send word up to a guest's room. The desk clerk told John James the number and let him wander the dank halls. Three raps and a man's voice bid him enter.

The yellow top hat sat at a forward tilt, obscuring the ring-master's gaze. His legs were golden stems outstretched. "Dan Pitch." He didn't rise, didn't even extend his hand. Nothing of the barker's singsong now.

John James flicked a glance about the room, scanning for bottles—whiskey-large or laudanum-small. He found none. Melancholy then, or plain fatigue. He stepped into the cramped room, drawing the door closed behind him.

"What is it you seek?"

John James would soon grow used to the ringmaster's peculiar mode of speech, but that first night it put a chill through him. At a loss for words, he turned side-on and widened his stance. Snaking his hands back between his legs, he followed their lead until his head, shoulders and a good part of his rib cage were through, armpits hooked at the backs of his knees. Craning his neck, he peered up under the yellow hat rim into the ringmaster's eyes.

"Well, well." Pitch sat forward, his face suddenly plain. He was all wax and hollows, an unlit taper of a man. "What shall we christen you? Rubber Boy? Rope Man? The Human Knot?"

John James released himself, swinging up tall. As the blood rushed from his skull, a face rose up to fill the void. Red Meg was pure memory now. Like so many of the city's females, she'd lost her looks, then her mind and finally her life to the plague of her trade. He'd caught sight of her from time to time over the past few years. Like standing vigil while a champion swimmer drowned.

"Bendy," he said, turning to face his new boss.

Dan Pitch nodded. "Bendy it is."

The tent was daunting, a giant bone-white molar set up two short blocks from the hotel among the ashy ruins of a warehouse fire. It sat back from the street, a long flap quivering in place of a door. Bendy called hello. Nothing. He felt foolish, entertained a moment's fantasy of retreat. Then took a breath, caught hold of the flap and gained the tent's white world.

Light like a thin cloud cover, trembling, diffuse. In the far corner, one of the wheeled cages stood alone, draped in plum-coloured cloth. Beside it, a minor mountain of straw bales. No sign of the ringmaster, but the clown stood dead centre in the ring. His back was turned, his arms outspread, heavy with birds. His head wagged slowly, side to side. He was chattering to them, a soothing cipher of whistles and words.

"Pardon me." Bendy felt the words sucked out of him, drawn upward into the hum.

The clown turned to reveal a row of faces—the fulcrum human, avian along either wing. Cleared of paint now, his features bore some resemblance to the ringmaster's. Slacker, though, underscored by a pouch of jowls.

"Show opens tomorrow night," he said, keeping his voice even, his flock calm.

"Oh, no. I'm J—I'm Bendy. Bendy Drown. Mr. Pitch hired me last night."

"Not this Mr. Pitch."

Bendy shifted on his feet. A long moment passed before the clown let him off the hook.

"You'll mean Dan."

"Yes, sir."

"I'm the brother. Camden." Again no hand came forward in greeting, though, to be fair, he hadn't a hand free. "He hasn't shown himself yet. Likely won't for a time yet." His gaze flipped inward then, as though in answer to a striking thought. He inclined his head toward the bird on his left shoulder, a lizard-footed brute with a flexing yellow crown. Letting a burbled whistle escape his teeth, the clown murmured, "Yes, Cocky. That so?"

Bendy jammed his hands into his pockets.

"Bendy." Camden Pitch came out of himself. "That your act?"

"Yes, sir."

"Contortionist."

"Sir?"

The clown gave a high laugh, setting both lines of birds squawking. "That's a word you'll want to know. Hush now, lovelies, hush." He pursed his lips and blew a stream of breath along each arm—ruffling feathers, quieting nerves. "You can work over there till he comes." He gestured with his chin to the crowded far corner. "Keep clear of the ring for now."

"Sure." Bendy followed the undulating wall, turned a sharp right angle and carried on to the hill of bales. Setting his pack down on the ground, he began limbering up.

Balance was key. It was one thing to tuck a foot behind your head while seated. Onlookers, put in mind of their own hips and hamstrings, might respond with wondering groans. Do it while standing on one leg, however, and they'd think not of their own bodies, but of trees made flesh and bone.

It wasn't easy to support the whole of his weight on one foot while he flung the other one up and back. He toppled backwards, hit hard-packed, sandy soil, untangled himself, rose and toppled again—half a dozen tries before he was blessed with an idea. Drawing the stubby knife from his boot, he sawed open a pair of bales and scattered himself a bed upon which to land. Knowing it was there behind him helped. On the next attempt he held steady for a full ten seconds before swaying and buckling back.

He sat up to find her watching him. Her cage door gaped, the purple drapery pushed aside. Dropping her left haunch to the cage floor, she slid her knees out from beneath her and dangled her feet out the open door. She pointed her toes as though stretching to dip them in a stream. This time she was clothed. Barely. A nightdress of sorts, but shorter, petal pink. Exposing the long pelts of her legs.

"Bendy, is it?" A low voice, softly mocking.

He nodded. For a second he considered adding *John James*, but the syllables seemed all wrong. A single turn of the clock and already his given name had the feel of a lie. He glanced over his shoulder to find Camden paying them no mind. The clown was balanced on a pair of short stilts, a monkey perched like a trapper's hat on his head.

"I'm Philomena. Pitch lopped off the *Philo* the day he took me on. Too much of a mouthful."

It was strangely thrilling to hear human speech issue forth from all that fur. Bendy realized he was staring. "You didn't mind?"

She smiled. "Small enough price to pay."

"For what?"

"What do you mean, for what? You just joined. You ought to have some idea."

He nodded again, though the force that had carried him to where he sat now was nothing so well formed as an idea. They watched one another for a long moment before she spoke again.

"Before he took me on, I was in a room. One room. Door bolted on the outside, one window, no curtains. You can part a curtain and peek out, and while you're doing that somebody might just chance to peek in. I had shutters. Shutters my daddy nailed shut."

Bendy swallowed. "All alone?"

"Not always. My mother brought me food, books. Sometimes we played cards." She paused. "Pitch got wind of a hairy girl and worked a deal with the old man. Out of sight, out of mind, I guess. I was thirteen when he sprung me. Been with the show three years." After a moment's silence she brought her hands together in a clap. "Try that trick again. Twelfth time's the charm."

Her regard made him worthy. His supporting leg became a pylon. An unseen plumb bob dropped from the tail of his spine. The bent leg swung up sweetly, heel cresting skull, hooking and catching hold. A single, tapering tremor and he had it. She smiled. He was rock solid. He could hop on the spot if he so desired. Maybe he'd try that next—he might even make her laugh.

Just then the narrow strip of tent that lay between them— between straw mountain and cage—parted. A hand came first, followed by the same bare, knotted arm Bendy had seen stirring the monkeys in their cage. Then a face. Again the Pitch features, but youthful and somehow flattened. The cageboy looked from

Philomena to Bendy, his gaze grappling along the sightline they shared.

Bendy's balance left him. The topknot of torso, head and leg sprang open upon impact. His wind was gone. The back wall of the tent healed over as Pitch the younger stepped all the way inside.

Bendy gulped and got nothing. Gulped again, caught purchase and hauled in a breath. One more, and he could manage a shaky sit. Raising his eyes to Philomena, he took in her terrible stillness, the hands gripped tightly in her lap.

The cageboy approached, each step a narrow lunge. He stood over Bendy, thrusting his groin out as though it were a chin or a kneecap, rather than a clutch of tender organs worn on the outside. He was making the most of the moment, his temporary advantage in height. Bendy contemplated rising, maybe even shooting up fast, but a twitch of dull wisdom made him wait.

"Stanley Pitch." The cageboy surprised him, reaching down a hand. Until Bendy realized that to take it would be to take a hand up.

"Dan Pitch's son," Stanley added, and Bendy saw then he had no choice. The cageboy's palm was rutted, his fingers blunt. In the sharp up-haul to standing, Bendy got a taste of his rival's strength.

It was full afternoon by the time Pitch finally showed. Stanley had long since disappeared through the tent's back flap with Philomena. Bendy had stretched himself sore and was lying on the scattered straw. Camden had his birds back in their cages and was arranging his props in a coffin-sized crate when the ringmaster shoved the front flap aside.

"Ah, you've come." He strode forward, high-stepping over the circle of mounded-up dirt that defined the ring.

"Yes, sir." Bendy rolled up onto the balls of his feet and walked to meet him.

"European tent." Pitch swept his arm in a loose circle, a gesture that encompassed the single ring, the four corner poles.

"Two-bit, he means," Camden added, grinning clear back to his puffy gums.

"My brother jests."

Looking around, Bendy found a single ring to be more than enough. As a child, he'd gotten used to gathering a crowd about him like a blanket, close enough so every comment stood clear—here the brash twang of a Sydney Duck, here the red tongue of a Chileno, laid haltingly over English or let slide down the grooves of its own design. Smells, too. No man could be a miner who hadn't made his peace with dirt, but dirt was the least of it, the cleanest. Their bodies were left to run on scraps and camp coffee for months of sweating blood, then dragged to town and gorged on whiskey, fried potatoes and fatty steak. Some managed to distinguish themselves, one man reeking of peppermint, another of hair oil, another of some putrefaction trapped deep inside. There would be no such discerning under the high white tent. His audience would be miles away.

Pitch flung his arms out wide. "A lot of space for a skin-and-bones lad to fill. Think you're up to it?" He rolled on before Bendy could answer. "You take me, for instance. You could lose sight of Dan Pitch if he turned sideways, but out here I'm a giant. Ever seen a cat backed into a corner? Puffs itself up double. Doesn't matter how you get there, terror, pride—point is, a man's as big as he believes."

This last elicited a grunt from Camden, laden with wire cages, crabbing sideways out the backstage flap.

Pitch stepped in close. "It gets to where you feel you could touch them, each and every one. Reach out a fingertip—" He grinned. "—or in your case a toe-tip, and lay it on whomever you please."

The ringmaster put him through his paces that day. They were a good hour into their rehearsal by the time the cageboy returned alone. Neither father nor son made a pretence of greeting the other. Pitch said only, "Bales, Stanley."

"What do you think I'm doing?"

The ringmaster waited a beat. "No idea."

Bent over between two straw bales, his fingers worming under twine, the son stiffened. "Bales. I'm doing bales."

Another beat, this one a hair longer. "I can see that, Stanley. It's quite plain."

Stanley straightened, his face working, wine-dark. Bendy averted his eyes. There was a moment's standoff, during which the monkeys struck up a muffled chorus beyond the sailcloth wall. Pitch ended things abruptly with a neat half turn on one heel. Over his shoulder he said lightly, "Well, get on with it."

While Pitch talked Bendy through pose after pose, Stanley worked at dismantling the golden pile. It took several slant-eyed glances for Bendy to determine the cageboy's purpose. Why cart heavy benches from venue to venue when even the most primitive mining town was sure to have a supply of straw? Stanley was laying the bales out in concentric circles beyond the dirt ring— staggered with sightlines and minimal legroom in mind. Once he got his head down, he proceeded like a Clydesdale, shoulders straining, eyes fixed and dull.

Bendy unwound himself from a particularly trying position in time to watch the cageboy drop the last pair into place. The mountain had shrunk considerably, to perhaps a dozen bales squared. It stood between Bendy and the tent's back flap. Watching Stanley duck out of sight behind it, he saw that it was meant to act as a sort of blind—performers appearing from behind a bright edifice rather than squeezing in through a fluttering slit.

Letting his gaze wander, he found the tent transformed. Light shimmered off the yellow seats, warming the ghostly walls. He felt a rush of promise in his watery limbs.

"Can you ride?" Pitch asked out of nowhere. "I could use a second in my act."

The question tipped Bendy back a little on his heels.

"Stanley used to manage it, before he got so thick through the chest." Pitch narrowed his eyes. "His mother's people, thick-chested, every one. Well?"

Bendy steadied himself. "I can ride."

— 23 —

May 21st, 1867

Dear Daughter

It is late and after much trouble I have managed to light the
candle and dip my pen. I was roused by one of Mr. Burr's
cries. You will not have forgotten his habit of screaming
himself awake from time to time. I will not sleep now with
my heart stuttering and him fussing on the far side of the wall.
He was not always such a man. The Lyman Burr I married had
many parts but life will draw out some and beat down others. I
was left with his weaknesses. For a time they made me strong.

Heaven only knows what brought it on this time. Maybe the
hog he butchered this morning with Kitty's help. I watched her
out my window clip-clomping across the yard to fetch him bucket
after bucket from the well. She will be tending to him now comforting him any way she can.

Dorrie I have told you there are many beginnings. Here is
another. Years ago your father did a terrible thing. Ten years
to be exact. He did not act alone. Some fifty Saints from

hereabouts took part and untold numbers of savages besides.
But I run ahead of myself.

In the late summer of 1857 a Gentile wagon train bound for
California struck a path through Zion taking the southern trail.
The bulk of them hailed from Arkansas where our beloved
Apostle Parley Pratt had so lately been cut down in cold blood
and McClean his murderer allowed to roam free. What was
more they had among their number several rough men of
Missouri that state so infamous in the history of our Church.
There were stories. At Corn Creek they had poisoned a spring
or some dead cattle or both. Several Pahvant Indians and a
young Saint had died. They had torn down fences and turned
their stock onto our pastures. They had popped the heads off
chickens with their whips. The Missouri men had harassed
women and uttered threats from town to town. Some had
bragged of taking part in the murders at Haun's Mill. One had
even gone so far as to claim he held the gun that shot Brother
Joseph at the Carthage jail.

The Saints refused them trade. It was forbidden to provision
the train in any way. By the time they had passed through Cedar
and were pulling south to Pinto feelings were running high. Do
not forget Dorrie at this time Deseret was under threat of
invasion by the Americans. Our militia drilled daily. We
expected at any moment the arrival of troops from both east
and west.

The Gentile train carried on southwest along the California
Trail and made camp at Mountain Meadows where lay the last
good grass and water before the Mojave's barren waste. They
would rest there or so they thought. They never left. They were
dispatched as are so many in this wild land by redskins. But also
by Saints. Fifty or thereabouts as I have written the leaders

among them men of high rank. I shall not take the chance of recording their names here but I believe in time they will be widely known. Truth will cut its own way. The Prophet's words Dorrie. I have finally taken them to heart.

Mr. Burr did as he was ordered. As you know Dorrie we Saints are counselled to obey the word of our superiors in the Church. Those who ordered the killing had been placed in power by Brother Brigham and therefore by God. And yet my husband is haunted as no doubt are his fellow murderers. As am I. It is crime enough to have kept the secret but I have done more. I have absolved him. Night after night I quieted his conscience even as I muzzled my own. The Lord only knows how Kitty manages it. I suspect she must smother his guilt with her young flesh. Doubtless she believes him plagued by monsters that live nowhere but in his own slumbering mind. I know better and so my methods were more elaborate by far.

When he would wake from the dream that his mouth was overflowing with blood I would tip a cup of clear water to his lips. And when he had drunk his fill I would sing to him. Not lullabies as you might think but battle hymns.

> *In thy Mountain retreat God will strengthen thy feet*
> *On the necks of thy foes thou shalt tread.*

Or sometimes

> *Remember the wrongs of Missouri*
> *Forget not the fate of Nauvoo.*
> *When the God-hating foe is before you*
> *Stand firm and be faithful and true.*

Often he would fix on one aspect of the thing and make a litany of it. Such as how they made camp on the meadow after the killing and how all night long he could hear a spring close by gurgling like a severed throat. On such nights I would read to him. How I scoured all Scripture for the passages that would suit. Many of them I read out so often as to have them by heart. From Elder John Taylor's statement recounting the slaying of the Prophet and his brother Hyrum I took this

> And their innocent blood with all the innocent
> blood of all the martyrs under the altar that
> John saw will cry unto the Lord of Hosts till he
> avenges that blood on the earth.

Or from the revelation given through Brother Joseph at Fishing River during the troubles in Missouri

> Behold the destroyer I have sent forth to
> destroy and lay waste mine enemies. And not
> many years hence they shall not be left to pol-
> lute mine heritage and to blaspheme my name
> upon the lands which I have consecrated for
> the gathering together of my Saints.

When he would bemoan having made a savage of himself by siding with the Indian horde I would remind him that our brown brothers are descended of the Twelve Tribes and are destined to rejoin the faithful so that we might rise up together in the final days. The revelation and prophecy on war became another favourite.

> And it shall come to pass also that the rem-
> nants who are left of the land will marshal
> themselves and shall become exceedingly angry
> and shall vex the Gentiles with a sore vexation.

Dorrie you see how I relied upon that which has been written but neither was I shy to invoke words I had heard spoken aloud. While Mr. Burr twisted in his sheets I bid him cast his mind back to the address Brother Haight delivered at Sunday Meeting in Cedar only days before the emigrants met their end. How he harrowed up feeling by recalling Haun's Mill and all those who perished there. How he swore to feed the Gentiles the same bread they fed to us.

At length Mr. Burr came to know stretches of unbroken sleep. Sometimes for months on end. The thing lay dormant but did not die. It rose up in him when word got round that a schoolteacher in Cedar had been shot dead for asking too many questions about the fate of the train. He woke bellowing night after night. Then again during the winter flood of sixty-one when he imagined the unending rains to be proof of the Lord's wrath. Remember wading out to the coop with me Dorrie? How the chickens squawked and splashed at least those that hadn't been fool enough to drown. Remember how Mr. Burr kept his bed while we struggled rising only after the waters began to subside?

Through all of it I ministered to him. Did I believe what I was saying? Did any of it make a difference to what he had done? I did my best not to ask myself such questions. When my husband howled in our bed I did what I could to console him. We never spoke of it during daylight hours. After a time it only ever seemed true in the dark.

Still it troubled him that I knew. The plan was that the killing was to be laid entirely on the Indians. Those Saints present on the ground had been forbidden to speak of what happened. Even to their wives. Even among themselves. To do so would be counted treason against the Church a crime punishable by death. Here I counselled him too. Were not a man and his wife one flesh? Was it not my sworn duty to share his life's burden? Was not a burden shared a burden halved?

I know now it is not. Not when that burden is knowledge of a great evil committed. I am become a vessel for his guilt. Look how I swell to contain it and still it will out.

Dorrie my hand fails me. I can write no more this night. From the next room come sounds of sobbing or love. I cannot say with certainty which.

All a mother's love
Helen Burr

24

THE MEAT IS COLD, left over from last night's roast. What's more, there's not enough of it on Lal's plate. He cuts his mother a sullen look, but her eyes are fixed on Baby Joe, who's sawing his own portion like a big boy. Her mouth is soft with pleasure. Lal looks away.

Reeling in his gaze, he lets it snag for a moment on Ruth. Her face, her lovely throat, rises from a great bulk of green fabric. He recognizes the dress as one resurrected from a previous confinement. An ugly, boxy thing, it houses rather than clothes her. He won't see her again in the shift. Gulping, he glares down at his meagre share.

It was the briefest of looks—a mere flickering—but it hasn't gone unnoticed. Thankful is staring at him. He can feel her augering twin points in his forehead with her eyes.

"Sister Thankful."

Lal flinches at the sound of his father's voice. He glances up to find Thankful's attention has shifted, husband and wife a closed couple now, alone at a table of twelve.

"Yes, Mr. Hammer?"

"That's a fetching dress you have on. You are a clever girl."

Thankful touches a finger to her water glass, catching a bead of its sweat. "Am I?"

"You know you are."

"And you, husband, are very generous to buy me such fine cloth."

Lal waits for the inevitable, Thankful twisting on her seat to include another in their talk. "Isn't that so, Mother Hammer?"

A quiet so cold it tinkles. Then, "Isn't what so, Sister?"

"Isn't Mr. Hammer a very giving husband?"

Lal scarcely knows whom to watch. He shifts from mother to stepmother to father—only to find Hammer's attention is nowhere near the sparking exchange. His gaze is intent upon Ruth.

A hardening comes over Lal's body. He presses the thumb to his lips, mouths urgently against it, "Do you see?"

Greedy, the thumb observes.

His mother speaks now. "Giving. I suppose *you* could say that."

Giving? the thumb whispers. *Hardly. Remember Emily Frye?*

How could Lal forget? It was less than a year ago, the Memorial Day picnic. The Frye farm lay some distance to the south; the last time Lal had laid eyes on the eldest daughter she'd been a yellow-braided rail. At the picnic she filled her good blue gingham like a jay fills its feathers. She stood closer than need be beside him, watching him over her chicken sandwich, taking sharp little bites.

It took him several minutes to think up something to say. "Blue's your colour." It wasn't much, but the look in her eye told him it would do.

He'd only just gotten the words out when his father caught hold of him by the shoulder from behind. "Here you are. Is he boring you, Emily?"

"Oh no, sir, I—"

But Hammer was already steering Lal away. It turned out there was work to be done, a plank floor to be knocked together for the dancing later on.

By the time Lal got free of his father, his good white shirt was stained with sweat. He searched the crowd for her anyway, spotted her standing before an older man in a dark, well-fitting suit. His grey beard working. Her grey eyes fixed on the ground.

It wasn't a month before Lal heard the news of their sealing at Sunday Meeting. For time and all eternity. What young man stands a chance? Little wonder he can't keep his eyes off Ruth.

What does he expect? the thumb breathes.

"What's the matter with you?" Hammer barks suddenly in his ear.

"Huh?"

"You gonna suck that thumb?"

"I—"

"Eat your supper."

"I—"

"You want me to eat it for you?"

Lal shakes his head violently. "I'll eat it." He grips his knife and fork, starts in on the first of three small medallions of beef. He'll fill up on spuds and bread as usual. "Pass the potatoes, Joe."

The boy doesn't move. No one does. After a long, stupid moment, Lal realizes what he's done wrong. The word nearly chokes him. "Please."

They're all abed. Ursula will go up herself soon, but for now she works the rocking chair like a cradle, wooing sleep. Why should a body so weary refuse rest? Because it's learned to. Because it's known far greater exhaustion and remained upright.

She will speak of that grim time, but only when the children press her. Even then it's up to them to draw out the details. It's wrong, she knows. The Church didn't die when Brother Joseph did. Its history—and her own, come to that—went rolling on.

I don't understand, Mother. Why did the Saints leave Illinois?

The same reason we left Missouri, Joe, and Ohio before that. The Gentiles drove us from our homes.

But wasn't Nauvoo ours? Didn't we build it to be our very own?

It was, son. We did.

So saying, she would feel the loss anew. *Nauvoo.* It was the finest city in the state of Illinois, built in a scant five years on swampland nobody had wanted—that is until, by the sweat of the Lord's Chosen, it was transformed into hallowed ground. Autumn 1845. The Prophet had been in his grave some fifteen months, Ursula's heart having chilled along with him despite the hot-skinned man who now shared her bed. She filled her days with preparations for the coming winter, laying strips of squash out to dry, bottling bent cucumbers with warty skins. All of it undone in the fire. The squash would have curled up black, giving off a sugary, stinking smoke. The pickle jars simmering before going off like bombs.

What about you and Father?

What about us? I've told you before, they burned us out.

And after that?

After that, an exodus to rival any endured in Old Testament times. They held out until February—still months before President Young had promised the Saints would leave peaceably, but when did a Gentile ever honour his end of a deal? It was a hurried leave-taking. Joseph's mansion was left standing empty, his body, so rumour had it, interred in the basement of an unfinished hotel. The mob helped themselves to all the Saints couldn't carry. In time they would go so far as to desecrate the Temple—broken bottles in the yard, vomit in the font, excrement on the steeple stairs.

The riverbank was little better than a mudslide. Ursula can recall lying back on the wagon seat, the rumps of the mules straining before her. The Mississippi boiled with ice chunks. A bone-chilling crossing delivered them to the Poor Camp at Sugar Creek, where Ursula watched a dry-eyed woman split her hope chest with an axe and burn it board by board. Where Joseph's people gathered and began in earnest to die.

Cold and hunger, croup and ague, black canker and bloody flux. Consumption. Axe wounds. Bad breaks splintering, poisoning the blood. All those who could manage it—the Hammers included—moved westward at the earliest chance.

Iowa was all mud. They wallowed in it, horses mired up to their barrels in evil-smelling sloughs, boots coated until they became black anvils that tortured the legs. Women and children goaded terrified teams while men laid their shoulders to sunken wheels. Some days they were lucky to cover four miles.

When the weather turned fine in mid-April, the grass sprang up high, providing cover for the snakes that came with it. A child's bare ankle, the soft, seeking nose of a grazing horse. Some only sickened. Others died. Those still walking learned to thrash the path before them with sticks.

In areas where game was abundant, wolves contented themselves with culling old or ailing stock from the margins of the herd. They grew bolder wherever the land turned mean. A great snarling bawl would be heard from among the makeshift pens, men bursting from their camp beds, filling the night with bellows and sparks.

The losses were many. The woman in the screeching wagon in front of theirs packed her dead baby along for weeks in the hope that it might be blessed by a member of the priesthood and properly laid to rest. She kept the tiny corpse wrapped up tight so that it might not lose cohesion, but not tight enough to fool the flies. Ursula watched them day in, day out, a black tail lifting with every jolt of the wagon's hind end.

It would be a lie, though, to say it was all hardship. Women, herself among them, wandered the grassy slopes, filling their aprons with wild strawberries. One night they gathered under starlight to bathe in the sand shallows of the Sweetwater, the men keeping their distance, having washed themselves earlier in the day. At times the air was so clear it flummoxed the eyes. The seam that held land to sky breached by jackrabbits, or was it Indians— Pawnee? Sioux? Or antelope? Everything made plain in the flash of a snowy behind.

Ursula comes close to dozing. Not all hardship. There were wonders. Things she's never told the children, and never will.

His knock is unlike any she's heard on her workshop door—a trio of clean, formal raps that play the old barn as though it were the chamber of a drum. She freezes, right hand gripping the saw, left hand braced against the workbench, fingers curled around a length of quarter-inch iron rod. Seconds elapse before it occurs to her that whoever knocked—and there's only one person it could be—is awaiting a reply.

"Come in."

The bad hinge gives a whimper. "I saw your light," Bendy Drown begins, his gaze already drifting right to take in the collective presence there. She says nothing. He turns his back to her to take it all in, but she catches the satisfying drop of his jaw. "Lord," he breathes, staring up into the motionless ranks. And again, louder now, "*Lord.*"

She allows herself a tiny smile.

"Did you—" he stammers. "Are these yours?"

She nods, an answer he must turn her way to see. As he does, she tucks the smile away, lowering her eyes.

"How long have you lived here?"

She lays the saw down on its side across the rod. Glancing up, she finds him staring at her hands. She takes a swift step back from the workbench and thrusts them into the pocket of her smock. "Three years."

"Three years." He shakes his head, and it is hard to credit, now that she thinks on it—the number of specimens she's mounted in that time, how far she's advanced in her craft. She knows a flush of quiet pride.

"But you're so young," he says. "You must've been—"

And now shame. She lifts her chin against it, the gesture working on him like a warning hand.

"Beg pardon." It's his turn to look down, inspect the straw-strewn floor. Abruptly, awkwardly, he wheels on one foot and once again faces the display. Then moves to the bottom tier and stoops over a rattlesnake's coils. "He looks mean."

The light there is poor, and Dorrie resists the urge to join him, lamp in hand. She could say so much about the diamondback— how her heart skipped a beat when Hammer dragged it from his kill bag, how its lank weight thrilled in her palms. It's no mean trick getting a snake to come smooth. The detail she's most proud of—the one everybody seems to overlook—lies in the rattlesnake's open mouth. It required such patience, such delicacy of touch, to slip her finest brush between its fangs and bring the bright palate to life.

All this and more she keeps to herself, waiting for him to speak. When he does, it has nothing to do with the snake.

"You always work at night?"

"Mostly."

He nods. "I don't sleep so good myself." He turns his attention to the next bale, where a pair of yellow-bellied marmots sit up tall. "Hello, boys."

"Boy and girl," she corrects him, and he shoots her an over-the-shoulder glance. "Brother Hammer prefers mated pairs. Families."

"That so." He watches her a moment longer before letting his neck uncoil. Tilting his gaze, he points to where the mountain lion claims three bales of the highest tier. "What about him? He's all on his own."

"It takes longer with some. You can't always bag a full set."

"Huh."

He stands still for a time, staring up. Then movement, the nature of which Dorrie can't begin to comprehend. It's as though he's melting, dropping to the ground in a boneless, unknowable mass. In the time it takes her to inhale sharply, the mass reconstitutes itself in the shape of a second lion—rump settled between haunches, belly long, chin resting on paws. Dorrie feels her own jaw drop, the purest of compliments returned.

"Bendy," she whispers.

"Yep."

For a moment they grin stupidly together—until an idea disturbs her delight.

The child went first. She had lived two years, learning early, laughing and grasping hold. Girl or no, she looked out through Younger Brother's eyes. This pained the Tracker—most of all when he caught a flash of recognition in the woman's gaze—but in the end the resemblance only added gravity to his love.

Just as the girl had taken shape at her mother's breast, so she dwindled in her mother's lap. She vomited while there was still anything inside her to bring up. The Tracker brought water, basket after pitchy basket, as fast as his legs would carry him, but her bowels ran faster, discharging a flecked and constant stream that reeked of fish. Little did he know he was hauling the source of her sickness, a river-borne gift from the Mormonee settlement upstream.

Crouching over mother and child, he reached out to feel the small heart racing, the delicate skin giving way. The eyes sank until they were no longer Younger Brother's. Until they were scarcely even eyes.

By the time the *Puagant* came swinging his crooked cane through the deepest pre-dawn dark, the child was already gone. His trip was not wasted, however, for by then the woman had begun to sweat. Symptom by symptom, she re-enacted the dying of her child. The Tracker sat twisting his hands while the *Puagant* did everything in his power to suck the disease away.

Again, death came with the sinking of the eyes. In the following breath, the Tracker felt his own soul tear free and leave him. He could have asked the *Puagant* to dispatch his spirit and retrieve it, but the old man was so wrung out from his ministrations he could barely stand, and the breaking dawn would drain what little power he had left. In any case, the Tracker was loath to have his suffering core brought home.

The sun hung directly overhead. After sitting for so long, he rose like a man still dreaming and set to work amassing her

things. Burden basket, water jug, bowls. The woven cradle, out-
grown but not discarded. Her hat, worked so neatly into the shape
of a beautiful breast. Every object was a testament to her industry, her skill. Winnowing trays, parching trays, treasure basket.
This last he didn't dare explore for fear he would come upon some
love gift from Younger Brother. It completed the pile, at the heart
of which lay his shrunken, beloved dead.

He brought a flaming pine limb, dropped it and backed away.
When the brush hut caught, the blaze was great. All who stood
witness backed away—all save the Tracker, who chose the most
direct and dangerous way to mark himself a mourner with the tra-
ditional singeing of hair. At length he turned to find the camp—
those who had not also fallen to the sickness—gathered behind
him. He met no eye as he passed among them, left their company
without a word.

Draped crossways over his bunk, his boot heels and the back of
his skull resting on the floor, Bendy feels this mildest of stretches
bring some relief to his weary back.

It's hard to say where he went wrong. True, he was overstep-
ping the mark by just being there—dropping in on the boss's
young wife while she worked alone through the night—but he
took pains not to spook her, keeping a fair distance between them
and, for the most part, keeping his eyes to himself. It was far from
difficult, there being plenty besides her strange little face to stare
at in that barn.

For a long moment after he stepped inside, he could scarcely
make sense of what he was seeing. He'd seen mounted antlers
before—deer, antelope, moose. A bear claw necklace, countless

lucky rabbit feet and tails. Even a grizzly head hanging high over a bar, so crudely stuffed its face had warped into a grimace more frightening than any it could've managed in life. Nothing, though, that had prepared him for that dark menagerie, the work of those bright red hands.

The air was heavy, hung not with the smell of animals so much as with that of their homes—nests and dens abandoned. Acrid, unnameable strains drifted above the musk. The base odour, a brackish undertow, seemed to emanate from beneath her workbench.

She was nervous of him at first, but her demeanour eased as she took in his awed response. "Did you—?" he stammered. "Are these yours?"

Pride brought her forward out of her collapsed posture—chin first, then chest. He thought he caught the edge of a smile.

We were fine, he thinks, stretching his arms out to lay the backs of his hands on the floor behind his head. We were getting along fine.

It had been her idea in the first place, him doing a wolf. He played the first scene that came to mind, evoking the rangy male he'd watched emerge from a river running wide and slow. Climbing inside memory, he assumed the dripping animal's form, planting his four paws, pausing for a moment before shaking himself shoulders to tail. She rewarded him with the briefest of smiles.

The back of his head and the rounds of both heels have grown warm—a shallow bone saucer and two matching cups collecting blood. Flexing up out of his flaccid arc, he rolls over onto his right side. The spaces between his left ribs expand as one ear and the outer rim of the corresponding boot meet plank.

"That's no use to me," she said coolly, as though the smile had never been. "I can hardly make one that's moving, let alone wet."

"Oh." He sat back in a human squat. "Right."

A second memory surfaced then, a dark balance to the clean renewal of the first. "Well, they're something to see when they're feeding." He was already looking inward by then, drawing the image down through trunk and limb. He dropped forward again onto his hands. "One time I rode through a valley the day after the sharpshooters had been through." He rounded his shoulders, getting the feel of a menacing hunch. "Buffalo carcasses as far as the eye could see. They'd taken the hides and left everything else to rot. Every one of those red mounds had a wolf on it, some of them had three or four." He lowered his head. "You wouldn't believe how loud they get, all of them tearing and snapping and growling at the same time. Sounds like a brush fire." He curled his lips back to bare his teeth, and, with a loud click, unhinged his lower jaw. Only then did he think to flick his eyes her way.

He wouldn't have thought she could get any paler than she already was. Wouldn't have dreamt a warm-blooded creature could turn the colour of midnight snow.

"Stop it." She was trembling.

By the time he'd resumed the shape of a man, she had the shaking under control.

"I've got work to do."

"Oh, okay. I'll be going, then."

"Yes."

Making for the door, he felt the glare of every false eye in the place.

25

ON OPENING NIGHT a late summer storm blew hard. The tent wept rain, roaring with every gust, while lanterns smoked and swung, wafting the fishy stink of whale oil. Camden got things started, running a frenetic course with his monkeys to whip up the crowd. When the moment was right, Pitch strode onto the scene and ushered the hairy fools on their way. Taking sole possession of the ring, he launched into his opening harangue. He had to bellow to be heard above the weather, but it was clear from the beginning that he had a way with words. That is, until the words began to have their way with him.

"Ladies and gentlemen, there are those who would brand this night's entertainment sinful." Pitch opened his eyes wide. "But I ask you, is a man's only respite from the hardscrabble, workaday world to be found in church?"

The crowd obliged him with a spray of laughter.

"God gave man dominion over the animals—witness the menagerie." He waved a hand in the general direction of the straw blind, the pathetic assembly of creatures that lay beyond the tent's back wall. The sight of Philomena's shrouded cage spurred him on. "Witness Mena, the amazing dog girl!"

Men whistled and bayed.

"Was not man made in God's image? How better, then, to glorify God than to bask in the splendour of the human corpus? See here." He stretched out an empty palm as though it held proof of the strike of a lifetime, a nugget the size of a cat's skull. He worked the fingers—crooking them one by one, wiggling the lot—then drew a loose question mark through the air with the thumb. "Miraculous!"

He was losing them. Bendy watched it happen from behind the blind—bottoms shifting on bales, hands floating up to fiddle with earlobes, collars, beards. It was a pattern he would come to know. Somewhere around the one-minute mark, an idea would sprout wings, lifting Pitch and his patter beyond the crowd's caring.

"Witness this very night," Pitch cried, "the heights this God-given body can reach. Feats of strength, of daring, of skill—performed by your humble ringmaster on the back of another of the Lord's creatures, the mighty horse!"

He paused, silence flowering. He'd forgotten himself entirely, lost his place not only in the monologue but in the sightlines of all those eyes. He stood rigid, blinking, as though shaken by the shoulder while out on a ramble in his sleep. Hecklers opened their mouths. Bendy counted them, seven sudden rents in the fabric of the crowd.

And then Camden ran in juggling, wearing a coat covered in birds. On his hat a brazen parrot parted its beak. "Shut up, blowhard!" it screeched, and the audience went wild.

Bendy came on after the clown had bled off some of the crowd's steam. Under Pitch's orders, Stanley had rigged him up a miniature stage—six tea crates lashed together and mounted on a spread of wheels, still sticky with a hasty coat of yellow paint. Hiss and spit of lamps above him, wooden echo below. He might as well have been naked in the hose and open vest Pitch had given him to wear. *Scarlet.* A colour he'd never laid hands on, let alone worn. He felt rare in it, raw.

He began with something simple, arching backwards to write with his body, a back-slanting capital P. Next he reached for his ankles and formed a narrow O. The audience was cool to him at first, unsure in the face of his wordless, shifting shape. He won them over by degrees. His human tree drew forth the gasps he'd hoped for. His waddling gull made the children squeal. By the time he became a cat—one foot stretched to the heavens while he licked his red tights clean—they adored him. In the glow of their regard, he became sensible of a spreading, penetrating warmth.

The true animals followed. The undersized bear let Pitch lead it about, placid as a moron child. The mountain lion fought the cageboy's chain, lunged and spat, but refused to chill the congregation with a scream. Saved for last, the dog girl put both beasts to shame.

"And now, ladies and gentlemen," Pitch bellowed, "I give you—Man's! Best! Friend!" Swinging the cage door open with a flourish, he greeted Philomena with a hearty, "Hello, girl!" Her cue to surge out of the shadows and begin joyfully licking his face.

Pitch lifted her down to heel at his side. He fixed a red leash to her glinting collar and paraded her before them, somehow stepping proud on her hands and knees. She rose up onto the balls of her feet when he loosed her and let her run, but kept like a good dog to all fours. Bounding to the verge of the ring, she sent the crowd recoiling with a snarl.

She fetched beautifully, driving her nose into the dirt, grasping Pitch's riding crop in her teeth, pausing to wag her hind end furiously to a chorus of whistles and hoots before wheeling and returning the prize. He made her sit. Lie down. Yip a mournful tune. Roll over and play dead, her dark, shapely limbs in the air. The closing trick was simple, brilliant. Pitch reached into his pocket for a biscuit. Philomena sat back on her heels and begged.

The audience ate up the dog-and-master act, but it was nothing to what would come next. Pitch was an unusual man on his own two feet. On horseback he became remarkable.

He entered at a trot. Without benefit of the yellow top hat, his head seemed unnaturally small, his hair greased to a shoe-black sheen. Knowing the worth of the mare's beauty, he made several plain circuits, letting the crowd fill their eyes with her before kicking into a canter and springing to a stand on her back. A cheer broke the crowd open wide. It wasn't the feat itself so much as the ease with which he managed it—as though a great transparent hand had descended to pluck him up by the scruff and set him squarely on his long bare feet.

The unseen hand held the ringmaster steady on one leg while supporting the other behind him like a rigid tail. From there it helped him safely to the ground, scooping him up the moment his toes met dirt to vault time and again over the pretty grey. Bendy marvelled at the man, but kept a portion of his admiration for the mount. Through everything, Belle held her canter, reliable as the sun.

Pitch dropped back into the saddle and, as though the great hand were twisting him like a cork stopper, began turning circles on his seat, his heels just clearing the tips of Belle's ears. He rode facing her tail for a time, then slipped down her inward flank and hung there Comanche-style, hidden from view. When next he stood on the grey mare's back, the hand flung him heels over head in a series of backward somersaults. Women screamed. For a finale, the invisible fingers guided him headfirst through a maze

of hoops held aloft by his brother the clown—the last of them
dancing with flames.

Pitch knew enough to end the show on a high note, standing
firm on Belle's rosin-coated back with his arms open wide and
his big mouth shut. The audience roared for him as he rode his
final circuit, forgetting for the moment the lack of tumblers and
scantily clad girls, the sad menagerie. They were still applauding
full bore as he rode behind the straw blind and out the tent's
back flap.

Bendy slipped out in time to watch him pull up short before the
mountain lion's cage. The storm had scudded on, leaving the
world sodden, the firmament clear. Belle stood steady, blowing
hard. Pitch slid to terra firma, becoming a trembling, sweat-
drenched thing. His bare soles sank in the mud. He'd removed
his tailcoat before the ride, performing in waistcoat and
trousers—the golden plush gone dark in cat-whisker patterns
about his crotch, sagging half moons beneath his arms.

The cageboy approached and caught hold of Belle's reins,
handing over the ugly top hat as though in trade. Pitch returned it
to his head without a word. Belle knew the drill. She followed
Stanley along the train of cages to its end, disappearing after him
into the stable he'd knocked together out of clapboard and sailcloth the night before.

Pitch flipped a tin feed pail and lowered himself to sit. "Fetch
me my coat." He pointed to where the garment hung from the
latch of the lioness's cage. A deeper, dirtier shade than the animal
on the far side of the bars, the coat was damp with rain, ripe with
Pitch's stink. Bendy held his breath and plucked it down, delivered it to the ringmaster's lap.

Pitch cradled the tailcoat loosely, one hand rifling its folds.
Retrieving pipe and pouch, he stuffed the bowl, struck a match

and sucked up a mouthful of fruity smoke. He didn't offer Bendy a pull—nor did he offer comment on the boy's debut. Hunched on his pail, he sucked and sighed as though he was alone.

"Mind if I get a little practice in later?" Bendy said finally. "Riding, I mean."

Pitch glanced up, smoke driven from his lips in a grey rush. "Thought you said you could ride."

"I can." Bendy toed a shallow puddle. "I want to get the feel of the ring."

Pitch let his gaze slip, the strain of keeping it tilted too great. "Not on Belle."

"No, sir. I thought I'd try the gelding."

The ringmaster eased himself up from the pail. "Come back when the crowd's cleared," he said around the pipe's stem. Turning side-on to the space between two cages, he sidled through the gap and was gone.

Bendy had intended only a short stroll—just long enough to let the last of the gawkers vacate the tent and its charred surrounds—but he found his limbs craved the plain swing of the human gait. He followed Second to where Montgomery angled off, and turned right on California, headed for the docks. Every dull heave of dune, every scrubby front garden, every salt-rotten whiff soothed his senses. At the foot of Central Wharf he found himself reluctant to turn back.

The grounds were lifeless by the time he returned. A lantern had been left hissing at the mouth of the corridor that ran between the tent's back wall and the train of cages—a beacon to those who belonged, a deterrent to those who would do mischief under cover of dark. Realizing he was one of the former, Bendy felt himself smile. He lifted down the lantern and entered the makeshift arcade. Above him, a strip of night. To his right, a pale expanse of canvas, to his left, the hunkering train. The cages were blind and silent now, their bars fitted over with panels of painted wood. Each bore an illustration, an ill-conceived rendering of whatever lay breathing within. Bendy paused before each crude portrait, holding the lantern close.

The bear was more grizzly than black, humped over a mess of unidentifiable gore. One foreleg twice the length of the other, snout flattened around a rat's nest of teeth. The mountain lion was worse, stretched all out of proportion along an elephant-grey ridge, its head a fat house cat's under coyote-sized ears.

The birds came nearer the mark, perhaps copied from the plates of a book. Inside, Bendy knew, fewer than half the wire birdcages hung. He'd learned the night before—shortly after learning he was to bunk in with Camden—that the clown routinely carried his favourites back with him to the hotel. Room number nine was already crowded by the time Bendy arrived, the birds tucked into themselves on various perches, Camden splayed like a tide-abandoned starfish across the bed. Bendy took the armchair, disturbing the fat macaw that clung to its back.

Last and perhaps strangest, the painted monkeys hung from ropy, lime-green vines. A single face repeated atop various configurations of limbs, the moony grin of an infant dosed with rum.

At the gallery's end, a second lantern spilled light down the stable's wall. If Stanley was within, he made no sound. Drawing open the door, Bendy held his light down by his thigh and made low, friendly noises in his throat.

Not one of them flinched. Not a rustle, not a single hoof stirring the straw. They watched him, mules and horses, motionless in their pinched stalls. For a moment he was puzzled, but then it came to him—he couldn't spook these animals if he tried. To a one, they'd dulled their senses to the wuffing of a bear, the shrieks of the deep jungle, even the feline musk of the ancient foe. These mules pushed through frenzied crowds as a matter of course. Belle and the brown gelding—and maybe even the old roan in her day—had learned to run rock-steady circles while no end of human nonsense took place on their backs.

Bendy lifted his lantern, fixing on the gelding's stall. By habit, he found himself treading softly, easing back the latch, murmuring as he took down a bridle and slipped it over the long brown nose.

The horse came quietly, Bendy leading him through the back flap and round the blind, past the draped darkness of Philomena's cage. Still no sign of the cageboy. Was it possible he'd sloped off somewhere, leaving his charges without a guard?

Bendy strode to the centre of the ring and set the lantern down on the beaten earth. He took a moment to stroke the gelding about the withers and neck, then tucked his boot into the near stirrup iron and rose.

Three trotted circuits and the brown horse broke into a canter on his own. Bendy let him have his head. Another turn of the circle and he felt himself on the brink of a gravitational trance. It shattered at the sound of her voice.

"So far, so good."

He hauled back on the reins harder than necessary, but the gelding took it, skidding neatly to a stop. Philomena stood poised on one of the bale seats, a furred creature at the limit of the lantern's reach. It hadn't occurred to him that she'd spend the night in her cage. But now that he thought about it, what alternative did she have? To step blithely through the front door of the Gillespie Hotel clad in nothing but her own glossy hair? Or worse, to belie her canine character by showing up there in a dress?

"Don't quit on my account."

She hopped lightly, gracefully to the adjacent seat, then the next, the next—a child crossing a creek on stones. Or not a child. Something fleeter, more certain of its feet. She breezed past him where he sat motionless astride his mount, bounding full circle, bale to bale. His head swivelled, eyes dogging her as they would a flash of something feral, thrill and misgiving made one. She closed in on her starting point, surpassed it and carried on, landing in moments on the bale nearest his suspended heel.

She gazed up at him, obscure in the melded shadow he and the gelding cast, wearing nothing but her own thick pelt.

"Or do," she said.

"Do what?"

"Do quit." Her teeth came clear in a smile. "On my account."

He was down on his own two feet before he knew it. When he glanced about for somewhere to tether the horse, she caught hold of his hand and said, "He'll stay put."

She pulled him after her, not looking back. Her grip was strong, her palm hairless, smooth. Her nails were pointy. They dug in a little, quickening his pulse.

As they drew up alongside her cage, she brought her face in close. "He's in there."

Bendy felt something tear free inside his chest cavity and rise. "He?"

She mouthed the next word. *Stanley.* The heart in Bendy's mouth beat hard.

"Don't worry." She made a bottle of her fist, tipped a thumb to her lips. "He'll be out for hours."

"But—" Bendy looked past her, contemplating escape.

"I don't invite him." She let his comprehension build for a moment before adding, "I'm inviting you."

All notion of fleeing left him. Together they passed the cloaked form of her cage, padding onward to the block of bales. She led him behind it—not, as he'd imagined, through the back flap to the rest of the world, but past it, round the far corner of the blind. There she dropped to all fours, fit her fingers around one of the bottom bales and, as though it were an oversized, golden brick, wrestled it out of the wall. In its place, the black promise of a tunnel. On her belly now, Philomena wriggled inside. In moments Bendy was faced with the twin swishing tails of her legs, the bald calluses of her upturned soles.

He followed. Never mind the risk, the solid fact of the cageboy— sunk in a stupor, but still mere yards away. The tunnel was close about Bendy's shoulders, heady with her scent. He squirmed forward the full length of his body before the dark opened into the shape of a den. Her hand came out to meet him. He clutched it and reached for more.

26

DORRIE DREAMS:

Dawn, and beneath me the sage clump quivers with life. The night was chill, but perhaps the child's fold of hillside held some of the day's heat. Doubtful. This high up, the changing time comes early, cold rising from the earth itself.

Her thirst must be terrible—how many dry days before her flock was freed, first from their camp, then from this waking world? Hunger too. This may be what's woken her, smoke wafting from the camp below, the smell of food being ruined over fire. Not that I'd refuse a scrap if offered. In the night my own hunger opened to swallow me whole. I can feel it in my wing tips, little flight left there, perhaps a mile or two more.

Who knows if the child can smell anything, wedged beneath that reeking bush. I have yet to catch a whiff of her—not her sweet, bruised flesh, not the deep, seeping scratches on her limbs. Not even her fear.

Dawn colours the scene below us in hopeful light, the bodies rosy now, shining with dew. The dog man's pack is rising, having filled their bellies with the usual human mess. Why make a paste of desiccated corn when it's so much sweeter straight from the ear? Their meat is worse, pig that tastes as though they found it floating in the reeds of a salt marsh.

Sated, they move again among the dead.

A whisper of paws on rock, and I look down on the grizzled back and black-tipped tail of a grey fox. Tree-climber, the sinewy bridge between cat and canine, a known threat to nestlings, but nothing serious to the fully fledged. A mocking caw, perhaps even a dive at the first click of those retractable claws—only, in my torpor, I begin to mistrust my wings. Hold still, then. Dead still, until the wave of its tail is gone.

See how the humans cache their kill, how they bow and scrape, swinging their heavy tools. Soon shallow patches have been scratched, and the dragging of bodies begins. Like weasels hoarding mice, they pile dead upon dead, dusting them with not enough earth to dissuade a fox kit. Some do even less, dumping corpses in gullies and concealing them with clumps of grass.

Willing the child to stay put, I stretch my hollow wings and drop, let the slope fall away before me in an easy glide. At grass level, I wing along deep and easy, skimming low over the waving green, mounting only when I reach the trampled bed where the females fell.

She is still there, one of half a dozen left. A male with hair the colour of a yellow martin stoops to take hold of her bloated ankles. He hauls her into the scrub, covering her with several branches in waning leaf. To the last, her hair calls the eye. A black, spreading wedge, like tail feathers landing or lifting off. It points the way to the rest of her, until the male kicks dirt over it and stamps it down.

27

A PAIR OF SHAPES dogs Dorrie's waking—one curved and gliding, the other triangular, terribly still.

She's been dozing since Bendy left. Any moment now the breakfast bell will sound, and if she fails to respond to its pealing, chances are good one of the children will be sent to knock endlessly at her door. Still she doesn't stir. Her body floats on its fatigue, a buoyancy she's reluctant to forsake, having experienced it only once before.

She'd been a member of the household for close to a year when Hammer announced there was to be a family outing: a picnic on the shores of the Great Salt Lake. Dorrie sat with the children in the buckboard, Lal taking the reins with Sister Ruth at his side. The first and third wives rode up ahead, wedged into the buggy with the man of the house. Dorrie's stepchildren fixed their ten eyes on the passing country while she fastened hers to the cart's jumping floor.

Lake seemed entirely the wrong word. Climbing down stiffly over the tailgate, Dorrie thought, *Sea.* Not that she'd ever laid eyes on one, or ever cared to. Lake, sea—whatever she called it, the great body before her was another gaping expanse to be endured. She made herself useful, laying the first of four blankets alongside a brine-encrusted thicket, so at least there would be something at her back.

Mother Hammer had put up enough sandwiches to feed a horde, and she made it clear she wasn't carrying any home only to find they'd spoiled in the heat. Her pickled cucumbers snapped audibly between the teeth, shooting vinegar into the sinuses. The children were used to them, knew to hold their breath and start gnawing, wary and persistent as mice.

Last came a mound of oaten biscuits, buttery and sweet. Everyone but Hammer and Sister Thankful ate their share. While Mother Hammer was busy brushing crumbs from Baby Joe's cheeks, her husband took the opportunity to rise from where he lay propped on one elbow and offer a hand up to his favourite. The pair of them set off together arm in arm to, as Hammer called back over his shoulder, *take the air.* Leaving the rest of them to take the waters.

Mother Hammer herded Dorrie, Ruth and the two girls into a thin cover of trees. Dorrie changed hurriedly, back hunched to the others, into a drooping costume that consisted of a linsey-woolsey dress and matching pantalets. A furtive glance showed Ruth undressing methodically, looking only to herself, while Mother Hammer fussed over Josepha and Josephine. Trudging down to the shore, Dorrie brought up the end of a uniformed female string. Lal and the three Josephs met them at the water's edge, clad in overalls and nothing else. Dorrie averted her eyes.

Mother Hammer kept Baby Joe and the girls close, but allowed Joseph and Joe to wade out after Lal. The eldest reached waist depth and plunged, striking out clumsily, kicking spume into his brothers' eyes. Joe let out a yelp.

"Lal!" Mother Hammer barked, and he stood up dripping, hands at his sides.

Ruth got no further than the shallows before she sat down, water creeping up the fibres of her bodice, darkening her breasts. Dorrie moved off on her own, not such a distance as to attract Mother Hammer's attention but far enough to escape the family's waves.

When no one called her back, she waded out a little more, turned to face the comforting curve of shore and dropped to her knees. Water to her neck. Until that moment, the creek that cut across the far acreage of the Burr farm had provided the only natural immersion she'd known. The water there only ever reached hip deep, but even so, you could feel the drag of it, its desire to suck a body down. There in the glassy lake, even the knit costume was weightless, unequal to the saline lift.

It required so little faith, such minimal movement, to let her knees slide out from beneath her. She tilted back in head-wetting surrender and found herself on the surface, trapped between planes. The sky yawned, so she drew down her eyelids against it. Her hands burned, but it was little enough to endure. Her ears knew only lapping. She could hear nothing of the others, and after a time she began to imagine they had forgotten her and returned to the ranch. And then to imagine that she too had forgotten, had abandoned her only body, setting it adrift.

That afternoon it was Sister Ruth's light touch on her floating arm that brought her back. This morning it is the angry, clanging bell.

Packed full of porridge and molasses, fried eggs and fatty ham, Erastus feels even lower to the ground than usual as he makes his way across the yard. It's as though Ursula has weighted him down on purpose, and not just with breakfast—the grace she delivered wound on and on while the meal lost steam. He listened long enough to determine the matter was the usual one, then stopped his ears with thoughts of the day ahead. Not that there was much to think of. A ride, certainly, but where? On his own he'd have to stick to the property. He could always look in on the Tracker, maybe beat the bushes for a male grouse to match the hen they bagged last year.

Hammer kicks a small stone from his path, pausing to watch it roll further than expected, its progress becoming unclear. Beyond, sunlight glances off the water in a trough, a brilliance evocative of Ursula's bowed head.

He was never a believer the way his first wife is. Ursula is steeped not only in feeling but in knowledge, well versed in Church history, Scripture and law. Weekly Meeting is more than enough learning for Erastus. Fiery sermons are best; when the topic is the need for continued vigilance, he's less likely to nod off.

Faced with the stable, he finds himself reluctant to go indoors. Instead, he veers left, leans into the corral gate and takes in the wash of the wide-open valley, letting his thoughts run.

It's always been the living religion for him, that great mass of cried-down people choking the road. Of course, one of those people—the tall, bonneted one he made sure not to lose sight of—mattered more than all the others combined.

He may have come to the new religion via things temporal, but as it turned out, he was fully prepared to believe. The Hammers were Baptists, his father in church when it suited him, his mother fond of face-down prayer, a gentle begging delivered nightly to the floorboards. From what Erastus could make out, the new religion offered all the benefits of the old—baptism to wash a soul clean, the theatre of tongues and healing, the happy threat of end times—and more besides. A bible story whose violent and miraculous chapters unfolded right here, rather than in some distant, sand-swept land. A vast, unconquerable kingdom, not only later, in the great beyond, but now. Best of all, a living prophet in direct communication with God.

Brother Joseph was a shepherd no man could fail to love—and yet, much as Erastus mourned the Prophet's passing, there was a part of him that leapt heavenward at the news. It wasn't long before that portion knew its reward. Ursula was more beautiful than ever in her grief—eyes cloudy and crimson-rimmed, hair stark under a bonnet of iron black. Having refused him countless times, she stared out from beneath its overhang and said yes.

Along with their marriage came the reign of President Young—a leader less winning, to be sure, but in the end no less loved. He may not have drawn gazes in those early days the way Brother Joseph did, but he draws them now, by God. The Lion of the Lord earned his place at the head of things. Joseph talked to angels; Brigham built Deseret—not one of many settlements the Saints would be driven from, but their own Zion, a desert fortress ringed round with stone. Land where it was said no white man could prosper—and look, twenty years on and Erastus Hammer stands amid orchards, pasture and stock. He takes satisfaction in the idea, squinting out over the fog and dazzle of his fields, then turning to survey his yard.

By habit, his eyes seek Ursula first. He finds her on the move past the clamouring garden—blue dress beneath a snow-bright apron, a lesser drift marking the large knot of her hair. Stooping to take up what must be a basket, she puts him in mind of the bright breakers he endured when, still a bachelor, he crossed the wide Atlantic on a mission to Wales. He converted precious few. Those he did manage to win came for the promise of acres as much as for the glory of God.

Movement shifts his gaze. A flush of reddish brown glimpsed among the mulberries—Ruth's undeniable hue. It runs like paint through the veins of every child he put inside her; doubtless the one she carries now will emerge with the same chestnut hair and gleaming, wooden eyes. What of his own colouring? Not one of them sprouted a thatch of black bristle in tribute to him—least of all his eldest, so like Ursula it troubles Erastus to look at him. What would he call a little Hammer if he got one—Erastus Junior? Ezra? No sense wondering. Naming is Ursula's privilege. Her own she called Lalovee after Erastus's father—a flowery name for a flint-hard unbeliever she never met. Erastus shortened the hated name the first time he uttered it, but the missing syllables still sound in his head.

After Lal—almost a decade after—Ursula began dubbing Ruth's issue, assigning each new arrival a variation on the only name she'd ever really loved. She did Erastus a favour in the end. On the rare occasion when he finds himself wanting to address one of the eerie brood, he possesses a fair notion of where to begin.

And soon there will be another. Ruth must be four months along now, the first of which Erastus spent waiting for Thankful to unlock her chamber door. It was scarcely fair. He wouldn't have been compelled to bed his second wife if the third would bear him a child. Thankful has been barren these six years, though—what are the chances she'll manage it now? Truth be told, Erastus is just as glad. He'd be expected to keep his hands off her until the thing was born, and anyhow, the notion of Thankful with a baby is all wrong. Like trusting a fox to carry a downy new chick in its mouth.

Lying with Ruth would've been crime enough in Thankful's eyes, but Erastus had gone further, allowing himself to enjoy it. He sighed as he descended into his second wife's warmth. Digging his chin into the depths of her hair, he couldn't help but moan. On the far side of the wall, the glass Thankful had been listening through splintered musically against the floor.

Still, it was nothing to the dry spell he'd endured when he'd dared to bring Eudora home. Thankful had gone wild. What did he want with a fourth wife—wasn't she a different woman for him every night? She knew he had two wives already when she accepted him, but she never signed on to be one in a long line. She must've been mad to marry him—a Mormon missionary! She'd pack her bags, go back to Chicago, back to the stage. He told her over and over, he'd married the girl for her hands alone, for what those hands could do.

"You think I'd look twice at a wreck like that when I've got a creature like you back home?"

"So why did you bed her?!"

"I had to, Thankful, a man has to stake his claim. It was no pleasure to me." And then the line that punctured her defences, the tip of the blade with which he would carve his way back in. "It was all I could do to finish up in there—a man'd have more fun at a knothole."

As luck would have it, he had no need of a lie. It really had taken him an age to finish. He'd felt the girl's flesh cool beneath him. No part of her, not even her pulse, had answered him back.

Erastus shudders to think of it, shakes the memory off. How long has he been standing here, back to the rails? He pivots, the door to Eudora's workshop sliding past with a leaden glint. Little chance of spotting her. She'll either be fast asleep or working, breathing the close, chokehold air of her art. In her own twitchy way, she may be the most contented of his wives. He holds to this idea a moment longer, then pushes back from the gate and makes for the stable door.

※

"Two more, please, Lal." Ruth's face in the crack of the silkhouse door, radiant, then gone. She always closes it quickly, afraid some small predator might be lurking in the weeds.

Lal hefts the two closest sacks, each giving a green sigh in response to leaving the ground. She opens the door to him and he sidles in fast, knowing this will please her. The racket is considerable, each worm-mouth growing wider, greedier, by the day.

"Are they from this end?" she asks, just loud enough to be heard. "Been shaded a good while?"

He matches her hush. "Yes, ma'am."

"Just there is fine." She points, and he sets the sacks down where she wants them, imagining the bulges of his bare forearms reflected in her eyes. When he glances up, her gaze is nowhere near him. A clean scent reaches him from the floor, the herb that is the smell of his mother's linen. He remembers creeping into her room and sliding open the middle dresser drawer, laying his cheek to the crisp whiteness therein. Back when he was stupid and small.

He searches for something to say—anything to draw out his stay in the close little house—but his head is empty, washed bare by the caterpillars' sound. Then, just as she looks round as though to ask *Are you still here?*, it comes to him.

"Why?"

She dips both hands into a sack, withdrawing them full. "Why what?"

He gestures to the sacks. "Why shade?"

"The leaves turn poison if they get too hot." She spreads her load over a tray.

"Oh." His mouth is empty, the brain above it blank. With the arrival of fresh food, the volume in the place rises. He feels himself take a step, then another—only two, but it's a small room crowded with shelves. He's beside her now, training his gaze on the bed of worms before them. The big green dress has gone dark beneath her arms. Her scent obliterates that of the flowers underfoot, painfully rich, like three Ruths distilled into one. He inhales hard. For one long, unreal second, he fears he will faint.

He steadies himself by plucking up one of her worms.

Ruth touches them all the time—he's watched her bestow light, loving strokes, occasionally taking one of them up into her palm— but never like this. Never, as Lal now finds himself doing, pinching one of them hard about its middle and watching it writhe.

The worm is the colour of flesh no longer living, the colour a finger might turn if he were to separate it from the quick force of a hand. He fights the urge to sniff it, see if it smells secretly of decay.

"Lal!" Ruth's voice is one he's never heard, panicky, high. "LAL!"

He blinks. "What?"

"You're killing it!" Her hands close around his bent arm, tugging at his biceps. A sensation he must prolong.

"No, I'm not." He resists her just enough.

"It's suffocating!" she cries, yanking now. "They breathe through their sides!"

"Oh." Lal knows he should set her precious worm down gently, contritely, but he doesn't want to. Her grip on his arm is beginning to pain him. She's staring as though he's some kind of demon, and maybe, just maybe, he is.

He flicks the thing like the burnt stub of a smoke. It lands amid its siblings with a nasty bounce. Ruth lets go. The look on her face is bad enough, but it's about to get worse. It seems he's upset more than just the one silkworm. He has, in fact, managed to terrorize them all.

One by one, and then tray by tray, the worms contract, drawing into themselves as though injured, swelling their ugly heads. Lal could show them what injured looks like. In his mind's eye he's all boots and knuckles, laying waste.

"Get out." Another voice he's never heard, this one terribly cold. He shifts on his feet, his mouth working a mute apology.

"Get out, Lal. Now."

After the passing of his woman and child, the Tracker left his camp on the Santa Clara River and travelled north. It was as good a direction as any, being the one he faced when he turned his back on the pyre that had been his home.

It seemed every Indian camp he skirted was dying, the People sick or starving, two men to every woman, scarcely a child or an elder to be seen. Many had given up on the land and moved to form shabby gatherings at the verges of Mormonee towns.

Each white settlement or solitary farm sat on country denuded by stock. Foreign cheatgrass and toadflax drove thick fingers into the surrounding grasslands, extending the damage done by the great herds. Flocks of flint-voiced English starlings darkened the sky. Here and there the mottled flash of a hunting house cat, the grey squirt of a Norway rat.

The Tracker passed scene after scene, watching, walking. There was a lightness to this new life—hunting when there was game to be had, now and then stacking crates for a soft-hearted shopkeeper or clearing brush on an expanding farm. He was careful to eat and sleep alone. For company he took to paging through the picture book every night, entwining the journey it recounted with his own.

He thought of settling. From time to time he would come upon some isolated spot that offered water, shelter and sign of game, and he would set to work gathering brush and cutting poles. It didn't matter how well he structured the hut; once complete, it would seem deserted—even when he crawled inside. Especially then. A day, or three, or five later, he would abandon it to follow the northward pull.

By the time he'd moved through Pahvant territory into lands inhabited by the Gosiute, he had lost both spring and summer to his wandering. He had no shelter, no cache, not so much as a single rabbit-skin blanket to lay down between his body and the slow, sleeping death that comes of cold. He could have joined a camp—in times of scarcity a good hunter would not be turned away. It was his best chance for survival, and yet, when he happened upon a large gathering, he held himself apart.

The Gosiute had come together just as his own people did, to harvest piñon along a series of slopes that had yet to yield to the axes of the Mormonee. And like his own people did on such occasions, they were dancing, arms linked in a great rotating wheel.

The Tracker took cover in the buggy scrub at the clearing's southern verge. The song was one he didn't know, the tongue several waves stranger than that which he'd overheard among the Pahvant. Still, he strained his ears, told himself he understood.

With a shift of the circle, a young woman's profile came into view. The Tracker felt his heart contract. It wasn't a case of resemblance—nothing so forgivable as that—but of beauty, pure and keen. Gazing at that face, turned full on to him now, the Tracker felt desire flare in his hollow insides.

She came to him for the first time then, his whirlwind wife, cool and drilling in the runnel of his spine. He knew her instantly, and the knowing nearly choked him with grief. Whether it was jealousy or something finer that had summoned her, the Tracker couldn't know. Sorrow, perhaps, or rage at having been forgotten, even for a moment, when she was barely six moons gone. He reached behind him with both hands to comfort her. Felt a shock like mountain runoff and then she was gone.

Gone also was the dancer's face when he opened his eyes, the circle having taken another turn. He set off before the fine features could come around again.

Some time after the whirlwind wife had made herself known to him—long enough that the nights had grown so cold as to remind him of her touch—the Tracker was making his way through a stand of young poplars when a sound brought him to stillness. The blowing of a recently tethered horse. He caught sight of it through the bony trees, a beast taller and blacker than any he had seen. It scented him and swung its great anvil of a head his way.

He gave it a wide berth, taking the gentle slope to the river's edge. There, above the water's low talk, he heard the horse's other half—a loaded tread, the rustle and crack of a white man on the hunt. Upstream a little way, in the shallows off the far bank, a blacktail stag had heard it too. It lifted its wet muzzle, lengthening up through its white throat and switching ears, out through its antlers' branched extremes. Every one of its fibres alight. An animal making ready to die.

The Tracker took a soundless step. Two, three more and he caught sight of the white man—a sun-riven profile beneath a hat's broad rim, eye squinting hard in its web of creases, sighting along a rifle's gleam.

There is no explaining to himself or any other what the Tracker did next. At that distance there was no way for him to know how skewed the hunter's aim was, how far the ball would go wide. Still, he slipped his rifle from his shoulder, aimed and loosed the ball, echoing the white man's wasted shot. The buck seemed to leap a little, then toppled to colour the river with its blood.

The white man's face buckled in an expression of disbelieving joy, then sagged as he took in the meaning of the doubled report. He looked about him slowly, as though he feared the second, unseen hunter now held human quarry in his sights. The Tracker had no earthly reason to approach with his gun slung over his shoulder and both hands where the hunter could see them. And yet he did.

Later, when the two of them sat facing one another across a dying fire—each with blood under his nails and a portion of the buck's haunch in his belly—the white man looked down at his breastbone and spoke. "It's my eyes. Been going this past couple of years. I used to be able to hit anything, you name it, a sparrow on the wing."

The Tracker understood enough. He held his tongue until the white man looked up. Then, laying a hand to his heart, he surprised himself again. "Tracker," he said.

"Is that so." The face buckled once more, this time with the force of a smile.

Hammer won't wake. Even if he did, Thankful would simply tell him she's making rosewater. Men know nothing of a woman's toilet. And anyway, he's well and truly gone, drumming the mattress with both heels, in the grip of his night's first dream.

She turns on her chair to face the mirror, the vanity's crowded top. A forest of tiny bottles and pots. Near the back, a fat pewter cup holds brushes—some fluffy, dusted with powder, others pointed as a mouse's tail. She closes her fist around the entire bundle, lifts and sets them aside. Taking up her nail scissors, she works the tip of the bottom blade into the seam of a plump sachet.

A moth, meaty and dull, collides with her lamp's chimney yet again.

Having cut through several stitches, she folds the pink satin back and upends the sachet over the heavy cup, working contents from casing. Once the cup's bottom is covered, she bends to take up her bed bottle from the floor.

Mother Hammer deigned to take notice of her tonight, pausing in her miserly larder count to find fault. "A bed bottle in May? Have you no blood in your veins?"

Thankful cradled the earthenware bottle to her breast. "Best ask Mr. Hammer." Such a treat to see those blue eyes twitch.

The cork gives her a little trouble, but comes loose with a low pop in the end. She tilts bottle to cup and smiles in the resulting scented steam. The moth, getting wind, moves off.

While her infusion steeps, Thankful takes up needle and thread and sews the sachet closed. A little limp, but it'll do. Next time she'll have to pick out the entire seam and turn it down. Such a clever trick. Not Thankful's invention, but she feels a surge of sly pride all the same.

Charlotte de Courcey was a woman of experience. Little wonder she handled knowing roles like Cleopatra and Lady Macbeth with such sensuous ease. Thankful kept her ears wide open when the house lead was dispensing advice. *House of Anjou. Tell them Miss de Courcey sent you.*

It was months before Thankful worked up sufficient courage to turn down the lane that would take her there. She was greeted, halted in fact, at the door, but Charlotte's name worked as promised, its syllables the teeth of a key. The shop was more than a marvel—it was an education. Notwithstanding her experience in the theatre, she'd had little idea of the costumes women might assume.

She would come to know the apothecary aspect of Anjou's perhaps a year later, the first time she felt the need. They were terribly helpful, terribly discreet. Her final visit to the little shop fell on the morning of the day she was to leave Chicago at Hammer's side. Monsieur Anjou himself came up with the solution. *It is usual for a lady to receive parcels from the city, is it not?* He made up a dozen sachets to get Thankful started, and he hasn't failed her since.

The first sip carries an initial hint of rose—like apple, if there existed a variety that was all scent and no flesh. The second taste is keener, its small-leafed source the business of the brew. Mint but wilder, reduced to a woody bite. Lowering the cup to draw breath, Thankful steels herself against the coming nauseous swell. A shred of petal clings wetly to her lip. The moth keeps its distance, thudding up the wall.

28

BENDY AND PHILOMENA were together fifteen times. He kept count. Once for every year he'd been alive.

The first time he was helpless. He'd been privy to enough hard talk to know he'd be allowed—expected, even—to suckle. Also that a triangular pelt would mark the spot. Not much use with a girl whose every mound and crevice presented fur. Philomena took over, parting the hair that hid her nipples, guiding him with a palm at the back of his skull. She found his britches buttons with ease. Released and maneuvered him in all that dark.

Fifteen times. Not every night. The cageboy always drank, but not always enough to put out the light in his head. More than once Bendy turned down the cage corridor with a spring in his step only to come upon Stanley dull-eyed and staggering.

Once, on a night livid with moonlight, he was partway along the corridor before he spotted the cageboy down the far end. Stanley's back was turned. He was sitting cross-legged in the muck outside the stable door, rocking side to side as though nursing something in his lap. After a time he curved down over whatever it was and began a concentrated struggle. Bendy stood watching, unsure. Should he back out the way he came? Or say something—*Evening, Stanley?* Or creep up and peek over the cageboy's shoulder, see what poor creature he'd gotten hold of, and whether or not it still stood a chance.

A flush of pity made him bold. He took several steps before a certain inward-delving gesture of the cageboy's brought him up short. In the following instant Bendy located the movement's meaning in his own limbs. The creature in Stanley's lap was nothing more or less than his own foot. He was bent on forcing it beyond its limits, on lifting and hooking it behind his head.

The curse Stanley let escape brought Bendy to his senses. To spy on a man engaged in an act so personal, so utterly hopeless, was wrong—more to the point, it was dangerous. He dropped to his belly and rolled out of the moonlit strip, into the shadow beneath the mountain lion's cage.

He could have kept on rolling out into the open, but he found himself arrested by the idea of what lay overhead. He could smell the big cat loud and clear—her scat on the planks above him, her urine in the earth beneath his back. He strained his ears to catch a shifting of haunches, a scraping of claws. Nothing.

Then Stanley swore again, and Bendy rolled, two further revolutions, out onto the charred grounds. Ash in his clothing, his hair. No Philomena tonight. He could go through with his nightly charade—lead the gelding into the ring and practise riding bareback, maybe try out a few tricks—but somehow he hadn't the heart. He lay with his eyes closed for a moment, refusing to look up at the night sky. Then rose and slipped quietly away.

There were times—three times, though he did his best not to count—when Bendy arrived to find the corridor empty. When he threw back the tent flap and helped the brown horse inside, only to be greeted by noises from beneath the plum-coloured cloth. A chorus of groans. All of them Stanley's, as near as Bendy could tell, but it didn't stop him seeing Philomena—on her back, on all fours—in his mind's bloody eye. Those nights he turned the gelding round and led him back, unexercised, to his stall.

Then there were the times when the cageboy was exactly where he ought to be—dead to the world on the stable floor, or on the straw pile in Philomena's cage—and something else got in their way. Pitch getting a second wind and showing up to check on Bendy's progress, talking a blue streak of pointers complete with the inevitable lengthy asides. Or Camden, struck with a fresh idea, hammering together little carts to be drawn by parakeets, monkeys swarming about him like children, climbing the curve of his spine.

Still and all, a month of nights had passed since the show first rolled into town, and Bendy had lain with Philomena for half of them. Always in the den at the heart of the straw blind. Always in silence. A sharp suck of air in place of a cry. Her soft, insistent panting in his ear.

He soon came to understand that the fur did not, as he'd first imagined, render any given part of her much like any other. On the contrary, Philomena's coat was all variation. It was long and slippery over her head, thin at her wrists, woolly in the cleft of her buttocks and between her thighs. Her face fur was soft, though her eyebrows bristled like any woman's. Finest of all was the hair that flowed south in the valley of her spine. Neck to tailbone, a thumb's-width ribbon of silk.

She smelled of good meat cooking. A joint in the oven, a chop in the pan. She smelled of salt. A little—he couldn't help grinning whenever he caught a whiff—of cat.

Fifteen times.

The last of which fell on a night when Stanley woke with a start, possessed of a terrible thirst. He bellowed for her, "MENA!"

and when she didn't appear, he kicked open the cage door and dropped to the ground. He was fast for one so bleary. He came lurching round the corner of the blind as Bendy was scrambling to his feet and Philomena's head was beginning to emerge.

A body can only bend so far before breaking, even the rubbery corpus of a freak. Stanley came at him bare handed to begin. Then, when Bendy was down and gasping, blind with his own blood, when Philomena had torn away into the night, loping a desperate track to the Gillespie Hotel in search of help, the cageboy staggered off to find a weapon. He was back in moments with a large wooden wedge, yanked from beneath the cage's wheel.

Swinging the block on its rope handle, he broke Bendy's collarbone, four of his ribs and the thinner of the two bones in his right forearm—they heard that one go. He was doing his best to ruin both legs when his uncle hauled him off. Camden had a good hold, Stanley's arms a thick bow at his back, his head drawn back by the hair. When Pitch doused his son with the contents of a water pail, the offspray caught Bendy in the face and helped him see. Clown and cageboy. Ringmaster. Dog girl nowhere to be found. He scuttled backwards on his behind, head singing, chest a bright butterfly of pain.

"Get off me!" Stanley lashed out behind him with his boot heels, but Camden was quick on his feet. "Get off!" He bucked and wrenched, and, giving up on words, let out a bellow devoid of sense.

The ringmaster watched Bendy struggle to his feet. "I'd be going if I were you."

"Going?" Bendy dropped a tooth with the word.

Pitch nodded. "Gone."

—

Bendy never knew how long Camden Pitch kept hold of his nephew—only that it was long enough for him to make a delirious getaway down Kearny Street to the plaza, spot a hollow beneath a watering trough and hide himself away.

Boots came and went, but none of them were Stanley's. With dawn an hour off, Bendy decided to crawl out of there while he still could. Wicklow would've taken him in, helped him back to the old narrow stall, called for a doctor, maybe even sat with him until the doctor came. The idea of it made Bendy's chest ache to bursting. In the end he chose an older path, dragging himself to Gripp's.

The rooming house was a miracle of sorts, survivor of a dozen great fires. The mountain man was wholly blind now, skimping on lamp oil, navigating like a grey steamer through the gloom. He let Bendy have his pick of a bunk—the place was three-quarters empty, a condition unknown during the rush—and he sent for the bone-setter, but that was no more than any man would've done.

Bendy was still there a week later—flat in his stinking bunk beside the open window, mending but not yet mended—when he caught sight of the show leaving town. The parade passed like memory—Pitch leading the lovely grey, Camden and his five bright balls. Bendy hauled the blanket up like a robber's kerchief, his heart thundering, as Stanley swung past on the tailgate of the lion's cage.

Philomena brought up the rear, motionless in her nest of straw. He was too afraid to call out to her. He rose up on his good elbow and, though it pained him, he waved. If she saw him, she gave no sign.

29

May 23rd, 1867

Dear Daughter

Can you possibly wish to know more? If I had you here before
me I might attempt to judge by your aspect though in truth you
were a closed book to me more often than not. In any case
you are not before me. No one is. And stories have a way of
unfolding themselves until they lie entire.

Mr. Burr rode for Cedar early on Thursday the 10th of
September 1857 saying only that the militia was called up and
he must go. I would not lay eyes on him until two days hence
when he rode into the yard at nightfall a different man on a different mount. You remember Dorrie the tall red mare named
Shade. He had ridden out on Pepper but now the poor fellow
trailed after him on a lead. My husband required help
dismounting. I watered the horses but left them to stand in
their tack. There were more pressing tasks at hand.

He was filthy. When I felt his forehead my hand came away
brown with grease. His clothing was stiff with dust and blood.

He stood silent while I undressed and bathed him suds the
colour of rust slopping on my kitchen floor. I wound him in a
sheet and helped him shuffle to the bed. He lay back when
I urged him but refused to close his eyes.

Next I built a fire in the pit out back of the house and burned
his clothes. Even his smalls were marked where the blood had
soaked through. His boots I soaped in the barn along with the
saddle I lifted from the sweating mare. And two items more. His
belt and threaded upon it a leather sheath. The knife it housed
was still sticky with blood. This I cleaned back in the kitchen.
I dried it carefully. After a moment's indecision I dropped it in
the drawer with the others as if it had been used to carve up a
Sunday roast.

I hoped to find him resting upon my return but still he stared.
He hadn't moved an inch the drying sheet still swaddled around
him tight. Will I bring you some broth husband? It never entered
my head to offer him solid food. He was not wounded yet clearly
he was not well. I felt a dull horror as I drew near him but
overcame it and skirted the bed to lie at his side. I was his wife.

When still he did not stir I drew his head to my breast. It
broke him. He wept so the tears penetrated my dress and
deeper. Now it was I who stared. Try as I might I could not
seem to string two thoughts together. I stroked his head as
though it were a cat come to purr on my chest. It seemed an
eternity before he could marshal sufficient breath to speak.
Even then he spilled his confession to my bosom not once looking up to meet my eyes.

I am no braver Dorrie. In truth I am grateful your face is not
before me so that I might set down that same confession in a
solitary scrawl.

By the time Mr. Burr's regiment reached Mountain Meadows

on the night of the 10th the emigrant train had been under siege for some three days. Dead horses and stock lay thick. Among them the surprised Gentiles that fell during the first attack and the unlucky Indians that met their returning fire. I say Indians Dorrie but I must tell you there were those who had made themselves so with horse tail wigs and paint. What is more their leader was no chief but a Saint of some rank known to all in these parts. Known to you my girl. Do you remember singling him out in Cedar? I thought Mr. Burr would unsocket your arm.

It was not until early the next morning that this man gathered the Saints there assembled about him to receive their orders. Mr. Burr was certain he had misheard. He had not. They were to kill the entire company save the small children who would be spared. The scheme was a treacherous one. The leader would lure the Gentiles from their stronghold with the promise of safe passage back to Cedar. He would claim to have struck a bargain with the Indians. The horde would stand down but only in return for all the wealth those wagons held.

Infants and small children would come first. They would be loaded into wagons with any wounded and most importantly with every Gentile gun. Next the women and older children would walk out in a herd. Following them at some distance would come the able bodied men. Each one of these last would be paired with a Saint in arms. Hard conditions but the leader had a way with words and in any case what choice did the emigrants have?

They could not possibly know that on a bellowed signal each armed Saint would turn on the man in his charge. Halt do your duty. It must have taken some time to fix upon just the right words. Nor could they know savages would leap from the brush to cut the women and children down. Again I say savages but I trust you take my meaning. Dorrie you will remember how my hand came away sullied from Mr. Burr's brow. Grease paint can be stubborn. A streak of it had clung to his hair line when he and the others knelt to wash their faces in a creek.

Which is worse? To turn and fire at arm's distance upon a man who has entrusted you with his life or to leap from behind a tree and cut a screaming woman's throat? And then another's. And then that of a ten year old boy. My husband did as he was ordered. They all did. In minutes the emigrant train lay dead. Save the small children. Those whose blood the Church has termed innocent and has forbidden any Saint to spill.

Dorrie I find I cannot go on. Can you see where my weeping wets the page? Salt circles in the margins. A pitiful offering indeed.

All a mother's love
Helen Burr

30

SHE WON'T LOOK AT HIM. It's been two days now since it happened, four meals at the same table and still not so much as a flicker of her eyes his way.

Bendy drags through his evening chores. Later, long after the windows of the ranch house have gone black, he leans up against Ink in her stall, pulling his fingertips down the tracks of her scars. Every stroke is a question—should he, should he not. Drawing the last of them to its conclusion, he decides.

He's out in the night air, kicking across the shadowy yard, before he can change his mind. He can't help but feel he should be clutching a spray of flowers—the picture of a man making amends. Instead, he brings only an idea.

She takes forever to answer his knock. He's grinding a slow turn in the dirt when the door emits a cry.

Running things over beforehand in his mind, Bendy saw himself surveying the collection again, asking a question or two, maybe even examining a few tools. Faced with the first touch of her gaze he's felt since the night before last, he spills his offering the moment he steps through the door.

"I watched this family one time. Not hunting or anything, just messing around outside their den."

She nods, releasing a flood of relief in his chest. He steps all the way inside, drawing the door shut after him.

"The den overlooked a river. Sandy slopes, you know, good digging. I was letting my horse graze on the far bank. They'd spotted me, all right, but the water was good and deep there, so they weren't too worried." He leaves a small pause, which, to his delight, she fills.

"What were they doing?"

He grins. "Not a whole lot. The pups were play-fighting. The mother looked beat. She was off on her own a ways, laying down. The daddy was keeping an eye on the pups, joining in every now and then. For a while they were crawling all over him."

"How many?"

"Huh?"

"How many pups?"

He thinks for a moment, bringing the tumbling mass clear. "Three."

"Playing." She says it to herself more than him.

"Uh-huh. Roughhousing, like."

Her face and neck flush suddenly, the thin tissue there awash with blood. She fixes him with a look, then turns her eyes, and his with them, to a spot on the floor halfway between her workbench and the first straw tier. Her meaning couldn't be clearer. He moves into her sightline, into an area the size of a modest stage.

Down on his belly in the near pasture, Lal imagines himself a rattler, all length and scale. He tilts his eyes up in their sockets to find the half moon bulging at its seams. He'd stretch his arms out long, try his hand at a slither, if it weren't so crucial he keep still.

Dead ahead, no more than a yard from the point of his chin, the grass shivers. His heart pounds, and he worries its rhythm will speak through the ground to the sensitive feet of his prey.

If it has feet.

A stab of fear now, as though a stone, sharp as a tooth, has cut up through the turf beneath him to catch him between two ribs. What if the disturbance in the grass was born of a diamondback—a real one? It's possible. He's made no sound, no movement, to warn one off for what must be at least a quarter of an hour.

The rustle comes again, and even through his fear Lal can tell warm-blooded scurry from reptilian flow. The tooth-stone sinks away. Moments later he becomes aware of a second small presence—this one closer still, somewhere off the crest of his left ear.

His jaw aches with waiting. He holds off until the grass blades before his eyes give a twitch and the rustling seems to emanate from inside his own skull. Then springs. Thrashes and flails, lets out a yelp as not one but both of his hands close around wriggling spurts of fur.

He rolls onto his broad back, clutching two fistfuls of mouse to his chest. Careful, don't smother them. Hold them hard, though, otherwise they'll bite.

Who's the hunter now?

Lal crosses the deep shadow at the horse barn's back, carrying the mice by their tails, two in one grip. They've left off squeaking. He holds them up before his face, sees both are alive and well, scrabbling in the air with their snowflake paws.

There would've been no need to go to such trouble if Drown wasn't so damn clean and tidy. A thorough kick through the corners of every stall hadn't produced so much as a skittering. The stable was Lal's place once. The horses still lift their heads when he has cause to pass among them, but there's a new flavour to their alarm, as though he were some foreign threat come slinking in, rather than the master in their midst.

He lifts his free hand, comforting himself with a bulge of knuckle against his mouth.

Never mind, the thumb murmurs. *We've got bigger fish to fry.*

The cow barn and chicken house stand quiet as he moves through the weeds behind them. A burst of speed across the open, mice swinging, and then he's into the mulberries, the black form of the silkhouse in his sights.

He creeps close, hunter quiet, hunter calm. The cottage is lightless within, but to be on the safe side he lays an ear to the perfectly fitted door. Nothing but the noise of their feeding. The mice twist and buck, swiping hairline claw marks across the jamb. Lal's thumb searches out the latch.

As the door eases inward, a rush of sound escapes, jangling his nerves. He'd pictured dropping the mice directly onto a worm bed—saving them the time and trouble of the climb—but now, inhaling the leaf-sweet, fleshy closeness, he finds himself unwilling to enter Ruth's little house. Coward that he is, he lobs the mice like a pair of tiny torches, yanks shut the door and runs.

Thus far, Dorrie's managed to cut the centreboard from a sheet of one-inch stock, shape and sand it to the depth of the runt's trunk, and nail four wooden blocks in the place of shoulders and hips.

These work to balance the board now, as she flips and rests it on the curve of its spine. Next she must affix the leg rods.

"Can you do the runt's legs for me?" she asks.

Bendy's been waiting patiently, lying on the old barn floor, staring up into the feathered forms that haunt the rafters. Now he folds his hands into paws, cycling his arms and legs as though in the grip of a fleet-footed dream. "How's this?" He flops his head her way.

She drops her gaze to the rough beginnings of the runt, sees nothing but lifeless wood. "I need you to keep still. Make the legs and hold them."

"Yes, ma'am."

He curls to take hold of himself by the shins. With a dual, muted pop his legs become hind legs, the crook of high canine ankles translated into unhinged knees. Reclining on the planks, he flips his elbows back on themselves, completing the pose.

"Thank you." Closing her eyes, she runs his description of the wolf family through her mind again. The runt lies in full submission, her brother standing over her. The third pup, another male, urges them on, teeth bared, hindquarters high. At a little distance, the father wolf sits watching. Beside him, the milk-white female rests.

He's been slung back in the yipping brother's pose for some time now—just how long Dorrie can't be sure. She yawns, laying her hammer aside. "You can stretch if you like."

She watches him draw back into a squat and bounce gently on his heels—three, four times—before rolling himself up tall. He takes a long stride toward the collection. Before she can speak, he touches his finger to the spot between a red squirrel's ears and rubs noseward, against the grain.

"Don't!" Lamp in hand, she slips out from behind the work-bench and draws up beside him.

"What'd I do?"

She doesn't reply, busy restoring the nap of the small red brow. The squirrel perches alone on a sapling stump, an acorn held like a fat apple to its lips.

"Hungry little fella." His voice is over-cheerful, making up.

She straightens, satisfied.

"I saw one eat a water beetle, you know, the kind with scissors for jaws."

She treats him to a narrow look. "Squirrels eat acorns. Nuts."

"Not only. I swear, he started in on the beetle's hind end to keep it from pinching his nose."

She shakes her head.

"Don't believe me?" He turns his attention to a weasel drawn up on its stubby hind legs. "How about this one. Back when I was riding the ponies, one of the station keepers told me how he saw a hawk swoop down on a weasel and snatch it up. Wasn't long before he could see the bird was in trouble. Sure enough, after a minute or so it quit climbing and dropped clean out of the sky." He swirls a splayed hand. "The hawk broke its neck, but would you believe that weasel up and scuttled off? Turns out he tore a hole in the hawk's sweet spot." He points to his own armpit, the place where a bird's skin stretches off into wing. "I'm telling you, the keeper swore blind."

"Hm."

He wanders to the far corner and gazes up at the bighorn ram. Dorrie follows at a polite distance. The great sheep has no mate, no young. Hammer and the Tracker heaved it up onto her work-bench two autumns ago. *It was work enough to bag one of the bug-gers. Tracked him for miles. Damn near dropped to our deaths.*

Hammer grinned to tell it. Beside him the Paiute bent his gaze to the rock-coloured sheep, its neck twisted, skull atilt on its head-dress of horn.

Bendy turns to face her. "You ought to hear the crash it makes when two of those boys come head to head."

She nods. This, at least, she's heard of.

"I watched a couple of them go at it high up over a pass. Came at each other from twenty, thirty feet, full speed. Crack!" He brings his hands together, hard. "Can't see how they come through it."

"Their skulls."

"Beg pardon?"

"Their skulls. The bone is extra thick."

He grins. "Trust you to know."

Her face flushes warmly.

Bendy gestures to the scene by his knee. Spanning the length of two bales, a large female beaver trails a pair of kits. "You ever seen a dam?"

"No."

"Don't get outdoors much, do you?"

"My work—I work inside."

"You ought to get out there on horseback, see a thing or two." He drops into a squat, looking the mother beaver full in the face. "You can sure see why the trappers are so mad for them. That fur."

"You can touch her."

He looks round, his neck seemingly boneless. "I thought—"

"It's all right. Just move your hand from head to tail."

"Head to tail." He turns his attention back to the dark, still animal and delivers a thoughtful stroke. "Lord."

When he stands, his narrow chest comes level with Dorrie's face. His shirt lies open at the collar, faded to the softest blue. At

his throat a puff of tow. For a second she contemplates reaching
for it, brushing it away. Instead, she takes a jerking step back,
turns and reaches for a grey squirrel mounted on a chunk of bark.
"This is the first one I did for him. He brought it to me on my
third night here."

"All in one piece?"

She nods.

"He must've barked it."

"Barked it?"

"Shot the bark out from under it. Stuns them. He must be
some shot."

"Most everything he brings me has just the one hole." She
clucks her tongue. "See here." She nudges her finger into a hollow
at the squirrel's hip joint. "He could use a bit of tow there, fill
that out. The ears, too. I didn't pinch them enough while he was
drying. They look frostbit."

Bendy peers in close. "Look all right to me."

Later, after he's gone, Dorrie takes up the grey squirrel again.
Fingering its tail, she recalls how readily the bone whip slid from
its fuzzy sheath. How, after she'd replaced it with a length of
number fourteen wire—anchored in the false torso, skeleton
strong—and sewn the little fellow up, she shaped the tail anew,
easing it first along the round of the spine, then back in an
answering curve. Now, making a ring of finger and thumb, she
runs it down the resultant S, tip to base, fluffing the fur. Springy.
Three years stuffed and still the creature responds.

It was getting on for dark when Hammer delivered the squirrel,
but Dorrie was wide awake, busy setting up her workshop. True to
his word, Hammer had purchased everything on her list, driving
straight from the Endowment House to the market. Tri-cornered

needles in cardboard, scalpels in burlap, plaster in powdery sacks. Countless bottles and jars. Crates overflowing with excelsior. Bales of tow, fat spools of thread. She was in her glory arranging it all, until her husband dragged open the door.

She was certain he'd come to escort her back to the house for a repeat performance of the previous night. What a gift when he grinned and produced a small grey body from behind his back.

"Brought you a little something." He laid it on her workbench.

"I'll get started now," she blurted. "If that's all right."

"Suits me." He was gone without a backward glance.

At home she'd been continually interrupted by chores or meals or bedtime, or by Papa taking exception to all those wasted hours. That night, Dorrie worked as she'd always dreamt of doing—without cease. She kept on until the squirrel came full circle, sat up and looked her in the eye. She was exhausted, exhilarated. It seemed a terrible comedown to return to the ranch house, pass chamber after chamber of slowed pulses, regular breath. And what if Hammer lay waiting for her in the dark?

She decided not to chance it. Kicking straw into a rough pallet, she dragged an empty feed sack over her body and slept.

Again the Father's footsteps have led the Tracker to the window of the old adobe barn. Inside, the child wife stands fondling some small, still creature—a squirrel by the shade of its fur. The Tracker watches until she sets it down and returns to her bench, then lets his gaze wander the framed scene of the barn. At length it comes to rest on a family of ducks.

Hammer had wanted him to shoot the canvasbacks, but the Tracker showed him a smarter, cleaner way. Entering the soup of the marsh from behind a blind of reeds, he bent his knees and sank to the level of his lips. A loose crown of rushes made a diminutive island of his head. He pulled himself slowly through water and weeds, half walking, half paddling, taking care not to bear weight on his feet and become mired in the rooty ooze.

On the surface, the woven mass that housed his breath drifted toward the resting flock. When he was within arm's reach of a complete family, he exhaled silently and submerged, leaving the crown to float empty. Eyes open in the murk, he rolled to gaze up into a thicket of twiggy legs. Webbed feet fluttered. A pair of adults bobbed directly overhead, one with a male's darker breast. Close at hand, several ducklings sat high in the water, scarcely breaking its skin.

It was then, staring up into those flecked, indistinct underbellies, that the Tracker first contemplated leaving this life. He could reach down and link arms with the weeds beneath him. He need never walk the earth again.

Instead, he reached up with both hands, grabbed the mother and father by their legs and dragged them under. Holding both in his hard left fist, he plucked and added ducklings to the thrashing bouquet.

When he burst up gasping into the air, the rest of the flock exploded into flight. He held the canvasbacks under until they ceased to resist, then rose from the marsh into Hammer's delighted gaze.

31

BENDY CAUGHT HIS LAST GLIMPSE of Philomena's glossy back in early September. By mid-October what little money he'd managed to save from his cut of the nightly take was gone, offered up to Gripp's stinking soup kettle and rat-lively walls. The mountain man was no longer content to let him lie on his back all day. Bendy was healed—every break knitted, good as new. He could get himself a job, or he could get out.

There was work to be had at the docks. A day's back-breaking labour paid roughly what he'd made on a good morning as a child, but the idea of cutting capers in the street seemed vaguely shameful now that he'd taken part in a travelling show.

The job suited bodies created opposite to his own: barrel-trunked trolls shuffling low to the ground, or men made of both height and brawn, bulls rearing up on their hind legs. They laughed at the reedy look of him, fell silent when they saw what sheer will could do. He kept up with the crew by day; by night he lay under the bug-jumping covers at Gripp's—paid for, secure—nursing his screaming joints.

True sleep came seldom that winter. More often he tossed under a dark rag-work blanket of noise. Sighs and breathy snores, undercover yankings, the occasional night-terror yell. Rain on the roof shakes and in seven pails—a tinny ring when they'd just been emptied, the timbre gentling as the levels rose.

After bed and what passed for board, he had a little money left over. Cash in a pocket runs through the fingers like silt. Cash stuffed deep in a boot, however, can become a nest of sorts. If asked what he was saving for, Bendy would've been hard pressed to give it a name. He'd know it when it showed itself, like every major junction in his life so far.

This one came on paper, a sheet of the *Alta California* one of the overseers had laid aside. He was lying on his bunk, reading by the flame of a tallow stump, when a word crackled through him like the touch of a longed-for hand. *Wanted.* He shifted his fingertip and read on.

Young skinny wiry fellows not over eighteen.

Me, he thought, the word pulsing down through the filth beneath his fingernail, inserting itself into the text.

Must be expert riders willing to risk death daily.

Expert? Near enough. More than willing. Eager.

Orphans preferred.

This he heard rather than read, the letters thrumming with a voice of their own. He scarcely dared read on.

Wages $25 per week.

He caught his breath.

Apply, Central Overland Express, Alta Bldg., Montgomery Street.

He lifted his forefinger and retraced the advertisement, giving it half a dozen passes before he felt he'd seen enough. Sitting up, he swung his feet—still in their boots, always in their boots—down to the floor. It was a good hour until dawn, and no office would open its doors until some time after that. Still, he rose. He'd miss a morning's work at the dockyards. The thought

had a long bright tail—he was done with grunt work. The change
had come.

"St. Joseph, Missouri, clean through to Sacramento." The man
with the shoe-brush moustaches swept his hand across the wall-
mounted map. "That's nineteen hundred and sixty-six miles in
two hundred and forty hours. Ten days."

The numbers meant little to Bendy, but he knew by the shiver
in the man's voice he was meant to be impressed. What did hold
some significance for him was the map. It was the first time he'd
seen the whole thing—a country in the making pinned up before
his eyes.

"Excuse me, sir," he heard himself ask, "does this map show
New Orleans?"

The man's finger took an angled course, unable to resist tracing
the route back to St. Joseph before turning southward. "Here,"
he said, reaching the black spot at the Mississippi's mouth. "Do
you have kin there?"

Bendy closed his eyes and saw her, plain as day. She was
standing on the wide verandah of that old mansion, her shopping basket on her arm. And then she wasn't. "No, sir," he said
quietly, "no kin."

He would answer many questions that morning. How old was
he? Sixteen. How much did he weigh? One-fifteen or so, last he
knew. That had been a year ago, when he was still at Wicklow's—
he and the other stable hands balancing themselves on the
feed scales on a slow day. If he'd gained weight since then, it
couldn't be much. If anything, his convalescence and Gripp's
filthy stews had whittled him a little. The dock work certainly
hadn't built any bulk, instead turning him stringy, like an over-
boiled bird.

Did he fancy himself a good horseman? Could he endure great hardship? Was he accustomed to a life spent out of doors? Yes, sir. Yes, sir. Yes, sir.

The man's face darkened then, becoming severe. "Do you drink?"

"No, sir."

"Not at all?"

"Not once."

Again and again Bendy felt his eyes drawn to the sprawl of the map—specifically to its far edge, the direction the ornate cross in the top corner identified as *E*. West's opposite. The land Bill Drown had so keenly despised. At last he worked up the courage to ask another question of his own. "Sir, is there any work to be had along the line?"

"Along the line?" The man's mouth contracted, drawing the dark brush down. "I'm hiring for the westernmost division, son."

Bendy took a step closer, reached out and slid his own index finger along the route. "Yes, but what about—" He almost blushed to utter it aloud, recalling his father's curled lip. He took a breath, blew it out across territories and states. "—the East?"

Stepping out of the Alta Building into morning light, Bendy finally knew where he was headed—all he needed was a way to get there. It was waiting for him when he got back to Gripp's. A played-out panner, back from working over the tailings of a played-out cut. Bendy took his measure in a moment. If there was anything more than a pinch of low-grade dust on the panner's sorry person, he'd eat a finger off his own right hand.

Gripp and the newcomer were alone, bent together across the plank table like old women grousing over tea—only they were silent, and the teapot was a cloudy bottle of gin. Bendy sat down at a little distance, his weight on the bench turning Gripp's moon-stone gaze his way. Neither man offered a glass, so he wasn't obliged to nurse a drink he didn't want.

Normally he would've kept to himself—perched on the sagging front step or stretched out on his bunk—but this time he had good reason to take part. On his way in, he'd noticed the panner's horse, a bald-faced yellow cayuse with white socks on her forelegs and stockings on her hind. She'd been let go—coat mud-streaked and dull, shoes worn to slivers. The panner had tethered her in the full sun without water. She was panting, a fact that let Bendy see the true animal beneath the neglect. She was deep-hearted, possessed of a good set of lungs.

Lingering by her head a moment, murmuring, Bendy showed her his hand before laying down several long, investigative strokes. She stood firm for him, let out a telling sigh. He crossed to the rain barrel and filled a bucket. It was a test as well as a gift, and when she thrust her mouth in up to the nostrils, drinking hard and long, she passed.

When the gin was three-quarters down—far enough to have loosened the panner's tongue and lowered the mountain man's eyelids, but not so far that they'd started fretting about where the next bottle would come from—Bendy made his move.

"That your nag out front?"

The panner squinted up from the pair of fresh shots he was dribbling out. "Nag? She ain't no—"

"I'll take her off your hands." Short and sharp. Let this kind get up a head of steam and they'd talk themselves to where you wanted them, overshoot and end up back where they began.

The panner made a show of drawing himself up. "Now hold on a minute here—"

"Cash." Bendy let his gaze slip to the bottle and rest there a moment, then reached down and began working loose his boot. The panner strained forward a little. Bendy produced two-thirds of the paper nest he'd formed with his heel and began slowly, methodically, to flatten and fan out the bills. The panner's answer was plain on his face, but he gave voice to it all the same.

"She's called Nugget."

Bendy nodded, pushing the money across the table. Like hell she is, he thought. Like hell.

He was packed in minutes and out Gripp's splintery front door without so much as a so-long. He put off tending to the mare, not wanting to clean her up where the panner could catch sight of what he'd lost. Riding her at a walk through town, he couldn't help feeling the pair of them were in disguise, weighted down by the evidence of lives now done. To pass out of the city would be a kind of passing away—one that preceded neither heaven nor hell, but a brand new birth, man and horse remade. But first a detour to the farrier's, where they began righting the panner's wrongs.

When the steamship *Antelope* set off that afternoon, Bendy and his mare were aboard. He was leaving San Francisco the same way he'd arrived—only now he was no longer a boy in thrall to his father, but a young man with reins in his hand. Another key difference—this ship took him inland, the first half inch along a line on a map, the one that had etched a corresponding groove in his brain. Moving up the Sacramento River instead of out to sea—into fresh, narrowing waters rather than an endless salt expanse—gave him a sense of direction, of having found the necessary path.

What could be simpler? He'd follow the Pony Express trail itself—or the foundations of it, anyway—until he reached its eastern end, stopping at each city, town or station to ask directions to the next. He'd be expert, all right, by the time he got there. The men in charge out that way would have to hire him on. Chances were he'd be their only rider who'd learned the entire route through his own horse's hooves.

The *Antelope* docked at Sacramento in the small hours. Bendy held the mare to a trot through the darkened streets, but let her run when they met open country. At a patch of tender pasture cut across by a stream, he dropped down and let her drink, then eat, her fill. Oblivious to the darkness and to his own fatigue, he brushed and curried her as she nosed along, freeing clods of dirt the size of knuckles, handfuls of hair. When she stood sated, he squatted and oiled her hooves, checking by feel the clinch nails on her new shoes. He stroked her brow until her eyes closed before setting to work on the knots in her tail. Kneeling by the starlit stream, he dipped his rag and rubbed the scurf from her filthy tack.

They passed the remainder of the night in a whispering copse. Bendy dozed under the saddle blanket, the mare's legs becoming four bright saplings when his eyes fluttered open at the screech of an owl. He named her then, half waking, murmuring, "Stand." She roused him at first light with the sound of her grazing, her keen lips inches from his ear.

— 32 —

DORRIE DREAMS:

Wolves. They've been waiting, biding their time, until the dog man's pack withdrew. Now, as twilight gathers, the hills are crawling with them. I can make out several from my perch, bristling along the far escarpment, threading down through boulders, through brush. The numbers lie to the west—the wind having turned to waft its happy message that way—but they move across these eastern hills too.

A deep-chested male pads by close to the trunk of my juniper, nose thrust into the blood-rich breeze, eyes on the valley below. His mate comes hard on his heels, her flank brushing the very bush that hides the child.

The breeding pair do not scent her, nor do any of their pack— a couple of rangy yearlings leading four of this spring's issue, fat-footed, overgrown pups. As the last of them files past the sage, a faint crackling issues from within. The pup hesitates, cocking his head. I caw, jagged and high, a note designed to trouble his ears. He looks up, spots me and shows a little fang. I sidle down my branch, draw a thin, silvery whine from between those glinting teeth. It's over before it begins. In the empty-headed way of the young, he suddenly recalls his purpose, the descent of his kind upon the field. He gives a growl for good measure, drops his snout into the current of rot and trots away.

A close call, yet I can't help but be heartened by the child's small stirring. She's been holed up in there since the middle of last night. Hours ago, when I returned from my survey of the humans at their burying work, the bush was so silent I began to wonder if she'd crept from its cover and scuttled away. I listened for her shallow breath, but could hear nothing over the echoes of human tools. In the end I swooped down from my branch, claws extended, and raked through the bush's crown. The child gasped and, on the exhale, released the softest of squeals. It was enough. I mounted to my post again.

For the moment no other wolves track over our particular rise. Perhaps all within reach of scent and howl have arrived. Territory means little now, enemy packs converging to answer the enormity of the call. Within the greater group, they keep loosely to their own. A skirmish or two breaks out along borders, but for the most part they are intent upon the surfeit of food.

Wolves are fine diggers. Watching them unearth the pitiful caches with such strength and skill, I feel a stab of envy, usually reserved for others with the gift of flight—the soaring ones, especially vultures, their bald heads a badge of purity, of dedication to the dead. Still, of all the ground-walkers, wolf is closest kin to crow. If we're patient and wait until they've had their fill, they'll let us dance through the bodies they've begun. It's a kindness coyotes never know. Wolves begrudge their little brothers and sisters, occasionally tearing a bold one limb from limb.

The coyotes are here too, a few within nostrils' range. For the time being they cling to the slopes, showing themselves here and there in a smear of yellow back, the twitch of an outsize ear. Not a yip to be heard. The sight of so many of their brutish big siblings gathered in one place keeps them quiet.

The wolves are co-operating now, large rings of them with noses down, pawing hard to reveal hands and bare rumps and heads. Teams of three and four haul bodies from the earth. Muzzles drive in through the open doors of mortal wounds. Where a shot through the skull or a knife in the back yield little, they make for the softest parts.

Near the heart of the meadow a red-faced female tilts over her find, dipping snout then shoulder in a delirious roll. Anointing herself with the odour of abundance and its brother, peace; the night meat lay ripe for the taking, enough to feed every member of every rival pack.

Wolves can be terribly quiet, pressing the earth with those soft, spreading toes, but when they eat, they give rise to a torrent of noise. I hear it now, and so must the child, the valley a bowl of sound. It grows out of a growl, steady and low, the organizing pulse of the pack. Tearing and gulping form loose, unpredictable strains. Bones wedged between molars crack.

Again a twinge of envy. What is a beak when compared with a mouthful of teeth? I imagine thrusting my face deep into a rib cage I've broken open myself, closing my jaws around the chewy wholeness of a heart. Then remember that teeth make a body head-heavy. Ashamed, I extend one long, fused finger, reminding myself of the irreplaceable span of a wing.

A sudden yelp calls my attention back to the field. A yearling prances near the foot of our hill, leading her brother in a game. She bears the prize in her mouth—a portion of leg snapped off at the knee, gnawed about the calf, the foot still strangely pristine. She twists to face her pursuer, grinning through the jagged clamp of her bite. Shaking the leg at him, she sends a chunk flying, unheeded by either of them, but glowing in my eye. Hunger freshens as I follow its arc.

I peer down into the sage bush, angle my head, listen hard through the hum of the feast. Sleeping, I tell myself. Deaf and blind. I could ease down the grade with barely a flap, land where the muscled chunk did, gulp under cover of grass. The child would be none the wiser. I'd be back in the blink of an eye.

33

RUTH CAN TELL something's amiss even before she opens the door. The worms are feeding—she can hear that much—yet there exists a dull spot in their sheeting sound. Her eyes take their time widening to the interior gloom, but once they do, the trouble is plain.

The mice are two trays apart, brothers in arms. In their greed they ignore any instinct to flee. Each regards her over a feast in progress—one gnawing a living worm, the other closing its teeth over a quiet tail end. Ruth has never moved so swiftly in all her life. Too late, the mice retreat, scrambling over worms like children over logs—only these logs are writhing, deadfall come to life. She plucks the little demons up, one in each fist, and brings her hands together in an almighty rodent-crushing clap.

The impact is great, yet not quite sufficient. A hind leg escapes her grip, kicking. Such a sight might give a woman pause, if it weren't accompanied by the sensation of needle-fine teeth sinking into her palm. Crying aloud, Ruth grinds her double handful from quick to quiet. Twist, crack, twist. Trickle of mouse blood down the crease between finger and thumb.

She stands in the middle of the room, her hands clasped tight. Inside her skull there is silence. Surrounding her, the soothing flutter of rain-not-rain. Miraculous—they've continued feeding, unperturbed. She bends her gaze to the worm bed before her. Her little charges are all softness and trust, equipped neither to fight nor to flee. If she didn't feed them, they would starve. A thought both comforting and sad.

She takes a breath and steps toward the door. She'll work the latch with her elbow. Once outside, she'll think what to do with the mess in her hands.

Thankful's husband prefers to face out into the room when she shaves him. He needn't watch in the mirror—he trusts her.

The middle boy brought the hot water this morning, halting at the door, refusing to look his Aunt Thankful in the eye. Doubtless her nightdress made him edgy, the bodice ribbons left untied. And, yes, she may have stooped a little lower than was strictly necessary to take the jug from his hands. Are they ever too young to learn?

Once she gets Hammer settled under the hot, wet towel, she flicks the shaving brush over the knuckles of his near hand. The hand plays dead, then springs, catching hold of her by the thigh. She squeals for him, and he squeezes hard, then releases, laughing through the steam.

She wets the brush and swirls it into the soap's hollow—brisk circles are best, folding in the air. She's good at this, one of the many skills a bit-part actress picks up to be sure and keep her job. While Charlotte de Courcey was busy rehearsing, Thankful learned how to sew far better than her mother could have taught her, how to sponge stage blood from a doublet, how to groom restive actors and otherwise tend to their needs.

Hammer's face is tricky, so many crags, even when he's relaxed. She nicked him badly the first time, just below the jaw. He didn't yelp, didn't even flinch. Just bled for her, pink through the lather, resolving into long red drops.

She lifts away the towel. He opens his black eyes halfway, regarding her for a moment before closing them again. She lathers the same pattern she will shave, beginning at his throat-apple, circling up and out. She's reached his right nostril when a knock sounds at the door. Two sharp raps, bolder than any delivered by the children. Mother Hammer has carried the breakfast up herself.

"Come." Charlotte's only answer to knuckles at the dressing-room door. Never a homely *Come in*. Or worse, the response favoured by Thankful's mother, *Who is it? Who's there?*

Mother Hammer pushes the door open wide as though she would air out the room, the breakfast tray balanced on one mannish arm. Despite herself, Thankful edges round to take a position at Hammer's back.

His head snaps up from the chair. "Ah, my good wife."

Mother Hammer crosses to the bedside table and deposits the tray, then straightens to survey the room. Her pale eyes pick out Thankful's costume from the night before, lying where she slipped out of it at the foot of the bed.

"Half a dozen eggs for you this morning, Mr. Hammer." The first wife stares Thankful in the eye. "To promote begetting."

Thankful spreads a hand over their husband's shoulder and feels it sag. He drops his head back and closes his eyes.

"You're very good, Mother Hammer, to wait on us so." Thankful should probably stop there, but her hand—the one not gripping Hammer—has other ideas. It rises to curl about the neck of her nightdress, drawing its frilled gap down. The air on her bare breast is shocking. She feels her nipple stand.

The first wife makes coins of her eyes.

"Was there something else?" Thankful hears the quaver and hates it. Hastily tucks the breast away. Mother Hammer's silence is frightening. The room seems to grow narrower as she leaves it, collapsing in on itself in her wake.

Ursula doles out the porridge like a punishment. Every male at the table shrinks back to avoid getting splattered—her three fine boys, then the hired man, then Lal. When Lal reaches to be first at the cream jug, she brings her spoon down across his wrist with a gluey thwack. He yips, his bright eyes rolling. The hired man lowers his gaze.

A moment passes before Joseph rises to take possession of the jug. He tilts it first over Baby Joe's bowl, then Joe's and finally his own. Ursula waits, spoon at the ready, arm aching to fall. But Lal thwarts her. Manages to hold his tongue.

Joseph passes the jug to Brother Drown, who spills a small stream over his portion and passes it on. Ursula skirts Hammer's empty chair and the one beside it, working the spoon like a chisel, gouging deep into the pot. She pounds a great dollop into Sister Ruth's bowl, glancing up to find Lal holding the cream jug, unsure what to do.

"What are you waiting for?"

He jerks a yellow surge from the jug's pinched lip, then shoves it, doily and all, across the table. Ruth takes up the cream and pours.

As usual, Sister Eudora has come to the table looking wild. Hunched shoulders and hollow eyes. Ursula ladles out a helping so large it threatens to overflow her bowl. Might put some meat on her bones.

Josephine enters bearing a platter of fried eggs just as Ursula drops a serving into her bowl. "Hurry up, girl. Cold food is halfway to no food at all."

"Yes, Mother." She follows in Ursula's footsteps, shovelling out two eggs to each of the boys, three to the hired man and Lal. She rounds the table's empty head. Two for Ruth, one for Eudora.

"For shame, Josephine." Ursula scrapes the last glutinous knob of porridge into her own bowl. "Would you have your Aunt Eudora waste away? Give her another."

Josephine complies, taking a lone egg for herself to compensate, then laying another down for her sister before sliding a pair of unbroken beauties onto Ursula's plate.

Brother Drown is the first to bow his head. The others follow suit, and Ursula proceeds to address the Lord with her mouth drawn tight. Opening her eyes, she glares at the pair of empty chairs. Half a dozen years gone since her husband returned from a mission among the hard-hearted Gentiles of the eastern states with his third wife in tow. Convert, indeed. Hammer sat grinning like a demon all through supper that first night, his new catch making eyes at him over her peach cobbler—not a pretty sight, given the stubby-lashed pebbles she had set in her head. Her dress, like every dress she's appeared in since, was a disgrace.

Hammer led his bride up the stairs long before any hint of dark. At least things looked hopeful on that front. It was difficult to be certain with all those petticoats, but the new wife appeared to be favoured with a decent set of hips.

Ursula laughs, a single *ha* that travels the table's midline as though it were a fault. To think she ever imagined Thankful would be delivered of anything so precious as a child.

She looks down to find a skin grown over her porridge, a white lacework of lard about the fringes of her eggs. A scarcely audible whimper issues from the place at her left hand. Josepha sits with knife and fork suspended over her lone egg. Having pierced the yolk and found it runny, she cannot bring herself to go on. Beside her, Josephine mops at the yellow leak with a sponge of bread. "There now," she murmurs. But Josepha's appetite has turned. She shakes her head slowly, her bottom lip swelling in a pout.

On another day Ursula might choose to indulge her youngest girl, tell her to go ahead and eat around the slime, perhaps even exchange the offending egg for one of her own. Not today. Today she lays the blade of her butter knife to Josepha's mouth. There is no risk of misunderstanding. The offending lip contracts. The child forks and swallows her food.

Having blanketed the last tray with leaves, Ruth can afford to sit down for a few minutes and rest. Her feet are bad this afternoon. They've never been so tender so early on, but then she's never asked so much of them before. The first five babies seem now to have been grown with little or no movement on her part, as though she were one of Mother Hammer's potato plants stuck waiting for harvest. Not this time. This time she has work to do.

She lifts her right foot to rest against the opposite thigh, taking it gingerly in both hands. It hurts to rub, but she'll pay for it later if she doesn't. Running her thumb down the upturned sole, she persuades trapped blood from ball to heel—three slow passes and she's awoken a burning tide. She closes her eyes and rubs harder, recalling the longest of roads.

After so many weeks of salt pork and sea biscuits aboard the *Thornton,* she was violently ill over her first plate of fresh vegetables and meat. New York City seemed a monstrous sprawl—it took forever to fall away beyond the soot-streaked windows of the train. It wasn't her first time in a passenger car—as a child she'd clung to her mother's side on the trip south to London, to an unknown life—yet she jumped when the steam whistle screamed, shut her eyes against the speed long before the engine hit its stride. Over the miles she came to trust the understanding between wheel and rail, and opened her eyes again to look out. The country streaming past her was huge.

At Iowa City the railway met its end. Under the direction of their many captains, the faithful made camp on the riverbank. It seemed not one of them had ever constructed a tent. When told to gather wood, the children wondered why, the fires of their acquaintance having fed exclusively on coal.

By the light of those first campfires, the converted made a sorry show. Most were thin, many were skin and bone. Hollow cheeks and fallen chests, scarcely a head over thirty years of age with half its teeth left. They ate well enough that night, the captains moving among them with butter, flour, beans. Once fed, they massed for evening prayer. Only then were they treated to the truth.

It is a great, a wondrous blessing that so many have answered the Lord's call. Would you have the Church waste money on wagons, on oxen, on mules, when those same funds might purchase passage to Zion for hundreds of weary souls? I feel certain, brothers and sisters, you would not.

They would walk to Zion. Well over a thousand miles. Pushing or pulling all they owned.

They camped on the bank of the Iowa River for a month, oppressed by a hovering, wet heat the likes of which Ruth had never known. The grass jumped with chiggers. Children flowered

in rashes of many hues. The only relief came in the form of buck-
eting rain, a fractured, bellowing sky. The men—few carpenters
and even fewer wheelwrights among them—laboured over the
handcarts they would come to hate. A knocked-together box on a
five-foot frame between a pair of waist-high wheels. The lucky
ones got iron axles, iron tires. The rest made do with unseasoned
wood.

It seemed they would never be under way. Then suddenly, one
sweltering mid-July morning, they were. Ruth was one of five hundred souls to set out under a missionary captain by the name of
James Willie. Men took their places behind crossbars and heaved-
to. Women carried infants or helped the older children push from
behind. The sad carts howled the news of their departure, drawing Iowa Gentiles to stare from their gates. Many laughed, but
those of a more serious turn of mind cried that it was a sin to
make beasts of human beings. The faithful replied with song.

By the time they made the Missouri River, hauling precious
heirlooms no longer made sense. Clocks and china, family por-
traits in ponderous frames—all were sacrificed to make way for
sacks of flour or the grievous weight of the weak. The flesh of the
living, the food it required. All else would be borne by memory
alone.

Beyond Loup Fork the land turned dry. The very air took from
them now, greedy for the moisture locked in skin, in green and
groaning wood. Both shrank and, when they could shrink no
more, began to crack. The converted gave up their soap, even
their precious bacon, for axle grease, only to draw more sand and
wear the soft wood away. Still they sang. Ruth knew by heart the
verses the clear-voiced missionary had sung by Mrs. Stopes's
hearth; she warbled along with the rest of the shambling horde,
All is well! All is well!

The days bled into weeks, into months. At some point the train was overtaken by a party of carriages, each drawn by four horses or mules in an unseemly surfeit of power. The carriages, dark and gleaming, disgorged men well dressed and well fed. Word travelled through the crowd that these were Saints of high standing, returning from missions abroad. One of the men took the time to deliver a speech concerning the need for continued faith, obedience and prayer. Watching him talk, Ruth found she couldn't quite focus her eyes. She blinked long and often, until the man closed with a prophecy that they would reach Zion in safety, come what may. Beside her a boy of perhaps five trapped a passing beetle and slipped it wriggling into his mouth.

Before they laid leather to horseflesh again, the missionaries requested meat. Captain Willie made them a gift of a sinewy calf. A woman wailed at its slaughter, confusing the skinned carcass with the body of the husband she'd buried in a sandbank some hundred miles before.

The good weather left them. Rations dwindled. Ruth could no longer haul the heavy blankets she would freeze without. The company made it two-thirds of the way into October before a river stole the last of their strength. Crossing the Sweetwater, Ruth felt herself abandon hope. Such promise in a name—and it was indeed a beautiful river, rolling clear over its rocky bed. A sight to lift the spirits. A cold to kill them. On the far bank many lay down and died—little struggle, less sound. The keen air swam with souls.

For days the faithful lay suffering. Nine gave up the ghost the night before rescue wagons came rolling from the west, loaded with beef and potatoes, blankets and buffalo robes, hale and hearty Saints. It took every ounce of will Ruth had to lift her head and survey the glorious scene. Deliverance. A short, hard-faced man approaching, centred between her deadened toes.

Another day gone. Thankful must try not to doze so much during the daylight hours—it makes for interminable nights.

Hammer sleeps like a dog—heat-seeking, fitful. Even after Thankful's worn him out, he snuffles on the pillow and kicks. Seated by the open window, she tires of watching him—the dull game of guessing where the covers will jump next—and turns her attention outward. As always, the peach trees, strict rows of whispering crowns. Their scent will be sickening come harvest, but for now it's pleasant enough. Other than that, a clear night sky, half a moon—and movement. Yes, movement, just there, where the orchard butts up against the track.

The moonlight catches, then releases, whatever it is, and Thankful feels herself stand and strain forward into the night. For a long moment she sees nothing. Then a fleeting glimpse as it crosses an open aisle. It gives more of itself away this time—a thing of four legs and alarming size, its colour changeable, its locomotion smooth. Chicago was home to dogs of all descriptions—needle-eyed terriers on ladies' leads, hip-high bone racks down snowy lanes—but never such a bulk as this. Never such beauty either.

The creature slips from between two trunks and turns right, following the dirt corridor toward the house. Thankful doesn't speak for fear it will lift its eyes and catch her spying. Instead, she takes a long step back and gropes through the covers for her husband's twitching foot. She squeezes gently, his heel hard as an apple in her hand, and he yelps himself awake.

"Shh!"

"What—"

"Shhhhhhh."

He blinks like a boy for a second more, then sits up, wakeful and wary, a man. She holds a finger to her lips, then crooks it to beckon him from the bed.

When they stand together at the casement—Thankful in a diaphanous gown, her husband in nothing but the hairy skin the Lord gave him—she points to where the animal showed itself last. He knows enough to hold his tongue in patience. Moments later it surfaces again, two rows over, this time following the hard-packed aisle away. Thankful gasps. It veers right, disappearing again, and she turns to find Hammer squinting into the night.

Wolf? she mouths.

His face is screwed up, unreadable. Finally, he nods. Stands there, arms at his sides.

"Well?" she hisses.

"Well what?" he says loudly. It will hear him and get away.

"Go get it."

"Now?" His laugh is louder still. "It'll be miles off before I'm out the door."

Her hands, clenched in terror now, find his chest. She would pummel him, but he already has her by the wrists. He walks her backwards to the bed. Her knees buckle and he covers her, quiets her, with his weight.

"Don't you worry, Thankful." His moustaches in the hole of her ear. "Nobody's gonna gobble up my girl."

She says nothing for a long stretch, sawing, hammering. Then stands back to cast an eye over what she's done. She sighs. "Can I see the father?"

"Yep."

Making dual loops of his legs, Bendy draws his tailbone down to form the centre knot of a bow. The human length of his fingers he doubles into toes. Having made forelegs of his arms, he lengthens from the root of his missing tail out through the top of his skull. If he could grow the ears to match the attitude, they'd be oriented forward, easy but erect. He inclines his head gently, training his gaze on his imaginary young.

After a time he steals a glance her way. "I used to do this for a living," he says. "Back in California when I was a kid."

She looks up. "Modelling?"

He's made her curious about him—a realization he experiences in his chest.

"Not exactly. More like what you might call a street show." For the first time ever, he can imagine telling the whole story. *I was in a travelling show, too. Things ended pretty badly. See, there was this girl—*

Instead, he says simply, "How about a break?"

She nods, releasing him, and he rises to walk out the kinks. Standing eye to eye with the blacktail buck on the second tier, he squints to inspect its seamless face. "I don't know how you do it."

His words have the desired effect. She comes to stand at his side, holding up her lamp.

"Deer heads are finicky." Her free hand floats up into the lamp's brightest field. "It takes forever to work around the horns." She stirs the air at the base of one. "You have to keep sharpening the knife."

His eyes leave the deer's scalp to settle on hers. If she were to grow antlers, they'd have to drive up through her dirty hair. Just there. And there.

"You have to watch out near the eyes," she goes on. "You never pierce the ball, but it's easy to nick the lid, too."

Here in the wick's wavering, he gets his best look yet at her eyes. They're unsettling in their depth. Beneath the near one, a hair's-width vein ticks blue.

"Here, too." Her fingertip touches the niche of the buck's tear duct. "The skin sticks to this little hollow in the bone."

It's hard to picture her crying, but for a moment he does—her sharp cheeks painted with tears.

She trails a pinky down the length of the buck's nose, crooking it up into the near nostril. "You have to get right up inside. Cut close to the skull. Otherwise you run out of skin when it comes time to mount."

Again, he can't help but compare. Her nose is severe in its descent, but softer, more appealing, at its tip. Like the ripe nub of a strawberry, a glory his tongue has known only rarely. He thrills to an imagined sensation—his teeth closing gently, the breath sighing out her nostrils into his mouth.

Her little finger finds its way along the deer's muzzle to the juncture of top and bottom lip, a spot that, on her own face, shows a bitter little crease. Above it, though, a small, incongruous plumpness. "It takes practice. The first one I did, I cut along the outside of the lip. Had to throw the whole thing away."

"It's very fine," he says quietly.

She withdraws her hand, as though she's afraid the deer might nip. Stands still a moment, then lowers her lamp and turns.

Tracing the Father's faint course through the mulberry trees, the Tracker can no longer deny the nearness of dawn. Soon the big house will spring to life, spilling smoke from its chimney, grim children from its door. He daren't risk being spotted skulking around the yard. No choice, then, but to abandon the wolf's trail and double back.

Only now, cutting at an oblique across the Father's loose, deliberate circle, comes a second, even fresher set of tracks. Soles long and broad, stride eager—the trail of an overgrown boy. Four trees on, the Tracker catches sight of the son, his head silver in the before-light, flashing between trunks. Beyond, the little log house, black save for a window's glow.

Selecting a tree behind which to hide, the Tracker stills himself against its bark before looking out. The son stoops, then drops to all fours and crawls for the rutted wall. He lays his cheek to it for a long moment before tucking his boots beneath him and beginning to rise. Lamplight turns the top of his head gold.

The Tracker understands. The broad-hipped, quiet wife is the only one of Hammer's women he can imagine wanting, the sight of her having stirred him distantly once or twice. The son's regard, however, is anything but distant—his neck a rigid column, his head cocked in a hungry stare. The Tracker shuts his eyes. Sees blackness and, in its far corner, the swish of an ancient tail.

Wolf's younger brother was never one to respect taboo. Coyote wanted the woman he couldn't have—some say daughter, sister, mother-in-law, some say all three. In every version, he comes to them in disguise. Once bedded, the women discover the trick. In their shame, they flee to the heavens, hardening their ruined bodies to become stars.

The Tracker cracks his eyelids on the first threat of light. Still he doesn't move. The scene at the lone window prevents him.

Slowly, almost delicately, the son unfurls the fist at his left side. Raising it up, he brings his thumb to his mouth. The Tracker can hear nothing, but it's clear the son is speaking—his lips churning with a pained and private voice.

A shiver runs through the Tracker, scalp to sole. Taking a step back, he feels the tree's impression come with him, written on his cheek and chest. The little forest presents many paths. He chooses one and makes his way down its length, resisting the urge to run.

❧

Dawn is breaking. Bendy left hours ago, yet Dorrie can still feel the effect of his unblinking eyes—a raw smarting wherever his gaze came to rest. She presses the tip of her middle finger to the corner of her lip.

It's very fine.

He was referring to the buck's mouth, of course, not hers. Still, the memory causes her to cross to the washstand in search of an object she hasn't handled in years. The hand mirror, like the hair-brush it lies beneath, is silver, degraded to iridescent black. What would Mama say if she could see her parting gift now, lying beside a yellowed basin and a battered tin jug?

Mama's hundred strokes. Dorrie never once brushed her own hair before coming to the Hammer ranch. Left to her own devices, she manages only the minimum required to keep matted clumps at bay, loosing and reforming her braid perhaps once a week. At least she still uses the brush; the mirror has lain untouched since the morning she removed her few belongings from the ranch house and took up permanent residence in the old barn. She's come to think of its oval face as a holder of sorts, a saucer to the cup of the brush. Stooping over it now, she peers into its gloomy return.

Very fine.

She shifts her gaze from one sore spot to the next, finding nothing but plain. Worse than plain. Strange.

It wasn't until she crested her first decade that things began to go wrong with Dorrie's looks. Her dark, deep-set eyes receded, moving from fetching to frightening—a pair of tracks sunk deep in snow. Her mouth, once pleasingly full, began to seem swollen, compressed between lengthening nose and chin. Only one feature held true. As long as Mama was around to look after it, Dorrie's black hair shone. But hair alone does not a beauty make. Papa was right, though surely he never meant for Dorrie to hear.

He and Mama must have thought she was still out in the shed, hard at work on the yellow barn cat, her most ambitious project to date. She was just slipping off her boots, about to pad through to the parlour in search of a spool of thread, when she heard raised voices from down the hall.

"It was a hell of a risk, but I took it. You think I'd have kept her if I'd known she'd turn out looking like that?"

"*You* kept her? If it were down to you—"

"All right, all right."

"Lyman, she's our child."

"That's as may be, but she won't be a child for long."

"She's thirteen!"

"And the way things are looking, we'll still be saddled with her when she's thirty."

There may have been more, but by then Dorrie was retreating, clutching her boots to her chest, easing the back door closed.

She stares into the dark puddle of the glass. So what if she isn't much to look at? If her three sister-wives are anything to go by, beauty is no bar to misery. At least Hammer is content not to touch her—save once, but she won't think on that now. Being plain and strange spares her the burden of his desire. But even as the notion soothes her, its shadow stretches long. *And every other man's too.*

34

GREEN VALLEY ROAD led to White Rock Road—pretty names, but Bendy never forgot he was passing through the land gold built. As he rode into Placerville, he couldn't help recalling its original name of Hangtown—a legacy of violence still palpable along the muddy streets. He kept his eyes to himself, asked directions of a plump washerwoman and pushed on through.

Mounting into the western summits of the Sierras, he encountered the first flaw in his plan. Though he'd only ever seen snow from a distance, he'd heard plenty of miner's tales—none of which had done it justice. He was surrounded by great shivering crests of the stuff, blinding mounds. The drifts were head deep in places, seemingly bottomless in the gullies and draws. Stand was undaunted, but she was only one horse. If it hadn't been for the trains of pack mules keeping the road open, they never would've made it through.

Buckland's Station in the Territory of Nevada presented the second flaw—talk of hostile Indians in the country ahead. Who knew how many of them watched Bendy undetected. The only braves he actually crossed paths with were too taken up with driving a herd of ponies to afford him a second glance.

At Carson Sink he came upon a team of station builders—several men axing and dragging willows for a corduroy road while others stamped barefoot in a bath of adobe mud. He asked the way forward, nothing more.

After surmounting the brutal Sierras, Stand proved herself more than equal to a series of desert ranges, as well as to the thirst and drilling winds of the barren tracts between. It seemed no privation was too great for her, and so long as she kept her footing, Bendy swore he would keep his seat.

He was in Utah Territory before he encountered a second station-building team. Leaning back in his saddle, he wound down a steep grade above half a dozen men who were piling up a lonesome dwelling out of stone. Again he asked only for directions. When the inevitable *where-you-headed* arose, he offered the lone syllable, *East*.

Meanwhile, despite what he told himself about the green and peopled stretches at the limit of the route, Bendy was falling victim to the desert's pull. And push. While drawing him through its vastness, it drove that same space inside. He carried its lovely, wrung-out weightlessness with him into the treed country around Utah Lake, up through the humming towns to the city that was the Territory's beating heart.

Salt Lake City wasn't exactly East, but neither was it the West he'd come to know. Yards were tended, porches neat. Fences stood whitewashed, upright. There were children everywhere, faces scrubbed, hands full of feed buckets, laundry baskets, books. Women—all women, it seemed—wore dark, high-necked dresses, unassuming prints. They kept their hair neat and plain, a knife's-edge centre part, two halves smoothed down from the temples, over the ears and back. Men called one another *Brother*—Bendy overheard them—hail after neighbourly hail.

He drew up outside the post office and let Stand take her time at the public trough, watching the human whirl out the edges of his eyes. He'd heard a thing or two about Mormons. He would learn soon enough not to use the word. Here in their own Territory, these people referred to themselves as Saints.

"Pardon me," he said, choosing one of them at random, "is there a Pony Express station hereabouts?" He'd asked the question many times along the route, but this time it felt different, vaguely electric on his lips.

The man turned and pointed to a grand verandah-fronted building across the street. Its swinging signboard read *Salt Lake House*. "Brother Egan—" He paused, looking Bendy up and down. "—Howard Egan's the man you want to see."

"Oh, no, I—"

"You won't find him in there, though." He arced an index finger westward. "They're out building stations in the desert."

Bendy nodded. He tipped his hat as the Saint moved on, then mounted up slowly, his mind a whirring expanse. What he did next confused him, confused Stand too. For the first time ever she resisted him, pulling against the reins for a moment, certain he'd made a mistake. After so many days spent moving toward sun-up, it made no sense to turn her white face back the way they came.

35

May 25th, 1867

Dear Daughter

Yes in spite of everything I carry on addressing you so.

How could I do it? I know a thousand questions must
crowd in upon you now but surely this will be chief among
them. How could I comfort my husband knowing what he
had done? How could I assure him he was innocent in the
eyes of the Lord when I knew in my heart I spoke a blasphemy?
Because I was his wife? Yes but the truth must be whole or it
is worthless. Dorrie I could do it because the Lord had seen fit
to give me you. You must remember. Some part of you must.
You were old enough when it happened six or seven years of
age at most.

With all the weeping and carry-on it took Mr. Burr an hour
or more to choke out the entire tale. Like the fool he is he left
the heart of the matter till last mumbling it into my lap in the
smallest hours.

I think maybe one of them scampered off he said.

Until then I had been listening through a kind of veil. It fell away at those words. I bucked his head up off my legs. What? I cried. What did you say? His eyes were popping. I was undoing what little calm I had wrought in him but I didn't care. Tell me I cried. He could scarcely speak. A dress he said I saw a little white dress. In among the bushes up on the hill. But I might have mistook myself. It was night. Show me I said. I didn't have to tell him twice.

It was a dark ride of two hours or more and the night was chill yet I was insensible of any hardship. Dorrie I believe I became inhuman for a time that night. So pointed was my purpose that I felt little revulsion and even less pity when we finally came upon the scene. The wolves had begun their work. Every grave was undone. The ground was littered with corpses and not one of them whole. Mr. Burr slumped in his saddle gibbering. By then he had given up begging me to turn back.

You will think me hard my girl but I had eyes for the living alone. More than eyes. Dorrie I could feel you. I could not think how a small child could escape so many men to survive uncared for in the wild yet in my bones I knew you were still alive. And so I called you. Over and over I voiced the plea I had borne in my heart for so long. Child child child. I would have called until the voice withered in my throat but Providence did not try me so. You answered and were found.

Dorrie I have never clasped another so tightly in all my life. I had to remind myself time and again not to squeeze the life out of you. You fit perfectly between my body and the saddle horn. The smell of everything you had lived through rose from you like smoke. Blood and filth and fear. And sage. My eyes burned with it over the miles.

You were so ill during those first few weeks. There were times when your pulse thinned to a thread yet I never once feared I would lose you. You had been given to me. You were mine and I would do anything to keep you. I would blaspheme. I would lie. Even to you my daughter. Most especially to you.

I will bundle this letter up with the others now as I am quite sure I shan't live to dip my pen again. My heart wallows Dorrie. It is well and truly mired. You may wonder at these words that are so much darker than any I have written in months gone by. I feel as though I have been sending you packets of pressed flowers only to surprise you with a parcel of some wild animal's flesh. I console myself with the notion that you of all people will understand both to be the stuff of life.

See how a plain-spoken woman might wax poetical in her dying hours. Dorrie those flower letters passed always through my husband's hands on their way to the post office in Cedar. I cannot say if he read them but I know a guilty man imagines every shared word to be a word against him. These last I will make certain he does not see. He is gone to town. He will return with some ribbon for Kitty and nothing at all for me. But I will not begrudge her. Did I ever truly? I knew from the start the thing was none of her doing. What is more their sealing was not the true betrayal. That came before she ever set foot in this house when he traded my only child away.

Besides now she is become my accomplice. I could not hope to wield the knife with such close and careful force. It seems she is capable of neat work when it is truly required. She manages a few pages at a time working where I can see her with the Doctrine and Covenants laid out upon the bedside table. Watching her I grow quiet as though I were observing the digging of a grave. She leaves the white margins just as I have asked and in time she has crafted me a clean and secret hole. She folds the book's insides into her apron pocket. As agreed she will set fire to them shortly in the stove. It is a sin to burn Scripture I know but we are both of us willing enough.

I trust her to do me this and one other final service. You will see she gets it? I ask her again. Along with the news? Beside her my hand is a bloated thing. She covers it with her own. I will Mother Burr she whispers. I do not bother to correct her. Thank you Kitty. I smile and watch her silly eyes fill with tears.

She has left me alone now to fumble at finishing the job. I can see my letters will fill the carved space nicely. Now at last you may hold the truth in your hand. Goodbye my daughter.

All a mother's love
Helen Burr

36

ERASTUS FINDS THE TRACKER sitting with his legs knotted like a sultan's before an ebbing fire. He slides down from the saddle, his boots touching ground alongside the Indian's rifle. Only now can he make out the bones of something insubstantial among the embers, the grease on his companion's lips.

"Had your breakfast already, I see."

The Tracker looks up at him.

"Got a wolf sniffing round the house." Erastus folds his arms. "Big bugger. Making himself at home."

No response.

"You seen him?"

"See him. Hear him."

"Yeah. Makes one hell of a racket."

The Tracker shoves the unburnt tail of a twig forward, stimulating the coals.

"Makes the womenfolk jumpy. We'll have to see to him."

The Indian rises. "No gun."

"No gun?" Erastus points to the Henry. "What do you mean no gun?"

"No gun this wolf."

"No gun this wolf." Again, Erastus finds himself repeating the Indian's nonsense. "Why the hell not?"

The Tracker toes something in the dirt. He takes his time answering, and when the words finally come, Erastus feels rather than hears them, three cool fingers laid across the stubble at the nape of his neck.

"This one smart."

He forces a laugh. "Too smart for shooting?"

The Indian shifts his gaze, staring through a break in the brush to some uncorrupted view Erastus can't hope to know. Then dips his chin in a single, irrefutable nod.

They are ten at table, Sister Eudora eschewing the midday meal as usual to keep company with her dead animals, Hammer busy chasing down more.

The hired man interests Ursula. Not as a man—only one has ever done so—but as a creature come into her fold. Wolf or sheep, it remains to be seen, though in her fibres she feels he is the latter. Still, a body can never be too sure.

Looking down the laden table, she takes his measure yet again. Wiry. Thoughtful. Not entirely whole. The kind to keep his eyes, his hands and, unless prodded, his opinions to himself.

Beside him sits a different sort of man altogether—and he is a man now, nineteen years since his crippling birth. Ursula's eldest son slides his knife under the skin of his chicken leg, causing it to jump. She registers a corresponding flinch in her own right arm. The urge to smack him is nothing new. It only makes matters worse that, when he meets her damning look, as he does now, it's through eyes that are brazen copies of her own.

Uncomfortable under her scrutiny, Lal shifts his gaze away. It's not something she'd ever give voice to, but Ursula's certain her son dug into her insides while she sweated and strove to push him out. She can picture him driving his elbows and knees into the walls of that red canal, making of his small body a sharp-angled star. She fought him for hours in that swaying wagon bed. Overhead, rain needled through the canvas, finding out the seams. Beneath her, the trail jolted on.

The Prophet had been dead four years, his people driven westward, scattered in temporary settlements across Iowa's breadth. Brigham was no Joseph, but there was no doubt the new Church President could lead. In the summer of 1847 he had done just that, seeking out the desert paradise Brother Joseph had foreseen. One year later, Ursula and her husband were part of the Big Company, Zion-bound. It ought to have been a time of glory.

Lal came tearing his own momentous path a fortnight early, when the company was scarcely under way. Ursula had known he would be born on the trail, but she'd hoped to get her bearings first. She wasn't the only woman bracing for such an ordeal. Some, having witnessed so much death, expressed a simpering pride at their bodies' capacity to begin anew. Ursula felt none of their satisfaction, only a grim sense of purpose. After four fallow years with Hammer, she was finally doing the work of the Lord.

She bested Lal eventually. Forced him out bloodied and bawling during the drizzling tail end of the storm. She insisted on rising the next day, leaving the baby in the wagon, well swaddled, immobilized in a crate of straw. *A mother knows,* she told Hammer when he questioned her. She wasn't about to lie still and let her blood turn bad—fresh air and exercise were what she required. She would rest when everyone else did, when night fell and the company made camp.

She climbed into the wagon box only when absolutely necessary. It was during those times—once the baby had finally quit
blubbering, clamped down on her rigid, burning nipple and drawn
its fill—that she changed the dressings between her legs. She
wadded up whatever she could bear to sacrifice from among their
scant possessions—tea towels, table napkins, winter socks. She
could have washed them of an evening—rigged up a rope-and-
sheet screen to be alone with her mess—but Hammer would
have been curious. Eventually he would have peeped.

Instead, she waited until he was taken up with the team or the
back axle, or had mounted up in pursuit of a flash of game. Freed
from his prying gaze, she would reach past the idiot trail hand's
knee, feel under her straw pallet for the latest bundle and slip it
beneath her apron's folds. From there she had only to drift to the
company's verge and duck into the first cover she met.

There was nothing strange about a body seeking a moment's
privacy—it happened all day long down the train's great length.
Unlike the other women and girls, however, Ursula didn't gather
her skirts about her and squat. She saved her water for the night
pot, knowing the holding would do her blown and ragged insides
good. Also, with the pot she could gauge parts of urine to parts of
blood.

Among the thickets that crowded the trail, she stuffed her dirty
rags into root tangles, or flung them deep into undergrowth too
knotted for a fellow human to breach. Not so the host of wild
things those long woods housed. Ursula knew full well some creature or other would sniff out and feed upon her secret. It was a
comfort to think she would leave no sign.

By the tail of the fourth day the baby was quietening, learning
to like its crate. The blood, too, was coming under control—a
scattering of scarlet coins on Ursula's drawers now, the sticky

wadding no longer required. To walk was all she wanted. She was getting her strength back now, her thighs no longer trembling with every stride.

She must have been getting her colour back too, for something fired Hammer's foolish enthusiasm, causing him to narrow the space between them and attempt to take hold of her hand. It was then that she let him know the way of things—not in so many words, but she gave him to understand what she herself had comprehended in the midst of her labour pains. She would not populate Zion, not even one small corner of it. One baby. One vicious, blue-eyed boy and she was ruined for life.

Dorrie's been struggling with the adult male mannequin for over an hour; no matter how she tries, she can't seem to reproduce the deep hull of the animal's chest. She's astride its back, passing twine under its belly, when Hammer yanks open the door. She knows it's him without looking up, his short-armed jerk producing a squawk from the bottom hinge. Besides, Bendy only ever comes during the night's second half.

"What's this?" her husband says.

She drops the ball of twine, straightening to face him. A black-tailed jackrabbit hangs by its feet in his grasp. Slung over his shoulder, the kill bag betrays the slack brown ear of what is undoubtedly the mate. He drags his gaze over the skeletal pack.

"Thought you'd be further along by now." He stands staring for another long moment, then crosses to her workbench and swings the jackrabbit up from his side. It lands with a muted thud. Blood trickles from the cleft in its upper lip.

Dorrie eases back off the mannequin as Hammer digs a hand

into the blood-stiff bag and draws out the female, a slightly smaller version of the first. This one he clutches by its ears. Again the jaunty swing. It lands alongside its mate, seepage from the wound in its hindquarters darkening the bench.

Moving closer, Dorrie feigns interest in the kill. "Big." She gestures to the male.

"Hm." Hammer pivots to survey the situation again.

"I'll just skin these two for now," she says quickly. "Mount them when I'm done the wolves."

"Good idea." He gives her a hard look, notwithstanding the sheen of reactive tears now evident in his eyes. His mucus too is beginning to run, already glistening in his moustaches. "I'm itching to see them." His hand lands on her shoulder, giving the stringy muscle there a squeeze.

"I know it," she mumbles.

A fat droplet spills from his left eye, and he lets go of her shoulder, reaching up to knuckle it away. "I'll leave you to it." Swallowing a cough, he chokes momentarily on its tail. He tries not to hurry on his way out, but his agitation is plain. He's desperate, almost gagging, to be gone.

Thankful has been left to her own devices again all day. She's filled the hours with sewing, and now the black and blue dress lies alongside her on the bed, complete but for the final hemming. She glares into the drooping canopy, brings both hands to her skull and presses, courting pain. When it doesn't come, she rolls and drives her face into the quilt. Smothering herself. Not long, just until her heart begins to labour. Then gasping, wrenching her face aside, catching sight of herself in the vanity mirror.

The light of a lone candle ought to be flattering. Hair like a mouse nest—how can it take so little to undo all her work? Kohled eyes turned to mudholes—why in hell is she crying? When did she start?

A little over four months have passed since Hammer lay with Ruth, but Thankful isn't the kind to let bygones be bygones. She tells herself he'd never have done it if Mother Hammer hadn't worn him down, but that's only part of the story. Hammer chose his second wife in the first place, remember. Got her with child five times before Thankful caught his eye. Worse than that, he still rests his gaze on her from time to time. Imagines he's getting away with it. Takes his third wife for a fool.

But Thankful is no such thing. She knows it's natural enough for a man's attention to stray—but to stray to an object like that? Ruth spends her days playing with grubs, staining her fat hands green. Her complexion isn't bad, and yes, her hair is enviable, but the rest of her scarcely merits a glance. She's built like a stack of corn sacks. Her belly, already ballooning, must be striped like a tiger's back.

Let a man breed you and it's the beginning of the end.

Charlotte de Courcey, peeling out of her costume and holding forth. On the night in question she was Desdemona, come backstage after the suffocation scene. *Mark my words, girls, the day he makes a mother of you, he'll be looking for a fresh field to plough.*

It seemed good as Gospel, given more than one poor dupe Thankful had known—not to mention her own mother's throwaway life. Words to live by, or so she believed. Yet it's clear Hammer would get across Ruth more often if Thankful let him. And Hammer's not the only one.

Less than an hour ago, alone and lonely in her room, Thankful conceived a craving for something sweet. She made her way downstairs to the kitchen, this time entering not when Lal was returning from his nocturnal wanderings but just as he was slipping out the door. She followed without choosing to, as though she were tethered to him on a lead. It was her first time setting foot outside in weeks, and she felt the night turn and regard her with hostile eyes. Wolf eyes, for all she knew.

He carried no lamp, but she found she could set a course by the moonlight in his hair. She could be stealthy when life required it. Years crossing backstage while others hogged the applause taught the trick of an undetected step.

He didn't go inside the silkhouse—didn't even approach the door—and in a way, that made it worse. To moon at a window like that, to risk so much just to fill his eyes. That was more than lust. It was worship.

Thankful watched him watch, and in all that darkness she saw, for the very first time, his singular beauty. He was something more than a reworking of his mother's looks, something separate and entire.

It was plain his vigil would be long. After some minutes she left him and crossed the dark yard alone.

Erastus plunges his nib carelessly, spreads the kill book and messes the page. Before him the lamp sputters, the table trails off into dark. Along its margins, empty chair backs loom. It's been a trying day, hours spent dogging the Tracker about the property and beyond, the only wolf sign to be found a single, days-old turd.

He returns to the ink blob—a shape that suggests nothing—and frets for a moment over whether he should commence writing beneath it or tear out the page and start fresh. His hands choose the latter, leaving a ragged edge as they uncover the dark ghost that's bled through. Resisting the urge to rip the second page out as well, Erastus dips the nib with care and employs pen against paper—the pressure of writing itself—to steady his hand.

26th of May, he scratches, *1867. Jackrabbits a fine pair. Blacktails. Flushed to a run in the far pasture.*

They hadn't been on the lookout for small game, but when the stupid creatures showed themselves, it seemed a shame not to pick them off.

Caught on the fly one shot each. Male in the neck. Female in the hind end.

Erastus halts, biting the pen's tail. She hasn't given him the particulars. He has no notion of weight or length, not a single figure to set down. His jaw tightens, the anger a rush he knows often, though rarely in relation to Eudora. He's asked little enough of her over the three years he's called her wife, and for her part she's done her work ungrudgingly and well.

Until tonight. Tonight she smiled—sniggered even, it seems to Erastus now—at his discomfort. And what about the wolves? He'd expected to find at least some of them back inside their skin.

He's been too soft on her, he sees it now. He'd march over there for the jackrabbit numbers right now if it didn't mean subjecting himself to that poisoned air. Besides, why should he go running? He'll send her back for the figures when she comes shuffling in answer to the morning bell. Tell her to comb her hair, too, maybe. Take off that filthy smock. Erastus nods. He'll have the family sit tight until she's back. Let the breakfast go stony cold.

Dorrie perches on her stool, her notebook open in her hand. Before her on the workbench lie the partly formed pups. She's fixed leg bones to rods, wired on skulls and shaped the crude bodies, but can't bring herself to begin the careful work of plastering. Her notes detail the location of every hollow and ridge, but they're only numbers, words.

"Can you do the barking pup again?" she asks.

"Sure thing." Bendy rolls up on all fours, rump to the rafters. His shoulder blades slip to vertical. Clicking his lower jaw out an extra inch, he bares his teeth.

She sets the notebook aside, takes up her block and sketches listlessly, wasting time. A line or two is the most she can manage before she scribbles and begins again. Perhaps using a model is actually clouding her vision. Or perhaps she's simply tired.

Beneath these and a dozen other excuses, a stream of truth runs cold and clear. None of that matters. Either you can do it or—*what if?*—you can't. Her pencil halts, clinging to the page.

"Brother Drown," she begins.

He barks.

"That's enough." She lays the series of aborted sketches face down on her workbench. "That's enough for tonight."

"Okay." He draws back into the high point of his tailbone, stands and shakes out his limbs. Then, looking about him, "You never did a horse?"

She shakes her head.

"Think you would've, living here."

"He doesn't want me doing anything he didn't kill."

"Huh. But would you want to, say, if one died?"

Clear as crystal, Dorrie envisions the huge mare, Ink. It would be a touchy job—thin hide, short, glossy hair, every vein showing through. Never mind the issue of size.

"Yes," she says finally, "I believe I would."

He plucks a straw from his shirtsleeve. Plays its tip over the palm of his hand. "That'd be something to see, a horse standing still so long."

She nods, only half listening, rebuilding Ink's great barrel in her mind.

"Don't see that with the wild ones."

"Hm?"

"Horses. They're always grazing or fighting or—" He colours a little. "—you know, moving." He tosses the straw aside. "You'd have to be a cat to catch them sleeping. They hear too good. Crack a twig under your boot a quarter mile off and the whole herd's up and away."

Dorrie blinks to picture it.

"Hell, most of the time they spook the second you lay eyes on them. They can feel it."

She brushes her fingers over the end of the runt's leg bone, the knob that will give rise to a paw. "Feel what?"

"Your eyes." He pauses. "Same as a hand."

Same as she can feel his now, her scalp tingling.

"Yes." A small word, out before she can swallow it. When she looks up, the barn has shrunk by half. The collection breathes down Bendy's neck. Birds dangle over his head, perilously close. Again she casts her eyes down, fixing on her scaly knuckles, peeling nails.

"Hey," he says, "let's you and me try it."

"Try what?"

"Close your eyes."

"Why?"

"Just close them."

She does, if only to avoid looking at him. Her internal darkness shrinks things further. It's as though she could reach out a hand and make contact with every creature in the place, from the red-tailed hawk to the bighorn—even Cruikshank Crow on his pillow beneath her cot. Even Bendy. She could easily touch him too.

"Where am I looking?"

She's startled to find his voice no closer, still a good three yards away. "My hands," she blurts, fighting the urge to hide their ugliness.

He sighs. "You're not trying. Try."

She bites her lip. Then feels it—a soft burning, dead centre between her eyebrows. She raises her right hand, touching a forefinger to the spot. "Here?"

He laughs. "That's more like it. Okay, now where?"

A flare at the tip of her nose. She touches it.

"Huh." No laughter this time. "Got it in one. Where now?"

Her finger moves of its own accord to the bone cradle at the base of her throat.

"That's right." He says nothing for a time. Then, "How about now?"

At first, her body is a blank. Then, sudden as a slap, her knees begin to sting. He's looking under her workbench. Tucked away beneath smock, dress and stockings, her legs might as well be bare. She snaps open her eyes, and he lifts his to meet them. Slowly. Not as though she's caught him doing wrong. As though she's interrupted him mid-page in a beautiful book.

"This is foolish." She jerks up off the stool. "You'd best be going."

"Yes, ma'am." He scoops his hat up off the floor. At the door he turns. "I'll come tomorrow night, will I?"

She says nothing.

"We can try the mother if you like." His grin is uncertain.
"I suppose."
"Good night, then." He hesitates at the door.
She turns her back to him. "Good night."

37

THE RUN HAD A LOGIC all its own, an inverted sense of things Bendy felt rather than knew. Working the desolate stretch between Fish Springs and Faust's Station, he risked death by a hoof put wrong, by frying or freezing, by an arrowhead embedded in the skull—yet each of these hazards held a balm of compensation at its core.

The possibility of a bone-crushing tumble came courtesy of great speed, the same speed that caused his blood to beat up and wash his insides to sparkling. In summer, blistering heat made the horizon dance, made his head hum on its stalk, made water— even the body-warm, sulphurous water of Fish Springs—a pleasure close to that which he'd known in the dog girl's den. His childhood had hardened him to damp and chill, but the desert winter shoved sere blue nails into places the coastal rains had missed. He felt those places crystallize; surfaces that might have been broken, their depths plumbed, could now only be skittered across. Besides, he'd heard death by cold was a close cousin to one of his dearest loves—a deep and untroubled sleep.

Death by Indian attack would be another matter. Still, there was something to be said for an enemy at the margin—glimpsed or imagined between greasewood clump and black volcanic boulder, known to be wreaking havoc just a few stations further west. There'd been the trouble at Williams Station and the resulting battle at Pyramid Lake. Seventy-six white men lost and another twenty-nine wounded, a hastily mustered body of volunteers trapped in the cottonwoods and picked off like bewildered deer. Rumour had it the whole mess had started over a squaw, Williams or one of his brothers or someone else entirely forcing himself on her and paying a heavy price. Pyramid Lake was the worst of it in terms of numbers, but the raids continued, several ending with riders or station keepers lying dead.

Most of Bendy's route lay through the wide open, where he'd spot any trouble against alkali flats or snow. Any mount he'd be riding would be a match for an Indian pony; nearly all the animals on Egan's division were just broken, fresh from the wild. They were fast the way only prey can be, and they feared nothing for their flint-hard hooves.

Of course, there were hills, passes where the land folded and closed in, where a war party could be upon him before he knew what he was about. In those narrow circumstances, he reverted to the old knowledge, the areas of his brain that had formed in reply to blind corners, darkened lanes. As it was, fortune smiled. In a year and a half of service he suffered neither ambush nor open assault.

Even the subtler dangers passed him by. The rigours of the schedule were a punishment to some, but Bendy felt the press of time and purpose like a defining embrace. St. Joseph to Sacramento, nearly two thousand miles, in just ten days. Seventy-five miles give or take between home stations, eight to fifteen of them per horse. The mail must go through. The mail must go through. The mail must go through.

Some who could handle the pressure buckled under the solitude. That portion of the trail sustained few inhabitants—only the hardiest of station keepers and hostlers, not one of them with a woman in tow. Game sightings were so infrequent they stopped the heart. With the exception of the mire around Fish Springs, even the swoop of a bird was rare. For a city boy, Bendy turned out to be a master at being alone. Because he wasn't. To consider himself solitary would have meant discounting the creatures on whose backs he rode—an idea that never once entered his mind. It would have made as much sense to disregard his own body, for, moments into any ride, he could feel the border between horse and rider begin to fray.

The rapid-fire strike of hoofbeats—right-hind, left-hind, right-fore, left-fore—chased by a hair's-breadth moment of suspension. *Glory.* He felt it down the inner traces of his shin bones, just two more ribs in the pony's cage. Felt it most of all in the fiery springs of his thighs. It beat a path to his heart, rebounded in a racing pulse. The sweat of his own effort melted into the animal's back lather. He began to blow along with the pair of great bellows between his heels.

Somewhere mid-route, after the second or third change of horses, he began to feel as though his eyes were slipping back to the sides of his skull. Then horse and rider looked out as one, Bendy's field of vision widening to encompass all but a narrow strip of forehead and a rippling wake of tail. By the time he reached Fish Springs or Faust's Station and passed on his *mochila* of mail, it seemed as though separating from his final mount would require a blade of some length, the spilling of considerable blood.

Attempts to puzzle it all through never progressed far. Thinking on the back of a galloping horse wasn't thinking at all, but a kind of blissful streaming—the mind relaxing its grip, giving up its holdings to the wind. He fared little better in the between times. Swing station stops were barely that, his heels touching down as Dan Pitch's had when he'd vaulted over Belle's forgiving back. Unlike Pitch, Bendy traded one horse for another, slipping his *mochila* free from one saddle horn and buttonholing it over the next. A fresh set of reins gracing his palm, he'd break for the horizon before his backside ever touched down.

At the home stations he knew the gift of true fatigue. As he slid down from the last of the day's ponies gone rubbery beneath him, he too would be close to collapse, his joints shaken so slack he feared they might give way entirely, leaving him tangled in the dirt like a mess of twine. After a plate of something salty and warm, and some bread unleavened by female hands, he was bound for the nearest bunk.

Two months into the job, continued raids forced a temporary suspension of operations between Salt Lake City and the Carson Valley. Through June, Bendy cooled his heels, tending stock at Fish Springs while stations further west were rebuilt, fortified and supplied with guards.

The springs wriggled with small silvery fish that fried up nicely in a smear of lard—a taste his coast-raised tongue had come to miss. To the west the trail cut through alkali glitter up into the hills, to the east it skirted marsh. Dawn and dusk were raucous with wheeling flocks. Fishing and stable work aside, the time lay heavy on Bendy's hands. He began to explore.

Prowling the marsh's verge, he found it thick with life. Bayonet grass sighed with muskrat, shivered with snake. Reeds, when parted, revealed nest after nest. Even the reek of the place was rich. Bendy penetrated further, careful of sinks. Coming upon a snowy egret fishing, he found he couldn't help but copy its shaggy dance. Tilt and shift the torso, lift one foot, make a lunging, beak-jabbing rush.

When the run started up again later that summer, Bendy found he loved the ride all the better for having made do without it.

There was more likely to be talk at the eastern limit of his route, where Doc Faust, the station keeper, was fond of telling tales. Bendy overheard portions from where he lay, the meat of each narrative bleeding into dream state.

Being the only non-Mormon among the riders and hostlers in those parts, he had trouble getting his bearings amid the storied landscape that began to unfold. He could never quite get a fix on the order of things—though it scarcely seemed to matter, as each chapter was more or less the same. The Saints gathered together, erected temples, planted crops and raised stock. They began to prosper. They were driven from their homes. Kirtland, Ohio. Far West, Missouri. A cursed hamlet called Haun's Mill. A fine city called Nauvoo the Beautiful, built up out of nothing, somewhere in Illinois. Only the town of Carthage stood apart. It was there that the Prophet himself met his end, plummeting through a hail of lead into the blackface mob below. Bendy tumbled alongside him, landing in a dark well of sleep.

Over time the frayed narrative wound into a single cord. One end led off into the ether, but the other looped around Bendy where he lay in his bunk. Every mention of persecution, of home-lessness, was a chafing tug. There was hope, though, a happy ending of sorts. Joseph Smith's people had made their way to a wilderness all their own. When their enemies had tried to drive them even further, the Saints would no longer be moved.

—

From time to time the captain of a supply train or a carrier for the mule-packed regular mail stopped in. Passengers were few and far between, the stage forsaking that leg of the route for months at a time. When they did appear, they were almost always male. An exception arrived one spring night when the ponies had been running for just over a year, a girl of perhaps nineteen, travelling in her uncle's care. She would've been fetching—dark, lashy eyes— but for the strawberry mark that had her by the throat. Three fat, red fingers curled up over her chin and across one cheek. She kept quiet. Kept back from the candle's glow.

The uncle was well spoken, the kind Faust warmed to, being a learned man himself. Together the two of them took on the story of all stories—the New World miracle at the core of the belief they shared.

"Imagine," the uncle began, "he was but a boy of fourteen when the Lord came to him in the grove."

Faust nodded. "Seeking counsel even then."

"Well, he was torn, wasn't he. So many factions."

"Methodists, Baptists, Campbellites, Footwashers, Shakers—"

"All of them corrupt, abominations in the sight of the Lord."

A deeper nodding, almost a rocking, from the station keeper now. "The Lord told him so. Told him to wait."

The uncle's head answered with a slow shake of its own. "Three long years until the Angel Moroni came."

Here Bendy saw the girl's eyes flutter closed, the loss of reflection carving two black pits in her unfortunate face. It was the smallest and most sensuous of movements. He felt his own eyelids follow suit, the resulting darkness giving rise to desire. It wasn't the act he craved so much as that which he imagined would come afterwards. It was a luxury he and Philomena could never afford—the pair of them closing their eyes as one, slipping together into sleep. He settled for toppling sideways on his bunk, following the great weight of his head.

The uncle murmured on. "Even then Brother Joseph had to wait. Four more years, four more visits from the Lord's messenger. Even after he'd been to Cumorah, unearthed the treasure, feasted his eyes upon the golden plates."

Bendy came close to letting go then, allowing himself to drift off. If the story was about gold, he'd heard it a hundred times before.

"Put them back, Moroni told him," said Faust. "The time for bringing the plates forth has yet to arrive."

Bendy's ear—the one not pressed to his folded-coat pillow—pricked up. *Put them back?*

"Ah, Joseph." The uncle gave a long sigh. "Such obedience. Such persistence when the time finally came to unearth the treasure and translate the story engraved thereon."

"He was no man of letters." Faust chuckled. "Little matter when you read with the eyes of the Lord."

"The world doubted him." The uncle seemed to sing now. "Some fought to discredit him. Some thought only of the gold, of melting the sacred plates."

"Let them try," Faust cried, indignant. "Let them mount up to heaven and try."

Bendy's head was a sack of sand. It split a seam, his consciousness scattering, whirling like the many desert storms he'd ridden through. Sleep curled itself around the one notion too weighty to blow away. Imagine a man who could drag gold from the earth and see nothing of its lustre on account of the message it bore. A man who, once he'd gleaned that message, returned the precious metal to its owner on high.

—

Nineteen months after two lean men on opposite sides of a continent kicked off on their inaugural rides, the ponies ceased to run. All it took was the meeting of two wires. Word crackled across the country now in a garble of dot and dash—electricity a current that put the rush of mere horseflesh to shame. It was early November, 1861. Bendy might have found work at one of the stage stations, or out on Egan's ranch at Deep Creek, but the idea held little appeal. Standing still in the heart of nowhere seemed a poor substitute for travelling breakneck along its spine.

All that hard riding had shaken a good deal of his old thinking free. He recalled an eastward impulse, but it had faded to a notion, and a vague one at that. Still, when he set out from Fish Springs the day after handing off his final *mochila* of mail, east was the direction in which he rode.

Anything slower than a gallop felt like riding through a saddle-high swamp, but it didn't seem fair to push Stand, not when they had so far to go. She too had done her time on the route. Unwilling to give her up, Bendy had worked out a lease of sorts, whereby she'd been kept to stations along his section of the line. Other men had ridden her, but this was a fact of no great concern. Cruel or careless riders seldom lasted long, being cheaper and more expendable than the animals they rode.

Still, the route had taken its toll. Stand was all wood and wire now, the long skull plain beneath her bleached-out face. She would carry him as far as the western bank of the Missouri. There, after a snow-whipped run that would've been routine to her only a month before, she would wait for him to dismount, then drop dead of a worn-out heart.

38

THE TRACKER WAKES with a start to find Hammer staring down at him through the hut's brushy mouth. Beyond, a black tower of horse.

"Hell, Tracker, why build a house if you're not gonna give it a roof?"

The Tracker sits up, pressing a hand to his skittering heart.

"Thought you weren't supposed to be able to sneak up on an Indian." The white man laughs. "What're you doing sleeping in the middle of the day, anyway?"

Getting his heels under him, the Tracker assumes a squat. Hammer blocks his threshold a moment more before stepping aside to let him stand. It's better, now he can meet the white man eye to eye. Still, to be caught off guard like that—and by a clay-foot like Hammer. The Tracker's first taste of oblivion. Mineral. Dark. A taste he could get used to.

"Thought we'd bag us a deer," Hammer says.

The Tracker steps past him, relieves his bladder against the ragged oak. "Deer," he says finally, buttoning back up.

"I know, we already got a full set."

The Tracker nods, memory sending a charge along his arm. A

swift downswing and the fawn no longer breathing, no longer struggling to stand.

He quiets the limb by making use of it. Dropping to one knee, he reaches into the hut and closes his fingers around the Henry's stock.

"It's not for the collection," Hammer tells his back. "It's a present."

Drawing the barrel alongside his shin, the Tracker turns in time to see the white man dig into his kill bag and withdraw a corked bottle of what appears to be salt. But isn't, the Tracker realizes. Nothing so benign. Hammer gives the bottle a happy little shake before slipping it back.

"What say we get started down along the ravine." Turning to the horse, Hammer hikes a foot up into the stirrup-iron. After a few levering hops, he mounts in defiance of natural forces, raw determination bent to resemble grace.

In lieu of a spoken answer, the Tracker rises, pivots west-southwest and sets off.

"Hey," Hammer calls after him, "aren't you gonna ride?"

"Not far."

"Far enough. I don't want it to be dark by the time we get there."

His eyes fixed on a dip in the horizon, the Tracker breaks into a run.

Stepping down from the kitchen doorsill, Ursula tosses her washing-up water over the flower bed that runs along the house. Come summer the dusty strip will be choked with black-eyed Susans. She smiles at the idea, a moment's pleasure before a small sound wipes her expression clean.

Listening hard, she scans the scrubby grass about her feet. Not far from the tip of her right boot a dead leaf trembles. She hunkers as quietly as her skirts will allow and slips a forefinger beneath its frilled edge. A grasshopper cowers in the sudden light. Ursula strikes before it can jump, tweezing it hard between finger and thumb. Its bent legs kick. She looks it square in its opaque-eyed face and twists off its head.

Why kill it? It's not one of the huge black crickets that come in plagues to smother the land, only a single green grasshopper, pretty in its way. Still, its destruction affords a rush of satisfaction she can only vent through a grin. She flings the broken body away. The bodies of those others—the grasshopper's filthy black cousins—don't bear thinking on. All the same, Ursula does.

Eighteen fifty-five. She and Hammer had been on their particular patch of Zion for seven years when the crickets came on like the worst kind of weather—unforeseen, unrelenting. As bad as the plague of '48, when a dark wave of them washed down into the valley of the Great Salt Lake, threatening the crops that had been sown to feed the faithful. Thousands would have starved if the Lord hadn't seen fit to send his angels, a great battalion of them disguised as gulls.

One moment a darkening waste, the next a fluttering, clover-white field. The gulls so bright as to be blinding. Where their wings showed grey it was the grey of a stone plucked up from a riverbed. A good, clean stone.

They gorged themselves, dragged their bellies spraddle-legged across the fields. Not a single Saint took advantage and scooped one up for the pot. The flock rewarded them by sending for reinforcements in the silent way birds do. They came and they came, until the foul rift that had given rise to that clicking black river finally healed. Their work done, the birds lifted and banked away. Beneath them, the fields stood swaying and green.

No gulls came to meet the swarm of '55. Seeing his people were settled, the Lord left them to fight that battle on their own.

Hammer could think only of his horses; it would be a decade yet before he would tire of them, abandoning them to Lal's care. The ranch looked burned-over, coal-black and glistening where the crickets still laboured, sere where they'd done their worst. He drove the herd south in search of grass they had yet to discover, leaving his wife and child alone.

Lal couldn't be counted on for much, so Ursula drove the buggy into Tooele the morning Hammer left and took a pair of town boys on for hire. All day long and deep into the night the three of them worked their shovels, Ursula rolling up her sleeves, her two arms more than equal to their four. The trench marked the western limit of the near pasture. It was the only decent grass still standing for miles, and Hammer had left her cows behind. The crickets would reach it within a day.

When the dark ranks came pouring, filling the long ditch like a fast black rain, Ursula and her helpers spilled a year's ration of kerosene, running end to end. Then lit their torches and set the trench aflame. The idea wasn't strictly her own. She'd heard tell that the Indians thereabouts were known to employ similar techniques—not to contain the onslaught, but to feed themselves and their children on the charred remains. Disgusting, but no real surprise.

Long after the town boys collapsed, Ursula laboured on. The creeping black carpet wasn't the only thing the fire consumed. Destroyed also was the mystique of sleep, as she learned how a body could thrive on the bright opposite of rest.

The smoke hid a foul grease in its folds. Ursula gagged on

mouthful after mouthful, even as she felt grateful for one small mercy—the stench had gotten Lal out from under her feet when even the sternest of her warnings wouldn't. When the last cricket had shrivelled and popped, and the trench was a smoking, stinking creek, Ursula opened her kitchen door to find him gnawing a green crust of bread.

The swarm would come again the following year, and again she would defeat it alone. She would have blamed Hammer more for deserting her, but there was no sense denying it—those horses were the best source of ready money they had. Besides, there was a sweetness to having saved the place without him. When he returned, she paid him even less mind.

Following the Tracker through close-knit trees, Erastus can almost bring the Paiute's outline clear. Almost tell the skin of those bare arms from the brown silk of his waistcoat's back.

It's odd, seeing one's castoffs animated in such a way. The Tracker wears whatever Erastus gives him until it falls to ribbons—or he would, if it weren't for a certain all-seeing eye. Ursula invariably notices when the Indian's pants are getting thin. Before any indecency can occur, she selects Erastus's oldest pair from the bottom drawer. His clothes still share a dresser with hers. He may bed down elsewhere, but there's never been any question of his effects going with him.

"Here," she said, passing him the most recent pair—the pair that moves through the forest before him now. "See to it he wears a proper belt." The backs of her fingers brushed his forearm, and she withdrew them quickly, as though they'd made contact with something unclean.

He held her gaze a moment. "Kind of you, Mother."

"You spend a good deal of time with that Indian."

"True."

"You must be fond of him."

He considered a moment, kinking his neck to her, drinking his fill of her eyes. "Does it matter?" he said finally.

"I should say so." Her gaze tilted to catch a shaft from the window. "If it keeps you from fulfilling your duty."

"My duty."

She gritted her teeth. "Yes, your duty. As a husband. As a *man*."

How long ago now? It was still full winter—he remembers the Tracker dropping his threadbare britches into a snowdrift and wriggling into the new pair. Erastus would give Ursula what she wanted not long thereafter—lying with Ruth, planting his seed—but just then he decided to hold his ground.

"My dear, are we not also duty bound to draw our red brothers back into the fold? I haven't your knowledge of Scripture, but—"

"Scripture!"

It was a rise such as he hadn't provoked in her for some time. He let her see how it pleased him, showing the first sliver of a grin.

She drew herself up. "'This people shall become a dark, a filthy, and a loathsome people.'"

"Indeed. But isn't there some nugget about the scales of darkness falling away come the final days? 'White and delightsome,' isn't it? Or have I got that wrong?"

He'd won. They both knew it, though Ursula acknowledged no defeat. Victory was fleeting. It departed when she did, leaving him to stand alone at their bedside, clutching a pair of old trousers like a fool.

Shifting, soundless trousers now. No matter how mindful Erastus is of his steps, he never comes close to matching the

Tracker's airy tread. It's as if those brown feet, clad though they are in a pair of Erastus's boots, are walking in a different wood— one where a body never quite makes contact with the earth. A lesser man might envy his companion, but Erastus knows silent soles aren't everything. They hadn't helped the devil he ran to ground near the settlement on the Provo River.

The Saints down that way had been too soft on their Ute neighbours—asking permission to put up houses, making them gifts—and they were paying the price. The band took what they wanted and answered any protest with gunfire. Erastus and some hundred and fifty others answered the call to give the region a good scrubbing out.

Seventeen years gone and still his blood beats hard to think of it. The wood was not unlike the one he and the Tracker pass through now. The cottonwoods a little older perhaps, and still naked, the ground blanketed with snow. His eyes could be counted on then—he spotted the brave when no one else did, got off a pair of shots and took after him, crowding his horse through the cover for all the beast was worth. The Indian should've had the advantage, being afoot in that narrow tangle, but a snow-deep root sent him flying. All Erastus had to do was draw up beside him and drop a couple of balls straight down from his barrel—one where the brave's shoulder blades met beneath his buckskin, a second where dark hair and feathers hid the base of his skull.

Erastus had killed men before, red and white, but never from on high, dropping lead balls as though they were swollen seeds. The Ute lay still, his right arm crooked where he'd raised it to break his fall—an image as clear and cold as the day that gave it rise.

The scene that lies before Erastus now is vaguer by far. The Tracker is opening the gap between them, gaining sufficient ground to render his form devoid of limits, discernible by motion alone. And now, by motion's cease. The Tracker raises his hand— a slow, exaggerated signal even a half-blind white man cannot fail to see. Erastus halts his own steps in answer. Remembers, for the first time since they entered the trees, the reason they've come.

The white man wants to lay the deer out where they can watch over it, but on the Tracker's insistence they deposit the body at the western edge of the far pasture.

"Wolf walk dying. Too close to house, take somebody with him."

Hammer doesn't need telling twice. He slits the doe's belly himself, beginning at the hole the Henry's ball opened in its breast, then salts her liberally with strychnine, upending the bottle to empty it along the length of the wound.

The job complete, the two men set off separately. Keeping the waning moon behind him, Hammer makes for the house at an easy canter. The Tracker turns his left side to the far ranges and heads homeward as well. Or so it would seem.

The moment the white man passes over a low rise out of sight, the Tracker turns back the way he came. A magpie beats him to the scene. He stoops on the move, swiping up handfuls of dirt, lobbing as many as it takes to drive the bird away. In sympathy, he feels his own hunger stir. He's eaten nothing since the night before. Crouching by the doe, he comes close to forgetting she's tainted, no longer food.

Poison. He recalls the she-wolf's skull, the child wife insisting he scrub its stain from his hands. He takes the doe by her uncontaminated forelegs and hauls her into the scrub, leaving a messy drag trail behind. Not what a wolf would do, but it's the best way he can think of to obscure his own tracks. Besides, for one who fancies himself a hunter, Hammer knows little of such things.

He's already decided where the doe will lie—close by the mother wolf's eyes but deeper. He'll take pains to pack the infill down and weight it with stones. He's seen the damage these white man's crystals can do, a single carcass spinning a wide spiral of death. Wolves and their younger brothers, foxes and skunks, weasels and wolverines—these and others leave staggering tracks as they abandon the kill, convulse and fall. Beyond the furred bodies, birds, the sky cut out from under them. Hawks and magpies. A mess of eagle. Always crows.

The first time he came upon such a scene, it radiated from the brown rise of a heifer. Some Mormonee farmer at war with the wild beyond his fields. The Tracker had left the ashes of his old life behind him just days before. Standing still in that littered pasture, a dead skunk reeking not far from his feet, he lost his bearings. The sun passed from above his right shoulder to above his left before he got them back.

Ursula is one jar away from reaching her tea box when Hammer shoves open the kitchen door. She doesn't flinch. Only replaces the peach quarts mechanically, their half-moon contents in slow commotion before her eyes.

"What're you up to, Mother?"

He knows enough to keep to the jute mat. Reaching for the bootjack, he cranes his neck to regard her.

She considers saying nothing, but silence might pique his interest further. "Cleaning." She slides the last jar into place and turns to face him, looking out from the confines of the larder into the open room. The light is poor—a single lamp, the glow at the stove grate—but she can make out the muck clinging to his boots, the dark smears of what is bound to be blood on his hands.

"Take off those filthy boots."

He waves the forked bootjack at her, then fits it to his right heel and, with a low sucking sound, works the foot free. His sock dangles empty inches. He drags it up with his bloody fingers—something else she'll have to soak and scrub.

"Can't you wash your hands?"

He fits the jack to the other boot heel, looses the foot with a sigh. "Pour me out some water and I will."

"Before you come in. Before you get blood all over my door handle."

"Your door handle, is it?"

She doesn't gratify him with a reply. Only crosses to the basin, taking up the kettle on her way.

He shucks off his coat and hat, hangs both on the nearest hook. "Kettle on the boil, I see. Now what would that be for?"

She keeps her back to him. "I told you, I'm cleaning." She pours out a steaming pool, tempers it with water from the jug. If she scalds him, he'll know he's gotten her goat. "Hurry up."

He comes to stand beside her, plunging his paired fists with a splash. He'll let his cuffs soak in the pinking water if she doesn't stop him. There's nothing for it but to reach across and wrench up his sleeves. He breathes on her cheek as she does so, hot and damp, the way she might breathe on a butter knife before rubbing it clean. She draws back, pushes the brown block of soap at him and crosses her arms. He washes loosely, sloppily, missing a red smudge at the back of one wrist.

"Are you blind?"

He grows still, as though unsure of her meaning. She points to the blood.

"Oh." He rubs diligently at the spot, swallowing it with suds, dipping the fatty lather away.

"What was it tonight," she says, "a barn cat? A lizard?"

He turns to face her, holding out his dripping hands. "A deer."

She drops a cloth over his cupped fingers. He wrestles his hands dry, tosses the cloth onto her clean table.

"A very pretty doe."

She plucks up the cloth and folds it over its rail. "You can't imagine they signify, these—trophies of yours."

"Signify?"

"Matter. Mean something."

"I'm acquainted with the word, Mother."

"Not to you." She turns her gaze on him. "To the Lord. You can't possibly believe He's keeping count."

He stares at her. "This again."

"Yes, this again. And again and again, Erastus."

He starts at the sound of his Christian name on her tongue. Seeing this, she wields it again. "Erastus, you know the Principle."

"I know it, woman."

"The more a man works to swell the ranks of the Church in this world, the greater his standing in the next."

"I said I know."

"Don't you want to be one of those who populates new worlds?" She lowers her voice. "'As man is, God once was; and as God is, man may *become*.' Would you be a mere angel, husband, or would you be a god?"

He lowers his eyes. "You have five children by Ruth."

"And what of the others? The dancing girl? That stick of kindling you keep out in the barn?"

"And another. Ruth has another on the way."

"Only because I made it so."

"*You* made it so?" He grins. "It's as I've suspected, then. You're not a woman after all."

"You—" She feels herself take a step back. "You know my meaning."

He matches it with a step of his own. "Are you, then?"

"What? Am I what?"

"A woman." The word thins at its conclusion, as though he can barely force it out. And then three events, so close in succession as to become virtually one.

His hand, clean now, reaching to take hold of her arm in its sleeve.

Then the reaction that flares in response to his touch—not rage so much as disgust, pity's cruellest edge. The idea that he should still try, still hold out hope after so many years.

Then the groan of a stair, a light step descending. Hammer makes no sign of having heard it—and why would he, his pulse drumming, his breath coming quickly, like a dog's.

The children do not wander. If they need her, they know to lie still and call. Ruth returned from her last feeding an hour ago and won't stir again for another three. Lal's tread is clumsier by far. Thankful, then. Coming to snoop at the sound of their voices. Coming to fill her beady eyes.

Ursula waits for the hall floorboard that squeaks, covering the sound when it comes with the last words Hammer can expect to hear. "You know I am, husband."

Then something he has no cause to hope for, let alone foresee. She lays her own hand over his where it wraps around her arm and, with a gentle squeeze, lifts and guides it to her breast. He sucks air like a man shot through the windpipe. She lowers her face, parting her lips to show him the tip of her tongue. He drives her back against the cupboards, levering up on his tiptoes to smother her mouth with his own.

Three, perhaps four seconds of his grinding whiskers and scrambling hands is all she need endure. Thankful isn't clever enough to slip away quietly and bide her time. She squawks like a pullet on the chopping block, stands shaking in the wide doorway, hair lank about the pale twist of her face. Hammer spins to face her, his hands in the air. Ursula meets her gaze over their husband's bristling scalp.

"Did we wake you, sister?"

And now, far too late, the ninny runs.

Ursula steps soundlessly to one side so that, when Hammer turns back to her, she's no longer there.

"I see now why she wears all that muck on her face." She smiles. "She's not much to look at without it."

"*Ursula,*" he moans, still not in possession of himself.

"You'd best see to your wife, Mr. Hammer."

He gapes at her.

She smooths the bib of her apron, erasing any sign of his touch. "Quick now." She treats him to one of his own hateful grins. "Before she draws the bolt on her door."

Striking out across the darkened yard, Erastus suffers a tearing sensation in his heart. Weakest of organs, it cleaves to her still. His first. His only. If he could, he would carve the bloody thing out whole.

He cannot seem to reach the horse barn. His stride is comically short—a feeling heightened by the sneaking suspicion that she's watching him from the kitchen window, perhaps even the open door. Eyes laughing. Mouth cruel.

And now those same damnable features come winding toward him out of the night. Lal is always slithering out of nowhere, this time from the blackness that clings to the stable's wall. He insinuates himself into Erastus's path, swivels and falls in step.

"You riding out again, Father?"

As a rule, Erastus would answer with a well-chosen word or two—*Man's work,* or *Nowhere you'd be of any use*—but just now he doesn't trust himself to speak.

"Father, I—"

Bereft of words, Erastus quiets his son with a single backhanded blow.

Alone in the parlour, Lal nurses his hurt cheek. It no longer throbs—scarcely even smarts—but remains painful all the same. He cups it in his palm, the thumb twisting up under his chin to rub at his bottom lip.

"It's not fair," he tells it.

No, it murmurs back, *not fair.*

Lal thrusts down through his heels, setting the rocking chair in motion. He's not allowed to sit here. No one is save her, but the household is abed, so his chances of getting caught are slim. In any case, there's nowhere he's not unwanted.

"Ruth," he moans softly.

"Speak up, Lal."

He starts, the chair dropping him back. Thankful stands before him by the time he rocks forward again. Her dress is a slippery petal pink. He doesn't know enough to realize the colour doesn't suit her—only that she looks washed out, maybe even a little green. He glares at her.

"All right, then." She gives a little quarter turn. "Don't tell me."

Scarcely a second elapses before she swivels back and covers Lal's hand with her own. Only then does he realize it's still welded to his injured cheek. He flinches, but Thankful holds steady.

"Somebody hit you? Was it her?"

He wants not to respond, but his head shakes itself slowly, his eyes fall closed.

"Him." An edge in the way she says it.

Lal nods. Her hand leaves his, hovers, and lands again, this time on his knee. Skirts rustle. He lifts his eyelids to find her kneeling before him on the braided rug. Up close she's definitely greenish. He wonders briefly, distantly, if she might be ill.

Then her other hand on his other knee. It's difficult to say who's to blame for what happens next, so equally do the pair of them take part. His legs spreading to the curved limit of the chair's two arms, Thankful dipping rapidly to nudge her sharp little chin into his groin. He groans an unlimited assent, but she's already standing.

"You like that?" She turns her back to him, crossing to take up a froth of crimson fabric from the low table beside the armchair.

"Uhn." The pain is exquisite, blood rushing to answer the touch she's withdrawn.

She turns, the bundle jammed beneath her arm. "He's in my bad books too." Her small teeth flash.

Lal nods, watching her move his way again. She halts just outside his reach.

"Ever heard a mouse scratch?" Thankful works a fingernail across her palm, producing the faintest of sounds. "Sometimes I hear a sound like that at my chamber door." She regards him keenly. "You know, in the middle of the night."

She sweeps past him, declining to wait for a reply. It's just as well—his throat and tongue feel as though they've been coated in salt. He wonders if he should rise like a gentleman now that she's moving to quit the room, but to do so would mean giving himself and his desire away.

Wrenching round to watch her go is better than nothing. She rewards him by repeating the sign—three light scritches written quickly over the lines on a palm. He spreads his hand and apes her, sealing the pact.

Erastus is in no hurry to return to the house, given that he'll be spending the night alone in Eudora's disused room. He plays with the idea of checking on the doe's carcass, but it's full dark now, and he's loath to come upon the wolf alone. The near pasture, then, is far enough. He lets Ink drop her great head and graze.

The knuckles of his right hand ring with the memory of Lal's cheekbone. The boy doesn't know how soft he's got it. His namesake, the first Lalovee Hammer, wouldn't have stood for a son who finished every day God sends with little or nothing to show. The other children work hard for Ursula, but they're too young as yet to be of any use to Erastus. Besides, they make him edgy—more like a clutch of blinking chicks than children. And anyway, it's a man's eldest son who ought to be his right hand.

Any work Lal does has to be laid out for him step by step. Tell him to see to the horses and you'll find them watered but not fed. Set him to cleaning stalls and he'll muck out every other one. Little wonder Erastus had to take on hire. At least that much is panning out. Drown earns his board and more, coming close to making up for the handsome sack of nothing Erastus is bound to call his son.

Truly, it's a lucky thing grandson and granddaddy never crossed paths. Erastus's father was a hard man in the Missouri backwoods mould. A devil of a shot, he took out every wild pig and redskin unlucky enough to set foot on his land. Besides clearing that willow-choked plot and planting it with corn, he'd had the foresight to build the only gristmill for miles around. It ran near constantly, his children put to work as soon as they stood as high as a fifty-pound sack. Erastus was the second of seven, black-haired Emmeline his senior by a year. He became the eldest when she was dragged by the hem of her dress into the works.

A hard, hard man. Folk thereabouts came to Lalovee Hammer's for more than the week's hominy and flour. Saturday nights they came in droves to watch men beat each other senseless on the patch of ground outside the delivery door. When he wasn't fighting himself, Lalovee was the one to call foul or declare a winner—the former heard rarely, as biting, eye gouging and blows beneath the belt were the order of the day. When the mill's owner was one of those who stripped to bare chests and braces, only one winner was ever declared. He wasn't a big man—shorter by a thumb's width, in fact, than Erastus would eventually stand—but he was wound tighter than any who dared meet him, and he could bite like a bloodhound, holding on until a finger or an ear, or once even a nose tip, swam loose in his mouth.

A man greatly respected, greatly feared. The same man who had pitched apple-weight stones at a son who dared strike out on his own, causing that son to see stars. It's some kind of love, surely, to try to kill the one who leaves you. Erastus can't imagine his own son leaving—can't even picture him filling a pack. One thing's certain. If, by some miracle, Lal ever did get up on that mess of a horse and ride out for good, Erastus wouldn't throw a blessed thing.

— 39 —

THE TRACKER DIGS the pit trap where the white man wants it—
some twenty paces out back of the cow barn. Hammer looks on
for the first yard or so down, during which time the son does his
share, steering the barrow smartly to and fro, clearing the telltale
mound of fill.

"Good and deep," Hammer says by way of excusing himself.

The Tracker glances up to see the son already laying down his
shovel. "Yes sir," he calls out after his father. "You heard him,
Tracker," he adds, once Hammer rounds the corner of the barn.
"Good and deep."

They lock gazes. As expected, the son shifts his away, turning it
skyward, acting the part of a man impatient with those in his
charge. A melody, thin and mocking, stirs in the Tracker's brain.
He works his jaw to its rhythm. The son is scarcely worth warning, but he sings a rough translation all the same.

> *Coyote*
> *on his tail*
> *he take him away*
> *take him away*

on his tail
Coyote take the child away.

The son glares at him a moment, then turns his head to spit. "What the hell was that?"

The Tracker cuts and tosses a shovelful. "Song."

"I know it's a song. Since when do you—why'd you sing it?"

"Song for bad child." The Tracker makes a third leg of the shovel, loaning it his weight. "Warning song."

The son shrinks visibly before the Tracker's eyes. "Get to work," is the best he can manage, barked side-on as he whirls away.

To the beat of the son's footfalls, the Tracker returns to the task at hand. Blade to earth, boot to blade, earth to sky. He puts his back into it and soon spills sweat from every pore. No one will think to bring him water. Nor will he be welcome at the well mouth, let alone the kitchen door.

By the time he stands neck deep, his thirst is turning dangerous. He floats rather than scrambles out of the hole and skirts the barn on the shady side. They will see him. From the garden, from the windows—the wives, the offspring, perhaps even Hammer himself, will catch sight of him on his knees, canting forward, lowering his face to the trough. They will laugh, or frown, or both. It matters little. The water is warm, fragrant with the meadowy mouth-slime of cows.

Having drunk his fill, the Tracker returns to his hole. Load after load, he diminishes the mound of earth. Pushing the empty barrow across the yard, he passes through a rich river of scent and knows the family to be gathered around the table for the midday meal. At the poplar brake, he cuts leafy switches and piles them high.

Back at the pit, he fixes the bait—a cottontail taken before he began digging. He ties one end of a long sinew around its neck, the other to the dead oak limb he's driven deep to overhang the hole. The rabbit dangles. He spreads the net over the mouth of the pit, then lays a loose weave of switches over that, saving the last of them to brush his traces from the surrounding ground. He will do so walking backwards, easing himself out of the scene. But first a sweeping glance to assure himself he's alone.

The Tracker kneels down at the pit's hidden lip. From the bag at his hip he withdraws a handful of rifle balls. Nothing smells more keenly of danger, but to be certain he nestles the cupped hand into the damp beneath his arm. Then holds it to his nose. Tang of metal, musk of man. Satisfied, he plants the first of them one knuckle deep. Leaving a hand's breadth between balls, he crabs sideways on his knees, circling the trap.

The clang of the supper bell comes as a great relief, Dorrie glad of the excuse to leave her work behind and trudge through evening birdsong to the house. She's the last to take her seat at the long table, her chair scraping when she pulls it out, drawing a matching sound from Mother Hammer's throat.

Hammer scarcely draws breath between muttering the blessing and making demands. "You made any progress on those wolves, Sister Eudora?"

Dorrie keeps her head bowed.

"I'll come and have another look after supper."

"No." A hint of shrillness. Her husband hears it too. He lays down his utensils. All eyes on the youngest, ugliest wife.

"I can't—" she blurts, "I'm having a little—trouble."

"Trouble? What trouble? You build a wolf, you cover it with wolfskin."

"I know." She looks up. "I am. I will."

He watches her for a long moment, until a hand in motion distracts him. Lal ravaging the butter dish. "Go easy on that butter, boy."

The eldest son jumps, yanks his knife back barely smeared. Glancing up, he catches Dorrie watching and twists his lip.

There is one at the table who would sympathize, whose eye she might seek if she dared. Instead, she forces her portion down in silence, rises when the rest of them do and hauls herself back to her cot.

Dorrie cracks an eyelid on blackness. She rises up on one elbow, strikes a match to light her bedside candle and finds herself faced with the same problem she abandoned at the peal of the supper bell. Sitting up, she blinks the crust from her eyes. The wolves haven't moved. Crowded together on the floor, they stand coated in plaster, ready to receive their skins. Ready as they'll ever be. Not ready at all.

To a one, the mannequins are lifeless. The runt is by far the worst—no suggestion of play, not even of submission, in its lines. Unless it be the final submission. Flat on its back with its four legs in the air, the smallest of the wolves looks dead.

Dorrie swings her feet out from beneath the covers, planting them on two uneven planks. She rises in a rush and crosses to her workbench. Reaching beneath it, she unhooks her hammer from its cradle of nails.

It's gone midnight by the time Bendy arrives. Dorrie is on her knees, prying staples from a slab of splintered wood. Around her, the floorboards tell the story of what she's done.

It's mostly plaster—dust and chunks, the odd shell-like fragment, smooth or faintly ribbed. Tufts of tow skitter, rushing for the vacuum of the open door. Some escape, others wheel back as Bendy draws it closed. Curls of excelsior sound beneath his boot heels. He walks a slow, crackling line to stand over her where she kneels. She says nothing, intent on the final staple, stubborn in the wood.

"I see you've done your worst."

She shoots him a glare.

"Never mind. You can always—" He's interrupted by a sound. Somewhere, neither proximate nor truly remote, a wolf sends up the first, low loop of a howl. Speech, even movement, is unthinkable. Only listening, the kind that takes place in the bones.

A second round ascends, ripples and trails away. The third is patchy, skipping over itself, splintering into a query of barks. On its heels a full-throated bawl. Each new vowel is both an echo and terribly new. It goes on forever. For a full minute, maybe even two.

Dorrie feel its aftermath in her skin, every last little hair rooted in gooseflesh.

"All on his ownsome." Bendy's voice startles her. "You heard him before?"

She nods.

"I saw a pack of them at it once. Maybe seven or eight." He shakes his head. "No two of them ever stick on the same note, but somehow it makes a song."

Dorrie's eyes have opened wide. She can feel them drying in her face. "Show me."

He cocks his head.

She scrambles to her feet, lunging for the sketch block. "Show me a howl."

❧

Erastus is cold. Eudora hasn't slept in this room for three years, but it's as though the bed remembers her lifeless chill. The quilt is dusty, but he drags it up about his neck all the same.

A man with four wives shouldn't have to sleep alone. He tried Thankful's door on his way past, but found it bolted. Ursula would laugh at him if he showed his face in her chamber. He could always put in with Ruth, but Thankful's already fit to be tied. No, best to wait his third wife out. A week, a month—whatever it takes. Patience is a hunter's virtue. A husband's even more.

In the dead of night, a thin sound at Thankful's door. She rises like a giddy girl to let him quickly, quietly in. They must be careful, Hammer snoring next door in the fourth wife's abandoned room, Mother Hammer like a mastiff down the corridor's far end.

The bed frame groans, so they lower themselves gingerly to the Persia rug. There can be no games—no hunt and capture, no costumes, no roles. And none are required. She need only lift her nightdress and he's wrenching his britches down. Thankful knows to help herself along, wasting no time with one so green. She swallows the cry when it comes, shoving her tongue hard against the backs of her teeth.

He leaves before he's entirely gone down, stuffing himself, elastic now but still large, back into the dingy folds of his smalls. Watching him slip out through her door, Thankful is swamped by an unfamiliar rush. She plunges her left hand down through the skewed neck of her nightdress, taking a nipple between finger and thumb. The unknown feeling comes clear. It is her own, and no one else's, desire.

❦

Back in his bed, Lal fights to control his body's trembling. He's a small boy with the ague. He's dying. His mother is busy in the cow barn—she won't come if he calls.

Idiot. He's a man of nineteen years, possessed of the knowledge he's longed for since the first of many growth spurts stretched him like a thief on the rack. Thankful. It was a blessing her bedchamber was dark. He wasn't called upon to confront her face—all angles where there ought to have been roundness, grey eyes where he wished for a deep, reassuring brown. The hair, too, was all wrong. He wanted it loose, wanted to follow its slick drop with his fingers to where it ended at the small of a back. He made do. Took a mass of spirals in his fist and held on.

As for the rest of her—breasts and spreading legs and hole— Thankful was a woman, all right. All right and all wrong. It hadn't stopped him losing himself inside her, burying his need.

Shivers animate every inch of him now, despite the night's warmth. He hauls the blanket up to his chin, the stubble there itchy upon contact with the wool. Thankful. Not Ruth. For a moment he considers the unconsiderable. Probably never Ruth.

The thumb is close by, just under the blanket's hem. He pops it out. "I don't feel good," he moans.

Good?

"She's—" Lal glances about in the blackness. "She's *his*."

He asked for it.

"He'll kill me."

He'll never find out.

Lal's teeth chatter. "He won't?"

The thumb nestles against his lips. *Trust me.*

40

THE TRACKER ARRIVES AT DAWN. The ranch house shows signs of life, but Hammer and the son have yet to emerge. The cottontail is gone, the sinew snapped clean through. The Tracker reads what happened on the ground at his feet. The initial approach. The warning scented, read full circle around the trap. The retreat, the turn, the bursting, bounding run—*the leap*. On the far side of the pit, the long skid of his landing, the triumphant trot away.

It's foolish, Erastus knows, but, just to be certain, he has the Tracker clear the brushy cover aside. Faced with the empty trap, he feels a similar pit open in the region of his bowels. First it drags off a poisoned carcass and now this?

Smart, the Tracker has said, but something in the Indian's hooded eyes hints at more.

What's it after? Not a single foal, not even a chicken, taken. The damn thing won't make a kill and won't clear off.

This one smart. Maybe, but a man can always outwit an animal. Erastus has an idea—a needle-sharp notion that mends his misgivings, sewing the internal pit closed. Dropping a smile into the hole before him, he glances up to meet the Tracker's gaze. "First light tomorrow."

He can count on the Indian to ask no questions. Just as he can count on him to show.

Ursula stoops at the edge of the vegetable plot, her back paining her just where a mother's will. Within eye's reach, three of her five little darlings work. Her girls are busy by the wash house—Josephine wrestling a mass of petticoats over the line, Josepha crouching over the basket, selecting the next sodden twist. Joseph is visible through the open door of the cow barn, shuffling forward and back, his shovel dipping. The other two are out of sight for the moment, but Ursula knows exactly where they are—Joe on his knees before the kitchen stove, Baby Joe beside him, filling his bucket with ash.

Any minute now, her youngest will scoot from the kitchen door, like as not sending up a ghostly cloud. She may be called upon to chide him for his carelessness, but she'll wait a moment before doing so, watch to see if he corrects himself. Who can say—the child might do as he's been told and take a direct path to the ash pile, swinging the pail only after he's emptied it. She's not overly concerned. He's still the baby. He'll grow up soon enough when he holds a brand new brother or sister in his arms.

Finding she's reached the end of a row, Ursula looks back over her trail of uprooted weeds. She straightens just as Baby Joe comes spurting from the kitchen door, her movement arresting him in his tracks. The smallest puff of ash escapes his bucket. He stands blank-faced for a moment, then hazards a smile her way.

Ursula's heart is suddenly full. She grants her youngest the rarest of gifts—the long, low trill of her laugh.

〆

Thankful is hearing things. It's the third time tonight she's hurried to unbolt her chamber door. No one. Not a soul. She closes the door slowly, locking herself back in.

Unwilling to return to her bed, she crosses to the window and looks down. The wolf is a silver memory. Not dead, though, despite Hammer's assurances; its singing reached her while she lay wakeful last night. She both looks for it and doesn't, unsure which is the more likely to keep it away.

Leaning out a little, she gulps at what passes for a midnight breeze. If only she could put more of herself out there, sit on the wide sill, dangle her legs in the air. Well, she could, couldn't she? What's stopping her? Her nightdress, for one. It drags at her shoulders, pools about her feet. Its folds would thwart her, send her toppling headlong to the verandah roof.

Most nights the idea would be enough to send her back to bed. Tonight she fights her way out of its gossamer mass. Forty pearl buttons drive her fingers mad. Then she's free of it. Showing herself at the casement like a naughty princess.

Easy now. Climb up in a crouch, work one foot out, then the other. She can feel the night's freshness. Wriggling her toes, she knows a sudden flood of promise, like a child laying claim to a swing. As the bare halves of her bottom widen across the sill, she pictures the arrowhead of dampness her sex is printing there. And thinks again of Lal.

As though conjured, her young lover appears below. He moves in the far left corner of all she surveys, his head illumined, dragging his dark body like a tide. She wills him to look up. He'll see her perched here like an exotic bird. Like Juliet without the burden of a costume. Like a woman he can't help but adore.

Only he's facing precisely the wrong way. He's leaving the ranch house, forsaking it for a much smaller structure hidden from Thankful's eye. Her heart slows with understanding, becomes a cool-skinned creature lodged in mud. She's not fool enough to imagine a tryst. It's worse than that. He's still pining for her—after all Thankful's given him, after all she's allowed him to do.

Let him scratch. Let him drag his damn nail over her door until it breaks and bleeds—she'll cut her arm off before she lets the thankless bastard in.

It's the arm that betrays her in the end. It strikes during the silence that follows the third scratching—the one where he might be deciding to give up—taking matters, in the form of the brass bolt, into its own trembling hand. His face in the crack weakens the rest of her. He slips inside with a smile.

Tonight he's bolder. He clutches at her rib cage, her buttocks, her calves. His hands are most certainly a farm boy's. He lifts her breasts as though weighing them, worries her nipples with his thumb to see what they do. He stops short of fingering her sex, approaching it blindly with his own.

Thankful has never felt anything like it. It's like being pawed over by some creature come loping from the wild. No knowledge, only want. A touch that could kill her, it's that clumsy. That powerful. That good.

Lal tries lying down, but the size of what he's done—*done again*—inhabits him, making him too large for his boy's thin bed. He considers leaving the room, the house, stalking about the yard—then imagines his bulk on the stairs waking his mother, rousing her suspicious mind. No outside, then, not this night. That much decided, he assumes the only bearable position, slouched at his open window. Here, at least, he can breathe.

And see. The sudden breach of the stable door—a cleft of darker dark from which the loose-limbed figure of Bendy Drown divides itself, becoming distinct. Out for a piss. No, a stroll. No. Lal feels a sudden buzzing, like a bright skullcap fitted to his crown. Drown is out to stretch more than his legs. He's crossing the yard in a hurry, a spring in his step. And now another barn door—this one showing a warm strip of light—takes him in.

Lal throws caution to the wind. He frees himself from his bedchamber, follows corridor to staircase, front hall to kitchen, creaking all the way. The latch on the kitchen door clatters. He's directly beneath his mother, but she won't mind when she learns what he's discovered. She'll thank him, Lal thinks with a flush, just as his father will.

He hasn't paused to drag on his boots, and the rough ground troubles his soles. Still, he wastes no time, threading between vegetable patch and wash house, sneaking up on the fourth wife's barn from behind. The window glass is wavy, but clear enough to show a pair of bodies stripped and tangled on a cot.

Only they're not. At least four paces lie between them, his father's wife tucked in behind her workbench, intent on the mannequin taking shape beneath her hands, Drown on the floor before her, all forearms—forelegs?—and settled haunches. Sitting like a dog.

Lal stretches out his disappointment, watching them a good long while. The girl's every movement is in fealty to the thing she's making. The hired man never even twitches a hair. They're nowhere near each other, and what's more, Drown is doing better than no harm—he's being of service to Hammer, helping the fourth wife get his precious trophies right.

Lal shifts his eyes to take in the tiered crowd. Beasts of half-light and haze, such as come to him rarely in dreams. His heart skitters briefly, then sinks. There's nothing for him here. He leaves them to it—animals, woman, man. Walks heavily back the way he came.

Nothing to record. And yet Erastus, pacing the dining-room floor, grips the kill book in his hands. For reasons as yet unarticulated to himself, the lamp remains unlit. Without benefit of its light, he can't even peruse the book's contents—a pastime he's not generally disposed to in any case. He turns its bulk in his hands. What, then? Why unlock the cabinet in the first place, why take the damn thing down?

What else is a man to do when he's woken in the middle of the night and there's no woman beside him in bed? This time it wasn't the wolf that roused him, but the sound of someone moving beyond his chamber door. Or the dream of a sound. The corridor lay dark and deserted by the time he stood peering down its length.

The book weighs against his fingers. It's high time he was making another entry. *29th of May 1867. No kill. No wish to.* Maybe Ursula's right. Would it signify if he never hunted again?

The moment the thought presents itself, he puts a shoulder to it, shoves it away. It's nothing to do with him. It's Eudora. She's taking so long—too long, dammit—to finish those wolves. What's the point of bringing her anything fresh? Did she even dress those jackrabbits like she promised? For all Erastus knows, she could have laid them aside to rot.

Again he turns the dark book in his hands. There are kills he hasn't recorded. Most recently, the look-alike brothers, mouldering some three years under the far pasture's crust. Not even a twinge of guilt there. They were fool enough to help themselves to what was his, and anyway, like he said at the time, it was doing them a favour to shed their sinful blood. The same couldn't be said for the many Gentiles he'd taken care of back in Nauvoo—not one of them died saved. But that was different. That was war.

Ursula had been his wife for a few short months, and already Erastus had given up hoping she'd remove the ugly locket ring from her married hand. He'd built a house for her, digging the foundations long before she accepted him. He'd had little choice but to guess at the layout she might want, for though he'd called on her countless times—were ever so many proposals laid down at a woman's feet to be so blithely kicked aside?—she had steered their every conversation down a single path. Always Brother Joseph. All he'd endured. All he'd created in God's name.

So it was that Erastus alone imagined, then erected, their first home. Logs hewn and dragged and fitted. Modest but well made. He set it in the midst of a hayfield—sown when he scarcely dared hope, high and swaying the day he brought her home.

The hay was drying in stacks the night marauders set fire to their farm. Erastus counted three of them. He let Ursula out the bedroom window, told her to run for the treeline and lie low. For once she did his bidding without question, without narrowing her brilliant eyes.

Having flushed many a creature from its cover, Erastus knew well what the trio of shapes had in mind. He was meant to belt it for the well in a desperate bid to save his house, making himself good sport, a clear target against the flickering yard. Instead, he let the log walls smoulder around him, waiting until the last possible moment before he took the back window himself and crouched beneath its smoking sill.

One haystack, set a little apart from the others, had yet to catch. Erastus crawled for it, rifle thrust out before him. Interring himself in its sweetness, he felt the mice around him burrow deep.

The Gentiles couldn't have known how long he would wait. Once they figured every Saint on the place had fled or burned, they began to move boldly about the yard. Erastus picked them off in sequence. The first taken unawares, the second firing a pair of guesswork shots before turning tail, the third running straight for the haystack in his panic, showing Erastus the space between his eyes.

It made sense to burn rather than bury the dead. Erastus dragged the bodies—two by their boots, the third by his armpits—as far inside the crackling cottage as he dared. He watched from a safe distance until the roof beams came tumbling, then set off for the woods in search of his wife.

That winter he rose through the ranks of the Nauvoo Legion, earning himself a reputation as a deadeye shot with an unflinching hand. Whatever he did, he did in the name of righteous duty, and in the fierce, undying faith that his side would prevail. That was before President Young relented, before the Lion of the Lord agreed his people would once again leave behind all they had built up about them. The defeat is still bitter to Erastus. Much as Brother Brigham was right to lead them west—much as Erastus and Ursula and so many others have prospered in the valley of the Great Salt Lake—the fall of that log house, of Nauvoo the Beautiful, pains him still.

No, definitely no remorse. Not for those three or any other. Excepting one. The one whose life he took without reason, before he even knew he was capable of such an act.

He fought because they all did. Because Lalovee Hammer was unbeaten among the men of Carroll County, and so his son must be unbeaten among the boys. In order to match his father's record, Erastus found he had no choice but to match his style.

The boy's ear was freckled like the rest of him—Erastus couldn't help but notice when he spat it out. It was more than enough to elicit a cry of *Uncle,* and that should have been the end of it, the extent of the damage done. Erastus heard tell of, rather than witnessed, the rest. The wound—perhaps dressed poorly, perhaps not at all—lay open too long, healing over only after a festering contagion had taken hold. The freckled face swelled, ripening cherry red through to a shade just this side of black. There was no talk of murder. Not a whisper. Men fought. Occasionally, one of them died.

With an iron tang in his mouth, Erastus returns suddenly to his present form, finding it hunched in his first wife's chair. The kill book lies closed on the table. His forehead resting on it God only knows how long.

Lying on his bunk in the small hours, Bendy absently massages his hips. He can think of nothing but Dorrie's hands. They are ugly, yes, but also terribly, inexplicably beautiful. It would seem there is nothing they cannot do.

Sound stirs the space beneath him, hooves shifting, restlessness passing like a secret from stall to stall. And now, bringing him up on his elbows, the high, inquiring whinny that signals fear. The brown nag. It'll be nothing—she's a flighty thing. Still, maybe he ought to descend, light the storm lantern, take a turn about the barn.

For a full minute Bendy regards the rafter blackness, straining his ears. They're settling now. Definitely nothing. He lies back. Lets fall the lids of his eyes.

Night draws toward morning. The howl is taking shape rapidly, Dorrie having finally hit her stride. In the midst of the five new mannequins, she tilts forward on her knees, setting the runt's left eye. Later, when she's mounted and sewn the skin—soaking, softening now with the others in the tub—she'll take the tip of a pin and draw the eyelid down over the ball. Bendy told her they close their eyes completely, but half-mast is as far as she's willing to go. She can't bear the idea of them wailing blind.

A current plays along her spine. She pays it little mind—another of the body's small complaints, brought on by her penitent's pose.

This time her work has progressed in cycles—runt to father to brothers, mother saved for last. Five centre boards traced, sawn and shaped. Twenty blocks nailed in place. Twenty leg rods stapled. Five skulls wired and affixed. She suspects this may be how she went wrong in the first place, by attempting to raise them up one by one. These are not individual specimens. This is a pack.

While the other four sit back on their haunches, the white wolf stands. The reason for this is simple—it's how Dorrie sees them, gathered on a moonlit meadow, the edges of which meet the steep inner slopes of her skull.

On the floor by her knee, what's left of a small batch of plaster glistens in its pot, enough to build up the little one's nose and lips. After that, she'll mix up a fresh batch and set to work on the adult male. She dips her putty knife into the pot, scoops a blob onto the bone peninsula of the runt's skull and begins working up the snout.

Digging out the right nostril, she feels again the tremor in her spine. It's stronger this time, an almost audible rush. She turns, chin over shoulder. The back window betrays an expression— canine, quicksilver, gone.

She stares into the blackened pane, her brain tumbling to make sense of what she's seen. First, *reflection*. Only none of her wolves has a long silver mane, a robber's mask of black. A trick of the angle? The lamp's dubious light? She releases her craned neck, hears vertebrae click and grind. She's thinking clearly now. Not one of her specimens has its fur on. Not one of them has a face to reflect.

41

THEY TAKE THE BUCKBOARD, a sure sign they'll be hauling something weighty back from town. Which is why the Tracker's been told to come along in the first place—Hammer only ever brings him when there will be many sacks and barrels to heft. Today the light is violent. The son rides up front alongside his father, leaving the Tracker to bounce alone in the back.

Tooele hasn't changed—the road hemmed in by houses, crowded with carts and wagons, mules and Mormonee. While Hammer and the son conduct their business, the Tracker jumps down and walks a little way, easing the track's unkindness from his bones. He knows to move slowly in town, keep his eyes down, stay within earshot of Hammer's call. He will stray to the corner of the block and no further. It is far enough.

On a narrow patch between buildings, six Indians sit facing each other, three on three. A moment passes before the Tracker understands they are gambling, a twelve-bone variation of the game. The marked bone hidden, then revealed. The men sing the accompanying song quietly, passing it from mouth to ear under a blanket of shared breath. Stock-still on the dusty road, the Tracker listens. Though not precisely the version he knows, it's close enough to start the plain tune stuttering in his throat.

"Tracker! You, Tracker!" Hammer's voice drops down around his shoulders. He turns and ventures back.

As expected, there are several barrels and sacks, plus a single crate. The Tracker curls his fingers under the wooden lip of a cask. In the old life, nothing save the largest game weighed so much, and a kill was rarely borne by one man alone. A shoulder net, a burden basket, these were the most a body was expected to bear. They lift the crate last, he and the son sliding it aboard. The Tracker rests his boot heels on it the whole way back.

He should have known. If he had let his mind wander down the track of Hammer's thinking just a couple of steps further, he would have. As it is, the crate's contents take him by surprise.

Hammer insists on prying the lid off himself, showing his teeth as the long nails screech and groan. It comes away to reveal straw. Hammer digs, not with his hand but with the curved tail of the crowbar. One, two hookfuls and the light finds metal, dark and cool. The son lets out a yip.

The white man decides where the leghold traps will go. One among the peach trees, where the painted wife sighted the wolf, one alongside the stable—Hammer himself spotted a full set of tracks there—and one at the far limit of the quiet wife's trees. All three laid where one of the family could put a foot wrong and lose it. The Tracker says nothing. It is not his place.

Hammer leaves them to it. The son stands back, clearly afraid of the teeth. The Tracker kneels over the first of the traps, beside him a basin of bloody scraps. The first wife had given them grudgingly, Hammer besting her with a few soft words—*Nothing a wolf likes better than children, Mother.*

As the son watches over him, the Tracker rubs the double hook of the drag chain with a fatty chunk of bait. Then the chain itself. Then, ever so gently, taking care to avoid the trigger pad, he treats the trap itself.

Ruth doesn't wait for the thunder to begin. She can feel the storm drawing closer, a wavering gloom at its leading edge. A fresh round of leaves laid down, she kneels to build the smallest of fires in the southwest-corner hearth. There can be no burning without heat—a pity, as the silkhouse is already warm. Lavender sags in the floor cracks, its perfume tired.

As the little fire builds, she opens her arms out wide. Can a body block air? She breaks a sweat, slippery beneath her breasts and in between her heavy legs. The lump of the child must be feeling it, held foremost to the grate.

The blaze begins to kick and spit, demanding more fuel. Let it. She requires embers, not flames.

And do you know what the peasants would do, Miss Graves?

No, Mr. Humphrey.

They would wave a coal about the place. They would sing. Anything to drive off the evil spirits that rode in on the storm.

She begins hesitantly, the first song that comes to mind. "All is well." The chorus as good a starting point as any. "All is well."

Outside, the thunderhead bursts with a vengeance, dumping its load of rain. It's up to Ruth to maintain calm. She doesn't glance round when the room brightens, doesn't so much as flinch when the explosion sounds. Still, she can hear the indoor rain song fading, giving way to the onslaught coming down outdoors.

He's promised himself he will no longer come here. Crouched beneath her window, soaked to the skin, he promises himself again.

The sky is hemorrhaging. At his back, rain invades the mulberry grove, fingering every leaf. One thin comfort—in this deluge he can hear nothing of her worms' torrential gorging. They'll be at their loudest now, only a day or two left before they abandon their green carpets and begin to spin.

Waterlogged, impatient, Lal inches up the wall. His crown, his brow, his huge eyes crest the sill. Ruth stoops over the small hearth in the corner, her back to him. Her beautiful, rounded back.

Lightning—its lustre raw, the colour of a slim sapling peeled. He feels it light up his face, the sodden slick of his hair. If Ruth were to glance his way, she would mark his every feature—stark portrait of a drowned man come to call. She does not glance his way.

Now thunder, the clap so loud it halts and restarts his heart.

Ruth straightens. She turns, shows him her swelling profile, and begins slowly to pace. In her hand, a pair of iron tongs. In their grip, a single living coal. Her lips move softly in time to her measured steps. She's singing. Something else he cannot hear.

Her face is drawn. She pauses, peering hard at one of the worm beds, and Lal strains through the watery glass to see what has her so concerned. Stillness. To a one, the worms have left off eating. A fright will do this, as he well knows. And now he remembers her telling him—thunder frightens them worst of all.

Ruth reaches out with her free hand. It hovers, then drops, bestowing a feather-light stroke. Rain tracks coldly down Lal's cheeks. He squeezes his eyes shut and moves backwards into the storm.

The sky cracks open wide. Moving between strikes, the Tracker freezes low to the ground whenever lightning illuminates the scene. Scarcely a breath passes between each bright fall of the great serpent and the deafening roar of its voice. In his right hand he carries a stick, such as an injured man might lean upon to walk. He spots his mark in a great flash, drives the point of the stick home under cover of the thundering cry.

One.

Run, Tracker.

Two.

He times each hit perfectly. No one, no matter how wakeful, will have heard the steely traps spring shut. He sprints on, heartbeat sounding in his skull. Only one to go.

Lal moves in spurts through Ruth's orchard, trunk to trunk. The mulberries offer no refuge. Branches clutch at his scalp, their huge leaves weeping, flapping like bats. A strike touches down, this one visible between the trees, touching pasture perhaps a quarter mile off. Thunder rattles his bones.

He can never remember—is a body more likely to be struck down in the open or among the black bodies of trees? The open makes more sense, God or maybe the Prophet getting a clear view, drawing a bead. Of course, a house is safest of all, but the idea never enters his head. He's a thing of the storm now, raining inside and out. Besides—the thought rinses through him—a lightning strike might not be such a terrible thing. Imagine being singled out like that, fingered and riven through with light.

The more he pictures it, the more fitting such an end begins to seem. What, if not sin, would draw the bright bolt down? And who more sinful than a son who adores one and defiles another of his father's wives? Unless it wouldn't be an end. He's seen trees burnt black and leafless continue to stand. Never again troubled by woodworms, by axe blades, by birds.

The open, then. His last, best hope. He doesn't consult the thumb—some steps so momentous they must be taken alone.

He tenses like anything about to break cover, a second's hesitation that changes the course of his life. Big eyes have their uses. A figure, dark but definite, hugs the verge of the trees. Lal tracks its progress through the maze of trunks, through sheets and sheets of rain. Another strike—brilliant, closer still—and the figure has a name. The Tracker. Running low and fast, something staff-like in his hand. Lal takes off after him, grinning into the thunder's deafening peal.

He halts when the Tracker does, witnesses from a distance of only three trees. The Indian lifts his staff like a spear, as though he would pin some scurrying thing to the ground. Lightning cuts the night behind him. A split second more and then he too strikes—driving the staff, yes, but hauling it just as swiftly back— just as the bolt's dark echo explodes.

Lal marks the flash, the steel jaws leaping from the grass. He's fool enough to have forgotten the trap was there; chances are, left to his own devices, he would have fed it his own foot. Not such a fool, though, as to mistake the meaning of what he's just seen.

The storm is dying, the old barn growing peaceful again. It turns out the simplest of poses is the hardest to hold. Cast in the shape of the standing mother wolf, Bendy finds his over-slung knees begin to complain.

"Any chance of a rest?" He cocks his head to find her kneeling beside the female mannequin, smoothing plaster along its back.

"Hm?"

"My knees."

She nods. He folds his legs beneath him to sit on his heels, slumping forward for a long moment before straightening back up. The rush of blood from his brain makes him reckless. He's speaking before he knows he will. "You ever think about leaving?"

She looks up. "Leaving."

"Yeah." His heart drums up double time. "Getting shut of this place."

Her eyes switch in their sockets. "And going where?"

"I don't know. Anywhere." He pauses, hearing the error in what he's said. "Anywhere east."

"East." She says it softly.

"Well, sure. We're already west. It's just more of the same or worse the further you go."

She stands abruptly. Taking up the pail of plaster, she returns it to her workbench, showing him her back. There on his knees behind her, he can't help but feel as though he's praying. His answer comes with her turning, the gleam in her sunken eyes.

— 42 —

THANKFUL'S DONE WAITING. With perhaps an hour to go till dawn, she looks both ways and cuts a fast diagonal across the corridor's dark. Lal's door handle is stiff. She works it with both hands, breath suspended, and then she's inside.

He's asleep on his belly, right arm dangling, knuckles grazing the floor. She wriggles free of her nightdress and climbs astride his back, tucking her hand over his mouth. He bucks upon waking, but she grips on tight with her knees.

"It's me." Her voice louder than she intends. He freezes. Mother Hammer's three little Josephs lie on the far side of the wall, sleeping with their matched eyes open, more than like. Let them listen. Let their dreams be troubled by what they hear. And what if their father should hear? What then?

Lal thrashes his head, and Thankful removes her hand from his mouth, rising up on one heel to let him turn over onto his back. It's a bit of a trick, the bed narrow, a boy's. He stares at her, coming fully awake to the fact of her weight on top of him, the shadows of her full, bare breasts. He's a young man, hard to the tip in seconds. She takes care of both of them quickly, hips grinding, fingers harsh. Then bends, panting, to his ear.

"Let's go away together." She daren't pull back to look at him.

For a time he lies unmoving. Then reaches up to tilt her head, a little roughly, with his hands. His lips graze her earlobe. "Are you crazy? He's my *father*."

She has yet to let him slip from inside her. She does so now. "I know he's your father," she hisses. "He's my husband. That's why we need to *leave*."

His hands turn cruel, hauling her down. "Keep your voice down, you stupid bitch."

Thankful feels her innards shrink. Why, why is she never best loved? *"I'll tell him."* Who ever dreamt a woman could screech so under her breath.

"You wouldn't dare."

"Wouldn't I?" This said in a voice that could carry.

"Shut up." He twists a handful of ringlets. "You'd be the one to lose. I could make a life for myself if I had to."

"So could I. I was—" She can scarcely say it. "I am—an actress."

He does his worst then, laughing at her, quaking soundlessly between her thighs. He keeps hold of her until he can speak. "There's only one job for a woman like you."

He has her by the head, but her hands remain her own. She reaches back between her legs and drives her knuckles into his balls. His strength deserts him. She's off him in a heartbeat, scooping up her nightdress, darting to the door.

Broken again. Ursula sucks the insides of her cheeks. Three out of thirteen eggs have fissures. One has cracked clean through and leaked its bright slime over the straw. He must have run with the basket again. She stoops over him.

"How many times, Baby Joe?" In the corner of her eye, Josephine takes up breadboard, knife and loaf, and filters away. "How many times?"

The child looks up at her.

"You. Never. Run. Not when you're carrying the eggs."

"I—" he attempts.

"Hold out your hand."

He does so, but keeps it bundled in a fist. Her youngest has a vein of his father running through him.

"Palm to heaven," she says quietly, and he obeys with a slow unfurling. She averts her eyes from his small, soft fingers, the leniency they might evoke. Busies herself with wiping porridge from her kitchen spoon.

One good whack ought to do it. Ursula gauges the force required, then doubles it on the downswing to be sure. Baby Joe may have a wilful streak, but he's not made of stone. He curls the injured hand inside the good one and presses both to his belly, betraying the stab of nausea that accompanies the sudden infliction of pain. His brown eyes widen, full to brimming with tears.

"M-mother," he moans, the first tear snaking loose as he lowers his face.

The word works on Ursula like a lineament, soothing, loosening her resolve. "None of that, now." She resists the urge to kneel and kiss him, press his hot cheek to her own. "Go and wash that muck off your hands, then maybe I'll let you ring the breakfast bell."

To her surprise, the child doesn't move.

"Mother," he says again, tilting his face up to regard her through dark and streaming eyes. "I want my mother."

This time the word is narrow, honed. It penetrates just where Ursula's breastbone reaches its ribbed conclusion—a pain so vivid, so pure, it demands to be returned. *Strike him,* it says, *hard.*

But the child is only six, his limbs padded with baby fat, a stubborn strata through which the milk of the one who built him still swims. Ursula contents herself with grabbing him by the shoulders. She kneels down before him. Descends to show him the pale discs of her eyes.

"I am your mother, Baby." She shakes him.

A glint of defiance taints his gaze. She sees she must be cruel.

"You think your Aunt Ruth wants you? You're mistaken, my angel. She'd much rather keep company with her worms."

His eyes dry as she watches. She gives him another shake for good measure before letting him go.

"Sister Eudora."

Ruth stands in the lee of the door—for how long, Dorrie has no notion. She's been driving pins through the mother wolf's fur, ensuring the skin will adhere. It takes her a moment to focus, her pupils having shrunk to pinpricks from staring so long into such whiteness. The frame of daylight around her sister-wife's form confuses things further. Dorrie realizes she's worked through to late morning, clean through Mother Hammer's bell. She rises from her knees. Save for a final brushing when dry, the white wolf, and therefore the pack, is done.

Ruth steps inside the barn, drawing closed the door. "My." She crosses to stand by the snowy hindquarters, knows without being told not to touch. "Such fine work."

Dorrie feels herself colour.

Ruth lifts her leaf-stained hand and closes it gently around Dorrie's wrist. "Eudora, your mother has passed."

Just like that. No, *I'm afraid I have some sad news.* Not even, *Sit down, dear.* Dorrie sways, just the once, pressing her thigh to the wolf's shoulder for support. Four paws planted. Legs of iron.

"She'd been ill for some time, I believe."

"Yes. Ill."

"She died on Sunday."

Ruth withdraws her hand. Delving into her apron pocket, she produces a parcel sewn up in burlap, untidy stitches traversing its spine. Dorrie reaches for it. The heft and dimensions are familiar, only the rough skin strange. Mama's *Doctrine and Covenants.* She had Dorrie fetch it for her every evening so that she might read a passage aloud. *For after much tribulation come the blessings. Wherefore the day cometh that ye shall be crowned with much glory; the hour is not yet, but is nigh at hand.* Papa listening intently, elbows on knees, head a great weight in his hands.

A high groan causes Dorrie to glance up from the swaddled book. Ruth is pushing open the door, letting in a slash of day. "I'm sorry," she says, her tone less one of condolence than of apology. And then she's gone.

Sorry for what? Not staying longer? Not even attempting to comfort Dorrie in her grief?

The truth is, Dorrie has no wish to be comforted. As for grief, she's having difficulty locating any—a quick internal inventory reveals only space, echoing and cool. Mama has died, she thinks, the words careful, clean. How could a mother be dead some five days and a daughter not feel it? Or not a mother. Not truly.

Maybe that explains it. If Dorrie never mourned the original, how can she spill tears for the one who took her place? It's a relief to think it, like discovering the source of a nasty draft. She sidles in behind her workbench, drags the stool beneath her and sits. She can cut open the parcel later. For now she sets it aside.

From behind, Hammer and the Tracker could be brothers. Two heads of pitch-coloured hair beneath matching battered hats. The same shoulder-slung rifles, same squat, solid build hinged in downward inquiry at the hips.

There are differences, of course, as there are between brothers. The Tracker is perhaps an inch taller, his hair longer, sitting jagged about his shoulders. Where Hammer's arms are clothed in shirtsleeves—parsnip-coloured, rolled to the elbow—the Tracker's hang bare, flanking the silken back of his waistcoat. As Lal approaches, he notes these and other discrepancies, yet every step closer to their twinned, stooping backs is a step less sure of himself. The thumb floats up to worry his lip.

"Brothers?" he asks it.

Mm-hm.

For a moment, Lal considers turning back.

Brothers can fall out.

Of course. He takes heart and strides forward, twigs snapping beneath his heavy steps. Both men glance back at him, say nothing, return their attention to the scene at their feet, the trap lying closed on its side. It will be the last time either one of them pays him so little mind.

"How in the hell—" Hammer says as Lal comes to a halt behind them.

"I'll tell you how." Lal hears himself say it, his voice deeper, clearer than he's ever known it. His father looks round, his expression sour, and in an instant Lal sees another way things could go. The Tracker could deny it. More than deny, he could pin the thing on Lal. And more. He could tell whatever he knows of Lal's own transgressions. *Song for bad child. Warning song.* Whose word would Hammer value more?

"Well?" His father glares at him. The Tracker keeps his eyes to the ground. It's not much to go by, but it's all Lal's got.

"He did it." The sure voice gone now. He lifts a trembling finger. "He tripped it, tripped all of them." It's all he can do not to garble the words. "The pit trap too, more than like, hell, probably even the deer." This last comes out in a squawk.

Hammer's face is rigid. Lal is done for. All the Indian has to do is speak. But he doesn't. He turns to face them, holds his tongue.

"You?" And then a sound Lal never could've imagined escaping his father's lips—a whimper, high and helpless, twisting its tail into a word. *"Why?"*

The Indian stares. Lal takes his chance.

"He doesn't want you to have it, Daddy." It's a child's term, one that's lain dormant since the days when Lal needed his meat cut for him by a big pair of hands. A term natural as teeth now, at home in his grown-up mouth.

"That true, Tracker?"

Still no word. Still the dark, unwavering gaze.

"You son of a bitch." Hammer forms the words slowly, as though trying them out for the first time. Then, like a blast of birdsong in Lal's ears, "Get off my land."

The Tracker doesn't run. Doesn't walk, either, but spins and sets off at a doggy sort of trot. His repeater bouncing. Nary a backward glance.

Lal knows better than to smile, and anyway, he's thinking too hard about what to say next. It matters terribly. His father is a wide-open door—the right words in the right order could walk Lal clean inside. The thumb would know, but to consult it would be to risk rousing his father's contempt. His brain churns. And then, from amid the slippery waste, a milk-white answer takes shape.

The Tracker sits for a time in his shelter. Not because he wishes to stay, but because he cannot, for the life of him, think where to go. He takes cover at the sound of hoofbeats, watches from the scrub until the son has gone. An easy shot let slip away.

It makes little sense to enter the hut again, even less to stand rooted when one is not a tree. In the end the Tracker sets off in the direction he's facing, thinking only that he must move.

He keeps up a good pace, despite having no notion of where he's bound. Only south, his feet seeking the tracks they laid when coming north some seven years before. Being feet, they are possessed of limited understanding; by undoing distance, they hope to undo time. They will carry the Tracker back to the old life, back to before the world went bad.

The idea—clearly impossible in the mind's bleak light—stops him dead. Looking about, he finds he's reached the southern boundary of Hammer's land. He stands still for as long as he can bear to. Then, as though spun by a great gust, he jerks a quarter turn.

To the west, the Gosiute scratch in the desert and starve. Turning further, the Tracker faces north—the half-life he's only just abandoned, Hammer and the son standing together against him, one flesh. Miles beyond them lies the site of the Bear River Massacre, Bear Hunter's band slaughtered, four winters gone. He turns still further, looking hard now into the east. That way even the mighty Ute are being driven from their lands, herded into wastelands set aside by the Mormonee.

The Tracker looks down on the scarred noses of his boots, watches them shuffle the last quarter, back to where they began. This final story is not one he's gleaned from Hammer's talk, or overheard while waiting for the white man in town. This is the story he would utter himself, if there were anyone in the world to tell.

To the south a long green meadow bulges with human skulls. In that sad valley, as in every other, swelling herds trample ancient seed grounds, drain water holes, drive game into the barren hills. The People follow the rabbits and deer or, worse, stay and cling like children to the skirts of towns. Many worship the Mormonee God in the hope that he won't abandon them as their own spirits have done. Their children steal or go hungry or wash white women's floors until they sicken and die.

To the south even the rivers, the land's life-giving veins, bring death.

DORRIE DREAMS:

Hoofbeats waken me, even as they scatter the lolling, meat-drunk wolves. I draw my beak from beneath my wing, watch as the last bloated stragglers push up into the scrub.

The horses have yet to come into view, but the ear determines there are two, weighty with riders. The wolves are right to go—it wouldn't be the first time those who came in the wake of a kill took the blame for the killing itself.

Despite hours of feeding, the packs have left much behind— many a face still possessed of its features, discoloured though they may be. It is the full of night, the chill having dampened the meadow's heady scent. The moon, showing horns now, shines a fair, cool light upon the pair of horses that emerge at a good clip from the northern draw.

The first is a grey, its rider female. She holds herself rigid above the bodies on the ground, looking left and right. Again and again she lets out a simple call, one syllable, half cried, half sung. Behind her a male hunches on a horse long-limbed and dark.

At the heart of the meadow, surrounded by the remnants of

her own kind, the female ceases calling and turns her mount flank-on to the male's. Then words, all hers, or if he replies it's in a rumble too low to carry up the hill to my tree.

Who can say if the child is sensible of their talk. I've heard nothing from her, not the smallest of rustlings, in hours. Come dawn, I have it in mind that I'll drag my claws over her hiding place again. There's only so long a body can remain still. If she stays curled there much longer, the crease of earth that cradles her may decide to sustain its hold.

Below, the female raises her voice, the male lifting his head in response. His arm floats up slowly, a lone finger tracing over these eastern hills, scratching an invisible trail. The female urges her horse forward, its pale nose pointed our way. In moments she gains the slope, leaving the killing grounds behind. The male kicks his mount to catch up, keeping its forelock to the tail of the sure-footed, climbing grey.

She resumes her calling now, bringing the sound up from low in her throat, spreading it like the purr of a grouse. I hold still, give the moon no cause to single me out. They draw closer, near enough that I can hear the horses' laboured breath, feel the touch of hoof upon hill in shivers through the juniper's bough.

When they are two trees away, their eyes almost level with mine, the female stills the grey. The male's horse follows suit. Neither of us makes a sound, child or crow, and I begin to believe it will be all right. Like the wolves, these humans will pass close and pass us by. Come morning I will chase the child from her hole, lead her first to water, then to food. I tell myself it can happen this way.

Again the female looses her call, a plaintive, enduring tone. Impossible to know if it wakens the child, or if she's been watching through a gauze of sage leaves all along. In either case she issues a cry of her own. It is broken, barely audible, but the head of the male snaps to attention, the female already slipping down from her mount. Even if they hadn't heard, they'd know she was in there now. The crown of the fat sagebrush parts. Up from its depths comes a trembling sign.

Foolish child. I harden my heart to her, harden my glittering eye. She's shown them her little white hand.

— 44 —

DORRIE WAKES IN DARKNESS, the hair at her temples wet with tears. She's slept through the supper bell and no one has come to fetch her. As always, she has only a single hook upon which to hang the dead weight of her dream. This time it is Mama. Lifting her small daughter, clutching her in a saviour's embrace.

Sitting up, she realizes what it is that's woken her. On the far side of the barn, a Hammer-sized shadow stands in the open door.

The Tracker hears her first—a fine buzzing, the glassy whirr of a fly. Then the chill he's come to know. Tonight, the whirlwind wife is not content to settle for his spine's valley. She drills through clothing, skin and bone. Once inside, she expands, filling him with light and air.

Behind them, far behind, the first wide-open note of the Father's howl. The whirlwind wife turns the Tracker on the spot. Such bliss to know what is required of him. He has never run so hard, but with her spinning inside him, he knows no lack of wind.

Ruth has dropped off, her feet propped pink and tender on the lip of a shelf, her back numb to the rails of her little chair. She comes to consciousness through a frothing ebb of sound. Opening her eyes, she finds there will be no need of fried onions this year. The worms are taking to the stooks without her encouragement, without so much as her say.

She eases her feet down from the ledge, her toes howling at the sudden influx of blood. The creature inside her stirs. No comfort there—just a reminder of the unavoidable childbed, the suffering still to come. Ruth drops her face into her hands. Her palms are fragrant. She rests there a moment, then rises to stand on her pain.

For more than an hour now, Dorrie's sat staring at the gap in the circular howl. Hammer offered no explanation, ignored both protests and pleas. Working his thick fingers under the she-wolf's wooden base, he motioned with his chin for Lal to take up the other end. His eldest obliged with a grin, pressing his cheek to the tail and shuffling out backwards, Hammer huffing after him, kicking the door shut when they were through. That was strange, too—not once in three years had her husband ever entered her workshop in the company of his son. Always with the Paiute, or, when the day's bag was small, alone.

She's playing it over in her mind when Bendy eases through the door. He takes in her stricken expression. Then, as though sucked into a narrow vacuum, he steps quickly into the white wolf's space. After a moment's pause, he drops to all fours.

In that instant a prickling, the lightest of caresses at the back of Dorrie's neck. She jerks her head round to find no one—the window faceless. Turning back, she draws a shuddery breath. "He took her."

Bendy nods. "Where?"

"I don't know." The last word devolving into a senseless, spiralling moan.

He makes a lupine, four-footed move her way. The second step finds him rising. He springs over the runt, clearing the black peak of its nose to land before her, fully upright.

No touch she's ever known has prepared her for the quality of his embrace. Not Mama's devoted service—a cool cloth on her fevered brow, a hairbrush tugging sweetly at her scalp. Not Papa's seldom-felt hand, a pat more suited to livestock, creatures with weathered hides. Certainly not Hammer.

With all of them, even Mama, there was a sense of shrinking, of willing herself to disappear. In the circle of Bendy's arms, Dorrie feels herself expand. His give is endless. Tilting her mouth upward, she draws his down and meets it. His right hand flexes at her ribs, the left rising to take hold of her chin. A second kiss, his tongue a keen pleasure now, her jaw aching, open wide.

The moon is sickle thin, but the mother wolf draws starlight, collecting it in her coat. She stands in the open, Lal and his father on their knees in the nearby brake of scrub.

It was a trial waiting for darkness. Lal rode out to check that the Tracker's hut was empty, but mostly to keep out of his father's way. Hammer had agreed to the plan, but only just. Lal wasn't sure he'd follow through until shortly after nightfall, when there came a knock at his bedchamber door. *Get your gun.* The sweetest words a son could hope to hear. Not that Lal was much of a shot. He'd never taken out anything bigger than a rabbit—he'd never been given the chance. Until now.

He holds his rifle propped at his side, just as his father does, muzzle to the sky. In spite of himself, he longs for no quarry, this paired waiting the nearest thing he's known to bliss. A simple prayer floats upward through the seams of his skull—*Stay away, stay away, stay away.*

It works like a charm against him. In the distance, the rogue wolf parts the night like a curtain, bursting onto the meadow's stage. His coat is the colour of armour. About his eyes a mask of black fur. He's upwind of them, upwind of the female's unnatural scent. Lal's breath catches. He hears a forced swallow, made audible by the stricture in his father's throat. The pack horse, hobbled at a good distance, holds its whinny.

The wolf runs to his mate, all caution thrown to the wind, a joyful, springing stride. She makes no move, no sound, to greet him, and still he runs.

Lal feels his father's rifle rise, and raises his own to match. The male reaches his goal, drives his nose deep into the white ruff and whines—a sound tangible in Lal's backbone, echoed in the wild shiver that animates the great wolf's length. Lal shoots his father a glance, shocked to find him sighting a wildly skewed shot. A moment's confusion bordering on panic, and then comprehension comes. It's a gift. His father trusting him to make the kill.

Ordinarily he'd buckle under the pressure, but there's nothing ordinary about this night. The male nuzzles his rigid mate, refusing to believe her gone. Lal takes a breath and feels himself quieten. On the exhale, his gun barrel grows, extending over the grey field until it presses its cold mouth to his target's breast.

They fire together, father and son. The powder flash is blinding, but Lal need not see to know the male is down, the female still standing, unmoved. If he understands anything, it's that his ball has hit home.

"Hell of a shot," his father says, and Lal feels his ribs in danger of cracking from within. Hammer heaves up onto his feet, kicking the kinks out of his knees. "Your daddy's a deadeye, Lal, always was." He breaks cover, moving cautiously toward the twitching kill.

Lal blinks like a child shaken awake. He watches as, with a mighty spasm, the wolf gives up the ghost, turning lumpen at his father's feet.

He's seen it done a hundred times. Still, meeting the black mare's gaze as she dips her head into the bridle, braving her long teeth as she accepts the bit, the Tracker knows wave upon wave of fear. The whirlwind wife helps him, lending torsion and lift as he hefts the dark saddle into place.

Cinching the girth brings him close to the mare's barrel—the depth of her breathing, the bulk of her heart. He works two fingers under the strap, the way he's seen the new man do, and the horse blows a trusting sigh.

He hasn't much time. He was closing in on the yard when he heard the belated human answer to the Father's call—the true shot folding the false one into its report. The briefest of detours past the child wife's window showed him his first glimpse of love in years—that and the space where the Father's mate had been.

The Tracker slings the carved saddlebags into place, steps back and unbuttons his trousers. The picture book comes free with a peeling sound, its cover damp with the sweat of the flesh to which it has belonged. His leg feels stripped without it. Resisting the urge to take a last look inside, he slips the book into the near saddlebag and lowers the flap. Still the leather thong dangles from his hand, the same cord that bound the drawings to their maker—that blue-white, lifeless thigh. After a moment's hesitation he shoves its thin length in after the book. The whirlwind wife is quieter now, a gentle churning, barely a hum. Threading tongue through buckle, the Tracker makes fast the flap.

Dorrie and Bendy hear nothing but the beating of their own two hearts. Not a distant, doubled gunshot. Not even a loaded pack horse shuffling to a stop. Nothing until the grey door screeches and they are no longer alone.

As they scramble to their feet, Lal twists to see what it is that's opened his father's eyes so wide. Together, the men let their burden fall. It hits the planks with a flesh-heavy thud.

Dorrie takes in the new trophy—a huge, silver-maned male with a raccoon's robber mask—and knows its features in an instant. It's the same instant Lal whirls on them, his eyes alight. Three skittering steps and he swings, an arcing roundhouse that catches Bendy at his temple, knocking him clean off his feet. Knuckles graze Dorrie's cheek, the blow's aftermath enough to send her reeling. She lands on her tailbone and slides, legs splayed, shoulders colliding with a bank of bales. Moorhens fly in all directions. Marmots leap.

The dark core of her brain expands. In the seconds it takes her to blink it back, a terrible scene evolves. Lal's rifle lies where he's thrown it. He's curled in a squat, his left arm pure violence,

levering down on Bendy's neck. Hammer stands at a little distance. His gun is nowhere in evidence—small comfort as he
draws a blade from the sheath at his hip.

"Hold him, son."

Dorrie crawls hard for the shelves, coming face to face with the
naphtha. Nothing better for cleaning blood from feathers. Also
the tallest, heaviest jar. She grabs it, already rising. A single leaping stride and it shatters beautifully, sending a shower of clear,
stinking liquid and splintering glass down the sweep of Lal's hair.
He rears and topples, his skull meeting plank with a resounding
crack.

Bendy scrambles back, Dorrie yanking him up beside her. The
two of them have their feet now, but Hammer's still the one with
the knife. He jabs the blade their way.

"You little bitch."

Behind him, the frame of the door stands empty. Then, sudden
as a ghost at a gateway, the Tracker fills its breach. The repeater
swings up from his side. He draws a silent bead—not on either of
the two young lovers, but on the back of Hammer's head. Reading
disbelief on the faces before him, Hammer glances over his
shoulder. If he's surprised, he doesn't show it. A last wave of his
knife, and he turns a slow, controlled about-face.

Shaking his head clear, Bendy balls his two fists into one and
brings them down hard on the older man's wrist. Hammer's grip
springs open. Dorrie swoops, plucking up the knife and sending it
hilt over blade into the shadows.

The Tracker advances, lifting his boots high over the father
wolf's body, grazing not a single hair. He doesn't stop until the
muzzle of his rifle meets Hammer's brow. "Horses." He gestures
with his head to the door, then looks Dorrie straight in the eye.
"Black one yours."

She takes a last, blurred account of the wolves—four sitting vigil, one missing, one lying dead on its side. There's no time to gather her tools, no time to reach beneath her cot and rescue Cruikshank Crow. Time only, as Bendy drags her by the hand toward the door, to snatch the still-unopened *Doctrine and Covenants* from the corner of her workbench, the final offering from a mother's hand.

Ursula cannot say whether she's been sleeping, only that she is now awake. Hoofbeats in the night don't signify trouble the way they used to, but she's not so incurious as to keep to her bed.

From her window she can make out the ghost of the track and, down its length, two figures riding hard away. Both mounts are dark, the larger of the two in the lead. Hammer dragging the hired man out on some fool's errand. A more suitable companion for him than the Indian, in any case.

Withdrawing from the casement, Ursula returns to the shadowy bulk of her bed. Should she lie flat and hold her eyes closed, hoping against hope to drift off, or light the lamp and stretch a fresh square of linen on her hoop? The answer isn't long in coming.

> *For behold, the day cometh*
> *that shall burn as an oven;*
> *and all the proud, yea,*
> *and all that do wickedly,*
> *shall be stubble.*

Hammer's eyes run bright streams. His breath is the breath of a labouring woman, his mouth the mouth of an expiring child.

On his knees astride the white man, the Tracker lays his left forearm across Hammer's windpipe and feels the resulting panic between his thighs. In his right hand, the Henry languishes. He meets the white man's bulging eyes briefly before tilting his gaze to take in the greater scene. The son stirs like a child dreaming, rolls groaning to push up onto all fours. The Tracker considers taking aim. Then sees he needn't bother.

The son sags, snakelike. Cranes his neck to look about him, his eyes fathomless, empty of sense. His golden head has gone dark with the loss of his own blood. He struggles past on his belly, reaching with his elbows, writhing. He makes the door, worries it open, slithers through. Leaving Indian and white man alone.

On the lip of the long workbench a lamp burns. Raising up his rifle, the Tracker finds its barrel to be just the right length. He swings a slow arc, upsetting the child wife's light, smashing it like a bright egg on the floor. A yolk of oily flame stains the planks. The Tracker watches its progress keenly. Beneath him, Hammer begins to quieten, what little air his body still harbours turning bad.

Crossing the yard to the horse barn, Lal evolves—now a crawling, a lurching, a loping thing. His father and the Tracker are friends again, practically lovers, the Indian straddling Hammer the way Thankful straddles Lal. There's only one path now, only one route clear to his father's heart. Catch the sinners—adulterers, betrayers both—and bathe them in the purest of streams. He gives no thought to his lack of weapon. He has hands and boots, a mouthful of teeth. Catch them, bleed them, bring them back. Father's wife, father's worker. The pair of them made quiet, obedient, clean.

He finds his horse by sound—a panicked wheezing that grows quicker the closer he gets. In the dark he hurts Bull worse than ever, wrenching the cinch, jamming and yanking the bit. He mounts in a bruising assault, clears the stable door and pulls the palomino up short. His dripping head is an owl's now, rotating on its stalk. His eyes dilate to take in the yard, the long grey tail of the track. Messy with mud and hoofprints. They've got a good lead on him, but sooner or later they'll stop and rest. Bull jigs beneath him. Lal kicks him up hard.

He makes it a scant half mile before the palomino imagines danger and digs in his heels. A headlong gallop ground to stillness. Lal flies from his saddle like an axe head forsaking its handle, turning bright-edged circles through the dark.

A thing of air now, the blaze rises, taking hold in feathers and fur. Beast after beast catches. Glass eyes fill to brimming with light.

Curling down, the Tracker brings his lips gently to Hammer's ear. The tale is an old one, the taste of his own language strange. Smoke rushes his open mouth as he forms the words, knowing his friend cannot hear them, would find them meaningless if he could.

ACKNOWLEDGEMENTS

FIRST AND FOREMOST, I would like to acknowledge the descendants of all those present at the Mountain Meadows Massacre. While *Effigy* is a work of the imagination, it does cross paths with history. It is a painful story, no denying. I have done my best to tell it with love.

Of the many books and websites I consulted during the course of my research, the following deserve special mention: *The Mountain Meadows Massacre* by Juanita Brooks; *Blood of the Prophets: Brigham Young and the Massacre at Mountain Meadows* by Will Bagley; *The Gathering of Zion: The Story of the Mormon Trail* by Wallace Stegner; *History of Utah, 1540–1886* by Hubert Howe Bancroft; *Wife No. 19* by Ann Eliza Young; *Brigham's Destroying Angel: Being the Life, Confession and Startling Disclosures of the Notorious Bill Hickman, the Danite Chief of Utah* by William Adams Hickman; *Beneath These Red Cliffs: An Ethnohistory of the Utah Paiutes* by Ronald L. Holt; *Handbook of North American Indians: Great Basin,* edited by Warren L. D'Azevedo; *Tracking and the Art of Seeing: How to Read Animal Tracks and Sign* by Paul Rezendes; *Guide to Taxidermy* by Charles K. Reed; *Mirror of the Dream: An Illustrated History of San*

Francisco by T.H. Watkins and R.R. Olmsted; *Saddles and Spurs: The Pony Express Saga* by Raymond W. Settle and Mary Lund Settle; *The Man Who Listens to Horses* by Monty Roberts; *Bird Flight* by Robert Burton; *Wolf Songs: The Classic Collection of Writing About Wolves,* edited by Robert Busch; *The Story of Silk* by Dr. John Feltwell; The Official Internet Site of the Church of Jesus Christ of Latter-day Saints at http://www.lds.org; The Virtual Museum of the City of San Francisco at http://www.sfmuseum.net; Pony Express Historic Resource Study at http://www.nps.gov/poex/hrs/hrs.htm; Utah Division of Wildlife Resources at http://wildlife.utah.gov.

Many thanks to the Canada Council for the Arts, the Manitoba Arts Council and the Winnipeg Arts Council for their support during the writing of this book.

I am grateful to the good people at Random House Canada, especially my esteemed editor, Anne Collins. My thanks also to my agent, the tireless and tenacious Denise Bukowski.

As ever, my gratitude to family and friends knows no bounds. To my husband, Clive, I say again and again, thank you.

The body of *Effigy* has been set in Fairfield, a typeface originally designed by Rudolph Ruzicka for the Linotype Corporation in the 1940s. The face references modern versions of such classic text faces as Bodoni and Didot, and, like its influencial forerunners, Fairfield is at its best when used in book-length text settings.

ST A

SEP 2 7 2007